LORD *of* SINS
BECKMAN

GRACE BURROWES

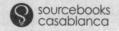
sourcebooks
casablanca

Published by Sourcebooks Casablanca, an imprint of Sourcebooks, Inc.
P.O. Box 4410, Naperville, Illinois 60567-4410
(630) 961-3900
Fax: (630) 961-2168
sourcebooks.com

Printed and bound in Canada.
MBP 10 9 8 7 6 5 4 3 2 1

To those of us who've been prodigals. May we know when it's time to come home, and recognize in what direction to travel.

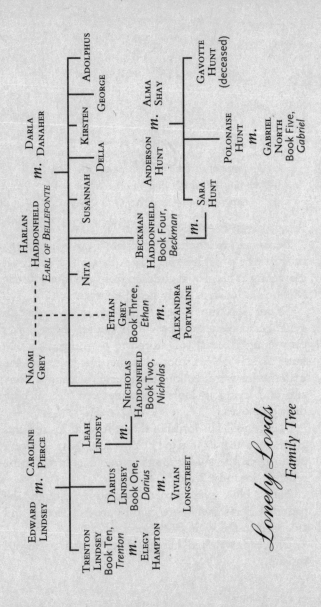

Lonely Lords
Family Tree

One

"HE INSISTED ON SEEING YOU OFF."

Beckman Haddonfield heard his sister Nita clearly, though she'd whispered. The Earl of Bellefonte, glowering at his grown children from the foot of Belle Maison's front steps likely heard her too.

"Your lordship." Beck stepped away from his gelding and sketched a bow to his father. Even at this early hour, the earl was attired in morning dress that hung loosely on his stooped frame. His valet and the underbutler were flanking him, each holding a bony arm and trying to look as if they weren't touching their employer.

"Leave us." His lordship didn't look at his servants as he gave that command. "You too, Nita. I won't perish from the cold, though it might be a welcome relief all around if I did."

Nita's blue eyes turned mutinous, though she gathered her shawl more tightly around herself and ascended to the wide front porch.

The earl watched her go then turned to regard his son.

He stabbed his cane in the general direction of the mounting block where Beck's horse waited. "Get me to the damned mounting block before I fall over."

Beck took his father's arm and assisted him to shuffle along until the earl was propped against the top step of the ladies' mounting block.

His lordship rested both gnarled hands on the top of his cane. "No dignity left whatsoever. Soon I won't be able to wipe my own arse."

The truth of this brought a lump to Beck's throat. "One shudders to consider the fuss you'll make then. If you're about to tell me how to find Three Springs, save your breath. I have directions."

"I'm about to tell you I love you," the earl groused. "Though such maudlin tripe hardly makes a difference."

Beck went still, hearing a death knell in his father's blessing. "One has suspected this is the case," Beck said slowly. "One hopes the suspicions have been mutual."

The earl's slight grin appeared. "Couldn't have danced around a tender sentiment better myself. You really should have been my heir."

"Stop disrespecting my brother," Beck retorted, but inside, oh, inside, he was feeling as decrepit and tired as the earl looked. His father loved him, something he had known without realizing it, but his father had also said the words aloud. More than the earl's frail appearance, this indicated the man was indeed making his final arrangements.

"I've said my piece, now get you off to Three Springs and put the place to rights. I've every confidence the solicitors have let it go to wrack and ruin."

The earl made as if to rise, something Beck suspected he couldn't accomplish on his own. Beck drew him up, but not just to his feet. With Nita trying not to cry on the porch, the underbutler blinking furiously, and the footman staring resolutely down the drive, Beck gently hugged his father.

"Papa." He barely whispered his words past his father's shoulder. "I don't want to leave you."

He had never wanted to be sent away, but each time, he'd known his banishments were earned. This time, try as he might, the only fault he could find with himself was that he loved his father.

The earl said nothing for a moment then patted his son's back. "You'll be fine, Beckman. I've always been proud of you, you know."

"Proud of me?" Beck stepped back, depositing his father gently on the mounting block. "I'm nothing more than a frivolous younger son, and that is the plain truth."

A flattering version of the plain truth, too.

"Bah. You should have gone to London with Nicholas and selected yourself another bride, though I suppose you've been trailing him long enough to be ready for a change in scenery."

He's sending me away, Beck thought, his self-discipline barely equal to the task of maintaining his composure. *He's sending me away, and we're discussing my possible marriage to some twit hungering for Nick's title.*

"When Nick is in the room, the ladies do not see me."

The earl thumped his cane weakly. "Balderdash! Nick is a good time. You are a good man."

"Nick is a good man," Beck said, a note of steel creeping into his voice.

"He'll be a better man and a happier man for finding the right countess. It is the besetting sorrow of my dotage that my sons have not provided me with grandchildren to dandle upon my knee."

His lordship loved a good scrap. Heart breaking, Beck obliged.

"You would not know how to dandle if the regent commanded it of you."

"That prancing idiot." The earl snorted. "I am glad I will be dead before the full extent of his silly imitation of a monarch can damage the country further than it has."

"It's too cold to be discussing politics in the drive," Beck said, ready to have this most painful parting over. "Particularly when you've had nothing different to say since the man had his father's kingdom imposed on him several years ago."

"You're right. It's been the same damned nonsense all along. Pavilions and parks, while the working man can't afford his bread, and the yeoman's pasture is fenced away from him at the whim and pleasure of the local baron. Pathetic. Absolutely damned pathetic."

Utterly. "Good-bye, Papa."

The earl leaned forward again, signaling Beck to get him on his feet. "You will be fine, Beckman. Keep an eye on Nick for me, as you always have, and think again of remarrying. Good wives have their endearing qualities."

"Yes, Papa." Beck mustered a smile, hugged his father again, and waved the underbutler and the footmen down the stairs. "God keep you, sir." He resisted the urge to cling to his father, knowing he'd embarrass them both if he stayed one moment longer.

"I wish to hell the Lord would see fit to take me rather than keep me," the earl muttered. "Perhaps patience is the last lesson He has reserved for me. Safe journeys, Beckman. You are a son to make a father proud."

"My thanks." Beck swung up, nodded to his sister where she stood clutching her handkerchief at the top of the stairs. He touched his crop to his hat brim then nudged his horse into a rocking canter.

He did not look back. It was all he could do to see the road for the chill wind making his eyes water.

∾

Sara Hunt took a final swallow of weak, unsweetened, tepid tea, looked out at the miserable day, and decided before the last of the light faded, she'd poke through the contents of Mr. Haddonfield's enormous wagon.

Lady Warne had written instructing the household to make her grandson welcome as he came to "take Three Springs in hand," but she hadn't said exactly when he'd arrive. If Sara was to make a proper inventory of the goods sent ahead of their guest, she'd best do it before the mincing Honorable was underfoot making a nuisance of himself.

She grabbed her heavy wool cloak, traded her house mules for a pair of wooden sabots, took up a lantern, and slipped out the back door. On the stoop she paused, listening to the peculiar sibilance of sleet changing to snow as darkness fell. If the sun came out in the morning, they'd have a fairy-tale landscape of sparkling ice and snow, the last of the season if they were lucky.

The barn bore the comforting scent of horses and hay on a raw day. The four great beasts that had pulled the loaded wagon into the yard the previous day contentedly inhaled great piles of fodder, while the wagon stood in the barn's high, arching center aisle.

Sara had just hung up the lantern when she realized something wasn't right. A shuffling sound came from the far side of the wagon where little light penetrated. The sound was too big to be Heifer investigating under the tarps, not big enough to be a horse shifting in its stall.

She shrank into the shadows. Damn and blast if a vagrant hadn't spotted the laden wagon and decided to follow it to its destination in hopes of some lucrative larceny. The country roads were not heavily traveled, and such a load would be easily remarked. Silently, Sara directed her footsteps to the saddle room, sending up a prayer for Polly and Allie—may her sister and daughter remain in the house, or anywhere but this barn.

She chose a long-handled training whip from the saddle room wall, then retraced her steps and heard muttering from the far side of the wagon.

"And what in blazes is this doing here?" a man asked no one in particular. "As if one needs to fiddle while rusticating. Spices, too, so we might not want for fashionable cuisine in the hinterlands."

A daft vagrant, then. Sara paused in her slow, silent progress around the wagon. Maybe he was harmless, and simply brandishing the whip would suffice to chase him off, but in this weather… She considered putting the whip down.

A man could catch his death in this miserable wet and cold. Times were hard and getting harder, and there were so many veterans of the Corsican's foolishness still wandering the land, many of them ailing in both body and spirit. Shouldn't she offer the man a little Christian charity before she attacked him for merely being curious?

An arm clamped around her neck; another snaked around her waist.

"One move," said a voice directly behind her, "and you will be the first thing planted this spring."

Without seeing him, Sara knew many things about whoever owned the rumbling baritone voice at her ear.

First, he was broad, strong, and quite, quite tall. The angle of the arm at her throat told her so, as did the heat radiating from the muscular chest to which she'd been snugly anchored.

Second, he was no indigent. The wool around her neck was soft, expensive, and clean, for all it had gotten a soaking. And beneath the stable smells and the aroma of damp wool, sleet, and cold, there was an unmistakable bergamot fragrance to this man. He bore the kind of scent blended from cologne, French soaps, and assiduous personal hygiene no vagrant veteran practiced.

Third, if Sara didn't diffuse the situation immediately, she could well end up dead. For herself, she had no great objection to that outcome, being in reasonably good standing with her Maker and profoundly weary of life.

But Sara's death would leave Allie an orphan and Polly without a sister, and to that, Sara had great objection indeed.

"Unhand me, sir. I pose no threat to you." Her voice quavered only a little. She raised her chin so the hood of her cloak dropped back, revealing her cap and, apparently, her gender.

"My apologies." The man dropped his arms and stepped back. "I'll put aside my knife if you'll drop that horsewhip. Beckman Haddonfield, at your service."

Sara took a deep breath and held her ground, not at all looking forward to being disappointed. No man's looks could make good on the promise of that voice. As a musician—a former musician—she was sensitive to beautiful sounds, and this man's voice was... too much. Too rich, too deep, too smooth, too lovely in the ear. His words sneaked along Sara's nerves and sank into her bones like a sweet, lilting adagio played on a fine violoncello. That voice had to belong to some low-browed brute, a backhanded gift from a Creator with an occasionally ironic sense of humor.

When she didn't turn, large hands settled on her shoulders and gently brought her around.

"And you are?" the intruder asked softly as he pried the whip from her fingers.

Sara looked up, and up some more, to gaze upon a face that more than suited the voice. Oh, damn, Polly would want to paint him. The thick blond hair, sculpted lips, and well-proportioned nose would have testified to aristocratic breeding if the height and stature had not. That nose bordered on arrogant but stayed just this side of noble. The chin was firm too, coming close to stubborn but stopping at determined instead.

"Ma'am?" In the dim light, a slight smile revealed perfect white teeth—of course it did—two rows of them, that disappeared with a sardonic lift of one blond eyebrow. And heaven help her, she let her gaze stray to his eyes.

Those eyes were a surprise, not what Sara would expect of a lordling off on a lark. They spoke of the weary humor exhibited by those inured to suffering. They had passed from sad to bleak to endlessly patient.

"Sara Hunt." She bobbed a semblance of a curtsey and wanted to draw her hood back up. "I gather you are Lady Warne's grandson?"

"Step-grandson, to be precise," the man replied, giving Sara the sense he was always *precise*. "I see my belongings have arrived safely, as have my father's horses."

"The wagon arrived yesterday." God help them, Lady Warne's *step*-grandson bore no resemblance whatsoever to a Town fribble. "Your rooms are ready, and I will inform our cook you'll need some sustenance."

A great deal of sustenance, from the size of him. Polly would be thrilled.

"I trust you are not the stable boy?"

Sara took a moment to realize he was teasing her. She had no idea how to tease him back, though his smile said he wouldn't mind such insubordination.

"Mr. North manages the livestock, but he's in the village today," Sara said, her words clipped. Big, gorgeous, and possessed of a voice that could promise a lady ruin at fifty paces, he had no business teasing the help.

Mr. Haddonfield glanced around, his smile fading. "Mr. North would be the steward?"

The barn was snug, tidy, and as clean as such a space could be, and while Sara drew breath, nobody would cast aspersion on North's efforts to keep it so. "Mr. Gabriel North is the land steward, stable master, house steward, arborist, harness maker, horse doctor, plowboy, blacksmith, whitesmith, drover, and much more. Your grandmother has not taken a direct interest in this estate for some years, sir, and you will find much evidence thereof."

Mr. Haddonfield's expression underwent a subtle transformation. The last hint of banter left his eyes, and by the shadowed lantern light, his features took on an air of resignation.

Not even one night on the property, and Three Springs was already taking its toll on the man.

Rather than gawp at his bleak countenance, Sara took the lantern down from its peg. "Come, sir. You have to be tired, and standing about in wet clothing is not well advised. Your rooms are ready, and a hot meal will soon await you."

"Then I have arrived to heaven." He hefted some soft leather version of a portmanteau, rummaged under the tarp, and emerged carrying an oilskin bag and—of all the unexpected things—a violin case.

Sara ignored the violin case but paused when they gained the stable yard. Full darkness had fallen, and the sleet had shifted to a thick, pretty snow.

"It was snowing over the South Downs," Mr. Haddonfield said, "and here I thought April was fast approaching."

"We get odd weather down here," Sara replied. The bleakness was now audible in his lovely voice. "The Channel and the Solent and the time of year conspire to make it so. How is Lady Warne?"

"My grandmother continues in great good spirits. She anticipates the Season as if she were making her come out each and every year."

Sara stopped and regarded Mr. Haddonfield by lantern light as snowflakes dusted his hair and eyelashes. He was a young man—a man in his prime, an earl's son—and yet he sounded puzzled that anybody should enjoy the social whirl.

Three Springs tended to collect refugees, and perhaps another had found his way here. The thought was dangerous, suggesting Sara might have something in common with this handsome, wandering man who knew enough to get a violin out of the elements.

She pushed open the back door to the kitchen hallway, only to be greeted by Polly and Allie, holding hands, both in cloaks and boots, and blinking at Sara and her escort.

"Mama?" Allie dropped her aunt's hand. "Who have you got there? He's quite interesting."

Allie would want to paint him. Oh, bother. Bother, bother, bother.

"Allemande Hunt," Sara said, trying for sternness, "you do not address a guest in such a fashion. Make your curtsey to Mr. Haddonfield and apologize for your manners."

Allie complied, but she continued to stare at Mr. Haddonfield with a combination of girlish fascination and artistic assessment. A polite version of the same expression—minus the girlish fascination—graced Polly's face.

"Polly Hunt." Sara's sister curtsied prettily. "And if you've been traveling in this weather, we'd best see to feeding you. I am Cook in this household, so you'll please excuse me that I might be about my tasks."

"I can manage on what's available," Mr. Haddonfield replied, offering Polly a smile all the more charming for the fatigue it conveyed. "And I've brought in some cooking spices. There's a particular muffin recipe I'm partial to."

"You make muffins?" Allie exclaimed. "You do, yourself?"

Sara braced herself to hear her daughter receive a much-deserved set down about children being seen and not heard, particularly the children of servants, but Mr. Haddonfield reached out and tapped Allie's nose with one long, elegant finger.

"I make muffins, but I require the assistance of competent help, and I cannot possibly bother Miss Polly when she has the entire household to cook for. Perhaps I might prevail upon you, for you are obviously a discerning young lady."

His countenance changed when he addressed the child. His eyes became clearer, and the smile dimmed to lurk around his mouth. He became not more charming, or not more charming in the way an adult woman might understand it, but... benevolent.

"Aunt Polly? Mama?" Allie turned her great green eyes on the adults. "May I? When Mr. Haddonfield bakes his muffins? May I help?"

Polly, as always, deferred to Sara on matters relating to Allie.

"You may," Sara said, knowing it was the wrong decision. "Tonight our guest is cold, wet, hungry, and likely exhausted. We must allow him his comforts before imposing on him to teach you a muffin recipe."

Though they had no real comforts to offer him, only the barest necessities, which added a dollop of embarrassment to Sara's feelings toward him.

"Shall you take a tray?" Polly asked him. "You have to be famished."

Mr. Haddonfield shrugged broad shoulders. "I can eat with the rest of the household. I don't relish a solitary meal above stairs. Is supper served in here when Lady Warne is not in residence?"

"We eat in here," Polly said. "We have two footmen-of-all-work, but they've gone into the village with Mr. North and will likely eat at the posting inn with him. The groom left at Yuletide to be with his parents over the winter but will be back when planting begins—we hope."

"So I'm to have the company of three lovely ladies at my supper," Mr. Haddonfield said. "I'd best get presentable then. I assume you keep country hours?"

"We do," Sara replied, wondering how an earl's son became presentable for eating with the servants in the kitchen. "By the time you've had your bath, Polly will have supper ready. Allie, you can take off your cloak and boots and help Aunt Polly while I show Mr. Haddonfield to his rooms."

"Yes, Mama." Allie's tone was deferential, though her gaze still strayed speculatively to their guest. Sara could see her daughter taking him apart visually then adding his features back together, one pigment and line at a time. Polly was doing likewise, though she had of necessity grown better at hiding her skills.

∾

Beck fell in behind the housekeeper as she departed the kitchen, his gaze fixing on the twitch of her skirts. He idly labeled it a pity a woman with such a pleasing shape and such glorious red hair—albeit glorious red hair mostly tucked up under a voluminous white cap—should be sequestered here, bailing with a teacup against an ocean tide of neglect.

"Are there writing implements to hand?" he asked as Mrs. Hunt preceded him along a chilly, darkened corridor. She held the carrying candle in one hand and shielded it with the other, there being no lit sconces that Beck could see.

"Of course." She didn't slow or turn to face him. "We've put you in the master suite, and you'll find most amenities at your disposal. Three Springs was well appointed when Lady Warne was younger. The house is still in good condition, though the land needs attention."

A polite way of saying yet again what the earl had put more bluntly: the estate had been neglected.

"I'm here to put the land to rights," Beck heard himself volunteer. "If that's possible before my father shuffles off this mortal coil."

"I did not know the earl was indisposed." Mrs. Hunt's bustling progress came to a pause in the gathering gloom of a sitting room. She used the candle to light a branch on the mantel above a cold hearth.

"His lordship is quite frail. My stay here may

be very brief indeed." Though Beck shuddered to consider crossing the Downs again, much less to attend his father's funeral.

Mrs. Hunt paused in circumnavigation of the room and gazed at him for a moment, but thank ye gods, there was no pity in her eyes. "And if the land cannot be put to rights while you're here?"

"That is not my decision. Lady Warne can sell the place, of course. She isn't likely to be leaving Town much when my younger sisters are poised for their come outs. This is a charming room." Beck saw sturdy masculine furnishings, thick Turkish rugs in burgundy and green, and three large windows covered with heavy burgundy drapes.

"Charming, if outdated," Mrs. Hunt said. "Lady Warne left the house much as she inherited it, and that was some time ago. Your bedroom is in here." She opened a discreetly paneled door and led Beck into the cold space beyond. "Had I known when to expect you, I would have lit the fire in here. My apologies for the chill."

Maybe he was hearing irony in her apology where none was intended, and perhaps threatening a woman's life was not the best way to make a good first impression, and yet, Beck hadn't known what or whom to expect on the far side of that wagon. He'd been cold, tired, and in unfamiliar surroundings yet again, almost happy to consider some thief might be attempting to steal from him.

Perhaps he'd apologize. Perhaps if she unbent the least little bit he would tell her he hadn't meant to frighten her, because that's what all this sniffy condescension was about, whether she knew it or not—he was big, strong, male, and he'd frightened her.

The fire caught—it probably wouldn't dare do otherwise—and Mrs. Hunt continued her speechifying.

"We typically bathe in the laundry rather than carry the water any distance in cold weather." She used the bellows to fan the flames, her movements casual and practiced, though they called attention to uncommonly elegant hands.

"I'll be down shortly to see to my ablutions," Beck said, unbuttoning his coat as he spoke. "And I'll make short work of this bath, since dinner looms like divine salvation."

"Until dinner then," she said, casting one last glance at him before leaving him in the chill and solitude of his comfortable, if old-fashioned, bedroom.

That last glance stayed with him as he rummaged in his luggage for clean clothes and made his way to the laundry. She was a widow, Beck recalled as he lowered his grateful, sore body into steaming water some minutes later. The look she'd shot him when he'd started on his coat buttons had been hard to decipher: fascinated, dismissive, and wistful, all at once.

Wistful was interesting, Beck thought as he started making use of the soap. No doubt the idea of a man preparing for his bath brought back memories of her departed husband. After Devona's passing, Beck had cast such glances at the wives being happily handed up into carts in the churchyard, at the matrons cheerfully dancing with their spouses at the assemblies.

Beck closed his eyes and shoved the memories away. He'd traveled like a demon, pushing Ulysses to the limit of the gelding's considerable capability, wanting to get them both out of the damned miserable weather. Sooner begun was sooner done, and his every instinct was telling him there was much to do here at Three Springs.

"Mr. Haddonfield?" A soft voice pierced the haze of sleep that had descended once Beck had finished washing. "Mr. Haddonfield? Sir?" He felt a hand on his shoulder but wished it away when sleep was a heavy, comforting blanket over his awareness.

"You'll not get supper," the voice warned him, "and your water will get cold, so you'll get the ague and perish without dessert."

Beck's eyelids lifted, just as that hand pushed a little harder against his shoulder.

"M'wake," he muttered, realizing the water was considerably cooler. Without thinking, he stood and heard a soft female sigh as he did. As his brain caught up to his body—his naked, dripping, exhausted body—he realized Mrs. Hunt was studying him.

"Mrs. Hunt?" He reached for his bath sheet, but did so slowly, struck by the peculiar expression on the lady's face. She wasn't horrified, and she wasn't attracted, but she was somehow interested.

"God above." The housekeeper exhaled. "Surely Polly would take up sculpting could she see you thus."

What an odd remark for a housekeeper to make about a cook. She offered no further explanation, just turned and left with a single shake of her head.

Two

"I'LL SEE YOU TO YOUR ROOM." SARA MADE THE OFFER OUT of civility. Mr. Haddonfield had been gracious over dinner and afterward had patiently explained whist to Allie, even going so far as to partner the child for a few rounds.

That did not mean Sara liked him.

"I should tell you your escort isn't needed," Mr. Haddonfield said. "However, because the house is unlit and I'm dead on my feet, it probably is very necessary." He winged his arm at her as he spoke, which surprised Sara into outright staring at him, then she gingerly placed her fingers on his sleeve.

Excellent manners were no reason to like a man either—Reynard had had excellent manners, when it suited him.

"What time would you like us to bring you your tea in the morning?" she asked as they traveled the cold, dark hallways and stairs.

"That won't be necessary. I can find my way to the kitchen the same as the rest of the household no doubt does. I'm a seasoned traveler, and I know how to make shift."

"We do break our fast in the kitchen, but Polly, Allie, and I have an apartment right off the kitchen, and it's warm and close to the larder."

"And where does the estimable Mr. North lay his weary head?"

"Gabriel has a room in the south wing," she said, though it was none of the gracious, considerate, polite Mr. Haddonfield's business, and if he was going to suggest that any impropriety *at all*—

"Good. I would not want ladies to be without protection in the dark of night this far from any town or village. This is my room?"

Maybe she did like him, just a penny's worth.

"Next door down." Sara reached forward to open his door then jumped aside, a shriek escaping her as a black-and-white cannonball of fur rocketed past her skirts. In that single instant, several things happened at once.

Heifer yowled his indignation as he shot down the corridor with uncharacteristic speed.

Sara's candle tipped off its holder when she jumped out of the cat's path.

She tried to grab the candle as it fell, only to yelp in pain and lose her balance without catching the candle.

The candle winked out as it rolled over her knuckles and hit the floor, leaving a stygian darkness in the hallway.

"Steady." Mr. Haddonfield's arms caught her when she would have overbalanced, but Sara's momentum was such that she pitched into his chest and would have fallen to her hands and knees had he not kept a firm grip on her upper arms. "Take a moment," he urged, his voice a rumble in the inky darkness.

Up close, he smelled as good as he had in the stables, only more so for having soaked, washed his hair, and shaved. Sara wanted to die of mortification, but in the complete darkness, her balance was hard to regain, so she savored the simple, long-forgotten pleasure of being held by a man.

"I'm all right," she insisted, except the words came out shaky and unconvincing, even to her own ears.

"Take small breaths." His thumbs moved against her shoulders in slow circles. "You've had a fright. Give yourself a minute."

She should pull away, Sara knew that, but he wasn't taking advantage; he was being everything that was gentlemanly, almost brotherly, and she simply lacked the strength of will to stand on her own two feet.

"That's better. Did you get burned?" He reached around and opened the door to his sitting room, letting a dim light leak into the hallway. "Let's have a look, shall we?" His arm slipped around Sara's shoulders as he shepherded her into the sitting room. Maudie, the maid-of-all-work, had left candles lit on the sideboard, and from the bedroom, more weak light came through the door. His rooms weren't exactly warm, but neither did they bear the bone-chilling cold of the unheated corridor.

"There's better light in here." He escorted her to the bedroom, as if waltzing along with housekeepers was a common pastime for him. "I thought the candle might have struck your hand."

"Not the candle, the wax. It's nothing, really."

He towed her over to the fire and examined her hand, using his thumbnail to scrape a drop of warm wax off her knuckle.

"At least the wax," he said, pulling out his hand-kerchief. He crossed the room and dipped the linen in a pitcher of drinking water on his night table. "This might take a little of the sting out."

He wrapped a startlingly cold cloth around Sara's hand, and it did indeed take the sting out.

"Sit you down." He pulled out the chair from his escritoire then leaned a hip on the desk, causing the wood to groan, but letting him keep hold of Sara's hand as she took the chair. "It will likely blister, as red as it is. Have you any aloe?"

"Aloe?" Sara looked at his hand, wrapped around hers. When was the last time she'd held hands with anybody save her daughter or her sister?

"It's a medicinal plant," he said, his grip firm and impersonal. "I spent a summer in Virginia a few years ago, right after the hostilities with the Americans concluded, and they've a number of plants we don't find here. I sent as many as I could back to my father for study and propagation."

"What were you doing in Virginia?" Sara asked out of sheer desperation. The continued grip of his hand around hers was making her insides unsettled, and while she might like him a very little bit, she did *not* like being unsettled. She'd seen this man in all his naked, Greek-god glory, and now he was holding her hand in dimly lit private quarters.

Though Mr. Haddonfield himself seemed oblivious to every one of those facts.

"My stated task was to assess the viability of investing in tobacco on behalf of my father's earldom." He let go of her hand, unwrapped it, peered at it, frowned, and soaked the cloth in cold water again. "I really ought to get you some ointment for this."

Tending to minor hurts was the housekeeper's province—her exclusive province. "You really ought not. Is your father raising tobacco now?"

"He is not." He let her scold go unremarked as he wrapped her hand once again, "Tobacco is profitable. It becomes a habit, and those who indulge in it are loyal to their habit, but it's hard on the land."

"Is that why the plantations are so large? Because they have to fallow a lot of acreage?"

"Everything in America is large. We think Cornwall is far from civilization, but consider that the distance from Penzance to London—not quite three hundred miles—might be little over a tenth the distance from Atlantic to Pacific coasts, and the Americans intend to lay claim to it all."

"One *tenth*? That is incomprehensible."

"Not to them. It takes half-savage people to deal with so much wilderness, and they will deal with it, inevitably."

"But you decided not to invest there. Why not?"

"The government isn't stable, for one thing." He let go of her hand to soak the handkerchief yet again. "Americans are terminally wary of kings and despots, elected or otherwise, and so they are miserly with their own government, haggling over every tax and tithe, clutching every little power tightly away from their own leaders. Then too, British enterprises are not regarded fondly in the current American climate, and finally, there is the issue of slavery."

That he would discuss his foreign travels with

her was oddly flattering. Maybe she liked him two pennies' worth. "So no tobacco farming."

"No tobacco, but I did bring back a number of medicinal plants, some trees, and a few wildflowers to see if they might be grown profitably here."

"Enterprising of you," Sara murmured, watching as he unwrapped her hand again.

"It doesn't look as angry," he decided. "I'd still feel better if you put something on it."

Sara took back her hand. "Then I will, when I get to the kitchen. I see Maudie turned down your sheets. The warmer for your sheets is by the hearth, and your wash water is in that ewer."

He smiled at her, making it even more imperative that Sara get herself down to the kitchen. "And my eyes grow heavier by the second. Good night, Mrs. Hunt, and my thanks for a pleasant welcome to Three Springs."

"Good night, Mr. Haddonfield, sleep well."

❧

Beckman watched the formidable Mrs. Hunt take her leave, watched the graceful way she reached up to appropriate the candle on his mantel. Did she realize she'd lost her cap in the scuffle with the cat?

Her hair was a glorious, vibrant red, though she'd caught it back in a severe bun. The sight of that hair had evoked a sense of déjà vu, the peculiar and unfounded certainty that he'd seen Sara Hunt somewhere else, her hair uncovered and the grace of her hands in evidence.

Which made no sense. She put him in mind of

nothing so much as home, bearing about her person the scents of lavender, lemon oil, laundry starch, and other domestic fragrances. Then too, she had hands that were both feminine and competent, not the hands of a debutante but the hands of a grown woman.

His hands had developed an itch to take down that hair and stroke it free and loose down her back. He recognized it as a remnant of the sailor's reaction to making port after a long, hard voyage, hardly an apt analogy for a little jaunt over the Downs. If he were lusting after a skittish, widowed—albeit pretty and curvaceous—housekeeper, then deprivation and fatigue were making him as indiscriminately randy as his older brother, Nicholas.

⁕

"That was the last of the wine." Sara let her head rest against the back of the armchair nearest the fire in her tiny sitting room. To call the space where she, Allie, and Polly dwelled an apartment was generous. They had three very small rooms and a sleeping alcove for Allie, though they'd shared far worse on the Continent and been grateful for it.

"She's asleep," Polly reported, peeking behind the curtain that provided Allie's bed a bit of privacy. "I'm surprised you were able to save a bottle so long—it was from Lady Warne's basket at Christmas, wasn't it?"

"It was, so unless we're willing to raid the strong spirits, we're officially an abstaining household hereafter. The occasional chocolate mousse will do much to console us, though. Whatever possessed you?"

"Winter megrims." Polly took the other rocking

chair, settling in with a sigh that was too weighty for such a young woman.

Part of that sigh, Sara well knew, was because the strain of megrim plaguing Polly had to do with Mr. Gabriel North, who would come home very late to find his favorite treat awaiting him.

Polly set the chair to rocking with a slow, rhythmic creak on the pitch of about… high G. "We need some sweetness in this life, you know? How straitened are we?"

Sara gave the same answer she'd been giving for months. "Desperately, though with the first of the month, we'll have another quarter's funds, and that's just next week."

"If Lady Warne remembers. Why don't you tell Mr. Haddonfield there is no money and there hasn't been enough for the entire time we've worked here?"

That Polly assumed Sara would decide what to say to whom rankled, but they knew no other way to go on.

"Lady Warne is elderly. One doesn't want to offend her, and in all likelihood, she's grown a bit forgetful. I will impart to Mr. Haddonfield what information is necessary, Polly, but not before it's necessary. He's a man, son of an earl, wealthy, and if we just humor him long enough, he'll likely go whistling on his way as soon as the Season starts up in earnest."

This was sound reasoning, except it had little basis so far in fact or observation.

"He'd better do more than just make work for us," Polly threatened darkly. "The household finances are tight, but I think the situation with the estate proper has grown unsalvageable, Sara. Gabriel won't say, but how does he expect to manage planting with only one team, and the one too old to truly do much?"

"That is Gabriel's puzzle to solve, and he hasn't failed Three Springs yet. We each tend to our own concerns, and we do that best on a good night's sleep."

Unfortunately for Sara, a good night's sleep was a necessity she frequently did without. Usually, it was the finances keeping her awake as she figured out ways to squeeze a spare farthing out of each penny or debated how to be more direct with Lady Warne.

Though lately, Sara's dreams were haunted by the future, by the prospect of more years, more decades even, sneezed away beneath ugly caps in a dusty old house. On the worst nights, she fretted that Tremaine St. Michael would find them, and she'd be denied even those dusty decades and the peace to be had as they drifted by.

❧

"Sara said there were matters you wanted to discuss with me, and after dinner I have every intention of seeking my bed posthaste." Gabriel North closed the laundry room door behind him, and yet a cold draft managed to eddy through the room as Beck stood wrapped in a towel beside the tub.

"I said that." Beck frowned, trying to recall what he'd been going on about. The day had been long, cold, and depressing, much of it spent in North's dark, growling, grousing, but never quite complaining company.

Every roof on every shed, barn, and outbuilding wanted repair. Every ditch and drain needed to be cleaned and unclogged. Every acre was in want of marling; every fence was sagging. The stone walls were nearly frost-heaved into mere piles of rock; the hedges were grown so high they didn't merely enclose the fields, they obscured them from view entirely.

The place was teetering on the edge of ruin, if not sliding down into the abyss. Beckman did not allow any metaphors to spring from that observation whatsoever.

North tossed him a bath sheet which was threadbare and scratchy but clean. "I'm listening."

"I wanted to discuss with you the possibility that we can render the twins productive members of the household. Either that"—Beck turned the towel on his damp hair—"or they're available for employment more suited to their temperaments."

"You want to cut them loose?" North drained the bathing tub then fastened it back in place. He was nearly as tall as Beck and dark where Beck was fair, but there was something about the look of Mr. Gabriel North that stirred Beck's memory. His features were harsh the way a man of the land came to look harsh— sun-browned, wind-scoured, crinkled at the corners, tried by biblical plagues and endless fatigue of the body and spirit.

And yet, women would find him attractive. As many foreign lands as Beck had traveled, women in all of them would have found Gabriel North attractive.

"I want to get Timothy and Tobias's lazy feet out from under Miss Polly and Mrs. Hunt's table," Beck said, shrugging into a shirt. "They take more than they give, by all accounts. If you see it otherwise, I'm willing to listen."

"They eat like a plague of locusts," North replied, swirling a large, blunt finger in the water in the warming tub. "And while they are not openly insolent with me, I seldom ask them for the time of day. They regard themselves as house servants and resent mightily that there's no butler, no male hierarchy placing them above the womenfolk because I refuse to trespass on what would be a house steward's domain. Sara occasionally inspires them to attempt some task, but they are adept at sabotage and have not enough honor to see that the women deserve their help."

"They're gone," Beck said, yanking his breeches up. "If they can't see how hard the women work, much less how hard you work, then they're blind as well as stupid. I can offer them to Lady Warne or just set them loose. God above…" He fell silent as North started calmly shedding clothes.

"I am not so pretty as some," North said as he tilted the warming tub to fill the bathing tub. "But then, I've no need to be."

"Was that a saber wound?" Beck asked, knowing curiosity was ill-mannered, but God's toes, North was lucky to be alive. The scar ran from his shoulder blade, across his back, right down to the curve of the opposite hip, thick, red, and ugly.

Few women would find that attractive—if any.

North sighed as he sank into the hot water. "A dirty saber wound, and tomorrow night, I go first and bedamned to your papa's title."

"You served King and Country?" Beck guessed, because sabers didn't commonly find themselves slashing at the backs of English land stewards.

"I did not. I'm going to have to appropriate your nancy damned soap, unless you're willing to retrieve mine from above stairs while I soak."

"And my dinner gets cold? Not bloody likely. Here." Beck proved himself the better man for all time and in all ways by not skipping the tin of soap into the tub, but rather, by handing it to the occupant. "You're dodging my admittedly rude question."

"My younger brother served," North said, his focus seemingly on washing one large male foot. "He was wounded. I went to fetch him home from the field hospital where he was not recovering to my father's satisfaction. As we made our way back to Portugal, some renegade Frenchmen set upon us, though we were both civilians at the time. The French were convinced they'd found officers out of uniform and were anticipating a fine time extracting information from us. My back was slightly the worse for having to differ with them."

"Oh, slightly," Beck allowed, wincing inwardly. A wound like that had to have pained him, had to have hurt like hell when he was tired, overworked, sweating like a beast… "You'll need my shaving kit too, if you're truly to make an impression."

"Needs must." North accepted the tin very civilly handed to him then studied the label at some length. "I'll need clean clothes too, damn it all. I came haring in here to heed your summons and anticipated I'd have to wait for my bath."

"My clothes will fit your scrawny frame," Beck said. "You needn't be so miserly with the soap, for God's sake. I can get more."

"Millefleurs was ever a favorite scent of mine. Hildegard will find me irresistible." Beck was waiting with the rinse water when North came up clean.

"You learned this before you got sent down from valet school," North suggested as he heaved to his feet.

"I learned this in a hundred different inns and hostelries. Cleanliness is a universal concept, often honored more in the breech." Beck dumped the water over North's head before he could reply. He'd been tempted to make the water chillingly cold, but as tired and sore as he was, he could only imagine North would have found some diabolical way to get even. "Your towel, such as it is."

"It's clean." North took the proffered towel. "And so, thank God, am I—even if I smell like an expensive whore."

"And you would be familiar with this scent?"

North met Beck's gaze then ducked his face back into the towel, and Beck had the satisfaction of knowing a shrewd and private man had just slipped. He'd slipped only a little, not enough to embarrass either of them, but he'd slipped.

"I'll take those clothes now." North hung the towel over a drying rack. "Unless you'd prefer I terrorize the ladies as I am?"

"That scar doesn't disfigure you." Beck assembled a stack of clothing and passed it to North. "You earned it, and it's a symbol of courage and bravery under duress. Nobody—no woman—who cared for you would see it as anything else."

"If you say so." North's tone was supremely bored. "Nice material, Haddonfield."

"Your clothing is just as well-made," Beck said. "Your boots are Hoby, if quite worn. Your waistcoat is Bond Street, perhaps Weston."

"Your point?" North wasn't quite as tall as Beck, but he packed even more muscle, and the clothes fit well.

"I don't judge a man for wanting some privacy," Beck said, "but if you're here under false pretenses, I won't put up with a threat to my grandmother's household, either."

Which might be a threat to the Hunt womenfolk, come to that.

"I'm no threat to anyone." North's expression was so bleak Beck had to look away.

"That makes two of us, then. Shall we go perfume the kitchen with our tidy selves?"

"Lay on, MacDuff." North gestured grandly with one arm, and Beck was struck by just how attractive a clean, well-turned-out Gabriel North appeared.

And how aggravatingly familiar... as he accurately quoted Shakespeare and filled out Beck's finery to good advantage.

Dinner was another surprisingly delicious meal, served in generous portions but without wine. Beck debated offering a bottle from the stores he'd sent down, but because North had helped him unload the wine crates and didn't remark it, he held his silence.

Dessert was flan, Polly having gotten her hands on both the oranges and the honey Beck had brought from Kent. Allie in particular made short work of her dessert, but Beck came in a close second.

"I have a request of you ladies," Beck said when everybody's bowl was empty. "I want to ask you to make a list of household necessities, things that are getting old, worn, or in low supply. I noticed the bath towels are nearly rags, for example, and the runner in the back hallway is nigh coming unbraided. The wagon is empty now, and the team is here. There's time before planting to make several trips to Portsmouth or even Brighton."

"That's very generous of you," Mrs. Hunt said, meeting Polly's guarded gaze, "but we're managing adequately."

"Lady Warne is a marchioness," Beck replied, and why had he anticipated having to coax this from them, despite the condition of the estate? "Her lineage is old, much respected, and deserving of a certain dignity. Three Springs falls short of that dignity, through no fault of present company, and I am charged with addressing the oversight. I'd like to see it done before I am recalled to the family seat, which summons might come at any time."

"Make your list, ladies," North said as he rose. "You won't get a better offer, and the poor man thinks a few towels and rugs will restore his grandmama's kingdom."

Beck kept his seat. "You as well, North. I realize the situation with the land is growing dire, so prioritize accordingly."

North sat back down and scowled mightily.

"The first priority would be sending those four mastodons that hauled your treasures here back where they came from. They eat everything in sight, and the new grass is weeks away."

The wagon had been heavily loaded and pulled

not by coaching horses but by the largest draft animals Belle Maison could spare.

"You're that short of hay?"

"I'll show you tomorrow what we have on hand," North said, scrubbing a hand over his face. "It's enough for our stock, if spring makes a timely appearance, but not much more. I sold off what we didn't absolutely need, because last year's yield was surprisingly good, given the generally miserable yields elsewhere."

"The past few seasons have been odd," Beck said. "I've made my requests, and if you'll all think on it, that's enough for the present."

"We'll think on it." Polly rose and caught her sister's eye. To Beck, the message was clear: *Not now, Sister; we'll talk later.* "Allie, I assume you'll want to scrape out the pan I baked the dessert in before we set it to soaking?"

Allie kept her seat, bouncing around on it in anticipation. "May I, Mama?"

"You may, and thank you for not bolting off as if the table caught fire. Did you put Mr. Haddonfield's clothes on his sofa?"

Allie looked puzzled. "You didn't ask me to."

Mrs. Hunt smiled at her daughter. "My apologies. I meant to, but then the scent of Polly's flan tickled my nose, and I must have forgotten. Mr. Haddonfield, if you want to gather your laundry, I'll light you up."

"I'll meet you in the laundry," Beck said. "Miss Polly, my compliments on another splendid meal. If you'll write the recipe down for that flan, I'll send it along to my father's cook. The orange zest is a magnificent touch."

"Of course." Polly looked pleased but wouldn't meet his gaze—though North was looking a bit disconcerted—so Beck contented himself with tweaking Allie's braid and bidding the child good night.

Beck cocked a finger-pistol at North. "Scrambled eggs at dawn, Mr. North. Last man out of bed has to clean up and take the scraps to the fair Hildy."

"I'll lie awake all night rather than suffer such a fate." North bowed with disconcerting elegance and disappeared up the steps.

Beck fetched an impressive pile of laundry, more than he'd realized a week of living could create. He'd arranged the load in a wicker basket when Mrs. Hunt joined him, a single candle in her hand.

Beck picked up the basket, lest she attempt to carry both the laundry and her candle. While they were wending their way through the darkened corridors of the house, Beck felt the chill seeping into his bones.

"I cannot recall a time when I was so desperately looking forward to my bed," he mused, mostly because his escort did not offer any conversation. "Whatever I expected of this place, it wasn't immediate exhaustion."

"You learn to pace yourself. It wasn't what I expected here either."

"How did you come to be here?" Beck asked, keeping his tone casual.

"My husband died while we were in Italy," she said, slowing to navigate a set of stairs. "Lady Warne was touring and had called upon us socially. She heard of Reynard's situation and offered us passage back here and employment for me. The packet landed in Brighton, and we've been here ever since."

This recitation struck Beck as a radically abbreviated telling of a more complicated tale. "And that was when?"

"A few years ago. A month after we got here, the old cook quit without notice, so Polly took over."

"She does very well with it," Beck said as they approached his room. Since his hands were full, Mrs. Hunt opened the door and preceded him into his sitting room. Once again, somebody had lit his fire, set his wash water by the hearth, and refilled the pitcher of drinking water. The room smelled good too, as if someone had freshened the lavender sachets hanging from the curtain sashes.

The effect was pleasant and welcoming, and yet Beck wasn't entirely comfortable with the notion that Mrs. Hunt herself had troubled over his comforts.

"I've added to your burden," he said, glancing around the room. "Just by being here, I make more work."

"But you lightened Gabriel's load." She lit the candles on his mantel and moved off to light some in his bedroom. "I'm surprised he allows it."

"He's an independent sort. I also think there's a bit of putting me through my paces going on."

"Maybe." She stood in the door between the two rooms and offered him a half smile. "Do you blame him?"

"Of course not." Beck put down his basket of laundry. "I meant what I said, Mrs. Hunt, about making a list."

Her smile became a quarter smile, then an eighth. "Of course you did. The question is, when you've replaced the towels and rugs, as Gabriel terms them, then what?"

"Then you have a livable property worthy of the Marchioness of Warne." Beck was tired and not up to deciphering females' moods.

"Or you have a saleable property, don't you?"

This again? "You think I'd turn out three females and a man who has worked himself to the bone simply to add to my grandmother's coffers?"

Her chin came up in a very unservile manner. "We're hired help, and you're the son of an earl. We live in an age of clearances and enclosures, Mr. Haddonfield. The working man can riot all he wants over the price of bread, but the price of bread doesn't change. You're perfectly within your rights to work us nigh to death and then sell the place for a song."

Beck advanced on her, fatigue letting his temper strain its leash. "Firstly, any decision to sell would be made by my grandmother, whose generosity of spirit has been proven by her dealings with you. Secondly, my task is to put the place to rights, not sell it. It's no more for sale now than it was the day you got here, Mrs. Hunt. Thirdly, I am a gentleman and would not leave you and yours to starve when you've served the family loyally under trying circumstances."

"I know better than to depend on any man's word," Mrs. Hunt said, her voice low and fierce as she glared up at him. "You mean what you say, now, Mr. Haddonfield, I'll grant you that much. But if your grandmother should die or the earl redirect your task, you can't stop the place from being sold."

Beck's brows came down in a frown, and he realized with a start he was not dealing with an arrogant exponent of the working class, but rather, a very tired, frightened mother and widow.

His second realization was that Mrs. Hunt employed a stage trick to make her presence more imposing: she remained always in motion. He'd observed her throughout the day, skirts always swishing madly. She dusted, she swept, she scrubbed; she beat carpets, boiled laundry, and bustled about, a rampage of cleaning on two feet. Standing this close to her, Beck saw she was in truth a slender woman of not much more than average height—and a tired slender woman at that.

"I cannot stop my relatives from dying or selling your home," Beck said, his tone much less belligerent, "but I can assure you they are honorable people, and when I convey to them the conditions under which you've labored, they will understand their debt to you, and to Polly and North. Mrs. Hunt—Sara—are you all right?"

༄

Mr. Haddonfield moved closer, close enough that Sara could catch a whiff of bergamot, an incongruous counterpoint to the roaring in her ears.

"I just need to sit," she managed. She felt the candle being taken from her grasp and then, in the next instant, felt herself scooped up and deposited on the bed, the scent of lavender bed sachets filling her nose.

"Head down." Mr. Haddonfield put a hand on her nape and gently forced her to curl her nose down to her knees. "You stay like that, and I'll fetch you some water."

She complied, not raising her head, the better to hide the ferocious blush suffusing her features. Her cap went tumbling to the floor, and she didn't try to restore it.

Mr. Haddonfield lowered himself beside her and let her ease back to a sitting position. "Better?"

"Better," Sara said. "I'm all right, really, but sometimes…"

"Drink." He wrapped her hand around a cold glass of water, peering at her with concern. "Your color is off."

"I'm pale by nature." Sara sipped the water cautiously.

"You're flushed now." His regard turned to a frown. "Are you coming down with something?"

"No," Sara said, handing him back the glass.

"I see." And perhaps he did see—possessed as he was of four sisters who each no doubt came down with the selfsame malady Sara suffered every four weeks or so. "I've wondered how women cope. Have some more water."

Sara stole a peek at him. He wasn't blushing or studying his fingernails or the ceiling, which was oddly heartening. They must be formidable sisters. "There's always a tot of the poppy when coping is truly a challenge," she muttered.

"I've seen my sister Kirsten wrapped so tightly around her hot water bottle you'd think it was her firstborn child. Susannah copes by tippling, and Della rages and breaks things, then gets weepy and quiet."

"I was like that," Sara said, knowing she shouldn't have this discussion with him. She'd certainly never had it with Reynard. "When I was younger, that is. I hope I don't rage and break things now, but the water bottle and the tippling sound appealing."

"Except you haven't a water bottle," he guessed. "And the only thing to tipple is the brandy I see in dusty decanters throughout the house, which might be a bit much."

"You're right, though I can put Madeira on my wishing list, can't I?"

"It's not a wishing list, it's a shopping list." He sounded both amused and exasperated. "You'll come to Portsmouth with me, because I've not shopped there in recent memory."

"The roads are miserable this time of year," Sara said, fatigue and the drops of laudanum she'd added to her tea making her eyes heavy. "We'll be stuck in town overnight, and that costs money."

And it would probably rain the entire time. Why did certain times of the month make a woman prone to the weeps?

"You should know Lady Warne is very well off, Mrs. Hunt. There's no excuse for her allowing this place to flounder as it has, except she delegated the land management to my father, and he delegated the task in turn to a pack of jackals posing as his London solicitors."

Mr. Haddonfield sounded very stern and a little bit far away, though he sat close enough that Sara could see a small J-shaped scar just past his hairline near his temple. She wanted to brush his hair back the better to examine the scar.

Sara refocused her thoughts to pick up the thread of the conversation. "The Three Springs house finances are still managed by Lady Warne herself. She sends down a quarterly allowance for the household, and separate funds for the kitchen. Polly and I receive salaries directly from her quarterly as well."

"So why are things in such poor condition?" Mr. Haddonfield asked. He reached out and brushed her hair back over her ear. The gesture should have startled Sara right off the bed, when instead it made her want to purr.

Like Heifer, who was probably the happiest member of the household.

"I've told Lady Warne the funds aren't sufficient as baldly as I might. It's as if she doesn't get my letters. Her notes are chatty and pleasant and wish us well, but the funding doesn't change."

"She'll read *my* letters. If I have to have Nicholas read them to her, she'll read them." He was very sure of himself. She'd expect no less of him.

"Who is Nicholas?" Sara's words came out sleepy, not quite slurred, and Mr. Haddonfield made the same gesture again, smoothing her hair back over her ear. She should rebuke him, except there was no disrespect in his touch.

Only an inability to abide disorder—Sara suffered from the same penchant—or perhaps a passing inclination to offer comfort.

"Nicholas is my older brother, the heir to the earldom, whose job while I'm immured here is to marry his prospective countess."

A little silence ensued, broken only by the crackling of the fire. He caressed her hair a couple of more times, his touch lingering.

"Mrs. Hunt?" Mr. Haddonfield's hand slid to her shoulder and shook it lightly. "Sara?"

"Hmm?" Her eyes fluttered open, and she focused on him with effort. Too much laudanum and too little sleep. What must he think of her?

"You're falling asleep. North claims it can be done with the eyes open. I can carry you to your bed."

"Carry me?" Sara straightened her spine through force of will, but between fatigue, the dragging of the poppy, and the mesmerizing pleasure of Mr. Haddonfield's hand, it was an enormous effort. "That won't be necessary."

His smile was slow and slightly naughty, like a small boy would be naughty, not a grown man. "If I wanted to carry you, you couldn't stop me."

"But you are a gentleman, so you will not argue this point with me."

"Suppose not, though I'll see you down the stairs, at least."

"I'm a housekeeper, Mr. Haddonfield." Sara rose, only to find her hand placed on Haddonfield's arm and held there by virtue of his fingers over her knuckles. "Your gallantries are wasted on me."

Though they were sweet, those gallantries. Sara liked them probably about as much as Mr. North liked his chocolate mousse.

"I respectfully disagree." He took up the candle and escorted her from the room. "If I lose favor with you, I'm out of clean laundry, candles, coal and wood for my fire, clean sheets, and God help me if I should split the seam of my breeches."

"God help us all, in that case." Sara gave up trying to hold her weariness at bay and moved at his side through the darkened house. "You really aren't going to sell the place?"

Beside her, Mr. Haddonfield stopped, a sigh escaping him in the near darkness.

He set the candle down and turned her by the shoulders, while Sara felt her heart speeding up for no good reason.

"You've managed as best you can, managed brilliantly, but you're battle-weary, Sara. You keep firing when the enemy has quit the field." He kept a hand on her shoulder, his thumb sliding across her collarbone in a slow, rhythmic caress.

He made no other move; he didn't use that seductive baritone on her in the darkened corridor, just circled his thumb over the spot where neck, shoulder, and collarbone came together. A vulnerable, lonely point on a woman's body.

Her mind did not comprehend what he was offering, but her soul longed for it, and her body leaned closer to his, then closer still. In the cold, dark corridor, she leaned on him, despite her pride, despite common sense, despite all the reasons she couldn't lean on any man ever again.

His arms came around her, and it felt so good. He'd called her Sara, and that had felt good too.

"I give you my word I will not recommend to my father or to Lady Warne that Three Springs be sold," he said, his voice sounding near her ear. "The house has good bones, and the resources are available to set it to rights. And even if Lady Warne should die and leave the property to some distant relation, I'll see you and yours situated. I give you my word on that too, and I've the means to do it, easily."

She lingered in his embrace for a few precious

moments, wanting to believe him but knowing only that she hadn't been held like this for years. It was worse, in a way, to be reminded of what she'd never have.

"Come." He turned her under his arm and slipped his hand down to her waist. With his free hand, he picked up the candle then escorted her in silence to the foot of the stairs. "Do you believe me, Sara?"

"I believe you mean what you say. I do not believe life often fits itself to our intentions, though."

"You're cautious. I can understand caution. To bed with you now, and you are ordered to make a nice long, expensive list for me, agreed?"

"I can manage that." She managed a smile too, albeit a tired one.

"Take the candle." He passed it to her, along with a smile that conveyed benevolence and something friendlier. His lips brushed her forehead, feather soft, like a warm breeze in the depth of winter. "Sweet dreams."

"Likewise." Sara turned without further words, feeling an equal inclination to touch her fingers to the center of her forehead and cry like a motherless child.

Menses. Damned, interminable, inevitable, toweringly inconvenient menses, and a tot of the poppy. That's what had put her in such a taking. It had to be her menses.

Three

ALLIE OPENED THE DOOR TO A LARGE, MOSTLY BARE room on the third floor. "This is my favorite place to play. I like the light best here, even on rainy days."

The light was abundant, Beck noted, mostly because what came in the row of uncurtained windows reflected off the gleaming hardwood floor and ricocheted off unadorned walls and a single large mirror.

"You paint." Beck took in the folded, paint-spattered cloth, the shortened easel collapsed against the wall, and the lingering scents of linseed and turpentine.

"I love to paint. I'm not allowed to paint human subjects, or portraits, but I will when I'm older, Mama said. This is what I finished a few days ago, so now I won't paint for a while. Mama doesn't want me to forget how to be a child, whatever that means."

She gamboled over to him, a small canvas in her hand. Beck took it from her, expecting to have to gush credibly over a crude rendering of some books and flowers.

"God's toenails." His carried the painting to the windows the better to goggle at it. George was the art connoisseur of the family, but Beck had been to enough royal exhibitions at various European courts and was enough his mother's son to have something of an eye.

"This is quite good. I expect Heifer to yawn and stretch right in my hands." She'd used brushstrokes to somehow render his fur nearly... pettable.

"The light on the mouse isn't quite right." Allie leaned over his forearm to peer at her work. "I'm working on secondary light sources, according to Aunt. She's my teacher. I got Heifer right, because he will hold still and let me study him, but mice aren't good subjects."

"You could study a painting of a mouse, or do sketches to work it out."

Allie looked intrigued. "I've never used a painting as a subject. It would have to be a good painting."

"If you go to the exhibitions in London, there are all manner of art students sketching the master-works," Beck said, still fascinated with the little canvas, because clearly, he was in the presence of a budding genius. Allie's quick mind and inherent creativity weren't suffering for lack of hide-and-seek. The child was built to focus on things more inter-esting and sophisticated than which playmate was hidden under the bed.

"You've got a whimsical touch, Allie." Beck tilted the frame. "You're deadly accurate too. Don't paint sad things, or you'll have everybody in tears."

Allie took the painting from him and frowned at it. "You don't think I should stick to watercolors?"

"Are you competent with watercolors?" Beck

asked, eyeing the room and seeing it made over into a studio.

Allie wrinkled her nose. "I'm competent. Watercolors are tedious, though, and best suited to tedious subjects, like weather and landscapes. For living things, oils are better."

"But you're not to paint portraits?"

"I am not." Allie heaved a martyred sigh. "So I did Heifer, and I rather like it myself. I think I'll do him again—Mama allowed it wasn't quite a portrait."

"You could also do my horse. There are people who make a great deal of money doing portraits of beasts for the very wealthy."

"I could be rich?" Allie was pleased with this notion.

"Or you could be in a lot of trouble." Sara's voice cracked like a whip from the door.

"Hullo, Mama." Allie's features arranged themselves into careful neutrality, and Beck felt as if the sun had disappeared behind a maternal thundercloud.

He donned a smile and faced the bad weather. "Good morning, Mrs. Hunt. You look rested."

She did. Rested and mortally peeved.

"Allemande, your aunt could use help preparing luncheon," Sara said, her tone softening. "And there's a bucket of scraps to take out to Hildegard. If you see Mr. North, tell him lunch will be ready soon."

"Yes, Mama." Allie scampered off, leaving a ringing silence in her wake.

"She's quite talented." Beck picked up the cat's picture. "Quite talented."

"She's quite young," Sara rejoined, but her tone was weary, despite her well-rested state.

"How are you feeling?" Beck intended the question to be polite but realized he truly wanted to know. She'd been dead on her feet the night before, and by his reckoning, had slept only eight hours. By the time he'd left Paris, he'd been capable of sleeping for days at a stretch.

"Rested." She took the painting from him and sank down onto a daybed protected by a Holland cover. "Or maybe not rested enough. I feel like my head is wrapped in cotton wool, and I could just sleep until the flowers are up."

"Laudanum leaves me feeling that way," Beck said, sitting beside her uninvited. Laudanum had left him within a whisker of permanent oblivion, truth be known.

"I used only a drop. I only ever use a drop."

"Good for you." Beck studied her hands while pretending to look at the painting rather than let the conversation wander over the relative merits of laudanum, absinthe, hashish, and other poisons. "She says she's working on secondary light sources. What are those?"

"Polly could explain it best, but if I tried to paint, say, the leg of that chair, I'd have to account for the effect of the sunlight coming directly in the window and for the light reflecting from the mirror behind the chair. One way to study it is to take away the mirror, then put it back, and so forth."

"But Allie's approach is more instinctive than that. She's an artist, not a technician. For a young girl, she's very, very good."

"She scares the daylights out of me," Sara said quietly as she rose and turned her back to him. "Any child is prey to the more powerful people in her life, but a talented child in particular. Allie is isolated here, I know, but I don't think she's unhappy. Polly is a good instructor, and there's more to life than painting as long as Allie is with us. My own mother…"

"Yes?" Beck's gaze went beyond Sara to the wide windows that opened on a bleak view of the snow-dusted Downs to the north. He had the sense this mother Sara alluded to lived off in that direction.

"She worried, like I'm worrying. Papa too."

He took a step closer. "Over Polly's talent? Allie said Polly is her instructor."

Sara looked momentarily confused. "Yes, they worried over Polly, but over me too, and Gavin."

"Who is Gavin?" Beck shifted again to stand beside her.

"Was." Sara glanced over at him, a mere flick of her gaze over his face before she was again inspecting the hills in the distance. "He was our older brother, but he died shortly before I married. Everybody called him Gavin, but his real name was Gavotte."

"Allemande, Gavotte… Was yours a musical family?"

"We were. My husband said he fell in love with my name."

Her tone suggested this was not a cheering memory. "Sarabande," Beck guessed. "It is pretty, and your sister would be Polonaise?"

"Polly for short, and I'm Sarabande Adagio." Her lips quirked up, as if a housekeeper ought not to have such a fanciful name. "I was Sara Addy when was I younger."

"That's lovelier than Beckman Sylvanus Haddonfield.

My mother wanted me to have a name that would stand up to the rigors of being the spare."

"Are there rigors?" This time, her glance lingered on him. "You don't seem like a man who's burdened by his birthright."

"That's the second time the topic has come up today." Beck shifted away from the substantial chill coming off the windows. "North quizzed me on it over breakfast, and his questions set me to thinking."

"About?"

"What is a land steward doing reading the label of my soap tin?" Beck asked slowly.

"Waiting for his turn in the bath?"

"The label is entirely in French, Sara," Beck said gently. "Florid, silly French. He quotes Shakespeare, and his clothing is made by the finest tailors in London. How much do you know about our Mr. North?"

"Not as much as you'd like to know, apparently," Sara replied. "I know this. Until he arrived shortly after us, the place was a shambles. Lady Warne hasn't been here for years and years, and if you think it's a disgrace now, you should have seen it before Gabriel put his shoulder to the wheel."

"I don't dispute that he works very hard." Beck regretted bringing the subject up at all, but if North hadn't served in the military, the explanation he'd given for his scar was somewhat suspect. "And a man's past is his own business, unless it's going to haunt him and those around him."

"We're all haunted by our pasts." Sara shifted away from the window, as if leaving the topic itself out there on the Downs. "Luncheon approaches, and that seems more worthy of attention at the moment. I trust Gabriel, and I do not feel comfortable discussing him behind his back."

"Not well done of me," Beck admitted. "I'm to spend the afternoon with him going over the books. Have you started on your shopping list?"

"I have not," Sara said, preceding him through the door. "I spent the morning cutting out a dress for Allie. Warm weather finally approaches, and the only bolt of suitable material I have is summer weight."

"And what about some new dresses for you and Polly?" Beck asked, putting her hand on his forearm. "You are females, and human, and that means a new frock from time to time is in order."

"We're managing. One needn't have an impressive wardrobe to bring Hildy her slops."

Beside her, Beck remained silent, but he felt frustration stirring. *Managing* was Sarabande Adagio Hunt's euphemism for eking out survival on a rotten, neglected estate far from meaningful society. He suspected some fear kept her here, grateful for her bleak, busy existence, but he railed against the compromise she'd made for herself and for her daughter.

Maybe she rusticated here, far from home and family, because she was afraid this was her only alternative to starvation.

Maybe she was still grieving the husband who died in Italy.

Maybe she feared the world's influence on her talented daughter.

And maybe—claiming to have been married but bearing the same last name as her unwed sister—Sara feared her own secrets might come to light. Beck felt that thought settle in the back of his mind, knowing it wouldn't let him rest until he'd gotten to the bottom of it.

∽

"I believe the hallmark of the term 'footman' is that those answering to the description be on their feet." Beck kept his voice down because no Haddonfield over six feet tall ever had to raise his voice to be heard. When he saw he had Timothy and Tobias's attention, he continued in the same chillingly civil tones.

"I wanted to give you two the benefit of some doubt." He glanced around the room. "But seeing—and smelling—the state into which you've allowed your own quarters to deteriorate, there's little likelihood you're just a pair of misguided, empty-headed fellows needing a firm hand to steer you back to the true definition of earning a wage."

"Now see here, guv." Tobias, the less odoriferous of the pair, managed to stand at last. "You can't come a-bustin' in here, tossing insults around like some… some…" He glanced at his brother, and support arrived on cue.

"Like some nabob new to his riches. Footmen wait on the family, not on the servants, and that's a natural fact." Tim didn't bother to get to his feet to deliver this pearl, but from his position lounging on his cot, he grinned at his brother.

Tobias nodded smugly. "Aye, like a nabob new to his riches."

"Because I am Lady's Warne's family, you ignore

my words at your peril," Beck said. "Firstly, you will wash your persons at the cistern behind the barn. You disgrace Miss Polly's table in your present condition, not to mention the memory of a mother who no doubt raised you better than this. Secondly, you will present yourselves, in livery, to Mrs. Hunt, and notify her that henceforth, you will be filling all of the wood boxes and coal buckets twice daily. You will trim wicks, refill the oil lamps, dust the entire library weekly, then start on the windows in the library, and continue on until every window on the house is scrubbed inside and out. Lady Warne pays good money to the Crown for the privilege of her windows, the least you can do is allow us to see out of them."

"You want us to wash?" Tobias looked utterly flummoxed. "In the *cistern*?"

"You aren't fit for the laundry. Should you find my direction not to your liking, I'll be taking the team into Portsmouth soon. You are welcome to collect two week's wages and seek other employment there, in which case you will need to clean this sty—Hildegard would disdain your chambers in their present condition—or the cost of cleaning it will be deducted from your severance. I'll tell Mrs. Hunt to expect you by two of the clock."

"Severance?"

The word hung in the air as Beck softly closed the door and took a few lungfuls of clean, cold air. They had a parlor stove in their room, and apparently felt no compunction about keeping it stoked with coal. The stench had been amazing, as had Beck's forbearance.

He couldn't stand a cheat, and these two had

been cheating his grandmother—step-grandmother, true, but an old woman nonetheless—for years. He sincerely hoped they caught their deaths scrubbing in the cistern.

"You look like you want to kill someone," North remarked conversationally.

Beck stopped on the back porch and took another series of deep breaths.

"How did you *not* kill them? Even a footman has a certain kind of honor. A damned potboy can know enough to earn his wages."

North glanced up at the sky assessingly. "In my experience, a lack of personal integrity isn't the exclusive province of the nobility. Are you ready to see the books?"

"I'm ready to hit something." Or to find the brandy decanter and become thoroughly familiar with its contents—which would not solve the problem at hand and would plunge Beck into a pit of self-recrimination.

"If you truly want a round of fisticuffs, I'm happy to oblige." North began to shrug out of his coat. "I've always wondered what Gentleman Jackson really accomplished with his young sprigs."

"North," Beck's tone eased, "you needn't oblige violent urges you didn't inspire. Besides, I wouldn't want to earn Miss Polly's everlasting ire by rearranging the features the Creator gave you."

North shrugged back into his coat. "As long as I can eat, Miss Polly will be content."

"I don't think you give your animal charm and sophisticated manners enough credit. She watches you eat the way I watch some women walk away."

North glanced at him, his expression unreadable.

"It's spring," he said shortly. "You're away from the pleasures of Town and seeing the sap rise wherever you look. But if I catch you watching Polly walk away with one hint of disrespect on your ugly face, Haddonfield, I will rearrange *your* features."

"I'm all atremble." Beck resisted the urge to probe, though Miss Polly's sentiments toward Mr. North were apparently returned on some level. "I can only hope the twins are trembling as well."

"My feelings regarding those two are mixed." North opened the door to the back hallway. "On the one hand, I hope they stay and become useful. Finding good domestics here in the provinces is nigh impossible. On the other hand, I will never trust them, because they've shown they lack honor but can be motivated by fear."

Beck followed him into the house. "You have a way of boiling things down to essentials that puts me in mind of Lady Warne herself, and perhaps my father."

"Flattery will get you nowhere," North tossed over his shoulder. "Shall we make a pot of tea to cheer us on?"

"And snitch a few of the biscuits Miss Polly baked this morning," Beck said, lifting the lid of a large crockery jar.

"That's only the decoy cache, you know." North rinsed out the teapot and refilled it from the kettle on the hob.

"Of course I know." Beck extracted a large handful of biscuits. "I also know Miss Polly would be insulted did we not raid it. Bring the honey. I refuse to face book work without something sweet in my tea, and do not think of reusing the damned leaves."

"Oh, the Quality…" North muttered loudly enough for Beck to hear. He loaded their tea tray with cream, honey, and mugs nonetheless.

Beck took the tray from the counter. "What did your expert agrarian assessment of the sky foretell in terms of the weather?"

"The same thing it's foretold for several weeks now." North grabbed a tea towel, draped it over Beck's shoulder, and followed him up the back stairs. "Spring is coming."

"My grandmother employs genius at every turn," Beck muttered loudly enough for North to hear.

"I might trip, you know?" North informed nobody in particular, "and bump into somebody else, who might drop our only good teapot."

"My second-favorite teapot sits ready to serve in the pantry," Beck tossed over his shoulder as they reached the library. "Please God, tell me you lit a damned fire in here."

"Wood, we have," North said, holding the door for him. "At least for another year or two, but when we catch up with the deadfall, we'll be buying coal like everybody else."

The room was high ceilinged, so the roaring fire in the hearth cast out only so much warmth, but the sofa facing it helped keep what there was from dissipating entirely. Beck set the tea service on the desk and poured them each a cup.

"You keep the books?" he asked, handing North his own cup to doctor.

"I do," North said, adding both honey and cream, much to Beck's satisfaction. "I incorporate the household expenses in the general ledger, but Sara has her own set of books, though why she bothers I do not know."

Beck sipped and decided that with cream and honey, strong black tea was almost a substitute for a stout tot of brandy.

Almost.

"Why shouldn't she track expenses and income?" Beck asked, moving to the sofa. North stayed by the desk, stirring his tea.

"I've met Lady Warne a handful of times," he said, "so don't come after me with fists flying when I say I've doubted her grasp of reality."

"My fist is wrapped around a strong, hot cup of tea. Perfectly happy there, too. Why do you question Lady Warne's sanity?"

"She must think a household runs on good cheer." North sank onto the sofa near Beck. "She sends along notes updating the ladies on the latest fashion gaffes made by the strutting dandies and preening peacocks in Mayfair—as if Polly or Sara care a damn for any of that. But she neglects as often as she recalls to send the sums they need to sustain life here. I suspect they both use their salaries to augment what is intended to be the household budget."

"As you use yours?"

"Drink your tea or it will get cold, and we'll be forced to dust off that decanter, which goes against my grain, as the help mustn't tipple."

"You're the help now? How movingly humble

you've become, North. So show me these books and then to the brandy."

He regretted those words. Drinking before dinner was ill-advised in the extreme. But he'd been good lately—appallingly good—and he still wanted to hit something and somebody as the enormity of the neglect all around him only became more obvious.

North had all but cheated the devil to keep any crop going on the place, and at a time when what a crop could fetch was precious little, and what it cost to farm was great.

"And it's not going to get better for some time," Beck said several hours later. "The general state of things, I mean. The weather for the past few years hasn't helped, but you can't cashier out thousands of able-bodied men who fought for damned near two decades and not see an impact. Then too, there are markets for what England produces, but it hardly pays to try to export with the taxes so high."

"We still have the free trade on this coast," North said. "Conditions on the Continent are far worse than what we suffer here, and there's a market for almost anything you can sneak onto a boat."

"I will ignore your casual observation." Beck sat back and let North pour them each a tot of brandy. The drink was good quality, which helped a man sip it, regardless of all temptation to the contrary. "What a bloody mess."

North enjoyed his brandy in silence, while Beck cogitated and drank.

With North's dark gaze taking in every movement, Beck set his glass down on a corner of the table not covered with ledgers. "My father's dying request was that I set the place to rights, because he felt the neglect here was a blot on his honor. I intend to see his wishes carried out."

"Your father is dying?" North put the question casually, no more weight to it than, "Your horse is a bay?"

Well, hell. In for a penny...

"Bellefonte is at his last prayers." Beck got the words out by staring at his half-empty glass. "Sent me off so I wouldn't have to see the final indignities. Sent us all off, except for my sister Nita."

"And this is why your brother is hunting a bride? You're the spare, why aren't you on the prowl with him?"

"Took my turn in that barrel, North." Had North offered condolences, Beck would have left the room and taken the decanter with him. "Even Papa won't ask that of me again. Started me on rather an unfortunate road, but Nick's the better fellow, and he'll manage. What do you recommend for Three Springs?"

North frowned—North was always frowning, so Beck tried not to ascribe significance to it.

"You ask my prescription for Three Springs," North said. "It will take more than money, Haddonfield. In the last century, this was a gracious, respected manor, and people were happy to work here. I've heard enough in the village to know they take the twins as the measure of the place. The locals won't throw in with Three Springs if they think you're just a nine days' wonder, down from Town to count the lambs then disappear. Somebody has to convey an abiding interest in this place. I nominate you."

North's grasp of the situation and logic he applied to it were unassailable.

"Nomination declined. I've two younger brothers who could use a property, and four sisters in need of a dowry. Let's nominate one of them, shall we? Then too, when Nick becomes earl, he can use this as one more excuse to get away from his countess."

"My condolences to his countess," North said in equally level tones. "In any case, you can't just buy Three Springs's way back to profitability. You have to earn its way back to respectability."

Beck leaned against the sofa's lumpy upholstery and silently railed against these simple truths, truths he'd thought applied mostly to people and not pieces of the English countryside. "You are a cruel man, Gabriel North. I like you."

North blinked then smiled, an expression both sardonic and sweet. "I like you too, Haddonfield. You preserve me from recruiting the fair Hildegard as my drinking companion, and smell marginally better than she."

They returned their attention to the ledgers, which were tidy, complete, and a study in economies. Beck thought of those economies when he finished off another generous meal in pleasant company. Sara offered to light Beck up to his rooms, and because the indignity of falling asleep where he sat had no appeal, he passed her the candle.

"Your servant, Mrs. Hunt." He bowed slightly and smiled at her, and they were soon treading the cold corridors.

"You're quiet all of a sudden, Mr. Haddonfield, as

if a candle has gone out. You were charming at dinner. Now you fall silent."

"Considering Polly and her swain," Beck replied as they approached his door. "You don't have to escort me up, you know, but I considered you might have wanted to leave them some privacy." He opened the door for her and admired her backside as she preceded him into his sitting room.

She was quick and graceful, and she smelled of all the lovely scents of a well-kept home. He hadn't spent dinner being charming. He'd spent dinner making infernal small talk, wishing she'd look at him and resenting the hell out of her stupid caps.

Too much wine with dinner perhaps, or not enough.

Mr. Haddonfield was in some sort of male mood. As he prowled along beside her through the dark, frigid corridor, Sara had to question her own motives. He knew where his room was now, and he was moving past the role of guest to temporary household member.

He did not need a housekeeper to tuck him in.

But Sara needed something from him. A few minutes of adult conversation that weren't about Hildy's slop bucket or Heifer's amours.

A hand on her shoulder, a smile unlike the ones he tossed out so liberally in company during a dinner that had felt interminable.

"I'll make sure Maudie turned down your covers." She brushed by him into his bedroom, hearing his footsteps behind her.

"Sara." Large male hands settled on her hips as

Sara flipped down his covers. She straightened slowly then froze.

Had her thoughts inspired him to this? He'd touched her before, and God help her, she'd liked it. He was comfortingly large, clean, and full of a kind of bodily masculine competence that reassured. She wasn't reassured—exactly—by *this* touch, and it wasn't in the least proper. Still, she merely stood and tried to draw air into her lungs.

"You should slap me," he murmured near her ear. "You really, really should." He remained like that, his hands on her hips, holding her lightly but firmly from behind; then Sara felt one hand shift, and her cap was gone.

"I'm asking you to wallop me, Sara." His voice was a low, soft rumble at her nape, and she felt his hand withdrawing pins from her hair. He kept his other hand around her middle, his fingers splayed just below her waist.

Over her womb. The heat from his hand alone threatened to buckle her knees.

"I just want…" He paused, and more pins went silently sailing to the quilt on his bed. Her braid came down and down, and then he unraveled it, slowly drawing his fingers through each skein until it fell to her waist in wild, curling locks.

"You hide your light," he accused softly, and Sara felt him nuzzling her nape.

This was wrong; she knew it was wrong, but in his world she was a widow and fair game. Nominally, she was out of reach because she was under his extended family's protection, but he was in truth just a visitor—and even according to the rules of his kind, she could stop him.

She *would* stop him, she vowed, just as he gently brushed aside the hair at her nape and settled his lips against her skin.

"Merciful God…" As heat ricocheted from his kiss through her body, Sara hung her head, knowing his arm was now supporting her, knowing the bed was right before them.

The bed…

She marshaled her considerable resolve and lifted a hand to cover the one spread over her belly.

"Mr. Haddonfield." She couldn't manage much more than a whisper, not when he was working his way to the side of her neck, the brush of his mouth so devastatingly tender she wanted… "Beckman, you have to stop."

He went still, and she felt his sigh against her collarbone. He turned her in his arms and folded her against him, resting his chin on her crown. She slipped her arms around his lean waist and silently thanked him—both for ceasing and for not expecting her to stand unaided.

"You should still slap me," he rumbled, his tone sad. "I would apologize, but that would imply remorse, and after this day, after listening to North's litany of economies and inconveniences, after tramping through mud for hours and missing… all I feel is frustration."

No, that was not all he felt. Plastered against his body, Sara could feel the contour of a nascent erection pressing against her belly. God above, he'd be… splendid. She wanted to push that thought away and push the man away as well, but he sounded so bleak, almost as bleak as she felt.

"No more damned caps, Sara." He rubbed his chin over her unbound hair. "They're a damned lie, and you're fooling no one."

He wasn't being charming and gracious now. Perhaps she was the one who'd been fooled earlier.

"I do not countenance untruths."

"Yes, you do." His tone was amused, but Sara didn't dare steal a glance at him. "We all do, myself included, if only to lie to ourselves. But you are not to wear those ridiculous caps."

"And you are not to go kissing me in your bedroom." She tried to pull away, but forgot the bed was immediately behind her and found herself unceremoniously sitting on it. She gazed up at his great height, trying to read his expression by the firelight.

"I haven't kissed you." He sank to his knees, utterly befuddling her. "Yet."

He remedied the oversight, brushing his lips over hers while he knelt between her legs. He wasn't an arrogant or clumsy kisser, thank God, because as long as it had been since her last kiss, Sara needed to be coaxed. He'd been clever by going to his knees, putting her a few inches above him, a position that suggested she had more control than he. His hand cupped the back of her head, gently burying itself in her hair as if he were hungry for even that simple touch.

But his mouth... he tasted of the cinnamon in Polly's apple cake, and his lips were cool while his tongue was hot and knowing, and full of delicate, dangerous invitation. Sara's insides fluttered, but she couldn't resist the temptation to touch his hair, to part her lips just a little.

Still, he didn't plunder but rolled his head back against her hand, rubbing his scalp against her fingers, then settling his mouth over hers again. Sara's other hand found his shoulders and went skimming over his arm and his chest, then joined its mate tangled in his hair. Such silky, thick hair he had, and such a silky, skillful tongue.

She sighed into his mouth, and the wistfulness of it surprised her. He broke the kiss and rested his forehead against hers.

The fire roared softly, while Sara sat on the bed, her hands in his hair, her mind as empty as the moors in winter, while her body... her body knew exactly what it wanted, with whom, where, and when.

"I'd just use you," Beck whispered. Sara didn't push him away. He sank down, his arms around her waist, and laid his cheek against her thigh.

"That would hardly be novel."

Nor tragic, and yet, she approved of him for regaining his senses. She did not like him for it—she positively resented him, in fact—but he was striving for honor, something Reynard would have found laughable.

When Beckman made no move to rise—to let her off the bed—she indulged the urge to pet him. His hair was corn-silk fine, and his jaw slightly raspy with beard. The scar near his temple barely registered beneath her fingertips, but she did feel it.

For long moments, he didn't stop her, so maybe her touch was soothing to them both.

"You deserve better, Sarabande Adagio," he said, loudly enough she knew he intended her to hear him.

"Maybe you do too, Beckman Sylvanus."

They stayed like that until Beck shoved to standing and drew Sara to her feet.

He frowned down at her, looking not at all like a man intent on dallying with the housekeeper. "I'm still not apologizing."

Sara frowned right back. "And I'll wear my caps if I blessed well please to."

Brave talk. He stroked a hand over the scandal of her unbound hair and smiled.

"Of course you will." He kissed her cheek and stepped back. "But it will be a lie, and we will both know the truth."

She was not going to allow him the last word. Sara brushed a hand through his hair, kissed *his* cheek, and swished past him.

"Go to sleep, Beckman," she called over her shoulder. "You are more tired than you realize, and tomorrow is a busy day."

Four

Like a good housekeeper, Sara—no plain "Mrs. Hunt" kissed like that—closed the door to Beck's bedroom to keep in the heat. The agreeable result for Beck was that her various homey scents lingered as well. He sat on the bed, canvassing his emotions, trying to find the shame and failing wonderfully.

What he felt was horny.

He also felt relieved—not quite proud—because he had stopped. When she'd asked it of him, he'd stopped. He hadn't even gotten a hand on one of those magnificent breasts of hers; he'd merely kissed her—and she'd kissed him back.

The wonder of that had him opening the falls of his breeches and extracting his cock from his clothing. He wasn't given to frequent masturbation, but the erection in his hand didn't deserve to be ignored. Typically, he refrained from onanism because his imagination wasn't up to the task of adequately inspiring his body. Recalling images of Sara's unbound hair glinting in the firelight and indulging in the fantasy of it brushing over his naked body, Beck let himself have his pleasure. When he was thoroughly spent, he stripped, washed, and climbed between the covers, his last thought a bet with himself that Sara wouldn't wear her cap tomorrow.

❧

Beck took himself down to the kitchen in the morning expecting to find only North, because the womenfolk made a religion out of rising early. To his surprise, he found Sara and Polly both, and the room redolent with the scents of bacon and fresh bread.

"Sleeping Beauty arises," Polly chirped from where she was taking bread out of the oven.

"It's getting light earlier and earlier," Beck improvised, stealing a glance at Sara only to find her stealing a glance at him.

No cap.

Her smile when he caught her eye was like a spring sunrise on a cold morning, slow, sweet, and powerful for pushing back the cold and the darkness both. She winked at him, and his pleasure in the day defied description.

He winked back nonetheless, thinking Nick would have winked first.

"I'll bring in some wood," Beck said, for that smile and that wink had parts of his body in need of the cold air.

"Don't bother." Polly took another fragrant, golden loaf from the oven. "North has seen to it, and Allie's helping him."

"Then I can help Maudie milk the cows." Beck was off to the back hall before Polly had a rejoinder for that too. He stood on the back porch, hearing the baritone of North's voice from the woodshed across the backyard and the higher-pitched tones of Allie's voice in reply.

North emerged, carrying a large armload of wood. "If it isn't the man responsible for the clearances."

"Good morning, Mr. Haddonfield," Allie piped. Her load was much smaller, but her posture copied North's exactly.

"What clearances? And good morning to you too, princess."

"The twins are gone." North paused to let Allie dump her wood into the wood box first. "Must have left after you reminded them of their options. Thank you, Miss Allie."

She curtsied and grinned. "I'm going to help Maudie."

"We'll tell your mama," North assured her, "and stay out of the stalls until we've mucked. You don't have your boots on."

She waved that admonition aside and took off for the barn.

Beck frowned at her retreating form. "Cheerful little soul."

"The women are all in good spirits this morning." North dumped his load on top of Allie's smaller offering. "Even Hildy seems to be smiling, which is unnerving from a lady uniformly out of sorts unless there's a slop bucket in the offing."

"Maybe there's a promise of spring in the air." Beck did not comment on a man who was confessing to reading the moods of a breeding sow.

"Maybe." North straightened slowly and braced his

hands low on his back. "And maybe the ladies were more uncomfortable with a pair of drunken wastrels on the property than I perceived, and for this I feel remiss."

Remiss was probably North's term for wanting to beat himself silly. Beck savored that notion in the privacy of his thoughts. "Do you think it's dry enough to risk a trip into the village today?"

North glanced around, likely seeing a thousand chores that would not complete themselves. "For what purpose?"

"To bring back a load of hay from the livery, to pick up the post, to ask about the twins, and to leave their severance at the posting inn. To lay in a few staples to tide us over until we can make it in to Portsmouth, to get the hell off this muddy patch of earth."

"Ah, youth." North loaded a wealth of amused condescension in two syllables.

"You're at best a few years my senior," Beck said. "Recall I've yet to see this thriving metropolis of a village."

"There's a whorehouse, if that's what you're not asking." North stopped on the back porch. "I'm told the ladies are clean and friendly, though it's not at all what you're used to."

"North…" Beck paused, because privacy was one thing, and North's opinion of him was something else entirely. "You do not know what I'm used to, and I did not ask you for particulars on the vices available close at hand. I am not, nor have I ever been, plagued with the tendencies that make my brother nigh infamous."

"Your brother?"

"Nicholas, Viscount Reston." Beck walked over to the porch railing and leaned a hip on it. "He is rather a favorite with a certain stripe of female, with any stripe of female for that matter. For those of questionable virtue and reasonable discretion, he returns their appreciation… or he did. He's bride hunting now, and one suspects this has curbed his enthusiasm for certain activities."

"He bride hunts while you rusticate. London's loss is Three Springs's gain. Shall we see to our breakfast?"

From North, that amounted to a ringing endorsement of Beck's chosen task, which North would, of course, serve up as casually as scrambled eggs on toast.

❧

"This is beautiful, Mr. St. Michael. Absolutely… I saw one like it in the villa of a Russian archduke near Sebastopol. It's likely Persian and worth a great deal."

Tremaine St. Michael did not let his impatience show by gesture or expression, because commerce was commerce, whether one peddled wool—which he did in great quantity and very profitably—or wanted to know what a very old and ornate amber-and-ivory chess set was worth.

Of course, it was worth "a great deal."

"Can you appraise it?"

Mr. Danvers, a thin, blond exponent of genteel English breeding, studied the set for a moment, kneeling down to peer at it from eye level. "Only approximately. The surest indicator of value is to hold a discreet auction for those with the means to indulge their aesthetic sophistication."

Aesthetic sophistication. This was English for *greed*. Tremaine's Scottish antecedents would have called it stupidity when it meant significant coin was spent on a game. His French forbearers would likely have called it English vulgarity.

Though it was a pretty game. Where Reynard had found it remained a mystery. Danvers was the English expert on antique chess sets; if he didn't know its provenance, then nobody would.

Which might be very convenient.

"I have some other pieces I'd like you to look at."

Danvers rose to his modest height like a hound catching a scent. "More chess sets?"

"Two, one of which might be older than this one."

The man bounced on the balls of his feet, and though he wasn't overly short for an Englishman, his enthusiasm made Tremaine feel like a mastiff in the company of some overbred puppy.

"This way, and then I'm going to need a recommendation for somebody who can appraise some paintings for me—somebody very discreet."

"Of course, sir. I will put my mind to it as soon as we've seen the chess sets."

Even Danvers, though, couldn't stifle a gasp when Tremaine took him to the storage room at the back of the house. For a man obsessed with chess sets, he spent a long time gazing about at the plunder Reynard had begged, bartered, or stolen from courts all over the Continent.

"You will need more than an appraiser of paintings, won't you, Mr. Tremaine?"

Tremaine sighed, because Danvers had spoken

not with the eagerness of a hound scenting prey, but with something approaching awe. Reynard's taste had always been exquisite, ruinously exquisite.

So much for discretion. "For now, let's start with the chess sets, shall we?"

❧

The weather held fair, and Beck's mood improved for being away from the house and having some time to assess the land itself while the roads dried and the ladies packed a substantial lunch.

The field before them was fallow, but from the looks of the dead bracken, the crop had been thin and the weeds thick.

"What about marling now, before planting, and letting it fallow over the summer, then planting a hard winter wheat in the fall?" Beck was thinking out loud as he slouched in Ulysses's saddle.

"What is a winter wheat?" North asked.

Beck was learning to read North's varied scowls, and this scowl connoted skepticism and veiled curiosity.

"When I was in Budapest, the mills were grinding wheat in mid-summer. I asked how that could be, and it was explained to me that on the slopes of the Urals there are strains of wheat you plant in the early fall. They ripen in June or so, and you have two months to harvest and fertilize before you put in another crop. We have plenty enough at Belle Maison to seed this field and several more."

North's scowl became more heavily laced with curiosity. "So if we're not planting until fall, how do you keep the cover from going all to weeds, and is there any corner of the semi-civilized world to which you haven't wandered?"

"Pen the sheep here," Beck said, ignoring the second question. "Same as you normally would over winter. Let them eat down the weeds and fertilize while they do."

"You've seen this done?" North's face conveyed the resignation of the typical man of the land, such fellows being inured to facing multiple variables and having little solid information.

"I've seen it done in Hungary. They're more partial to goats there."

"I am not raising goats at Three Springs."

Lest there be a species underfoot more stubborn than North himself? "I'm not asking you to, though they make a respectable poor man's cow."

"So if we don't plant here, where do we plant? The place can't go a whole year without a crop to sell."

"We break sod, North." Beck raised an arm. "There, where the drainage is equally good and the land looks like it's gone halfway back to heath. It's fallowed plenty long enough, and the field lies low enough we could irrigate it from that corner if we had to."

"We could, if we're to bloody well break our backs digging ditches and serving as plowboys."

Our backs, because Gabriel North would not permit others to work while he sat on his horse and supervised—any more than Beck would.

"You can't keep farming the one patch forever without letting it fallow," Beck argued. "And a better use of the place might be to farm produce and sell it in Brighton."

"Brighton is a damned long day's haul, usually two days. Just how many teams and wagons do you think Three Springs owns?"

This was North's version of taking time to think something over, so Beck did not raise his voice. "Three teams. My four can be worked in pairs, and two wagons, because I'll not be returning the one to Belle Maison. We can use your old team to haul produce."

"Why in God's name are we hauling produce to bloody Brighton?"

Beck grinned, because *this* was North's version of enthusiasm for an idea with promise. "Stop whining. Our bloody Regent has nominally finished his bloody Pavilion and must show it off to all his gluttonous, bibulous friends. Your little patch of coast has become frightfully fashionable."

North's habitually grim features became even more forbidding. "Brighton is already a horror. The Pavilion will bankrupt the nation so Wales can pretend he's some Oriental pasha before his drunken guests."

Beck pulled a doleful face. "You flirt with treason, Mr. North, and a singular lack of appreciation for Eastern architecture." Beck did not lapse into raptures about Prague or Constantinople, though it was tempting. "We'll have to broaden your horizons, North."

"Spare me." North nudged his horse into a walk. "I'm sufficiently sophisticated for Hildy, Hermione, and Miss Allie, so we'll leave the broad horizons to you."

Beck let Ulysses walk on beside North's mount. "You do not account yourself sophisticated enough for Miss Polly?"

"Stubble it, Haddonfield." North's tone was

deceptively—dangerously—mild. "Polly Hunt has seen every capital in Europe, converses passably in a half-dozen languages, can out-paint most of the Royal Academy, and out-cook whatever Frog rides the Regent's culinary coattails. I will never be sophisticated enough for her." North fell silent while his horse crouched in anticipation of leaping a rill. "But you might be."

Ulysses chose to wade the little stream. When he was again parallel to North's mount, Beck studied his companion for a moment before replying.

"Polly Hunt is a lovely lady, but she doesn't look at me the way she looks at you. You matter to her."

"I matter to her," North said patiently, "because she is a good Christian woman, and I eat prodigious quantities. You matter to her on the same account, as does Hildegard."

"How flattering. I am likened to a market hog."

"Not a market hog, our best breeding sow."

"Our only breeding sow. North, you are truly obtuse on the subject of Miss Hunt. Don't compound it by seeing competition where there isn't any."

"You are not competition. I'm not sure what you are, but you're an earl's son, and Polly deserves at least that."

"You're daft." Beck urged Ulysses up to a trot, and North's mount smoothly followed suit.

"What?" North cued the beast to a canter. "You're a *picky* son of an earl? A woman as accomplished as Polly won't do for you?"

Beck scowled over at him. "Polly is in every way lovely, but she hasn't got…"

"She hasn't got what? No title? No pedigree? No dowry?" They'd gained the lane, such as it was, and North's voice had gained an edge.

"She hasn't got the right color hair."

Beck tapped his heels against Ulysses's sides, and the race was on.

∽

"I thought you had a thousand things to do today." Polly set a tea tray down on the low table, clearly intent on a rare late-morning respite.

"Perhaps only a hundred. I can smell that pot of tea from here." Sara's nose told her the leaves were fresh, Polly hadn't skimped, and the blend was heavy on the Assam.

"A bit of bliss, courtesy of Mr. Haddonfield's Wagon of Wonders." Polly did the honors, adding cream and sugar to both cups. "Weren't you going to clean out the carriage house, scrub the floor to the back hallway, change the sheets on the men's beds, and"—Polly paused to pay homage to the steaming cup of tea she held before her nose—"about eight other things?"

"Morning light is best for fine work." Sara hitched her embroidery hoop a bit closer for emphasis. All those chores and tasks and duties could wait for a single, perishing hour, couldn't they?

"You look different today."

When an artist made that sort of observation, evasive maneuvers were in order. "I'm sitting still for a change, perhaps? With Allie busy sketching, the twins banished, and North and Mr. Haddonfield in the village, it seemed like an opportunity to enjoy a bit of peace and quiet."

While pondering the feel of the man's palm, pressed snug low against her belly, or his lips grazing across the back of her neck.

"You're not wearing a cap."

The tea was excellent—stout without a hint of bitterness, fragrant, and perfectly brewed. Sara savored one swallow, then another. "I don't always wear a cap."

"You didn't used to always wear a cap, but lately, you've done so more and more." Polly wasn't making an accusation, she was reviewing historical facts. The accusations would come soon.

"I approach the age of thirty, and I am a widow in service. A cap is appropriate to my station."

"A widow who is using her maiden name. If I had hair that color…" Polly muttered.

"Be grateful you don't. Be grateful you sport dark auburn hair, not this, this… regimental scarlet gone amok."

Polly's artistic gaze narrowed, as if she'd launch into a sermon about light, luminosity, and points of interest. Then, "North has teased you about your caps. North seldom teases outright about anything. I was sure he'd flirt you out of them eventually."

"Polonaise Hunt, you well know the difference between teasing and flirting, and Mr. North never flirts."

Polly's gaze shifted to the day outside the window, one leaning a bit in the direction of spring, at least as far as the morning sunshine was concerned. "North flirts with that damned pig. I thought he'd get you to budge on the matter of your silly caps."

"I am not Hildegard, Polly."

And North was not Beckman Haddonfield.

❦

The village was a modest little widening in the cow
path between the South Downs and Portsmouth.
It wasn't exactly isolated, but it wasn't aswirl with
commerce, either. Beck was comfortable in such
places, far more comfortable than in the rarified
artifice of Vienna or London. The two years he'd
spent mucking stalls had taught him that much,
at least.

He left the team at the livery, paid in coin of the
realm for a full wagon of hay, and made arrangements
for some oats to be loaded on as well, while North
took off to do actual shopping for the ladies. By the
time Beck had made a circuit of the streets intersecting
at the green, midday was closing fast, so he went to
find North at the inn.

The innkeeper sized Beck up with a practiced smile
as Beck approached the polished plank bar. "What'll
you have, then?"

"Have you a decent winter ale?" Beck detested
the dark, hearty quality of winter ale and could trust
himself not to drink much of it.

"We do." The innkeeper got down a pint glass.
"Until the first of May, at least. Some years, it seems
we're never without. Will you be having some tucker
to tide you over, sir?"

"No, thank you." Beck turned around and lounged
back against the bar. "Have you any mail for a
Beckman Haddonfield, Three Springs?" North was

nowhere to be seen, but the ladies had wanted a bit of this and that, and depending on custom, Beck could see their errands taking some time.

"Be ye him?"

"I am." Beck kept his back to the bar. "Decent ale."

The innkeeper reached under the bar and withdrew a thick packet of mail. "There's notes in here for them Hunt ladies, too. The best of it's for ye, though."

"My thanks." Beck pushed away from the bar, left a coin, and scooped up his mail, then turned with careful nonchalance. "You haven't seen Tobias and Timothy since last night, have you?"

"Them two." The innkeeper's ruddy features contorted into a scowl. "Me missus done run 'em off the last time yester eve. She had the hostlers and stable boys toss 'em, in a wagon headed for Portsmouth, and their haversacks with 'em as they was sayin' as they'd been turfed out from Three Springs."

"I take it they left an unpaid tab?"

The innkeeper nodded. "Missus is right when she says they'll never pay as much as they drink and carry on."

Beck passed a small pouch across the bar. "This is intended as their severance, their employment at Three Springs having indeed come to an end. I'm sure you wouldn't mind keeping it safe for them, for a reasonable period?"

Not by a blink or a twitch did the innkeeper hesitate.

"I'd owe it to 'em as loyal customers." He slipped the pouch into his apron pocket. "Missus would agree."

"A woman of discernment, your missus." Beck smiled pleasantly and took himself, his mail, and his beer to the snug, where he could see the whole room, be seen by few, and have the table space needed to set his correspondence down in private.

Lady Warne had written, her florid feminine hand evident in the largest packet, and Nita had written as well. There was a thin epistle from a location obscured by the rain having gotten to the sender's direction—Beck supposed it to be from one of his factors on the Continent—and a note from Nick.

Nothing was banded or sealed in black, so the news couldn't be that awful. That he didn't yet have to leave Three Springs came as a relief, and not simply because it meant the earl yet drew breath.

Pushing his beer across the table, Beck opened the note from Nick first. Nick was the realm's largest grasshopper, shifting about from one residence to another, one friend's holding to another's, one county to another with a speed and frequency that left his family dizzy.

But he made up for it by being a good correspondent, in two senses. First, he was conscientious, and second, he was to the point.

Becky Dearest,

Am up to my miserable arse in dancing slippers, cravats, and interminable small talk. I do not wish you were here, not when I feel about as comfortable with this charade as the Regent would riding a lame donkey. No countess yet, and I shudder at the potential candidates. They all look as desperate as I feel. If you ever have sons—for

*I shall not—don't make them promise to marry
until they're at least forty.*

*No bad news from Nita. I've asked her to keep
you well informed while you are in the provinces.
Lady Warne is delighted you're on premises down
there, and says to warn you the women on staff are
her personal friends—I don't know if she means
you are honor bound to flirt with her collection of
relics, or you're honor bound not to. I know Papa
appreciates the effort you're making, as do I. When
the day comes that the title befalls me, the last thing
I'll have time to do is racket around the South
Downs, restoring Three Springs.*

*Don't let the old dears pinch your tender bottom
too hard. If you should make a progress to Sutcliffe
and run into Thomas Jennings doing the same, I
specifically told him to leave you in peace, but recall,
Linden is just a few hours the other side of Brighton if
you need reinforcements. He says Loris fares well and
is nowhere near as big as a freshening heifer. If you're
going to bide there for a spell—and I encourage you
to, the scenery up here being pathetic—then I'll have
Nita send you some pigeons.*

*Papa would want to hear how you go on, as
do I.*

Love,
Wee Nick

Beck set the letter aside, vowing to return fire
soon. Nita's letter was equally brief, but reassured
Beck the earl was comfortable, if "fading." Nita's

guess was the old man would hang on until Nick had chosen his bride.

The letter from Lady Warne was indeed accompanied by sealed notes for Polly and Sara, but the tone of Beck's missive was puzzling.

My dear boy,

Trust I am keeping an eye on that imp of a brother of yours. I will not allow him to indulge in too much folly in the choice before him. Still, one wishes you could be two places at once, because your ability to discreetly manage our Nick would come in handy. Instead, you have been set to checking up on my property, for which I am grateful. Nicholas has hinted all might not be in order with Three Springs, but I have assured him you have my power of attorney and will soon address whatever minor neglect has occurred.

You will please ensure the enclosed are delivered to their respective addressees in person, because there has been a peculiar quality to my correspondence with my staff. While the Misses Hunt are most amiable and competent ladies, I've found their attendance to epistolary matters oddly unreliable. They write only sporadically, seldom answer the direct questions I put to them, and often remark on matters of random interest. I'd be concerned, except Mr. North's quarterly reports arrive timely into the hands of my secretary, who assures me they are current and complete.

When you are done rusticating, you must come up

*to Town that I may sport about on your arm and be
the envy of my friends—and their granddaughters.*

> *Your loving grandmother*
> *Della, Lady Warne*

The letter explained at least one thing: Lady Warne
was not reviewing North's reports herself. She left
them in the hands of her secretary, a cheerful, practical
little man who'd looked exactly the same since Beck
had first been introduced to him fifteen years ago.
Three Springs, alas, was falling through the cracks,
with the secretary certain the earl was managing it, and
the earl comfortable to leave it to his shifty solicitors.

And as for managing Nicholas, Beck attributed
that to harmless flattery or willful misdirection on
Nicholas's part.

The other part of the letter, the almost querulous
description of communication from her house staff at
Three Springs, that bothered Beck, and put him in
mind of Sara's comments regarding Lady Warne's own
letters and notes.

"Whiling the morning away as I work myself to a
nubbin." North grunted as he slid into the snug beside
Beck. "Any news?"

"My father lives so you will not yet be rid of
me, my brother is not yet married, and Mistress
Innkeeper has cashiered the twins into Portsmouth
because they were foolish enough to disclose they'd
lost their livelihoods."

North caught the eye of a serving maid. "All in all,
a good report. I've bought out the shops for the ladies

and heard there was a young lord buying up hay at the livery. Big devil, but spoke like a toff."

"Village life makes up in charm what it lacks in privacy," Beck said. He slit open the final, flimsy missive and then set it down. "This is not for me." He flipped it over and eyed the address more closely. The ink was slightly smeared, on both sending and receiving addresses, but it was clearly sent to Three Springs.

"Perhaps"—he slid it over to North—"it's for you, *my lord*."

North eyed the single sheet of paper with distaste. "Bugger all."

Beck took another sip of his ale and waited in silence. The letter had begun with a florid, obsequious greeting to his lordship, Gabriel, Marquess of... And Beck had folded it back up, lest he read more that he didn't want to know.

North scanned the letter, scowling mightily, then folded it into an inside pocket as a serving maid approached.

"Your pint, Mr. North." She set it down and curtseyed, her gaze running over North with veiled appreciation.

"My thanks, Lolly. How're the boys?"

Lolly's tired countenance lit up. "Growing out of everything they own. Can't wait until I can turn them loose in the garden and get their noise and rumpus out of the cottage. They're still learning their letters this winter, and it's hard for 'em, but Gran and I insist. It's all their pa asked of me, and I intend to see it done."

"They won't regret it," North assured her. "And neither will you."

She left the table, a little more bounce in her step, and Beck tilted his head to consider *his lordship*.

"Tell me this much, North. Is there anybody who will be coming around, out for your blood and uncaring of the welfare of those around you?"

"No." North was emphatic. "You have a right to be concerned, because the appearances are troubling, but no. I have no enemies who've tracked me to Three Springs, and the ladies have nothing to fear."

"Jolly good for them. You, however, will have a considerable enemy in me if I find whatever game you're playing threatens harm to them or Lady Warne's assets. Are we clear?"

"Oh, cut line, Haddonfield." North's tone was weary. "I ended up at Three Springs intending to stay only a season or so—that was my initial arrangement with Lady Warne—but the place needed somebody, and I couldn't leave it to the twins, could I?"

"So you'll leave it now that I'm underfoot? North, any day, any instant, I may be called away."

North was quiet, and Beck realized he was deciding the answer in the moment.

"I won't jump ship until fall, at least. I won't plan to. We'll get your Russian wheat in, and that's as much as I can commit to. If I can't manage that much, I'll try to warn you of my departure."

Beck stared at the murky liquid in his mug, knowing what it was to be far from home without friends or family. "North, is there something to be done here? My family has influence in various spheres, and if it's a matter of finances, my own assets are not inconsiderable."

North's smile was sweet, making his harsh features astoundingly handsome, charming even. "Haddonfield, you are a dear, and I can see why this miserable job was put on your very honorable shoulders, but no. I am not hounded by creditors. There are no angry papas gunning for me. I am not listed on some warrant for murder most foul. It's a family matter."

"And those," Beck said, "are sometimes the most difficult." His thoughts roamed back to when Nick had hauled him bodily from Paris, and for the first time, he considered what Nick went through, having to scout every brothel and hell in a very sinful city, at a time when an unmistakably large, blond Englishman was risking his life just to be seen on the streets.

"You are kind, Haddonfield," North said as they walked back toward the livery. "One forgets the aristocracy can produce men like you." On that cryptic comment, he went ahead of Beck and inspected the hay piled high on the wagon.

By the time they departed, Beck was eyeing the sky, hoping the huge quantity of fodder they hauled wouldn't get wet.

"You're quiet," North said as they gained the last mile.

"I think I've puzzled something out." Beck steered the horses through a badly banked turn. "Who picked up and delivered the mail for Three Springs, North?"

A beat of silence, and then, "The bloody, bedamned, sodding twins, of course." North shot a disgusted look at Beck. "I'll bet if we checked, we'd find much of the correspondence from Lady Warne that conveyed household funds never made it into Sara's hands."

"And Sara's letters detailing the extent of the needs

here probably got cast aside as well, with only the more social correspondence being allowed to make it through. Your reports, by the way, are falling into the indifferent hands of Lady Warne's secretary, who is not a man of business. But what of your correspondence?" He steered the wagon onto the Three Springs lane. "Do you get the sense it has been tampered with?"

"That is a possibility," North said. He took the letter out of his pocket and scanned it again. "It is a distinct possibility."

He kept his silence all the way to the stable yard, then got down and swung open the barn doors so Beck could drive the team right into the barn aisle. The men spent a hot, dusty hour pitching most of the hay up into the loft, leaving the last of it below for immediate consumption.

"Will that last us?" Beck asked as they unhitched the team.

"Depends when the grass comes in," North said. "Turn around." He swatted a quantity of hay from Beck's clothing and hair, and submitted to the same service in return. Still, they were dirty and sweaty, and minute wisps of hay had insinuated themselves beneath their clothing, necessitating a bracing trip to the cistern.

When they reached the house, North disappeared up the back steps, and Beck realized the man was still preoccupied with his letter. Beck let him go without comment, knowing all too well what it was like to be at an awkward distance from family and friends.

God willing, North would find his way home more successfully than Beck had.

Five

SARA BLUSHED, A HOT FLOODING OF COLOR NO housekeeper ought to be blushing. "I saw both of the men today. When I was scrubbing the windows in the carriage house, they bathed in the cistern behind the barn, and God's nightgown, Polly... Your pencil would be smoking, did you sketch what I saw."

Polly stabbed her needle into a hoop of linen but didn't pull the thread through. "How is Gabriel's scar?"

Sara was too consumed with the images in her head to sit, and yet, the little parlor hardly allowed room to pace. "I don't know if it's the cold or the passage of time, but I thought it somewhat faded compared to last summer. In any case, it didn't seem to inhibit his movement. But, Polly, I also saw Beck—Mr. Haddonfield. Would to God I had seen such a man as a young lady, and I would have been utterly bored with Reynard's silk-and-lace affectations."

She'd seen him *again*, not in the dimly lit confines of the laundry, but in the broad light of day, sunshine kissing every wet, muscular inch of him.

"Lace affectations were only part of Reynard's

charm," Polly reminded her, setting the embroidery aside. "I don't have to guess at Mr. Haddonfield's appeal in the nude. He's taller than Gabriel but more sleek, without any lack of brawn. My fingers itch to sketch him. I envy you, Sister."

Sara shook her head, though her lips curved in recollection. "Don't envy me. They were magnificent, the pair of them, but the sight of them will keep me up nights for many a week to come."

"Is there anything you miss about Reynard?" Polly asked.

Sara paused in her circumnavigation of the parlor, hearing the careful delicacy of the question—delicacy they should have been long past.

"Not one thing. He was not a good man, Polly, and his dying when Allie was young was divine justice."

"I suppose." Polly considered the hoop that had been set aside. The beginnings of a Tree of Life sprouted up in soft greens and muted golds, and a peacock strutted about its base. "It's good you can say that, good you can be that honest."

Sara kept her gaze on Polly's domestic artistry. "Do you miss him?" An even more delicate question.

"I used to. I never understood exactly what he was up to, Sara, and he was always kind to me, as long as I behaved, that is. But then I see that Allie is almost ten, and I realize I was fourteen when Reynard came to St. Albans—I thought I was so grown up then, as all little girls do, but I was a child. He exploited a child, and that child was me. So no, I don't miss him."

"I miss things I thought I could have had with him," Sara said softly. This realization was... sad enough that Sara took a seat in her rocker.

"Could you be any more tentative?" Polly's smile was sad too. "Things you thought you could have had?"

"Dreams," Sara said. "When he proposed, I had dreams for a happy marriage. When he talked of travel on the Continent, and touring, I had dreams of artistic recognition, of making some contribution to music. When we bought the villa in Italy, I still at least dreamed of good things for my sister. Despite all the hardship and travel, and… all of it"—even in this extraordinary conversation, Sara could not be more specific—"I dreamed, Polly. Now I fret."

"What do you fret about, Sara?"

"I fret about Allie. I fret whether we're doing the right thing for her. Beckman complimented Allie's talent, and I almost took his head off. I fret Lady Warne will die, and we'll be begging for crusts or worse. Allie is so pretty…"

"You can't think like that," Polly rejoined earnestly. "We can go back to St. Albans, pride be damned, Sara. Mama and Papa would provide something for Allie, at the least. We both have trades, and we'd have characters. Beckman sees clearly what we've been up against, and he'd make provision for us in any case. An earl's son knows people, and I've a little put by. We'd manage, Sara. We would."

"We always have." Barely and badly, sometimes not even speaking to each other, but they had. "Mr. Haddonfield assured me he'd find something for us, but he's a man, Polly, and here on some sort of lark or familial obligation. He could be gone tomorrow. We can't rely on his word."

"We might have to," Polly said, "though for

the present, I'd say things are improving. North is certainly more sociable with another man shouldering some of the load, and Allie seems to like having more company as well. Can you believe the twins were pilfering our household money?"

"Yes, I can believe it. What I can't believe is none of us guessed it."

"Just as he spotted that problem," Polly went on, "I think Mr. Haddonfield can bring a fresh eye to the whole undertaking here. North works like a demon, but it's as if he's already too tired to see the larger perspective."

Sara did not ask if Polly's interest in the man was part of that larger perspective. She did not have to. "He does have a weariness about him. I fear I've acquired it too."

"Then, Sister"—Polly picked up her hoop and frowned thoughtfully at the unfinished peacock— "you must allow Mr. Haddonfield to bring you a fresh perspective as well."

"I still say he's married." Any man that fine looking had to have been dogged with opportunities to marry. "He's just too… canny, too at ease with females in the kitchen and the laundry and the still room."

Polly stabbed the thread through the fabric. "If he's so married, then why hasn't his wife written to him? Why hasn't he written to her? Why doesn't he wear a ring? Why doesn't he get a faraway, missing-his-wife look on his face when he lingers over his last cup of tea? Why does he watch your fundament at every turn, and why, when I heard North telling him of the boarding house in the village that caters to men, did I hear Haddonfield disdaining to know of it?"

"Polonaise Hunt, you are a naughty, naughty girl—for eavesdropping so, and for not telling your only sister sooner."

❧

"I want to show you something, Mr. Haddonfield." Sara's tone made it plain, if the crisp *Mr. Haddonfield* did not, that she wasn't going to show him how much she'd missed him that day. "Come along, we haven't much light left."

Beck ignored the glance exchanged between Polly and North, ignored everything except Sara, rising from the table and moving off to the back hallway.

"Polly, my thanks for an excellent meal." The compliment was sincere. That he'd again beaten North to expressing his appreciation for Polly's cooking was no little satisfaction.

"Where are we going?" Beck asked as Sara held his coat out for him.

"A short walk. I won't keep you long."

Pity, that. When she would have swished off ahead of him across the yard, Beck instead captured her hand and put it on his sleeve. "I'm not in any hurry, and I think Polly and North might appreciate a few minutes' privacy."

North might also kill him for it, but men were fools where true love was concerned. This truth might not be universal, but in Beck's experience, it was at least international.

Sara's steps slowed. "Do you think so? I used to be able to read my sister like a simple etude—you look at the melody on paper and you can hear it in your head and feel it in your fingers and your bowing arm. Now I must interpret her cooking spices and her silences."

"While I interpret your caps and the way your skirts whip and swish as you rampage through the house." They reached the end of the garden, and Sara kept moving Beck away from the house. "I'm glad you're not avoiding me, Sara. Did I offend last night?"

He wasn't going to mention her lack of cap. He was instead going to hope that if he had offended, he'd also disappointed a bit too, when he'd chosen to limit his offenses.

"You did... not offend. I'm a widow, not some pampered lady."

She was taking him in the direction of the trees that formed the hedgerow of the home wood, a dark, tangled mess sporting two decades of deadfall and windfall.

"I'm told widowhood can be lonely." God knew, being a widower was lonely. "That it can feel like an ongoing wound, an indignity, not just a loss. I've wondered why you and Polly use the same last name."

And yet if she was lonely, like him, she hadn't remarried.

"Lonely is a good word, an honest word, but I don't think you mean lonely, exactly."

"Where are you taking me, Sara?" Because she was leading him down a declivity, such that the house had disappeared from view.

"To the springs."

"One suspected a property named Three Springs might boast some of same." He switched his grip on her as they approached the trees, linking his fingers with hers. They circled around the side of a medium-sized pond and traveled a little ways into the woods along the stream feeding the pond.

"Hot springs?" Beck guessed. Steam rose from the water in the deepening twilight, creating a land-of-the-faery quality. He took a whiff of the air. "And not sulfurous. Shall we sit a moment?"

Because hot springs were worth noting, but they weren't the reason she'd dragged him away from home on an increasingly chilly night, nor why she'd dodged his question about her surname.

"We can't sit for long. It will be dark in just a few minutes."

Dark enough for kissing? As a very young man, Beck had cadged a tumble or two under the stars, but always with the benefit of a blanket and some congenial weather. Then too, Sara was giving off not a single hint she intended to tumble him.

Which ought to have occasioned more disappointment than it did. If Beck coaxed Sara Hunt into intimacies, he'd be using sex with her as an antidote to lust and something else—grief, maybe. That she would use him wasn't the comfort it ought to have been.

"There's a bench." She tugged him over to a rude plank and arranged her skirts while Beck came down beside her. "You should have Gabriel bring you here. His back gets to bothering him, and he's too stubborn to find what relief he might."

Beck took her hand as an experiment in modest comforts. Sara's weight settled against his side, perhaps her own version of an experiment.

"This is a pretty spot, Sara. Thank you for showing it to me."

The location was peaceful and attractive, not just to the eye but also the ear, graced as it was with the sound of gently flowing water.

"I resumed the use of my maiden name because I wanted to forget most of what transpired while I was married. I wore my caps because it was appropriate to my station."

Beck looped an arm around her shoulders—the evening was chilly, and the sun was all but gone. "You wore your caps because they meant you had a kind of privacy, but housekeeping is an occupation, not the sum total of who you are."

The longer she remained silent, the more Beck pondered the rightness of his words. She was Polly's sister, somebody's daughter, Allie's mother, and much more that he could only guess at but was sure of too, somehow.

The first star winked into view on the western horizon.

"I am not just a housekeeper, Beckman, and Three Springs is not just a list of purchases and tasks. It has beauty and dignity and value—also hot springs some people would find a very valuable addition to their holdings. Most people."

Another star winked into view against the darkening sky. Beckman rose and offered Sara his hand, which she took. As they strolled back in the direction of the house, he admitted that making love with Sara Hunt—who also had beauty and dignity and value—might be about more than loneliness and lust after all.

❧

"I love that sound," Beck said as North set a mug of hot tea down before him.

"What sound?" North sat across from him at the kitchen table and shuffled a deck of cards.

"If you're quiet," Beck said, "you can hear the murmur of the women's voices in their apartment. They're discussing the day, trading opinions, making plans for tomorrow, and so on. It's the same cadence and rhythm in any language."

And it put him in mind of the music of the stream by the springs.

"You notice odd things. Prepare to be defeated."

"I notice you're still disconcerted by today's letter," Beck said. "One hopes you'll be able to concentrate on the game."

"With your witty repartee to distract me," North drawled, "the matter is in question." He played carefully but made the occasional chancy decision, and they were evenly matched halfway around the cribbage board.

Beck moved his pegs. "I have a question for you."

"You always put your fives in the other fellow's crib," North said, which was fine advice provided a man wanted to lose badly.

"Earlier today, you said Polly spoke six languages and had been to every capital in Europe. Were you speaking literally?"

North appeared to consider his cards. "Sara, as well. I don't think Allie was much more than an infant when they returned to England to visit. Why?"

"So Sara speaks all those languages? Sara's been to all those exotic places?"

"She has." North tossed down a card. "If what Polly says is true, Sara was touring."

"Touring?" Beck glanced over his cards. "As in being a tourist, seeing the sights?"

"That too." North waited for Beck to play a card. "Sara has musical talent, as a violinist. She performed all over Europe. The Continentals aren't as stuffy about women on stage as we are."

Beck set his cards down as a curious prickling sensation ran from his nape to his fingers. "She was *that* good, and she's spending her days washing the lamps and polishing the silver?"

"I believe it was her choice," North said. "She has a child, if you'll recall, and that effectively ends a career before the public, even on the Continent. Or it should, in the minds of most."

"Why isn't she at least giving lessons? This place... you don't keep house at a place like this if you have other options."

"Beckman"—North's voice took on that patient, long-suffering quality—"we all have other options. You, for example, could be with your brother, flirting and gaming your way across London during the Season, but you're bathing in cisterns and mucking stalls here at Three Springs."

"Valid point." And while he did want to be at Belle Maison, Beck did not want to be racketing around the vice-ridden terrain of Mayfair in spring. "You're impersonating a land steward, and Polly—who I assume is a talented artist—is impersonating a cook."

"I cannot vouch for her artistic ability." North

counted up his hand. "Allie says her aunt is as good as anybody she saw in London."

"Allie's been to the museums?"

"I gather she would have been four at the time." North moved his peg. "She remembers what she saw."

"Sara…" Beck ran a hand through his hair, mentally revising and reassessing things he'd tried to tally up before. "She's hiding then too."

"What do you mean?" North appropriated the deck and began to deal the next hand.

"You're hiding."

"Earlier today I was entitled to privacy. Now I'm hiding. And what of you, are you hiding?"

Beck smiled a little. "Probably. When I keep company with my brother in Town, there are too many females willing to tolerate my attentions in exchange for an introduction to Nick. It's safer for me and Nick both if we move independently."

"I'm familiar with the problem," North said. "I'm told you first become aware of it when some sweet and naughty young thing rises up from your sheets and asks if you ever carouse with your brother."

Beck's eyebrows flew up. "And here I thought I was the only one."

"We always do," North said, glowering afresh at his cards. "We always think we're the only ones when it counts, though in fact, we never are."

❧

Beck finished a quick lunch under a shady tree, soreness reverberating through every muscle and sinew of his body. At least the crushing fatigue of spring plowing had kept him from misbehaving with Sara again.

She hadn't dragged him to any more pretty corners of the property, and no longer offered to light him to his room. Allie was a good and constant chaperone, and ye gods, the child was sharp. She was waiting for him when he got back to his team, grinning as she stroked the nose of the nearest horse.

"Watch your feet around these fellows," Beck warned, checking the harness. "One misstep on their part, and you'll have toes like a duck."

"I'm wearing my half boots."

"So have you come to help?" Beck surveyed the ground yet to be turned. Thank all the gods, there wasn't that much of it. Just another few backbreaking, arm-wrenching, hand-blistering, gut-wearying hours of work.

"I have come to cadge a piggyback ride on old Hector. Mama said I might, because it's a lovely day, the chores are done, and you're to send me back to her if I'm a nuisance."

"Duly noted." Beck hefted her up into his arms. Hector took the outside position on the left, which, given the direction Beck turned the team, put him on the inside of each turn, and gave him the least to do. He could carry a little girl without even noticing the weight. "Up you go."

Allie scrambled onto the horse's broad back and, predictably, began to chatter. Not so predictably, she also scooted around, swinging a leg over the beast's withers, then another over his rump, so she was sitting on him backward.

"This is more polite," she informed Beck as the team turned into the first furrow. "So when are you going into Portsmouth? Mama says you might also make a trip into Brighton, because you're thinking of selling the vegetables there later this summer. I think you ought to sell our flowers."

Conversing with somebody facing him while he plowed was oddly disorienting. Beck had to look past Allie to fix his gaze on some object at the end of the furrow. Plowing straight was an art, and Beck would have said he had the talent for it, until Allie sat between him and the end of the furrow.

"What sort of flowers, princess?"

"All kinds. I don't know all their names, but I can draw them. We put them all over the house when summer comes. Before the strawberries even come in, we have bunches and bunches of tulips and irises—I know how to separate those—and there are roses too, but Mama despairs of them. I like to draw the roses—they're complicated."

"What have you been drawing lately?" Beck asked, reaching the first turn.

"I always draw. In my head, mostly, which Aunt says is good practice. Mama saw you and Mr. North without your clothes, and Aunt said she wished she could draw you."

"That's nice," Beck muttered. Turns were tricky, especially with horses hitched three across. "What else do you—she saw *what*?"

"You." Allie grinned beatifically. "Without your clothes. Both of you. Mama and Aunt Polly saw Mr. North in the pond last summer, but after you unloaded hay, Mama was up in the carriage house and saw you bathing in the cistern. She said the sight would keep her up at night for weeks, which is silly. It's just skin."

Beck tried to divide his attention. "Allemande, you can't go repeating such things merely to provoke a reaction. I'm sure your mother was mortified, and had we known, North and I would have been mortified as well. Modesty is a virtue shared by most decent folk."

"Not Aunt. She says artists have to study nudes because human subjects are the most complicated. She drew naked people all the time when we were in Italy. I will draw naked people again too one day." She wrinkled her nose and sighed in resignation. "I draw naked pigs and cats and so forth now. From what little I've done with them, I don't expect people will be much different."

"We aren't going to talk about naked people. Or naked pigs or cats. What's for dinner tonight?"

"Aunt is making roast chicken with smashed potatoes." Allie smacked her lips dramatically. "And she said she's making a chocolate cake *with icing* to sweeten Mr. North's temper, because plowing makes him cranky."

"Plowing, not getting much sleep, and dodging busy little girls with nothing better to do than plague their elders."

"I'd paint if Mama would let me," Allie groused. "Am I really plaguing you?"

"Of course not," Beck assured her, though she absolutely was. He wanted to carefully examine his recall of the day they'd unloaded the hay wagon, and go over every detail of his dunking in the cistern.

They'd both stripped down completely; that much he was sure of.

"I've decided I would like to paint Mr. North's hands," Allie went on happily. "It's not quite a human subject, because I'm forbidden those, but I like hands."

"Your mother might not approve. She was not even comfortable with your doing Heifer's portrait."

"But she told me it turned out well, and Aunt agreed. Aunt is never one to spare feelings at the expense of truth. She says an artist has to be ruthless."

"I can't like the idea of you being ruthless," Beck said, thinking a relatively carefree Allie was challenge enough. "But tell me something, oracle of the plow, when was the last time you heard your mother play her violin?"

"I haven't heard her play since I was little. There's a pianoforte in the downstairs parlor, but she only dusts it, she doesn't play it. She and Aunt argue about that too."

"About dusting it?"

"No, silly." Allie lifted her arms to the spring day in casual joy. "Aunt says Mama should teach me a little so I am suitably capable at the keyboard, but Mama gets all tight around her eyes and does that cranky-without-saying-a-word thing, and then Aunt gets quiet, but that never lasts."

"Most mamas know how to do what you describe, sisters too."

Allie lowered her arms and shuddered. "Papa could do it. I was little, but I remember him glaring and glaring. Mama wouldn't play for him and his friends, and it was awful."

She glared herself in recollection.

"I thought you were very young when you came back to England, Allie." The plow hit a subterranean rock, and the team stopped.

"We came back when I was four, and we saw everything. That's when Papa found out I could draw like Aunt. Then it was back to Italy, and I got lessons and everything. Aunt and I both had lessons. Then we came back to England again, but we didn't see anything except Brighton and Three Springs. Papa was dead. Mama said I didn't have to wear black if I didn't want to."

Beck urged the team forward and hefted the plow over the rock, his back screaming at the abuse.

"Did you want to wear black?" Beck tossed the question out as a distraction, unwilling to pry more directly. From Allie's account and Sara's own comments, Sara's marriage had had its share of rough spots and challenges.

Allie smoothed her hand over the horse's broad rump. "Of course not. I'm to have more long dresses in the fall."

"You are growing up," Beck said, wishing it didn't have to be so. He missed his sisters badly and wanted nothing so much as to leave the team in the field, mount Ulysses, and see his father one last time. The realization blended with the plowing-ache to form a peculiarly poignant misery.

Allie heaved a great sigh. "I know it's not all bad, growing up. When I'm older, Mama won't be able to tell me what to paint. Hermione's udder is dripping on both sides."

"Thank you for telling me." The plow hit another rock and sent jolts of pain up both Beck's arms into his shoulders. "For good measure, I think you ought to tell Mr. North as well."

"I'm being a nuisance." Allie grinned, nuisance-ing apparently being great good fun in her lexicon. "See if I share these biscuits Aunt sent out for you, Mr. Haddonfield."

Beck signaled the horses to halt at the end of the furrow. "If you want off that horse, my price is one biscuit."

"Here." Allie passed him a sweet and drew one from her pocket for herself. "They're still warm." They shared a companionable moment, munching their bounty, then Beck swung her down.

"Don't sneak up on North. His language is colorful today."

"His back hurts," Allie said, her tone serious. "Aunt says he needs horse liniment, but he's too stubborn to admit it. Mama agrees."

"Then it's unanimous. Where is the horse liniment?"

"Mama makes it." Allie began to trot off to the next field. "It isn't really for horses, and it's in the still room with a purple flower on it. 'Bye!"

Leaving Beck to try to recall if, on the occasion of bathing in the cistern, he'd scratched his ass, pissed in the yard, or otherwise disgraced himself. He didn't think so, because the business of the moment had been getting clean.

And Sara hadn't just peeked, she'd peeked and told and was plagued by the memory of what she'd seen. He decided this was only fair. In the past weeks, he'd seen Sara on four occasions with her hair not only uncovered, but flowing down her back in a shiny, thoroughly unforgettable braid.

His sore, aching hands itched with the frustrated desire to undo that braid and touch the silken glory he'd known once before. His groin started to throb, until the plow hit another rock, and pain once again served to displace desire.

Six

After dinner, an uncharacteristically sociable North had accompanied Beck to the hot springs, and a medicinal soak had followed. As Beck hung up the new towels in the laundry to dry and made his way to his room, it occurred to him his sojourn at Three Springs was different from many of the other trips he'd been sent on.

Here, while the typical traveler's propensity for observing hadn't left him, he was not among strangers. He was among the same people day and night, and he was becoming familiar with them in ways a lone wayfarer in a distant land did not.

He was, in short, growing attached. Whatever plagued North, Beck wanted it resolved, not out of a need for tidy endings and neat answers, but because it weighed on North's soul, put shadows in a good man's eyes, and kept him scanning the horizon rather than focusing on the bounty at his feet.

And then there was Sarabande Adagio herself. Beck's feelings for her were growing complicated, beyond the simple, powerful lust of a man who permitted himself only infrequent attractions. He watched her moving around the house, taking down this set of curtains for a good washing, polishing andirons in that unused parlor, mixing up a salve for burns to keep in Polly's kitchen.

Sara was preoccupied, biding her time, doing what the situation called for, but she had an eye on the horizon as well, and it was an anxious eye. Beck wanted to banish her anxieties, to carry her burdens for her and offer her the comfort of a shoulder to lean on—and so much more.

Except she deserved to be able to rely on the man she bestowed her favors and her fears on. Rely on him utterly and exclusively, and Beck was not that man. He sank down on his bed, frowning, as something nagged at the back of his mind, something from the day's flotsam of conversations and silences.

Hermione's dripping from both sides.

Allie's casual information trotted up from the back of Beck's mind, pushing him to his tired feet even as he cursed the need to check on the mare. He took a lantern and a jacket from the back hall and shuddered at the chill of the spring night.

As soon as he spied Hermione in her stall, Beck knew he wouldn't be going back into the house any time soon. She was slowly circling, pawing at the straw, her belly distended, her eye both restless and resigned. She swung her gaze at Beck as soon as he approached her stall.

"It's only me, sweetheart." He kept his voice low and relaxed, because a mare could stop the foaling process if she became disturbed. "I've come to tidy up your nest. Thought you might want a bit of company on a chilly night."

While Hermione stood along one wall of her stall, pawing occasionally, Beck mucked out her loose box and heaped extra clean straw in one corner. He scrubbed out her water bucket next and forked her a mound of fresh hay into another corner, then left her in peace to resume her pacing.

"I'm told"—he spoke softly to the horse—"I'm good at foaling. Nick says the mares like me, which is fine with me, because I certainly like them. One wonders, though, who the papa of your foal is, Miss Hermione Hunt. You were a naughty girl, going courting without an escort that way…"

He pattered on, until with a heavy groan, the mare went to her knees then lay down on her side. She began to strain, and Beck went silent, standing outside the stall and praying for nature to do what nature alone could do best. A few minutes later, a very undainty hoof emerged from beneath Hermione's tail.

Beck had assisted at many, many foalings, from the time he'd been a boy at Belle Maison right up through the past two years in Sussex. He was good at it, and he enjoyed it. If the size of that hoof and the one appearing next to it were any indication, Hermione had taken up with a damned draft stud.

She couldn't help that now, of course, so Beck waited another couple of anxious minutes while the mare made no progress.

Resuming his quiet monologue, Beck eased open the door to the stall and approached the mare.

"Not cooperating, I take it." Beck knelt and

stroked a hand over the mare's sweaty flank. "Children are like that. Ask my papa. What say I lend a hand, and we'll see if we can't persuade the Foal Royal to join us sooner rather than later?"

Hermione rested her head in the straw, lying flat out as if dead, which was only prudent when she was between contractions. God willing, the old girl would need her rest. Beck continued stroking and talking until he was positioned behind the mare, his hands wrapped around the foal's hooves. When Hermione began to strain again, Beck exerted a steady, increasing pull on those hooves, and the foal started to shift in the birth canal.

"Come to Papa," Beck gritted through clenched teeth. The mare was laboring to the limit of her strength, Beck's aching back was screaming with his efforts, and progress was agonizingly slow. The contraction ebbed, and Beck released his hold as the foal slipped back a few inches.

"Next time, my girl, we are going to have a damned foal," Beck panted, getting his breath while he could.

Hermione grunted and thrashed and began to push again, so Beck went back to work. It took two more back-aching, harrowing attempts, but on a rush of fluid, a sizable filly was born. Beck peeled the placenta back from the foal's nose, made sure the little beast was breathing, then sat back in the straw, leaning against the sturdy wall.

He beamed at the mare, who had shifted to start licking her new treasure. "Would you look at that? Look what a lovely little business you've done here. She's gorgeous and hale and full of beans already."

The filly was shaking her head and trying to prop her front feet out before her, while Hermione methodically licked her baby's coat dry.

"Beckman?" Sara's voice came from the aisle way. "To whom are you speaking?"

"My newest goddaughter." Beck rose slowly, careful not to disturb the mare and foal. "Hermione has tended to the Creator's business tonight, and done a splendid job."

He eased from the stall, moved, as he always was, by the spontaneous joy of seeing a new life begin. Hermione was acquitting herself like an old hand, but Beck would stay around to make sure the foal nursed in the first hour of its life and the mare passed the afterbirth. After that, there was little he could do to keep the odds running in the filly's favor.

Sara, wrapped in a thick wool shawl, peered over the half door. "What a little beauty."

"A big beauty," Beck countered. "Hermione has an eye for the draft stallions, I think, but the filly's elegant for all her size."

"She's gorgeous."

Beck was taken aback to see a sheen on Sara's eyes. He moved in close and wrapped his arms around her. "Mother and baby are doing fine, and all's well."

"I know." This sounded more like lament than agreement. "But she's so... dear. Precious." Beck said nothing, thinking dear and precious applied to the female in his arms as well. When he stepped back, he kept hold of her hand.

"I'll mind them until the baby nurses," he assured her. "Sit with me over here. They'll do better with a little privacy." He tugged her across the darkened barn aisle to sit on a trunk outside Ulysses's stall. The gelding noted their presence without a pause in his consumption of hay.

"What made you come out here?" Sara asked, her hand still in his.

"Allie told me the signs were pointing to sooner rather than later, and mares are famous for dropping foals in the quiet and privacy of the night," Beck said. "How about you? What drew you out here on this chilly night?"

"I saw your lantern light." Sara's voice was soft, as if she were mindful of the peace conducive to a newly forming bond between mare and foal. "I don't think North could have been any help, so badly is his back hurting."

"Does it pain him often?" The ladies seemed better attuned to North's back than the man himself was.

"When he overdoes, which is to say, yes. Last year, he tried to do the plowing alone, and it did not go well for him. Polly made him hire help for the haying and the harvest, or he'd still be sitting in the hot spring, cursing and refusing help."

And the ladies would have been without any meaningful protection. The precariousness of Sara's existence at Three Springs loomed more clearly in Beck's mind.

"North and Polly are stubborn, but Three Springs requires stubbornness, I think." Beside him, he felt a little shudder go through Sara's smaller frame. "You're cold." He tucked an arm across her shoulders. "Budge up. I'm good for warmth, if little else. So when are you going to let Allie make another painting?"

He drew away again to drape his jacket around Sara then used his arm about her shoulders to draw her close to his side.

She made no protest, and the feel of her against him comforted in a way that had to do with the mare and foal and with being far from home.

"I should let Allie paint again soon. She needs to paint the way Polly needs to cook and North needs to stomp around the property cursing the weeds, the fences, and the foxes."

"And what does Sara need?" A safer question than what Beck himself needed.

"To see the people I care for happy and safe," Sara said. "That's what I need, Beckman. What about you?"

"This is a mystery." Beck resisted the urge to nuzzle her hair, was which flowing down her back in one glorious fat plait. "For now, I need to be here in this barn with you, and I need that little filly to thrive with her mother."

"Good needs," Sara said. "If only for the near term."

"Your hands are cold." Beck covered hers with his own where it rested on her thigh. "I should shoo you back into the house, Sara. You haven't the luxury of the periodic cold or sniffle."

"I won't go back to sleep until you tell me the little one is nursing. And what if you hadn't been here? North is worn out, and Polly and I wouldn't have known what to do. How would we have managed?"

His question exactly. "Nature usually knows what to do, but you and Polly need more help here."

Beside him, Sara pokered up but didn't move away. "Without family in residence, there's no reason for hiring more staff."

"There is every reason to," Beck said, sitting up to watch as the filly tried to thrash to her feet. "The estate needs the help, even if you don't."

"Should we help her?" Sara started to rise, but Beck tugged her back beside him.

"She has to figure out where her feet go," he said softly. "If she struggles so long she's getting too weak to stand, then we'll intervene, but give her a chance to work it out for herself first."

"That's a very difficult part of parenting." Sara sighed as she settled against him and brushed her nose near the jacket lapel, where the fabric would carry his scent. He resettled his arm across her shoulders and took a whiff of her hair.

"Difficult? Watching a child's first steps?" Beck folded her hand in his again, and again, Sara made no protest.

"That, and the whole business of letting them struggle, letting them find their own balance. I am protective of Allie, sometimes I think not protective enough."

As if worrying about her very livelihood and the entire manor house wasn't enough?

"What's the worst that can happen to her? Short of a tragic accident or illness, such as might befall anybody?"

Sara was silent for a moment; then she tugged his jacket more closely around her.

"She might meet the wrong type of man," she said, "and let him take her from all she's ever known, fill her head with silly fancies about fame and art and wealth, and discard her when her usefulness is over."

Beck heard the bitterness and the bewilderment too.

"We all have the occasional unwise attachment,"

Beck said gently, for it wasn't Allie whom Sara was discussing. "And nobody chooses a perfect fit."

"Was your wife a good fit?"

Well, of course. He should have known Sara Hunt, quiet, serious, and observant, might ask such a thing. The sense of... rootlessness in his belly grew as he considered an honest answer.

"We were not married long enough to assess such a thing." A version of the truth. "We were both eager for the union, and our families approved."

"How old were you?"

"Not old enough. Not nearly old enough."

"I'm sorry for your loss. I have been grateful, on occasion, that Reynard lived long enough for me to see his true colors, to hate him. I cannot imagine losing a spouse with whom there was potential for a lifetime of happiness."

What did it say, that a woman professed to be grateful to hate her own spouse? Beck's arm over Sarah's shoulders became less casual and more protective.

"I would have been grateful for a few years of contentment," Beck said. "It wasn't meant to be." And what a useless, true platitude that was.

"How long were you married?"

"Little more than a summer. At the time, it seemed like forever, and then she was gone, and forever took on a very different meaning."

"I was married for nearly a decade. That was a forever too."

A decade was forever to grieve, forever to carry guilt and rage and remorse by the barge load. "So how do you manage now? What sustains you?"

"Allie," Sara replied immediately. "Polly."

"But what sustains *you*?" Beck pressed. "Allie will grow up, sooner rather than later, and Polly could well bring Mr. North up to scratch. Five years hence, Sara Hunt, will it be enough to polish silver, beat rugs, and mix vinegar to shine the windows?"

Would it be enough for Beckman to spend most of his year traveling, to hear more foreign tongues than English, and to be always planning the next journey, even as he turned his steps for home?

Sara was quiet, and Beck regretted the question.

He squeezed her fingers. "Don't answer. I am feeling philosophical because my father is at his last prayers, and he was always such a robust man. I am aware that any day I could be summoned to his side, and you'll no longer be plagued by my larking about here."

"You are on good terms with your father?"

How to answer? "Such good terms, he sent me down here, rather than allow me at his bedside."

"You're hurt by this," Sara concluded. "You mustn't be. Men are proud, and they can't admit when they need to draw comfort from others."

He did not want comfort, he wanted to *go home* and have his father be there. He wanted…

What he wanted astonished him and made perfect sense. "What of you, Sarabande Adagio? Can you admit you might need to draw some comfort from another?"

She made no answer but didn't protest when he shifted on the trunk, untangled their hands, and used his free hand to turn her toward him.

"Would you let me give you some comfort, Sarabande?"

∽❧∽

Beckman was going to kiss her, and she was going to let him. Sara felt heat not just radiating from him but welling up inside her body, filling the tired, lonely depths she'd learned to ignore. His lips brushed over hers, and then again, a soft, warm hint of pressure behind the caress.

This kiss was different from the last one, more personal. Sara liked it better and returned his initial gesture, dragging her lips over his as her fingers burrowed into the silky hair at his nape. On a soft groan, he lifted her to straddle his lap, again placing her slightly higher than him and giving her an advantage of sorts.

A control or the fiction of it, even as he so casually demonstrated his superior strength.

Balanced on her knees, Sara was free to explore his body with her hands, to stroke over the breadth of his shoulders, and learn the curious curves and textures of his ears. His hands roamed too, slowly, carefully, tracing the shape of her elbows, the span of her hips, and the bones of her back.

"Settle," he whispered, urging her to let him have her weight in his lap. She sank onto him, feeling the tumescence of his arousal against her sex. She knew what that was, knew what it meant, and rather than feel embarrassed, she was reassured.

Somebody—a man she esteemed and desired—could feel desire for her, even at her great age. Even though she was mother to a growing girl, measuring her days on some forlorn, neglected estate, she was still desirable.

And—even better—*she* could still feel desire. Reynard hadn't taken that from her after all, not permanently. She smiled against Beck's mouth, the joy of that realization fueling the warmth inside her.

"What?" Beck pulled back and traced her lips with his finger. "Am I amusing you?"

"Not amusing. This isn't funny." She curled down against him and felt his hand trace down her spine.

"But you smiled, Sara," Beck said, his other hand cradling the back of her head. "I like that I can make you smile."

"This is wicked." Lest he think she condoned her own behavior—except in a sense she did. His behavior too.

"To find a little comfort isn't wicked." Beck kissed her check. "Though it is wicked to take a lady unawares. I can't offer you much, Sara. I don't know how long I'll be here, and I don't intend you any disrespect. You can decline my advances, and I'll understand you aren't interested in what I'm offering. But while I'm here, I can… share pleasure with you, if you'd like."

His tone was careful, measured, and that, more than his words, helped Sara surface from the haze of sentiment and physical pleasure clouding her judgment.

"I hadn't considered this." That was a lie. She had considered this, particularly since having seen Beckman at the cistern. She'd considered little else.

She lifted her face from his shoulder to peer at him in the shadows. "I am not… sophisticated, Beckman. For all the time I spent with Reynard, who was sophisticated, I still did not discover the knack of dallying."

He kissed her nose. "I am not as proficient at it as you might think. I am attracted to you, regardless of common sense, regardless of the dictates of gentlemanly behavior, regardless of being physically exhausted. I do not think I am going to plow you out of my system, Sara Hunt."

Somewhere in his words lurked a compliment, but Sara was too overwhelmed by what he offered to puzzle it out.

He would be *lovely* in bed. Sumptuous, generous, considerate, and good-humored. He'd be patient with her inexperience, tender with her sensibilities, cherishing of her body. How could she not…?

"And if I conceive a child?" Sara asked, some of the bloom wearing off her pleasurable anticipation.

He did not heave out a manly sigh of long-suffering at a question that would douse most men's passions. He traced her hairline with the side of one thumb, a caress that beguiled with its very simplicity.

"I understand you have a dim view of marriage, Sara. My own experience with it was not encouraging, but I can provide for you and a child easily and well. You could live anywhere you pleased, in fine style, if that's what you wanted, but I would not want…"

He paused to nuzzle at her throat.

"You would not want…?" Sara prompted, even as she angled her chin to encourage him to continue.

"I would not want to be a stranger to my own child, and I have to tell you"—he bit gently on her earlobe—"I have an illegitimate half sibling, and I cannot relish the thought of bringing bastardy down on any child of mine."

"Nor would I relish such a prospect," Sara managed. He was suckling at her earlobe, and God above, the sensations that evoked were strange and wonderful.

"So we'll take precautions." Beck left off touching his tongue to the pulse in Sara's throat, which was fortunate for her sanity. "I will take precautions, and there will be little chance of a child."

"*If* we dally." Sara willed herself to focus on the words, not on the glorious, naughty, unlooked-for sensations he was creating.

"If we dally," he agreed solemnly. "You'll think on it and let me know your decision."

"I will." Sara sank against him and realized that big, warm hand of his was stroking her *calf*. In all her years of marriage and fending off the advances of Reynard's drunken friends, no man had put his hand on that portion of her body. The caress was different, slow, soothing, and yet… His hand shouldn't be there, and she loved that it was.

His thumb traveled over the joint of her knee, tracing the bones, bringing a melting warmth that traveled up her thigh. Sara rested against him, listening to the sensations her body was experiencing. Who would have thought a knee could be so receptive to tenderness? Who would have known an earlobe was capable of sensation at all?

Beck's lips traced over Sara's cheek, and she lifted her face to meet his kiss. When she raised up on her knees, the better to frame his face with her hands and kiss him back, she felt Beck's hand on the small of her back, holding her against him.

"Let me pleasure you," Beck whispered, his hand

now stroking slowly over her thigh. "Let me touch you, Sara."

Of course she was letting him touch her, letting him chase away the chill, the darkness, the years and years of isolation, and the self-doubt that never yielded to common sense or stern admonitions. With a start, Sara realized exactly where Beckman sought to touch her, but just as she would have drawn back to protest, he slid a hand around to cup her breast and gently close his fingers over it.

Sara groaned against his neck as heat and arousal coursed through her from that one gentle caress. "I feel…"

"Tell me." He did it again then set up a soft, slow rhythm of pressure and release on her breast even as Sara felt the backs of his fingers brush over the curls at the apex of her sex.

"Too much," she breathed. "This is too much."

"Not enough," he countered, his fingers closing around her nipple, intensifying the sensations with a more focused caress. "I want you utterly undone."

When his thumb brushed upward, Sara whimpered with the intensity of the sensation.

"You must not," she whispered, flinching.

"I want to put my mouth on you here," Beck rejoined, his whisper growing hoarse as his thumb found her again. "I want to taste you and make you scream with pleasure."

"Beckman…" Sara's grip on his hair tightened. "I can't stand…"

He silenced her by sealing his mouth to hers, using his tongue, his thumb, and his hand to destroy her ability to think, much less speak. She began to rock shamelessly against his hand, her body damp with desire for more of his caresses.

"I want… Beck…"

"Let me give you what you want." His voice was a low, rasping command. "Stop fighting the pleasure, Sara. Stop fighting yourself."

He increased the pressure and speed of his thumb, and she stifled a moan against his neck. Her hips picked up the tempo, and then she was lost, overcome with pleasure, keening softly and riding his hand with mindless determination. When her pleasure finally subsided, she was limp in his arms, panting and without words.

Utterly undone.

And despite his own unappeased need, Beck was apparently content to hold her, to stroke her hair and her back, to fit his breathing with hers and to wait for her to regain her equilibrium.

"Love?" He kissed her cheek. "Sara, sweetheart?" He patted her backside gently, and she lifted her head then tucked her nose against his neck.

"What did you do to me?"

"Petted you a bit. Cuddle up, or you'll take cold." He tucked her closer, wrapped his arms around her, and rested his chin against her hair. "Talk to me, sweetheart. A woman gone quiet in her dallying is not a reassuring prospect. Are you all right?"

Sara tried to assay her bodily state and found the results did not lend themselves to articulation. The confusion of her emotional state defied any description whatsoever.

"No. I am not all right, but I can't be more

specific." Part of what was amiss had to do with these affectionate, cherishing little touches being every bit as overwhelming as what had gone before.

"I wasn't too rough?"

"Of course not." She let him see her eyes, see the truth of that. "You were…" She hid her face again. "So tender."

A silence spread, not uncomfortable. Tenderness was the furthest thing from a transgression, and yet Sara felt as discommoded as if Beck had committed some domestic misdemeanor.

"She's nursing," Beck said softly. Sara twisted to peer over her shoulder and saw he was right. The filly's tail was twitching, and her mother was contentedly lipping hay while the baby fed.

"They'll be fine now, won't they?" This mattered terribly. If anything should happen to either the mare or the filly now, Sara would lose her mind.

"They should be." Beck lifted Sara so she wasn't straddling him anymore but was across his lap instead. She was full grown and well fed, and he moved her around as easily he might lift Heifer. "What about you, Sara? Are you all right?"

"I think so." She bit her lip in thought. "I will be, I am just… That wasn't what I expected."

"So are we dallying?" Beck's expression was utterly unreadable as he studied the mare and foal.

"I must not decide this now." She tucked into him as she said it, gathering a scent that was a combination of bergamot, hay, and horse. "I cannot think, Beckman. I cannot think one sensible thought just now."

"Good." He sounded smug and relieved both.

He lifted her in his arms, had her take the lantern down from its peg, and carried her back to the house. When he set her on her feet at her apartment door, he didn't kiss her, but he did take her in his arms.

His voice rumbled under her ear where she'd laid it against his chest. "Even if you decide we shall not dally, Sara Hunt, I will be in your debt for the comforts you shared with me this night. All the comforts."

When Sara wished he'd kiss her again or at least hold her for a few more moments, he disappeared up the steps to the cold and darkness above.

❧

"May I ask for your help with something in the barn this morning, Miss Allie?" Beck tossed an orange into the air, caught it, and began peeling it.

"You may." Allie tried to toss her orange, only to have Beck pluck it out of midair. He started over on hers, then set both oranges on the counter. "Mr. North hasn't come down yet, so I'll help with his chores."

"Give him a little time," Beck said. "I doubt you'd manage to get his chores done by Tuesday, so conscientious is our Mr. North. Put your sabots on, please, so we can see to this task before your aunt is done making breakfast."

"What if Mr. North died last night?" Allie asked, clumping out the back door in her wooden shoes. "Or took off for Portsmouth like the twins?"

"What if the fairies took him and dropped him in the hot spring?" Beck suggested, "Which is just about as likely." He held the barn door for her, provoking a shy grin from Allie. "Are you ready to help?"

"Yes. But with what?"

He led her over to Hermione's stall and hefted her up to stand on a trunk.

"You have to help someone learn to make friends," he said, nodding toward the occupants. "There's a little girl in there ready to take the world by storm, but she needs a friend to scratch her neck and pet her and show her what brushes are for."

Allie's eyes went round, and her shoulders lifted with glee. "A baby for Hermione, and you say it's a girl. She's gorgeous, absolutely bee-yoo-tee-ful. I must sketch her this instant, and then, she must have a name."

That sketching came before naming struck Beck as significant. He spent a few minutes acquainting Allie and the filly, until Allie was gently scratching the little beast on its fuzzy neck.

"I must get my sketch pad."

Beck rose slowly from the straw so as not to spook the filly. "I suggest you eat a decent breakfast, feed Hildy, and do whatever other chores are expected of you before you start, or you'll just have to stop midway."

A jutting chin was his answer. "That is not fair. That is just not fair. She's all soft and pretty and cute *now*, and I want to sketch her now."

Beck tweaked a braid. "She'll be here, Allie. When you get back to the house, be sure to wash your hands. Be thinking of a name while I take care of mucking and watering."

"I will." Allie turned abruptly to dash out the door, caught herself, and left the stall at a dignified pace. She even walked to the barn door before breaking into a dead run across the backyard.

Beck had mucked the stalls, refilled the water buckets, fed the chickens, and pitched fresh hay for the horses and the milk cows when Sara appeared, the egg basket over her arm.

"Good morning." Beck smiled at her as he hung up his fork. "How fare you on this fine, frigid day?"

Sara kept her gaze on the foal, who was in fine fettle. "It is colder, isn't it? Is she doing well?"

"She couldn't be better. What of you, Sarabande Adagio?"

No cap. He would go to his grave pleased in some measure to have rid her of her caps.

Sara glanced at him, but only fleetingly. "I'm fine."

Sara's variety of *fine* did not invite a good-morning kiss. In Beck's breeches, the sunrise lost some of its glory.

"Are you truly fine, or wishing the ground would swallow you up?" He leaned in and pitched his voice to a conspiratorial whisper. "Or are you a trifle sore and anticipating the next time you come upon me all alone late at night?"

"Of course not." She put more surprise than dismay in her words.

Beck lingered close long enough to catch a hint of her scent before aiming a naughty grin at her.

She fought a shy smile and lost. "Oh, maybe a little, anticipating, that is, but maybe not."

"Well, there's a rousing endorsement of a fellow's opening moves."

"This isn't a chess match," Sara said, watching as

the foal teetered around in her bed of straw. "But whatever it is, I don't know how to go about it."

She sounded genuinely perplexed and not exactly pleased.

This again, though not, Beck surmised, for the last time. "It's a friendly dalliance, Sara, and it's not complicated. Here's how it works: you indicate to me my advances are welcome, and I offer you what pleasure you're inclined to accept. There is no obligation and no particular significance to it beyond the moment. I would ask, however, that we observe a certain exclusivity in our dealings for whatever duration it suits you."

To add that condition cost him some pride. Would that he'd clarified his stance on the matter of exclusivity with his poor wife.

"Just like that?" With the toe of her boot, Sara pushed bits of straw around in the dirt of the barn floor. "You wait for me to drop my handkerchief, and we go at it?"

"I wait for you to encourage me," Beck corrected her, "and then I have your permission to persuade you to my bed."

"You're thinking of bedding me right now, aren't you?" Sara's tone was puzzled. "And you've thought of it before."

"I have," Beck replied, trying to fathom the direction of her thoughts. "I can only hope you've had reciprocal thoughts about me."

"And I can rely on your discretion?" She peered at her egg basket, as if the contents might be getting up to mischief if left unsupervised.

"Sara…" Beck's tone was patient. "I won't maul you before your daughter, and I won't discuss you with North, if that's what you're asking."

"I suppose it is." She rearranged the eggs. "I don't know how to go on, Beckman. In the cold light of day, I don't know why I would want to—though… I do. Want to go on. I think."

Were she being coy, he would have flirted and flattered and charmed, and they would soon be climbing the ladder to the hayloft. Sara was not being coy; she was being honest, and while the rutting male part of Beck resented it, the part of him far from home and a little sick with it valued her for her genuineness.

"I'll remind you why." Beck took her free hand, cradled it between his own, then brought it to his face and rubbed his cheek along the backs of her fingers. When his gallantry elicited a soft sigh from Sara, he pressed her fingers flat and planted a lingering kiss on her palm, then folded her fingers around it.

"I'm reminded," Sara said, snatching her hand back a little breathlessly.

She disappeared in a swirl of skirts, leaving Beck to admire her retreating form.

"You're reminded," he murmured, "and so am I, Sarabande, so am I."

Seven

"YOU HAVE MAIL AGAIN." BECK'S VOICE STARTLED Sara where she bent over the makings of Allie's dress. When she straightened, her back protested the shift in position.

"Here now." Beck stepped in behind her and settled his hands on the small of her back. "Can't have you competing with North for least able to hobble about." He kneaded the muscles running along her spine, and Sara gave up even pretending to ignore him.

"You shouldn't be doing that, but you can stop five minutes from now, while I lecture you about people walking in the parlor door unannounced."

"Who's to walk?" Beck did not desist—she had hoped he wouldn't. "North is flat on his back, Polly is putting together the midday meal, and Allie is sketching the filly. Not a one of them could be dissuaded from their present course by anything short of a French invasion."

"Don't say that, not even in jest. If you'd seen what the Corsican's ambitions did to most of Europe, you'd know nothing associated with him is humorous."

"I have." Beck's arms slipped around her waist. "I spent most of a year in Paris not long ago, and I've seen many other once-lovely towns and villages devastated. In the end, the man's penchant for supporting his armies by foraging helped do him in, particularly on the Peninsula, and at what cost to the countryside?"

"Foraging?" Sara's tone became bitter. "More like pillaging, and from the innocent people who had no notion of the glory of France or the glory of anything, save a decent meal and a roof that wouldn't leak."

"Those things are glorious," Beck said, and he sounded sincere. "As is your hair."

He sounded sincere about that too, blast and bless him.

"My hair is a disgrace," Sara said, angling her chin to accommodate him. "Your manners are a disgrace."

"Shall I ask?" Beck kissed her below her ear. "Sara, may I please hold you for a few moments in the middle of the day? May I remind myself how delectable you taste? May I offer you a little teasing and affection before you sit down to lunch?"

He turned her and wrapped his arms around her, but when she didn't banter back, he let her go. "Who's the letter from?"

"I don't know." Sara glanced at the missive he'd passed to her. "I don't recognize the address. I take it you nipped into the village?"

"I did. I made it a point to tell Polly I was leaving the property. I should have told you as well, and in future, if I'm rambling beyond the estate, I will."

This from a man who'd be leaving any day to assume a place as an earl's heir?

"Have the twins been back to collect their pay?"

Beck's mouth—his beautiful, tender mouth—creased with disapproval. "The twins are nowhere to be seen. I ran into a relation of mine in The Dead Boar."

"In *our* village?" He was related to an earl, for pity's sake. "Are we to have company?"

"Not at present," he said, finding a seat on the arm of a sofa. "My brother Ethan was on his way to Portsmouth to look in on some peach seedlings he'd had shipped from Georgia. It was probably a chance encounter, as most of ours are."

Sara studied him, catching the scent of some unresolved family difficulty. "You seem to like your family. Is this Ethan not agreeable to you, that you meet him only by happenstance?"

Beck reached for her, and she let him take her hand. "In truth, I hardly know the man. He was booted off to boarding school under a cloud of drama when I was nine, and never did come back to Belle Maison. My father's situation may be inspiring some sort of rapprochement between Ethan and the earl, but at the very least it was good to have a cordial exchange with my brother."

Beck referred to the earl's illness as a *situation*, and even that passing mention dimmed the light in his blue eyes.

"Only cordial?" Sara brushed her free hand over Beck's hair. "I would hate to be only cordial with Polly. Loathe it, in fact."

"Cordial is better than civil." Beck turned his face so his cheek rested against her palm. "But then, Ethan has his reasons for keeping his distance, and they're reasons I can understand. Sometimes I want to shake my father, so stubborn is he in his convictions."

"Fathers can be like that." Sara moved a step closer of her own accord, and without leaving his perch on the arm of the sofa, Beck again tucked her against him.

Beckman Haddonfield was an affectionate man. This posed a greater threat to Sara's self-possession than the fact that he was also a lusty, handsome man. "Your papa is a despot?"

"A loving despot." Beck's hand stroked over Sara's hair, a sweet, tender gesture with nothing carnal about it.

"Mine is too, or he was. I haven't seen him for years, and we don't correspond."

"You should," Beck said, rising and wrapping his arms around her. "For Allie's sake, if nothing else, you should make the overtures, Sara."

"And if the overtures are rejected?" And that was the real problem, wasn't it? With Beck's arms around her, she could admit that much to herself.

"You can make them again another day, or at least know you tried. I've been astounded at what can be forgiven between human beings, and how completely. My parents would argue vociferously at midday only to be billing and cooing over supper."

"Your parents loved each other, I suppose?"

"They did. Even when you love somebody, you can lose track of them, as we've lost track of Ethan, and he of us—and all over a misunderstanding."

"All families have misunderstandings and secrets." Sara moved away, and again, Beck let her go. He'd always let her go, and that was also something she valued in him even as it occasioned some sadness.

When his father died, she was going to have to let him go too, wasn't she?

"Is Allie a secret?" He posed the question softly, the understanding in his gaze more than Sara's limited store of composure could look upon.

"My parents haven't met her," she conceded. "They know I have a daughter."

"What happened, Sara? I trust they approved of your marriage. You were underage, and you haven't mentioned eloping. Polly had to be even younger, and yet your parents entrusted her to Reynard's care as well, even to the point of letting her travel with you on the Continent."

"They approved my marriage, and they did send Polly with us when Reynard and I departed on tour. Polly was to receive instruction from the Continental masters, according to Reynard. Things did not go as my parents planned, though, and by law and custom, my husband's dictates prevented their welcoming me back home."

Dictates. Beck wouldn't like her word choice, but it was legally accurate.

"Your husband no longer has dictates," Beck pointed out gently. "Do as you will, Sara. Your parents love you, and they've had time to reconsider their positions."

"How do you know they loved us?" Sara posed the question idly, but it had gnarled roots wrapping around both present and past.

"Because of how you and Polly are with Allie. She knows she's loved, and you can't give away a love you've never experienced yourself. If you allow this, this *silence* to remain between you and your family, it can grow. Like a pernicious weed, it will grow without sunlight or water, without marling, until it chokes out the love you still bear each other."

He used an agricultural image to make an effective point, and the stillness in his gaze suggested he knew of what he spoke.

Sara looked away rather than ask him what besides the loss of a wife illuminated the sadness in his eyes. "Our parents loved us, but not as they loved Gavin. Still, it's in the past, and if you and I tarry here much longer, Polly will be reduced to ringing the kitchen bell. It will go hard for us if she does, though Allie might be forgiven her artistic absorption."

He looked at her for one more instant, long enough for Sara to understand that he was *allowing* her to close the topic, just as she allowed him to hold her.

He looped an arm over her shoulders when she would have marched for the door. "If you're ever ready to talk, Sara, I'm always ready to listen. My own family isn't a study in uniform happiness, or good choices and tender sentiments. We don't always trust each other or take the kindest option among ourselves. It can't be that different from your family."

"I suppose not." Sara pressed her face to his shoulder, a moment of weakness—yet another moment of weakness. She had the surprising thought that when Beckman reached for her, those might be his moments of weakness. As she went on speaking, she addressed the solid musculature of his shoulder.

"When there's a title, one expects a larger-than-life existence—an earl might have an illegitimate son, his countess a little affair, his firstborn be estranged. My father was a lowly squire who enjoyed scribbling the occasional composition for the choir at St. Albans, my mother a vicar's daughter who made a solid, comfortable match. Our story should have been prosaic."

She slid out from under Beck's arm, having given up enough of the difficult tale that was her old life. Her existence at Three Springs was prosaic in the extreme, tiresomely so, and yet, she could not say it was exactly comfortable.

⁓

"Polly and North haven't come in yet?"

"You are not to fret, Sarabande Adagio," Beck said, flipping the last muffin out of its pan. "I can assure you, North is in no condition to threaten anybody's virtue. He's still moving like an eighty-year-old veteran of the Colonial wars. If he asked Polly to introduce him to the new foal, then that's exactly what's afoot."

More or less. A man did not need a supple back to kiss the woman he loved.

Sara stood, arms crossed, watching him arrange muffins on a rack to cool. "It will take him a few days to come right. A trip or three to the springs wouldn't go amiss."

"I'll suggest it to him tomorrow, as it's the Sabbath, and he's not up to any work anyway." Beck fetched a pat of butter from the window box. "Join me?"

"For a few minutes." Sara preceded him to the table. "And yes, I will have a muffin as well, just so your feelings won't be hurt."

"Such a considerate lady." Beck put the butter on a tea tray with three muffins and brought it to the table. "And while we enjoy my baking, there are things I want to discuss with you."

"This sounds ominous." Sara sugared her tea, half a teaspoon then a second half teaspoon.

"Not serious, but needful. First, you should know I rounded up some help today from Sutcliffe Manor for the harrowing and planting, so Polly might have some extra cooking to do at midday come the first of the week."

"Is this why you added some stores from the Saturday market?" She dabbed a little butter on her muffin, then a little more.

"In part. You should also know I made the acquaintance of Mrs. Grantham, the Sutcliffe house-keeper, who might well be calling on you and Polly."

Sara closed her eyes and inhaled a whiff of her muffin, looking like some decadent kitchen angel. "Susan Grantham? Tallish, blonde, and goes about with a not-to-be-trifled-with look?"

Beck did not snort at that observation. "I would have said it's a housekeeperish look, but yes. She's isolated at Sutcliffe. The roads between there and here are miserable, and I gather she doesn't have a riding mount. I will notify the property owner of the oversight, but if it holds fair tomorrow, she might be over with the farm help."

"I'll let Polly know." Sara took a sip of her tea. "Allie will be excited."

"Planting is an exciting time, or it should be. But when the planting is done, Sara, we'll need to make a trip into Portsmouth, and I will want your company for that excursion."

She paused in dabbing yet more butter on her muffin. "My company? Why not Mr. North's?"

"For one thing, I don't think hours on a wagon will appeal to his abused back," Beck said, for which Beck really ought not to be so grateful. "For another, I would rather he and I are not both gone from the property overnight."

"Beckman, we manage here by ourselves often enough."

"You shouldn't have to. Besides, North has no idea which tea towels will go with what's on hand, how many lamp chimneys need to be replaced, or whether we're lower on lamp black or boot polish. I can speak for the needs of the land and the buildings, but you are the one who must address the needs of the house."

"We'd have to spend the night."

The very point of the outing, since goods could be ordered by mail and hauled overland if a man preferred to spend his coin that way.

Which Beck did not. He appropriated the butter knife from her and doctored his own muffin with a generous dollop of butter. "I know of several very reputable and discreet inns in Portsmouth, Sara." Beck held his muffin up to her lips. "And honestly, the prospect of having you to myself, away from the rest of the household, appeals greatly."

She nibbled a bite off, peering at him curiously while she chewed. "Are you offering to *go shopping* with me?"

Lest she attribute to him saintliness beyond his aspirations, Beck replied honestly: "I suppose I am, among other things." He topped up their teacups and bit into his muffin from the same spot she'd nibbled. "But I'm warning you, Sara, when we're in Portsmouth, I expect to spend a great deal of money, and some of that on you and yours."

"Don't say that. You need not spend a ha'penny on us, Beckman, particularly not on me."

"I mean you no insult."

"I did not mean to imply…" She covered his hand with hers for the duration of one quick, warm squeeze, which was something—a small bite of a tasty muffin. "Don't be offended, I'm just… not used to generosity. My parents were frugal, and with Reynard, we rarely left town but that the creditors were nipping at our heels. It was no way to live."

She was coming to Portsmouth with him. He could afford to be not just generous but gracious. "How exactly did he support his family?"

"He purported to be a gentleman, one of the many exponents of the dispossessed French aristocracy—a *comte* who did not use his title, of course."

"I'm sorry. I know what it is to be disappointed in a spouse, but my wife wasn't particularly evil, she was just a victim of circumstances."

"As are we all." She worried a thumbnail then stopped herself.

"Will you come to Portsmouth with me?"

She knew what he was asking and what he was offering. She'd all but accepted, but he wanted to hear the words from her.

"After planting, we really must tend to the shopping, Beckman, and if I go with you, I don't want to tarry. I've not been away from Allie for a night before, and I don't want her to fret."

Maternal fretting he could understand—up to a point.

"Polly and North will look after her, and you have a couple of weeks to accustom her to the idea."

Sara nodded but took to staring at her tea as Beck passed her another half of a muffin slathered with butter, holding it out to her and waiting for her to take it from his hand.

"Sara?"

Her chin came up, as if prepared for confrontation.

"I will not force my attentions on you," Beck said. "Not ever. Going to Portsmouth, sharing a muffin, even sharing a kiss, does not obligate you to anything more."

She took the muffin.

He did not smile, but the moment was sweet. "I'll arrange for our trip in a couple of weeks, and you and Polly should finish up your shopping lists. I already have Allie's."

As a change of topic, as a distraction, that apparently served well enough. "Allie made a list?"

"I asked her to, and, Sara, there is not one damned thing on that list for the girl herself. She wants me to get you some dress fabric and two new bonnets, the same for Polly. She says North needs a new set of farrier's tools and two new shirts, as well as winter stockings. For Hermione, she wants harness bells, and for Hildegard, she wants one of Mrs. Radcliffe's novels. She claims the pig ate such a book last year then had thirteen piglets."

"Even North laughed when Polly pointed that out." Sara smiled in remembrance.

"As did Mr. Hildegard, no doubt." Beck smiled as well, glad for the lighter mood. "You have to believe you're doing very well with Allie, Sara, and I would like to buy her some paints and books on art when we're in Portsmouth."

Sara's smiled faded into a staring contest with her last bite of muffin. "Is it important to you?"

"I think it's important to her," Beck countered. "If something important to her is denied by her elders, it will eventually foster rebellion in the child. I don't gather any of the Hunt womenfolk are possessed of malleable spirits, and talent like Allie's isn't simply going to fade."

"We're not weak spirited," Sara agreed, reluctantly. "We haven't had that luxury, in any case. Just don't…"

"Don't what?"

"I don't want Allie's art to consume her, to sweep away her common sense and put her in the path of licentious, profligate dilettantes who think a little art excuses a lot of immorality."

He didn't ask—Is this what befell you and Polly?—but he would ask, eventually.

"Forgive me." Sara rose and picked up the tea tray. "Again, I blunder onto difficult subjects, and it's growing late. My thanks for the muffin, and I will look forward to seeing Mrs. Grantham on Monday."

"I'll walk you to your door, unless you want me to casually tuck Hildy in and shoo your sister back to your worried arms first?"

"That won't be necessary. I'd like to send Hildy to go shoo my sister inside, because Hildy is a very conscientious and forceful parent. Polly is an adult, though, and Gabriel is a gentleman, but he's going to leave, isn't he?"

"Why do you say that?" When she set the tray

down, he slipped his arm around her and began walking her toward her apartment.

"Because for two years Gabriel has hidden his regard for Polly from all, including himself sometimes. He arranged to spend time with her tonight, privately, and at some length. I can't imagine him permitting himself such a liberty except in parting."

"If he is leaving," Beck said as they reached her door, "I am sure he has been absolutely honest with Polly about his plans, Sara. Maybe she can permit herself to acknowledge their feelings only for the same reason." He knew far too well the emotional dynamics of leave-taking. Beck wrapped his arms around Sara, held her for a moment before kissing her on the mouth and stepping back. "Sweet dreams, Sarabande. I'll see you in mine."

"Good night, Beckman." She rose on her toes and brushed her lips across his. "I'll dream of shopping with you in Portsmouth."

In the kitchen, Beck poured himself another cup of tea and wondered if he would wait up for Polly—or North—had Sara not expressed concern. He appropriated pen, ink, and paper from the library and started on a list of his own. A good hour later, he heard Polly's voice in the back hall, followed by the less distinct rumble of North's baritone.

About damned time.

North ambled into the kitchen, clearly having sent Polly to her bed. "You're still awake?"

"Making my list." Beck pushed the teapot toward North. "How's your back?"

"Aching." North lowered himself to a chair—slowly,

slowly. "Thank God it's merely aching, not cursing and making me wish I were dead."

Beck put his pen down and considered his companion. North's saturnine features held the usual complement of banked suffering. "Does it really hurt so much?"

"The physical pain is only part of it." North stirred a little sugar into his tea, sipped, then added cream. "I know that's likely temporary, and can cope with it. The indignity, however, remains intolerable even as it becomes mere memory rather than fact. But I suppose your golden life has not taught you this, yet anyway."

Beck took off his glasses and waited until North was done stirring his damned tea.

"My brother had to carry me, bodily, covered in my own filth, from an opium den in Paris, and I fought him to my last breath to be left where I was. I cannot recall a great deal about months of self-indulgence in the same spot, but I can recall clearly the look on Nick's face when he realized which bag of noisome bones was what was left of his little brother."

North picked up Beck's glasses and started polishing them on his handkerchief. "One would find that a tenacious memory."

"He cried," Beck said. "They weren't tears of disgust or rage, though they should have been. They were tears of relief, because I was still alive."

"Beckman..." Some of North's characteristic gruffness slid away. "It isn't that I'm ungrateful... I had last rites in Spain, you know, twice. It's just I've made a muddle of things, and one grows... weary of one's situation."

"So you hare off," Beck finished for him, knowing

exactly the terrain North called home turf. "You leave, and you hope the change of scenery or people or horses or whatever helps, and it doesn't."

"We'll have to see about that, won't we?" North poured more tea for them both.

Beck waited while North appropriated the cream and sugar. "Sara worries about Polly and Allie, but I worry about you."

"You needn't." North rose very slowly with his teacup. "I'm fully breeched, and I've made my bed, Haddonfield. One copes."

Beck slid his chair back to look up at North. "Tomorrow one is going to cope by making a visit to the springs, and in the light of day, before the temperature drops back down to nippy, North."

"Not a bad idea." North sipped his tea and aimed a look at Beck. "Did you mean to kill yourself in that opium den?"

"I thought I did. I'd tried running and drinking and stupid risks and all manner of idiot means to deal with the low cards I'd found in the hand life dealt me, but I also made halfway sure Nick knew where to find me, and eventually, he did. Part of me just wanted to know somebody would try."

North set his mug on the counter. "When I leave, you needn't engage in such heroics, Haddonfield. I have a trade, and some means, and will land on my feet. But as for you…" He turned to go. "I'm glad this brother of yours found you in time."

He left before Beck could reply, while Beck hoped wholeheartedly that there was a brother out there looking for North.

Eight

"NORTH IS LEAVING."

The studied calm in Polly's voice didn't fool Sara for an instant. She put aside the pinafore she was mending, and put aside the urge to give Gabriel North a stern talking to as well.

"Why now?"

Polly sank into her rocking chair and sat still. "He says he must, that it's a family matter, and that Three Springs will come around in Beckman's care. I'm not to worry."

So much had been taken from Polly, it seemed wrong that North should try to deprive her of her justifiable concern too. "He didn't ask you to go with him?"

Polly shook her head once, a gesture of defeat and heartache.

"What will you miss the most?" If Sara didn't ask, then Polly would bottle all the misery up inside, making extravagant desserts out of it, and subtly spiced dishes fit for the Regent's pavilion in Brighton.

The kitchen would be spotless—more spotless—and there wouldn't be a weed within ten yards of the spice garden.

"I'll miss his voice. I love Gabriel's voice. I love the way he cleans his plate at every single meal. I'll miss the way he talks to Hildegard as if she really were some society dowager. I'll miss the way he and Heifer commiserate without a word."

Polly turned her face away, as if the darkness beyond the window held some consolation.

"When Beckman goes," Sara said, "I'll miss his scent."

Polly glanced at her. "Bergamot and some other notes. It's… soothing."

"I'll miss the way he puts his hands on me, like I'm precious but not fragile—even if he's walking with me in the garden, he handles me confidently. I adore that."

Polly's lips quirked up in a sad smile, and both sisters spoke in unison.

"Men."

⌒⌁

Monday arrived, bright, mild, and more May than April, much to Beck's relief. He'd marched North to the springs the previous day, and the soak had done them both good, but North was still in no shape to man a team of draft horses.

A half-dozen men showed up from Sutcliffe Manor, five of them in a farm wagon and one driving a dray, a willowy blonde on the bench beside him.

"Mrs. Grantham." Beck assisted her to the ground. "I'm pleased you could call. The Hunt womenfolk are much in need of company. I'll show you to the house while North gets the men sorted out."

Beck had escorted his guest to the front door, an entrance he hadn't used since arriving at Three

Springs weeks ago. The front approach, he realized, was neglected. Weeds cropped up through the crushed shells in the driveway, bushes sprouted willy-nilly much in need of pruning, and flower boxes sported nothing so much as robust… weeds.

When he introduced Mrs. Grantham to Sara and Polly, it took about two minutes to realize he was *de trop*. The ladies launched into an intense discussion of the best layout for a spice garden, so he returned to the barnyard. North had a harrow hitched up behind one of the Sutcliffe teams and the second team standing in the traces waiting for its harrow to be secured.

Beck sidled up to North. "It's killing you, isn't it? To send others out to do the heavy work?"

"Not killing me, exactly. I'm just used to doing it, is all."

"Mrs. Grantham says you were born to give the orders, not take them." Beck patted the leader of the second team.

"Susan Grantham is one to talk. This team is ready to go."

Beck stepped back, and the second harrow scraped and dragged its way out of the yard. The next task was loading some barley and spring-wheat seed into bushel baskets, so it could be sown broadcast in portions of the field not congenial to the seed drill Beck had borrowed from Sutcliffe.

The third and final harrow, owned by Three Springs, was hitched up behind a team Beck had brought down from Belle Maison, and one of the rangy, muscular Sutcliffe plowmen took up the reins.

"Mind the ladies bring us some nuncheon," the

fellow cautioned. He signaled the horses to move out, and soon another piece of heavy equipment was bumping and dragging its way toward the field.

Only to come to an abrupt halt before even gaining the farm lane.

"What's amiss?" Beck hustled over amid the plowman's cursing; North followed more slowly.

The plowman hopped around, shaking one heavily booted foot. "The bedamned, blighted harrow is come undone." He wrapped the reins, fanned himself with his battered hat, and pointed at the harrow. "If we'd been in the field, this would have taken m'foot clean off."

"The bolts are loose," North growled, squatting carefully beside the heavy iron frame. "Those two sheared just now, and the rest are likely to at the next bump or rock. God above, I should have checked this over. I should have seen this."

"Good thing yon beasts is well trained," the plowman said. "If they weren't so quick to mind, they would have pulled me along, regardless."

Beck knelt to examine the problem. "Can it be repaired?"

"It will be a damned pain in the ass." North rose stiffly. "We'll have to get the parts in to the blacksmith and hope he has the means to weld and bolt on hand, then get the whole business back here somehow."

"It can wait," Beck said. "We've two in the field, which is twice what we had on hand, and Sutcliffe can spare the help."

North gave a terse nod but gestured with his chin to indicate they needed some privacy.

"Is your foot all right?" Beck asked the plowman.

"Right enough. It got a good stubbing, but no real harm, thank the good Lord."

"Unhitch the team, and you can assist with the seeding," Beck said. "We'll switch teams at midday to rest the horses."

"Right, guv." The man moved to the horse's bridles, pitching his voice to the horses as he did. Beck accompanied North to the side of the barn and waited, because clearly, North had something to say.

"I did check that equipment," North began in a low, angry rumble. "I work largely alone here, and I don't relish the thought of bleeding to death trapped beneath a faulty piece of equipment. I checked that thing over before I put it up last spring, and I checked every piece of equipment on the property as part of the winter inventory. I checked it again when we finished plowing."

"What are you saying, North?"

"Somebody broke our damned harrow. It's the only one on the property still functional, and the repair will take at least two weeks. Even if you went to Portsmouth for a replacement, by the time you got one here, you would have lost several weeks of spring growing."

"I believe you, North, but who would have had access to the harrow?"

"Any damned body in the neighborhood. The hinges on the sheds and barns are so rusty a determined old woman could get into any building on the premises."

"Or she could just peel off the rotten shingles and

drop down from the leaky roof. Who would be motivated to do such a thing?"

"Anybody who wants to buy the place," North said. "Anybody with a grudge against me, Lady Warne, or the Hunts."

Beck eyed the steward thoughtfully, because this was the first time he'd seen Gabriel North truly upset. "Are those lists long?"

North glared back at him. "How the hell should I know? I have no enemies here that I know of, but perhaps you have an enemy. Three Springs has been rotting on the vine for years, but malicious mischief passed us by until you showed up."

"True enough."

"Hell and the devil, I didn't mean that the way it sounded, it's just… who would think it amusing to take off a man's foot?"

"I don't know. We're going to have to have a frank talk with the women, and with Allie in particular, North. If there are vandals on the property, that child cannot be scampering around unsupervised."

"Holy Infant Jesus." North closed his eyes and marshaled his temper with visible effort. "Polly and Sara don't need this, but it makes the prospect of hiring help more urgent."

"I thought we'd start with your friend Lolly. Maudie is a maid of all work, but there's enough for her to do just in the scullery. Three Springs could use another maid, and those boys of hers could be put to use all over the property."

"They eat a lot," North said. "Polly will like that."

"We need some men, though, and good labor is in short supply."

"Will Sutcliffe let you keep some of his for a time?"

"I suppose. We have walls to mend, roofs to repair, hay to take off soon, more sheep to shear and dip, and God knows what else."

"My back is protesting the mere recitation. You're right. There's plenty enough work, if you've the coin to hire the labor."

"Three Springs has the coin," Beck clarified. "If Sutcliffe turns us down, we have other options."

"Such as?"

"Portsmouth, if not in the village. I meant to tell you last night I've secured Sara's agreement to accompany me there on a shopping expedition when the planting is done."

"Are you sure it's a good idea to leave the property with this going on?" North gestured toward the broken harrow.

"If everything stays quiet for the next week or so, then yes. We need more than the village can supply, North. Shingles, hinges, locks, lumber, nails, paint, you name it, if it goes into the building or maintenance of a structure, we need it."

"Suppose we do. The ladies are looking forward to putting the house to rights, too."

Beck sent a wary glance toward the house. "One shudders to think of disappointing them. Which reminds me, we need a gardener as well."

"Can't you buy one of those in Portsmouth?"

"I intend to try, preferably a very fit, muscular specimen who has a way with a rose bush and a blunderbuss."

"My thoughts exactly, and I hate to say it, but a footman or two wouldn't go amiss."

"I'll write to my sister at Belle Maison and send word to Nick. They'll likely have a few stout fellows to spare, at least for the summer."

"I'd write to Lady Warne," North said. "This is her damned property, and lady or not, it's her interests that will be affected if we can't get a crop in."

Interesting that Beck turned to his siblings for help, while North pointed out the more appropriate choice. "We'll get a crop planted. One piece of broken equipment won't stop a Haddonfield from his assigned task."

As the week progressed, the weather held, and they did get the crops in. Through correspondence with Baron Sutcliffe, Beck gained permission to offer employment to two of his farm hands, both stout, reliable fellows. Lolly and her two adolescent omnivores were recruited from the village, and letters went out to Belle Maison, Nick's London townhouse, and Lady Warne's residence.

While Polly reveled in the need to keep more mouths fed, Beck set Sara to taking the gardens, lane, and porches in hand. Lolly's sons were put to use as undergardeners, pulling weeds, rebuilding flower boxes, and putting in a huge kitchen garden in the field closest to the barns. With her mother's help, Allie proved surprisingly willing to tear into the challenge of setting the front beds and main approach to the house to rights. She divided irises and daffodils, pruned roses, moved daylilies and daisies and heaven only knew what according to some design she carried in her busy head.

Sara had been mindful of the need to keep Allie close to the house, leaving Beck a little concerned when he didn't see the child puttering away in the front gardens on Friday afternoon. It wasn't sums day or wash day, and for most of the morning, Allie had been planting her posies in the flower boxes on the side terraces.

She wasn't in the lower reaches of the house, so Beck made his way to the third floor, finding Allie in her studio of choice, much to his relief.

Beck ambled into the room, knowing Allie when sketching was an absorbed young lady indeed. "I had wondered where you'd gotten off to."

"I'm hiding from those odious boys." Allie's tongue peeked out the side of her mouth.

Beck lowered himself to sit on the day bed beside her. "They might be odious, but they plant an impressive kitchen garden."

And they made for good sketching subjects, Beck saw. Just as she'd done anatomical studies of the filly—Miss Amicus, by name—Allie was visually taking apart Lolly's sons, piece by piece. The odd quality of the adolescent male wrist was drawn from many angles and positions. Unruly boyish hair stood up in a dozen different inelegant coiffures; strangely graceful, young male hands grasped this or that tool, or flattened Heifer's disgruntled ears in a thumping pat to the cat's head.

"I could plant the kitchen garden," Allie said, putting the finishing touches on an image of a long, dirty boy-foot toe-scratching at a skinny boy-calf.

"But then you'd still be outside, hands muddy, covering up potato sprouts or pulling weeds," Beck pointed out. "Not honing your craft."

"Mama says it's a hobby," Allie countered, considering her final effort. "But is it a hobby if it's something you simply *must* do?"

"I don't know." Beck chose his words carefully. "My brother must build a birdhouse every so often, but he would say it's a hobby."

Allie considered the boy-foot. "He'd say it's a hobby because he's a man and all grown up, and a gentleman cannot work with his hands in any case. I am not a gentleman."

Beck flicked her nose with the end of one of her braids. "For which we are all very grateful."

Allie didn't dimple and giggle as Beck had intended. "If I were a boy, I'd be getting art lessons again, and there would be talk of apprenticing me."

"You really love to paint and draw, don't you?" Beck asked, eyeing her work.

"More than anything. Mama says I get lost when I do, but I feel like it's when I get found. It isn't that I forget time or where I am, it's that I'm where I'm supposed to be."

Beck slid a large hand down Allie's back, feeling the sharp little bones of her shoulder blades. "Sometimes, princess, you have to allow for people not understanding you, even though they love you and you love them."

Sometimes, you have to let them send you away, because they love you and you love them. Beck thought of his father, his brothers, his sisters...

"You mean like Mama?" Allie tucked herself a little closer to him. "That's the thing, though. She *does* understand, not about painting, but about art. She used to play for people, for important people, and they would pay her money, make her do three encores and everything. Now she doesn't play, and she forgets. I think it's my fault."

"Why would you say that?" Such little bones to carry so much responsibility.

"Because when you're a mama, you can't forget the time or the day," Allie explained patiently. "When you're a mama, you have to always be... where a mama should be. That sort of thing. Making beds instead of making music."

"Have you ever asked your mother to play for you?" Beck wondered, as the question left his mouth, if he were fomenting treason.

"I don't." Allie set her sketch aside. "I think it would hurt her feelings to remember, and she's afraid she'll forget about the beds, and then where would we be?"

"Here's where you are." Beck searched for a way to convey his thoughts *safely*. "You and your mother love each other, and you want each other to be happy. The beds have to be made, but it might be possible you have to paint too, Allie. Your mother is a very smart lady, and if she needs to get her violin out of its case, trust her to know that."

Allie kicked at the bed idly. "She can't play her violin. She sold it, but she buys me paints."

"Maybe she sold it because she was done with it."

Allie didn't say anything but leaned in against Beck silently, reminding him of many such gestures and conversations with his younger sisters. Whoever thought little girls were full of simple impulses and silly dreams had never spent time listening to one.

"I enjoy your art, Allie," Beck said. "I think your mother does too, but what will count in the end is if you enjoy it."

"Maybe." Allie shifted away, and Beck let her go. "She likes what I do, but it bothers her too—like I do."

Beck drew her back for a growling hug. "It is the job of mothers to be bothered by their offspring. Now go see if your mama needs help. She's unpacking the crates my sister sent down from Belle Maison, and I suspect Nita might have tucked in some maple candy, for we raise both bees and sugar maples."

"Maple candy?"

"Go." Beck closed her sketch book and handed it to her. "And don't stop sketching, Allie, not as long as it makes you happy."

She grinned and nodded, casting off her pensive mood in the fashion of young children. And then she was gone, leaving Beck to ponder what had changed in Sarabande Hunt's life that she'd traded in her violin for wrinkled sheets and dirty andirons?

৩৯

Appraisers apparently considered it their purpose in life to state the obvious, repeatedly and emphatically, as Henri Bernard was doing now.

"They're unconventional, very unconventional, but the brushwork is…"

Extraordinary, Tremaine thought, wanting to kick something—or someone.

"Mr. St. Michael, I tell you the brushwork is nothing short of extraordinary. Absolutely, utterly extraordinary. And the use of light—the mastery of it—beyond extraordinary. Words fail, they simply fail. Have you more works by the same artist?"

He had a good dozen more, larger and just as well executed, the subjects conventional enough for a dowager duchess's drawing room—provided her grace had exquisite taste in paintings.

"Let's start with these three. I need a value on them." Which was the same point Tremaine had made nearly forty-five *absolutely*, *utterly*, *extraordinary* minutes ago.

Bernard stuffed a quizzing glass in his pocket and straightened. "Are they to be sold at private auction? An auction for gentlemen, perhaps? Christie's will do an excellent job, and there are smaller houses, too, that I can highly recommend."

Because each of those auction houses would pay the dapper, so-French Monsieur Bernard a healthy commission for bringing these works to the block.

"I'm considering my options," Tremaine said. "The first step is to determine a value for them."

"That will take some time, sir. I must correspond with colleagues on the Continent, research sales of paintings of a similar nature."

Damn the French and their confounded, mule-stubborn delicacy.

"How long will you need," Tremaine asked, "and how much will it cost me?"

❧

Beckman set an idle pace across the yard. "My money's on young Cane."

"Your money?" Sara liked that he'd escort her like

this on a simple trip to the pond, and liked even better the way his hand rested over hers on his arm.

"In the great sweepstakes to win Maudie's heart," Beck went on. "She spends more time goggling at the scenery than she does helping Polly. We'll have to get two scullery maids, one to serve and one to stand as lookout. They can take turns."

"Cane is a handsome boy, but he's only fifteen. My guess is Maudie is more impressed with the older fellows. Angus is too old, but Jeffrey has a nice smile."

"Jeffrey's too old for Maudie too. If I find him walking out with her, I'll have to say something." Beckman sounded very stern over this business of calf love among the infantry.

"Maudie will be sixteen this summer. She's plenty old enough to marry, and if her parents don't object, you haven't anything to say to anyone."

"God's hoary eyebrows." Beck's idle pace slowed further. "Maudie doesn't seem that much older than Allie."

"Because she isn't." Which was an alarming notion every time Sara came upon it. "Allie will have some height on her soon."

"Allie will always be your little girl." Beck brought Sara's knuckles to his lips for a kiss, then replaced her hand on his arm. "She worries about you."

"Me?" Sara stopped and peered at him. "Why would Allie worry about her own mother?"

"She thinks you've forgotten your music," Beck said, his tone so very casual. "She's worried raising her has cost you your art."

"My art." Sara snorted derisively. Of all the causes

for worry, this one did not signify. "I might, once upon a time, have aspired to the title of musician, but by the time I put away my instrument, I was a fiddling strumpet."

"I have a certain fondness for strumpets." Beck's tone was mild. "I gather you mean the term as a pejorative."

"I most assuredly do, and my so-called husband was my procurer," Sara replied flatly. "When I met him, I had a little talent, a lot of dedication, and a confirmed love for music. Within two years, my technique had slipped badly, I wasn't fit for solo repertoire anymore, and I was so tired of performing the programs he chose that I was tempted to smash my hand just to put a stop to it."

And that was describing the situation in euphemisms.

"But you didn't."

"Within two years," Sara's tone softened, "there was Allie. I didn't dare stop playing. We had bills, and the child deserved to eat."

"Why had your technique slipped?"

Brave man to ask such a thing. "It might seem to a nonmusician that frittering the day away spinning melodies is the next thing to idleness, but it isn't," Sara explained. "Not physically, as one stands to play the violin properly, and that requires strength of the entire body, but especially the arms, back, and torso. And mentally, if you are going to improve, you must attend what you create, and attend it closely. With Reynard controlling my schedule, I simply became too tired to practice and to perform day in and day out."

Because she had her hand on his arm, Sara could

feel the tension her recitation provoked in the man beside her.

"How old would you have been?"

She needed to change the subject, but Beckman would only come back around from a different angle of inquiry. "I was seventeen when we left England. I was a girl, with stars in my eyes, ready to love the world, my husband, and my music. I was determined to do my brother's memory proud, because I was going to play better than I ever had, and everybody would love me for it."

"But instead…?"

The memories rose up, mean, heavy, and miserable. "One ratty inn after another, one leaking tenement after another. I'd try to stay up practicing after performances while Reynard went out 'seeking patrons,' as he put it. We were supposedly on our way to his family's chateau, there to put Polly in the tutelage of an old master. One city led to another, and another, as I was transformed from a relatively decent, if young violinist, into the Gypsy Princess, a hack sawing away in vulgar costumes, barefoot, and made up to look like a cross between a ghost and a streetwalker."

The memory was so worn and tattered, to speak of it should barely hurt. To discuss it with Beckman made Sara sad, though, made her wistful and tired.

If she'd had her violin, she'd be playing Beethoven slow movements. As it was, she had Beckman's escort and a spring evening with more promise than many other nights had held—though it was temporary promise.

Let that be enough. Let some other younger, more

innocent woman have the Beethoven. Sara no longer deserved it.

                         ✍

Beck strolled along beside Lady Warne's housekeeper, shock silently coursing through him.

"So how did you stop playing?" He was surprised to hear his voice sounding so steady.

"I just… stopped," Sara said. "When I was young, Reynard was my business manager—also my husband—and deserving of my loyalty on that basis alone. Then, as we toured, I was too scared, too innocent, too blasted ignorant to be able to get along without him. He began to take for granted I would do his bidding and eased his grip on me. He drank more, he gambled more, he was less and less discerning regarding his liaisons, and I grew less and less intimidated by him. I took over the finances, dealt with the various house managers, began to schedule my own performances, and so forth. When I had enough put by to afford it, I told him we were purchasing a modest property in Italy and finding a teacher for Polly."

"But he became ill."

"He was always ill, ill in his spirit, but yes, he became ill in body as well, but not before he'd gambled us right back into enormous debts."

"Did you consider touring again?"

"I did, only briefly. A woman at seventeen is a very different resource from a woman at twenty-five, and I'd already robbed Polly of her most marriageable years, exposed her to all manner of wickedness and unsettled living. I wanted better for my daughter, and anything seemed better than facing another drunken, roaring, leering mob who excused their rudeness in the name of appreciation for art."

She wasn't wrong in her assessment, and that made Beck hurt for her all the more.

"So you've been retired now for, what—several years?" They'd come to the pond but not to the end of their discussion.

Sara smiled sadly. "I've been a housekeeper for several years."

"Don't you miss it?" Beck seated her on the bench near the edge of the water. "Don't you miss the excitement, the adulation?"

"The stinking, yelling… No. As a musician under those circumstances, one has to learn to hold back, to not feel, or one… perishes, and not feeling takes great effort."

He settled beside her, knowing there was more and worse to the tale but unwilling to dig for it. Not feeling did indeed take great effort, or dedication to some form of poison, to achieve.

"You're happy, then, as housekeeper at Three Springs?"

"Happy is a luxury few can afford," she said as Beck settled his coat around her. "I am content."

"Your husband." Beck took Sara's hand in his. "He was… unkind, then?"

She was quiet for so long he wasn't sure she'd answer, but he couldn't very well ask outright if the man had beaten her, denied her food, or intimately abused her.

"In the eyes of Continental society, Reynard was merely unconventional, managing his wife's talent, but he wasn't unkind. He could convince you, even you, Beckman, he was simply ensuring the God-given gift of my abilities was shared with a deserving and appreciative audience. What's more, he'd convince you he did this not because it was his personal choice, but *for me*, and for the sake of art itself."

"What about in your eyes, Sarabande?"

"One has to have a conscience to be susceptible to labels such as kind or unkind." Sara looked out over the pond, where the fading light had turned the water's surface to a gleaming mirror. "Reynard was not burdened with a conscience, except where it suited his convenience."

"And your parents." Beck began to rub his thumb over the back of her hand. "They were taken in by his charade?"

She was again silent—Sara Hunt, former musician and housekeeper, knew silence in a way Beck was fathoming all too well—but then she leaned over, resting her weight against Beck's larger frame as Allie had done earlier in the day. "They were grieving my brother's passing," she said at length. "I tell myself that explains their initial willingness to be taken in by Reynard. It's hard, you see, because I'm a mother now, and I cannot imagine letting any of the Reynards of the world within two counties of Allie. Not ever, not while I draw breath."

"You were grieving your brother's passing too," Beck pointed out, tucking her more closely still.

She cocked her head. "I was, as was Polly, but she was so young…"

For long moments, Beck waited, hoping she'd say

more but knowing she'd already disclosed a great deal, for her. The sky went from pink to orange, to gray then purple, and still he waited, his arm around her shoulders.

"He died in spring," Sara said, almost to herself. "Gavin did, and I was married in spring, and Reynard died in the spring too." She turned her face into Beck's chest and slipped her arms around his waist. He didn't realize she was crying until a spot of damp warmth bloomed near his collarbone.

Nine

"BECKMAN? MAUDIE NEGLECTED TO…"

Sara's voice trailed off when she didn't see him in his sitting room, so she opened the door to his bedroom. Her eyebrows rose as she fell silent, taking in the tableau before her.

He was absolutely, utterly, without-a-stitch *naked*, and absolutely, utterly, without-a-doubt *breathtaking*.

"My goodness." Sara stood there, feeling drunk, unable to move, holding a pitcher of water between her hands. As casual as you please, Beck strolled over, took the water from her, drew her into the room by her wrist, and pushed the door closed.

"A pleasure to see you." He leaned down and nuzzled her neck, barely touching her but bringing his heat and the clean scent of him near enough for Sara to sense both. And in just a few words and a few steps, he'd shifted his species, going from a hard-working man partway through his bedtime routine to a prowling beast bent on seduction.

"Beckman?"

"That would be me." In no hurry whatsoever, he

picked up a blue velvet dressing gown and loosely belted it around his waist. She watched him, even when he was decently covered.

Beck smiled, and not the smile of a hardworking man preparing to retire. "You look at me like that, and I am reminded that for a week I have been a perfect gentleman—a long, difficult, profoundly frustrating week."

Sara knew he expected a reply, but she was entranced by the naked skin of his throat and chest. Her hand came up as if to brush along his sternum then fell self-consciously back to her side. The week had been very long indeed, and he was not the only one who'd been burdened by good behavior.

"Touch me, Sara." Beck kept his hands at his sides. "It has to have been a long week for you too."

"This isn't wise." But even as she spoke, she did stroke a single finger down his sternum. He closed his eyes, fisted his hands, and she did it again with two fingers, pushing the material of his dressing gown a little aside as she did. In the light of the candles gracing his room, the trail of hair down his midline gleamed like gilded fire.

Beckman opened eyes bluer than his velvet dressing gown. "Indulge yourself. Investigate me, Sara. Investigate me beyond a walk to the pond or a tour around the rose bushes. See if what I offer is worth your consideration, lest you make a decision on supposition rather than fact."

"You want me to inspect you, like a horse?"

"I want you to take your time," Beck said. "To assure yourself you know all you need to decide your course. Consider this a trial ride, and see how I suit you."

He was smiling at her, a maddeningly coy and relaxed smile.

"I'm not ready for that," Sara said, resenting his poise. He'd barely even touched her—barely—and her insides were already turning liquid, her thoughts slowing, her awareness filling up with sensations instead: his bergamot scent, the way his skin gleamed by firelight, the feel of smooth male muscle beneath her fingertips, the warmth he gave off, and the soft light of desire in his eyes, even as he waited for her to choose.

"I'll inspect," Sara heard herself decide, "but no more." Had they not taken that walk to the pond, had Beckman not listened to her silly tale of woe, she would not have made that choice—maybe.

"Inspect to your heart's content. I take it Allie is off to bed?"

"She'd already tucked herself in," Sara said, "and Polly was right behind her. We've all had a busy week."

Beck shrugged out of his dressing gown.

"What are you doing?" Sara tried to keep her voice level and did not move one inch from her post by the closed bedroom door.

"Getting ready for bed myself." He yawned and scratched his chest, giving her a shadowed look at the front of him before propping one foot on the raised hearth. "I assume you'll want me on the bed, but regardless, I'm fastidious by nature."

She knew that and liked it about him. He bent to use his washrag on one sizable foot, and the play of firelight along the curve of his spine and buttocks nearly had Sara's knees buckling.

He straightened. "Perhaps you'd like to do the honors?" He wrung out his rag and held it out to her.

"Me?" She took a step closer.

"Or I can finish myself." He dipped the cloth and started on his other foot, bending forward again. "I truly enjoy washing my feet, which probably has some biblical connotation, but it keeps the sheets clean, and it's really nobody's business but my own. Shall I wash your feet, Sarabande?"

"What else do you like to wash?" She'd moved to the end of the bed, a few steps closer.

He shrugged. "I just like to be clean. I was teased for that by my brothers, but they're as fussy as I am."

"I don't think of you as fussy," Sara said, watching the muscles of his forearms and biceps flex as he wrung out the washcloth again.

"I certainly hope you don't see me as fussy." He swiped the rag along the back of his neck, though from the scent of him, Sara suspected he'd completed his ablutions before she'd arrived. "Shall you finish this job for me?"

"You look clean to me." He looked naked to her, naked, desirable, and completely at ease with it. She'd never seen Reynard entirely naked, never wanted to, but she knew the view wouldn't have been half so impressive as this.

"I've missed a spot." Beck smiled at her. "An important spot." He tossed the rag at her and held her gaze as she caught the cloth. "Go ahead, Sara. Indulge your curiosity."

"I am indulging it." She licked her lips but couldn't help darting one glance to his genitals. Turned as he was, his groin was still shadowed, but she thought she could see a hint of tumescence to his... To him.

Had *she* inspired that?

"You are tolerating your curiosity. Lying again. Indulge it."

She read a challenge in his expression, but something much more seductive than a simple taunt: behind his cool humor, his overweening male confidence, his patience even, there was *tenderness*, a willingness to abide by her wishes out of genuine regard for her.

A form of kindness.

She'd told him too much at the pond. Were she not aware that Beckman could on any day be summoned to leave the property and not come back, she might have found the strength to walk away from that tenderness.

"Touch me, Sara. I'll not beg, and you'll not regret it. Let me give you what you want."

"Turn around." She closed the distance between them and grasped Beck by one arm, turning him to face the hearth. He watched while she moved the basin and took a seat on the bricks beside it. "You'll tell me if I misstep."

He nodded, his expression becoming unreadable as Sara positioned herself, realizing only as she did that her face—her *mouth*—was nearly level with his groin.

She laved his thighs in slow, rhythmic strokes, but sweet, holy, perishing saints... "Turn."

She spent a long minute admiring his buttocks, then used the washcloth to make measured trips over his flanks then the backs of his thighs. "Turn again."

She heard him take an audible breath before he complied, keeping his hands at his sides but planting his feet half a step wider. His cock was showing unmistakable signs of interest in the proceedings, and he didn't try to hide that from her.

Sara frowned at his genitals, but wrung out the flannel and this time used it on the insides of his thighs.

Rinsing the cloth again, Sara slid it in a careful, general pass over his groin.

"Not like that." Beck closed his hand over hers and brought the washcloth directly over his cock. "Like this." He swabbed himself with her grip, up and down several times, the angle of his erection increasing as he did. He bent and picked up her other hand. "And then you tend it like this."

Holding his cock up against his belly, he showed her how to use the washcloth on his testes, then let his cock go so it bobbed against the back of her hand. She snatched her hand away, glaring up at him accusingly.

"And now I'm clean enough," he said. She took a breath, set the washcloth and basin aside. When she would have risen—would have lost her nerve—he reached out and cradled a hand along her jaw then stroked it down over her head from her crown to her nape. "When we're in that bed, you'll touch me, Sara. However you please."

She wanted to. Sara was ruthlessly honest with herself, and she admitted she wanted to. That wasn't surprising, because he was right: she was curious. She could resist temptation if she had to, but there was something unusual about this encounter with Beckman Haddonfield.

Men had often attempted to seduce her—practiced, polished, worldly men, some of whom had been musically literate. Reynard would have crowed with glee had she taken lovers, because lovers would mean gifts, even extravagant gifts, and gifts would mean more good food, decent wine, and late nights at cards for him.

Those men had looked at her with desire, and a few of them had even been handsome, intelligent, attractive men.

But the lust in their eyes hadn't been bounded by the *respect* she saw on Beck's face. He would not pressure her, and if and when she capitulated to her desires, he would want it to be an independent decision on her part, not a lapse she could blame on him or attribute to a weak moment.

He wanted her to choose him, but for her sake as much as his own.

Beck hunkered on the rug, letting her hide her face against his shoulder. "Come to bed with me, Sara. You can indulge all of your creative impulses and allow me to explore a few of mine, too."

She nodded against his naked, muscular shoulder, no longer recognizing herself. God help her, but she wanted to put her mouth on his shoulder, taste him there, open her teeth on him while her hands ran riot over the rest of him.

"Come." Beck straightened and raised her to her feet. While she stood, docile and self-conscious, he undid her dress, took off her stockings, stays and slippers, and then untied the bows of her chemise. He paused and met her eyes to ask the question.

She considered, finding she wanted to be as naked as he was, and that too was something that hadn't ever happened with Reynard.

Which, she realized, made her fiercely glad. Reynard had been flawed, troubled, and morally diseased, but it had been easy, particularly as a young woman and a new wife, to think the flaw had lain with her.

Well, it hadn't. The look in Beck's eyes, the reverent feel of his hands as he drew her chemise off her shoulders, they told her, if nothing else ever had, she was desirable, wonderfully, wildly, irrefutably *desirable*.

"Come to bed with me." He held out his hand and let her see in his eyes his pleasure in her nakedness. When she put her hand in his, he drew her to him and enfolded her against him. "Just one more thing…" She stood patiently while he drew the pins from her hair, until her braid was swinging down her back, brushing against her naked backside.

"That is an odd sensation." Wicked, peculiar, and ticklish.

"I want it all the way undone." He drew her braid over her shoulder and brushed the tip of it over her breast.

"You want *me* all the way undone." Sara retrieved her braid from his hand. "This will have to do for now. Oh, dear…"

Beck had pulled her close again, and his erection arrowed up along her belly between them.

"I want you," he murmured as his slid his hands down to cup her derriere. "This should not be surprising. You are lovely, sexually appealing, intelligent, and thank all the gods, naked in my arms."

"You mentioned something about the bed, Beckman." She tried for a convincing version of prim, but when she saw him stifle a smile, she knew he heard the hesitance in her voice.

"The bed with both of us in it." Beck dropped his arms, seized her hand, and towed her the last few steps toward the bed. "Naked."

"One can hardly forget that part." Sara eyed the bed with sudden misgiving.

"In you go." Beck patted her behind gently. "I'll lock the sitting room door."

Happy to get under the covers, despite the obvious appreciation in Beck's eyes, Sara obligingly lifted the bedclothes and scooted across the mattress. Beck closed the bedroom door behind him and climbed in beside her with a complete lack of ceremony.

"Now what?" Sara had the covers up to her chin, and she was on Her Side of the Bed, staring at the ceiling. Beck came bouncing and rocking across the mattress, causing Sara to scoot farther toward the edge of the bed.

"Stop that." He wrapped long arms around her waist and hauled her back to the middle. "I won't bite, Sara, unless you want me to. And then I'll kiss it better."

"It's just…" She paused while Beck rolled her to her side and wrapped his body around hers. "I'm not used to situations like this."

"So it's been a while." Beck's arm threaded under her neck, and he gathered her close. "You'll recall the particulars, with a little reminding. Scoot a bit, if you please?"

He need not have bothered asking. With his size and complete lack of self-consciousness, Beck had arranged her in his arms and himself around her.

Mostly.

"You're blushing." His tone indicated he was pleased with himself.

"You are… your *parts* are intimately situated."

"So enjoy them," Beck suggested, rolling his hips to rub his cock against her sex. The angle was wrong for penetration—Sara could figure that much out—but intriguing for other purposes.

Sara wasn't blushing, she was *mortified* as the great, thick length of him was snuggled right up against the parts of her body Sara rarely touched except to wash. Having the bulk of him between her legs brought an odd comfort, but it was disquieting, too. Impossible to ignore, like a beautiful picture hanging crookedly directly across the room from where one sat.

And yet, she did not want to leave that bed. She wanted to learn him, to become as familiar with his body as he was. She ran her hand over his flank, liking the curve of it, the way muscle and bone became a lean, elegant leg.

Sara's fingers found a scar crossing the crest of Beck's left hip.

"Riding accident as a child. There's another one on my wrist, and a scar here"—he brought her hand to his collarbone—"where I broke a bone in another fall."

"Little boys are so reckless. Men are no better." Sara rubbed her thumb over the scar on his hip.

Beck slipped his hand around hers. "This man

would very much like you to wax a bit reckless too."
He slid their combined hands down and positioned
her fingers over his cock. "A lot reckless wouldn't go
amiss either."

～～～

Tremaine surveyed the tally before him, knowing
that even the sizable total on the last page was not an
accurate figure when it came to the booty Reynard
had sent back to England "for safekeeping."

"There's a bloody fortune here."

The cat in his arms, Harriette, named for the famed
courtesan whose behavior she emulated whenever
allowed to roam free, purred audibly.

"I've cast my first lure but gotten no response." He
paused before a small painting for which anybody with a
discerning eye would have paid a fortune. "A marmalade
cat was a much better choice than you would have been."

The cat in the figure made perfect graceful counterpoint to the nearly naked woman with whom it
slept. "Black is trite, overdone, and probably not very
interesting to paint."

The beast leapt from his embrace, her back claws
pushing away from Tremaine's ribs with enough
emphasis to make Tremaine grateful for both waistcoat
and shirt. "Be that way. See who lets you cuddle
up on his bed when I'm off to deal with Reynard's
womenfolk. Some of us appreciate the treasures that
come our way."

The cat, tail held high, strutted from the room,
paying him no mind whatsoever.

～～～

Sara Hunt was driving Beck past the controlled, careful wooing he wanted to give her. His plan was not motivated by generosity but by the conviction that a more precipitous approach would fail.

And Sara would allow no second chances.

"Other men aren't built like you, are they?" She'd shifted to her back and sent her hands running riot over his person and his… parts. She began to shape and stroke one part of him in particular, while Beck struggled to keep his breathing even.

"We all have pretty much the same accoutrements," Beck managed, though it was an odd question for a widow. But then, some husbands were painfully modest—*he* certainly had been.

"Like a pony has the same parts as a horse," Sara said. "When you're like this"—she closed her fingers around his shaft—"it means you're impassioned."

Was that a question or an observation? When he was with her, it was an understatement in any case.

Beck let his hand wander over her shoulders and down to the slope of her breast. "Or it can mean I've awoken with a need to use the chamber pot."

"Really?" She seemed intrigued. "How odd. What are you doing, Beckman?"

"Appreciating your parts, as you are appreciating mine," he temporized, but he hadn't even really touched her breast yet; he was merely scouting the territory. "I'll stop if you prefer."

"That's…" Sara closed her eyes as his fingers grazed the soft flesh right under her nipple. "Not necessary."

"Tell me." He repeated the caress. "What exactly do you like, Sarabande? And how do you like it?"

She'd closed her eyes, and her hand had gone still on his cock. "I don't understand the question."

"Come here." Before her eyes were open, Beck was lifting her above him and positioning her astride his lap. "Better. No, don't start lecturing."

"But I'm…" She crossed her hands over her breasts and turned her head so as not to meet his eyes.

"You're modest." Beck covered her hands with his. "With me, you should be proud, Sara. You're beautiful, in the way only a woman can be, and I want to look at you and touch you until you feel as beautiful as you are."

"Must you be so kind?"

"I'm being honest." Perhaps Sara thought him both, for she allowed him to peel her hands away from her breasts and place them on his chest. Still, he sensed an awkwardness from her, as if perching upon a man's aroused sex had not been in her marital vocabulary of intimacies.

Beck reached up to cup her nape and drew her down within kissing range. This hid her magnificent breasts from his view, of course, but it also let him get his mouth on her somewhere, thus avoiding the utter collapse of his sanity.

And this was better, Beck decided as he touched his lips to hers. Kissing let him spare them both the burden of speech and much of the burden of thought as well.

She sipped at his mouth then slipped her tongue along his lower lip, while Beck teased and coaxed and encouraged. When she grew a little bolder, he growled his approval and framed her face in his hands, the better to hold her still for his reciprocal invasion. Her fingers tangled in his hair, and the way they gripped at him suggested she was passing the point of mere comfort with their kissing.

Unable to resist the temptation any longer, Beck slid a cautious hand to Sara's waist. By degrees, as their kiss grew more heated, he stroked his hand up, over the nip of her waist, to her lowest rib and up farther. His tongue found its way into a slow, penetrating rhythm just as his palm settled over the fullness of her breast.

She arched into his hand, and Beck felt a spike of simple joy in her response. Without breaking the kiss, he offered her a cautious pressure with his fingers, and her hips stirred restlessly.

Thanks be to heaven… He raised his hips, the better to accommodate her, and immediately, Sara's body thanked him by settling more firmly on his cock.

"What are you…?" She tried to lever up, but Beck caught her by the back of the neck.

"Kiss me, love." He urged her back down. "We're just getting started." She hesitated, her mouth a half inch from his, but then he gave her breast another gentle squeeze, and she closed her eyes and found his mouth with her own.

And that was just fine. Beck adored his prize with his fingers then went so far as to brush his thumb over Sara's nipple in slow, languorous teases that drove her to moans and whimpers.

"Move on me," Beck whispered, curling up to get his mouth on her nipple. She cut off in mid-whimper, her hands cradled the back of his head, and she moaned outright when he suckled her.

In his heated, lusting bones, Beck knew he was with a woman who could come and come hard, just from attention to her breasts.

But why should she have to? He rubbed his cock teasingly against her sex. She was damp for him now and not the least shy about the contact.

He cruised to her other breast. "Please yourself, love. Move on me."

She might have heard him, she might not have, but she did begin to slide her sex over his cock, forward and back, a deliberate, purposeful stroke to which Beck could time the way he drew on her breast. Her hand came up and closed over his, showing him she wanted more pressure—a lot more pressure—and held longer, more tightly.

"Better?"

But she was beyond forming any answers, other than with her body. Beck's body had become a torrent of articulation too, screaming at him to bury his cock in her wet heat and have her over the edge in three hard strokes, but he held back.

Trial ride, he reminded himself. *Trial ride; you promised her.*

If she decided to change the angle and plunge down on him for her own pleasure, Beck would enthusiastically oblige, but the decision had to be hers.

"Beckman…" Sara ground against him and trapped his fingers around her nipple with her free hand. "I can't stand…"

Somewhere in the mental brawl between carnal need and self-restraint, Beck comprehended that Sara did not know how to enjoy and prolong her own arousal. She was *hurting* with a lack of satisfaction, and he had to show her where relief lay. Anchoring one arm around her back, he slipped his hand between their bodies and got his thumb into the wet folds of her sex.

"It's here," he rasped against her breast. He pushed hard and rhythmically with his thumb until she recalled how to push in counterpoint to that most gratifying pressure. Seizing his self-control with both fists, Beck bit gently on her nipple and felt her body ripple with the pleasure of it.

And off she went, battering his self-discipline as she writhed and keened, letting him give her two long fingers pressed deep into her sex to send her back out of her mind just when he sensed her satisfaction might be cresting.

And God above, *she was snug*. Her sex clamped down on his fingers, hard, repeatedly, until Beck gave up and let his own orgasm go rocketing through him. He barely got a hand around himself to deflect the worst of the untidiness onto his own belly before he was groaning quietly with the sheer, wringing pleasure of his release.

He couldn't recall when he'd come that hard, not even in the act, and he wasn't sure he'd survive it if such pleasure befell him again.

"Beckman?"

Sara sounded as dazed as Beck felt, and he realized his fingers were still hilted inside her. He eased his hand from her and felt her shudder with an aftershock of pleasure.

"On your back, sweetheart." He levered up and kissed her cheek. "Careful of the sheets."

She pitched awkwardly to the mattress, leaving Beck to get up and fetch the basin and washcloth.

"I'm... buzzing inside," Sara said, consternation in her tone as she waved a vague hand below her waist.

"Is buzzing a good thing?" Beck brought the basin to the night table, wrung out the cloth, and scrubbed it over his belly and groin.

"Different." Sara lay on her back, knees drawn up, her modesty apparently not yet within reach.

"The water's a little cool," Beck warned her, wringing out the cloth again. She let her knees fall to the sides but turned her head as he swabbed gently at her sex. "Sensitive?"

She nodded, saying nothing until he'd folded the cloth against her and applied a comforting touch of pressure.

"And you, Beckman? You found... pleasure too?"

Beck smiled at her just for asking, and still pressing the cool cloth to her sex, leaned in and kissed her. "A wagonload of it. I hope I didn't hurt you?"

"No. Overwhelmed and buzzing, but pain is not part of it."

"You'd have to tell me if it were." Beck believed her, but still... he hadn't been anywhere near as gentle as he'd intended—and Sara hadn't been restrained.

"Why are you smiling?"

"I'm happy," Beck said, the truth of his answer surprising him. "Very happy. Now scoot over. Company is coming to call, Sarabande Hunt." He tossed the washcloth into the basin and climbed in beside her where she lay on Her Side of the Bed.

"None of that tea-with-the-queen business, love." He seized her under the arms and hoisted her back over him. "We're friends now. Cuddle up. There's my girl." He patted her bottom, and then his touch shifted, stroking up her back. "What?"

"I feel like crying," she blurted out, folding forward onto his chest.

"I'll hold you while you cry," Beck said, his brisk humor disappearing as tenderness swamped him. "Tell me honestly, Sara, was I too rough?"

"No." She burrowed into his chest, and Beck had the odd thought that they were—finally—getting to the real lovemaking. "I'm just… sentimental."

"It's spring," Beck finished the thought for her, "and it has been a long time for you, and your daughter is facing her birthday, and you have no one with whom to share these things the way you ought." He gathered her closer and felt a sigh go out of her. "How was your trial ride, Sarabande?" Beck kept his caresses on her back slow and soothing, but—though he would leave any day and likely never see Three Springs again—her answer mattered to him. "Will I do?"

"You." Sara's breath puffed against his chest again. "You know very well you are not the one whose condition has to be assessed. You probably have a different dalliance for every season."

Beck's hands went still. "No, I do not. You would be mistaking me for my brother Nicholas, who has a different dalliance for every day of the week when he's in a certain mood."

"You're not exaggerating, are you?" Sara raised her face to peer at him. "You're not, I can see this. You must worry for him, this Nicholas."

Worry was not the first sentiment that Beck would have named in conjunction with Nick, but it was… applicable. Maybe more applicable than exasperation, frustration, or even anger.

"I do worry." Beck traced the dimples at the base of her spine. "Just when I think much of Nick's reputation is merely gossip and rumor, another of his cast-off lovers will assure me the facts are understated, not overstated. I don't know what drives him, but it isn't a happy impulse."

"You said you were happy a moment ago. Maybe your brother wants that happiness."

"Maybe," Beck allowed, but he wasn't convinced he'd ever understand what drove his brother. "Are you happy?"

"Disconcerted," Sara rejoined all too readily, "but not unhappy."

"Talk to me," Beck said, appreciating her honesty, even if her answer wasn't what he wanted to hear. "Tell me about being disconcerted."

Sara rubbed her cheek against his chest. "Has it escaped your notice that we are naked, tangled upon each other, and having a discussion?"

"And which of those disconcerts you?"

"The three of them." She raised up enough to frown at his chest, then settled back down, a bit to the left. "The three of them together. How do I face you in the morning?"

She fell silent, and then the quiet took on a busier quality as Beck felt her tongue slide experimentally over his nipple.

"Behave yourself, Sarabande."

She did it again then settled back. "Does that make you feel the way you make me feel?"

Beck smoothed his thumb over her jaw. "Now how would I be able to speak for how you feel? I can tell you I like it, it's arousing, and I can feel it right down to my vitals."

"Good. I'd say the same, were you to ask me—which you shall not—but you've avoided my question."

She sounded shy and brisk, and Beck found both appealing. "About facing each other in the morning?"

"The very one." She batted her eyelashes over his nipple this time, suggesting an inventiveness that boded ill for Beckman's remaining wits.

"You are a delight." He closed his arms around her in sheer affection. "An absolute, utter, unequivocal delight." A dangerous delight. A shaft of misgiving went through him, because leaving this delight behind when it came time to return to Kent would be difficult.

"But a housekeeper too," Sara reminded him, "and delighting is not on my list of duties, though when you hold me like this, you make me want to rethink my list."

"Delight belongs on your list, Sara," Beck said in all seriousness. "I am not your lover yet, but I would dearly like to be."

"You can be my lover, but only if I can discern a means of becoming invisible thereafter, Beckman. I cannot hold in my mind at the same time the way we are together now, the way I behaved with you earlier, and the need to ask you to please pass the cream at the breakfast table tomorrow."

For a widow who'd just found her pleasure, she was

peculiarly reluctant to experience it again. "So skip breakfast. Have me instead."

Sara tongued him again for his insolence. "I can't help but feel everybody will know. They'll be able to see by looking that I've cast my morals to the wind and embarked on a life of dissolution."

"Oh, indeed." Beck drew his hand down her braid, which had gotten satisfactorily messy. "You spend one hour a week in my bed, and now you're a flaming strumpet. How much time does Allie spend drawing and painting?"

"Hours and hours."

"And in the past week," Beck went on, "how much time has Polly spent in North's exclusive company?"

"Several hours at least. They walk out. She takes him his lunch. I think he reads to her some evenings."

Good work, North, Beck wanted to retort, but he had a point to make.

"And how many hours in a week do you spend in housework?"

She was silent a moment. "Seventy, at least."

"But you think this one hour with me will define you to the exclusion of those seventy? I'd say you're entitled to one hour a week, Sara, at least one, to be pleasured, held, and talked to like an adult. Surely you don't begrudge yourself that little respite?"

Surely he didn't begrudge it to himself?

When she didn't answer but went back to playing with his nipple, he knew she was considering his argument. He could tell this, he assured himself, by the *thoughtful manner* in which she was driving him beyond reason with her mouth.

She fell asleep on his chest, much to his relief. He indulged in a long, long hour of holding her and letting his hands travel at will over the soft planes and hollows of her skin before wrapping her in his dressing gown and carrying her through a silent house to her bed. When he was convinced she wouldn't wake, he returned to her room with her clothing and slippers, kissed her as she slumbered on, and sought his own bed.

Not until he was almost asleep did it occur to him that a married woman, of all women, ought to have a nodding acquaintance with a piss hard, particularly if she'd traveled with her husband in close quarters.

But to Sara, the whole idea had been terra incognito—as had the idea of sexual pleasure.

Interesting.

Ten

NICK HADDONFIELD RODE ALONG BESIDE HIS HALF brother Ethan Grey as their horses trotted the perimeter of one of Nick's farms in Kent. Long ago, as boys, Nick had not needed to speak with his brother, so thoroughly familiar had they been with each other's hearts and minds. And now… the silence had taken on a taut, unhappy quality that made Nick want to gallop off in any other direction.

They *could* not discuss the earl's failing health—what would be the point?

They *would* not discuss the weather, Ethan having no tolerance for idle talk.

They *should* not discuss Nick's attempts to find a bride before the earl passed away, lest Nick end up babbling to his brother about impossible things best kept silent.

Ethan rubbed a gloved hand down his horse's golden neck. "I ran into Beckman down near Portsmouth."

Beck was a fine topic for discussion, a safe topic.

"I gather from his correspondence that Three Springs was much in need of attention?"

Ethan shot Nick a look that suggested the topic was perhaps not so safe. "Beck is plowing and planting like a yeoman, Nicholas. His muscles rival your own. I begin to think his sense exceeds yours or mine too."

Nick steered Buttercup around a mud puddle, while Ethan's gelding shied at the comparable hazard in the parallel rut. "Beckman is very sensible, except when he's not."

The next look from Ethan was easier to read: Nick was spouting nonsense. "Beckman will see Three Springs put to rights, provided you or the earl don't banish him to some foreign shore once again."

Nick silently scolded his grandmother for carrying tales to all corners of the family, even corners estranged from one another—banish, indeed. "Better that dear Becky take a repairing lease overseas from time to time than be the object of unkind talk."

"Hmm."

Nick was an older brother many times over. He knew older brothers took special delight in finding the most aggravating delivery possible of even a single syllable. In future, he noted to himself, he would not "hmm" quite so often at his younger siblings.

"What, Ethan?"

"God forbid a Haddonfield should engender talk, particularly talk more interesting than that caused by the Berserker of the Bedroom."

As broadsides went, that quiet observation would do nicely. "You aren't in possession of all the facts. The death of his wife rather knocked Beck off his pins. He's done better lately, but one worries for him."

"For him, or for the consequences to his family?

From what little I know, Beckman has been widowed nigh eight years. For the last three of those years, I haven't heard a single word regarding him when there's a Haddonfield to be gossiped about."

The retort Nick was prepared to deliver never made it past his lips.

Three years? Had it been *three years* since he'd dragged Beckman out of that cesspit in Paris?

No, closer to four…

"You're silent, Nicholas. When you might be describing some fool's errand in the far north for our younger brother or a repairing lease in, say, St. Petersburg, you're silent. I beg you not to spoil such a boon. One thanks God for the occasional small favor."

Ethan nudged his gelding into a canter, and Nick—rather than offer a reply—let his mare speed up to keep pace.

❧

"What has you in such a good mood?" Polly drizzled brown sugar icing over the sweet buns she'd taken from the oven, interrupting Sara's humming with her question.

"I slept well," Sara replied, which was not a lie.

"I looked in on you before I came out to start the bread dough," Polly said. "You were sleeping *well* in a very large blue dressing gown, and your clothes were draped across the bottom of your bed."

Sara wished a blight on concerned sisters the world over, even if they did bake up delicious sweet buns. "Why would you look in on me?"

"I often do. It's an old habit, from when you

performed and were never there when I went to bed. I'd check on you first thing when I woke up, and last night, Sister dearest, you were not there when I went to bed."

Sara felt her lovely mood wafting away. "Are you going to be difficult?"

"I am not." Polly considered the buns, which were dripping with sweet icing. "I am going to be concerned for you. Just…"

Her thought was interrupted by a cold breeze from the back hall, followed by the sound of North's voice sporting its customary irritable edge.

"The ladies will have to decide where to put them," North was arguing. "I am not an arborist. Good morning, ladies. Are those sweet buns I spy on yon counter?"

Allie crowded in behind the men. "Wash your paws. Aunt will smack your fingers if you don't, and she's got good aim."

Sara smiled at her daughter, glad for the interruption. "Good morning to you, too. Gentlemen, when you've seen to your hands, you can tell us what you're arguing about."

"I'll tell you now," North volunteered as he approached the sink and worked the pump. "Haddonfield's esteemed brother has sent him a half-dozen peach trees, for pity's sake, and now we must find them a sheltered, well-drained but fertile location, as if we've that to spare."

Beck joined him at the sink. "It's the first remotely civil gesture my brother Ethan has made in years— many years—and the gift isn't to you, it's to Lady

Warne. It isn't as if you're expected to plant the deuced things yourself."

"Deuced." North shook his wet hands out, spattering Beck liberally. "That's precious. I say the ladies can find a place for your *deuced* trees."

"We can," Sara interjected, as clearly, North was a bear with a sore paw—or back—about something. "And the walled garden strikes me as one possible location. Polly, do you need help with that? There are at least two healthy, full-grown men here capable of carrying food to the table."

Or possibly, a pair of oversized, hungry little boys.

"And me!" Allie reminded her indignantly.

"Well, of course there's you," Beck piped up. "Though your paws have yet to be washed."

Breakfast was noisy, and Sara was grateful for the hubbub, for she was, as predicted, having trouble meeting Beckman's gaze. He left her in peace, for which she was also grateful, and moment by moment, the meal progressed.

"See?" Beck whispered as he held her chair for her to rise. "No thunderbolts, no cataclysms, and you look lovely this morning."

"I slept well."

"Mama…" Allie's tone approached whiny. "You said we could try my dress on right after breakfast, and it's after breakfast."

"I did say that, and the last of the alterations are done, so let's be off. I'll bring it to our apartment, while you get your boots off."

Allie was off like a shot, so Sara hurried up the steps to the small parlor she'd used as her sewing room.

She gathered up the dress then draped her sewing apron over her head, reaching behind her to tie the sash. A crackling in the pocket had her frowning then reaching down.

"Oh, dear..." Her fingers closed on the letter she'd received almost a week past, the one she'd forgotten about entirely. She put it back in the pocket—nothing would be permitted to delay Allie's final fitting—and hurried from the room, only to run smack into Beckman Haddonfield loitering in the hallway.

"And now"—he settled his hands on her upper arms—"for the other greeting, the one I've looked forward to since I woke from my dreams of you." He lowered his mouth to hers while she was still blinking at him in consternation. When he'd thoroughly greeted her—scattered her wits to the compass points—he drew back and smiled down at her.

"Now, it is truly a good morning."

He sauntered off, leaving Sara nigh panting with... well, not indignation, which would have been a proper response, but maybe surprise and a bit of appreciation as well.

It *was* a good morning. She smiled to herself and hurried back down to her apartment, finding Allie prancing around in her new finery.

"May I wear my new dress today, Mama?" She twirled dramatically. "Can we put my hair up? Just to see?"

"We can try a few things with your hair, but your new dress should be saved for a special occasion."

"This material makes my eyes really green," Allie said, swishing her hips to make the fabric swirl around her calves. "Mr. North would look nice in this color."

"Mr. North would look a lot nicer in any material if he'd just smile," Sara said as she undid Allie's long coppery braid.

"His back still hurts," Allie said. "I think he's homesick, too. He went to London last year just after planting. Maybe he should go again, particularly when Mr. Haddonfield, Jeffrey, and Angus are here. Ouch. And the Odious Boys, too."

"Sorry." Sara freed a skein of Allie's hair from a hook. Allie had a point: North hadn't gone up to Town for at least a year, though he'd darted into Brighton and Portsmouth. "You have such pretty hair."

"Mr. Haddonfield said so too." Allie preened, sliding her hands over her dress. "He also said what's under my hair is just as impressive and likely of greater value."

"He paid you a compliment. Now, pay attention. You've a decision to make. Do you prefer it twisted up like this, bound in a coronet like this, or swept back to your nape like this?"

"Do them all," Allie crowed. "I have to see them to choose, but this is fun!"

It was fun and sweet, and soon Polly came in to offer advice and commentary and suggest accessories. Allie eventually settled on a double coronet, which was simple to do and very secure "for painting."

When the new dress was hung lovingly on a hook in Allie's alcove and Allie had bounced out to visit with Amicus and Hermione, Sara sat down beside her sister.

"Thus ends the short and illustrious childhood of Allemande Adagio Hunt."

"There, there." Polly patted her hand. "She still doesn't like boys, unless they're Beckman or North."

"And who wouldn't like that pair? She likes Soldier as well."

"We're getting old," Polly observed. "Our little Allie is dreaming of putting her hair up."

"At least she liked her dress," Sara said, rising and hearing again the crackling in her pocket. "My heavens, I've never neglected a piece of mail quite so consistently." She sat back down and slit the little epistle open with her thumbnail.

"Oh, dear saints…"

"Sara? What is it?"

"Polly, he's found us." Sara put the letter down only partly read. "He's found us, and he's asking after Allie."

❧

April passed into May, and the trip to Portsmouth grew closer, but matters between Beckman and Sara did not move forward. She hadn't reneged on their trip, and she hadn't been exactly chilly, but neither was she quite as… warm as Beck had anticipated, based on their encounter in his bed.

And perhaps this was for the best, because daily, the probability grew that he'd receive a summons from Belle Maison.

So he stayed busy ripping the bracken from what should have been drainage ditches, trimming the trees whose limbs encroached over the gutters and sheds, and mending wall. North groused and griped but heeded Beck's admonition to stay away from the heaviest work, and occupied himself supervising the four other men when Beck was otherwise engaged.

As the days went along, Beck began to feel as if the next task to be supervised was a sound beating of one Gabriel North. North argued, resisted, and grumbled at every turn, to the point where Beck was increasingly willing to let the man tend to the stone walls single-handedly, bad back be damned.

When Beck suggested that barley straw sunk in the pond would reduce the algae growing on the surface, North came back with a lecture about straw floating and lordlings who would be best advised to limit themselves to making muffins.

When Beck wanted to investigate certain crosses for the sheep that would result in more twins and two lambings a year, North informed him that they were not in Dorset, where such sheep thrived, though perhaps Beck might enjoy a visit there.

As they took their noon meal beneath the hedgerow of oaks, Beck mentioned planting some American sycamore trees to dry out a boggy patch of one field. Around bites of ham and buttered bread, North lapsed into a sermon about leaves creating shade, which contributed to the bogginess.

"We're planting the bloody trees," Beck bit out and found North looking at him in sharp consternation.

"I do believe," North replied slowly, "this is the first time you've actually given me an order. Of course we'll plant the trees if you feel that strongly about it."

Beck scowled at a cinnamon bun. "A steward on

this estate willing to take direction is a frighteningly humble thing."

North rubbed his chin, surveying Beck speculatively.

"The truce," North said quietly, "the one I'm negotiating with Polly—was negotiating? It isn't going well."

"Sara's got the female complaint," Beck said, still studying his bun. "Maybe they're synchronized, like a harem or a brothel."

"The naughty little things you know, child… Polly is not having her menses."

Interesting that North should know such a thing, and volunteer it.

"Are they arguing over Allie's painting?"

"Polly defers to Sara in all matters pertaining to the child. Allie said something the other day, suggesting she's noticed her elders are in a taking about something."

"What did she say?"

"Something to the effect of 'what's the fun of putting up your hair and having a new dress if everybody's in a bad mood all the time anyway?'"

"You don't suppose Polly is objecting to Sara coming into Portsmouth with me?"

"Who can fathom the mind of the female?" North sighed the sigh of Every Man. "I have some reason to believe Polly encourages the outing, and not entirely out of sororal selflessness."

"Does this have to do with that truce you mentioned?"

"A man can dream." North studied the clouds beyond the filmy new leaves on the oak.

"Maybe the argument goes the other way," Beck

suggested. "Maybe Sara is getting cold feet, and Polly is being obdurate."

"Polonaise Hunt could write the book on being obdurate."

"With a forward by your lovely self."

"Beckman?"

North's use of his given name had Beck studying the clouds too.

"Hmm?"

"I don't mean to be so contrary, at least not all the time." North rose very carefully.

"So who is telling the meek and selfless steward on your estates what to do now?" Beck asked.

North braced his hands on the small of his back and arched slowly. "The rightful heir, of course. Now let's be about planting your magic trees." North's reply was airy and unconcerned. When he quickened his step, Beck let him move on ahead alone, for that seemed to be how the man functioned most comfortably.

❧

"Tremaine is Reynard's *brother*," Sara pointed out for the dozenth time. "There is no giving him the benefit of the doubt. Even Reynard didn't trust him."

"He never struck me as cut from the same cloth as Reynard," Polly argued. "And he kept his hands to himself."

Sara spoke more quietly, when she wanted to scream. "You were a girl, Polly. At the risk of opening old wounds, your judgment of a man's character was not necessarily your best feature."

"My judgment of some men's characters was

miserable, I admit it. But Tremaine wasn't one of those men, and I credit him for that. And when we did run across Tremaine, Reynard received him with every evidence of affection."

"Reynard would have received the devil with every evidence of affection if Old Scratch's pockets were full, but *I* did not receive Tremaine with every evidence of affection, and neither should you."

Polly folded her arms and braced herself against the shelves of the small pantry housing their altercation. "At least write back to him, Sara. Tell him his niece is provided for. Tell him to stay in perishing France, impersonating a *comte* or whatever he's doing."

"He's not in France," Sara said miserably. "He rents out the chateau—*Vive le roi!*—and he's bought a place not far from Oxford."

"Near St. Albans?" Polly verbally cringed.

Sara stopped pretending to arrange the rack of spices Beckman had brought with him. "Quite the coincidence, don't you think?"

"You have to warn Mama and Papa," Polly pleaded. "He'll call upon them, and there will be no end of fuss."

"I doubt it. We haven't made a secret of where we are, not to Mama and Papa, Polly. If they wanted to fuss, we would have heard from them."

"I have left the decision of how to deal with them to you, Sara." Polly's tone became thoughtful. "If you're tiring of that responsibility, I can change my position."

Sara regarded Polly narrowly, but when she saw Polly's offer was genuine, her shoulders dropped.

"You miss Mama and Papa." Sara missed them

too, and Allie didn't even know them, her only maternal relatives.

"I miss them, and I can't help but think Allie has the right to know them. She can't know her father's parents, but Mama and Papa are decent people, Sara. Stubborn, true, and misguided and provincial, but they'd love her."

They would. They would love the child regardless of her origins. "You'd want to tell Mama and Papa all the sordid, sorry details, Polly. They aren't that forgiving."

"That is not the decision before us," Polly countered gently, uncrossing her arms. "The decision before us is if, given that Tremaine is making overtures, we can continue to cling to the fiction that we'll be safe standing alone and ignoring him."

"We do stand alone." Sara was never more miserably sure of anything. "It isn't a fiction, and Tremaine isn't making overtures, he's making threats, saying he has been remiss not to play a role in Allie's upbringing, and so forth."

Polly planted her fists on her hips. "I thought he was apologizing for his absence."

"He's French," Sara shot back. "That was a threat, couched as an apology. They excel at it. 'So sorry, your head, he got in the way of my guillotine. *Quel domage! Zut alors!* And such the mess!'"

Polly's lips quirked at Sara's parody. "Half French, and the other half of Tremaine's heritage is Scottish. They don't apologize for anything."

Sara managed a weak smile. "Our poor Allie."

"Go to Portsmouth and put this from your mind. You can always write back to Tremaine later, but I think you'd be best advised to make some reply, lest you give him a reason to jaunt down here and see for himself that Allie thrives. Then too, Sara, you have another alternative—we have, rather."

"What is that?"

Polly ran a finger over the nearest shelf, as if dust might have had the temerity to gather in her pantry. "You can put this situation in Beckman Haddonfield's capable hands. He's big enough to intimidate anyone, well connected, wealthy, a gentleman, and enamored of you. He'd take any threat to Allie very seriously."

Abruptly, the tidy little pantry with its interesting scents of exotic cooking and clean aprons felt stifling.

"Tell Beck…? And what would he think of us; Polly Hunt, did he know how far we fell from his polite, titled world? He knows I performed, but he never saw my bare feet on the stage. He doesn't know about the private performances. He doesn't know the leverage Tremaine possesses should he seek to make our lives miserable."

And of course, Polly had an answer for that: "Tremaine likely doesn't know the leverage he possesses. We have to hope that's the case."

Sara did not hear hope in Polly's voice; she heard thinly veiled, old despair. "And how long will you punish yourself for that?"

"I don't punish myself for it, but it's always there, Sara."

"I know." Sara slipped an arm around her younger sister and hugged her. "There are some decisions we make it seems we never stop paying for. I still don't think I should go to Portsmouth."

"You're going," Polly assured her, hugging her

back and stroking a hand over Sara's blazing hair. "You need to loosen your grip on Allie and let Beckman spoil you, as a woman needs to be spoiled."

Sara slipped away. "Will you let North spoil you?"

"It's as much a matter of letting me spoil him, though we're working on it. Seriously, Sara, use this little trip to put your troubles aside, enjoy some time with Beck, and come back here refreshed and restored."

"You will not let Allie out of your sight, Polonaise. I mean it."

"I will let her paint, with your permission," Polly countered. "She's dying to do another canvas, Sara, and trying not to pester you for it."

"You're right. Beck points out, and he's right too, she'll just sneak and dodge her way around my permission if I don't allow her reasonable access to her paints. You corner her on the subject matter of this one before she starts, though."

For the first time in their exchange, Polly smiled. "I can do that. I ought to make her do a study of Hildegard and challenge her to make the pig beautiful."

"She could do it," Sara said. "She really could."

Polly tucked Sara's braid over her shoulder. "If she sees beauty in a wallowing pig, Sister mine, it's because you showed her where to look."

❦

The trip to Portsmouth took the entire day, much of which Sara spent reading *Mansfield Park* to Beck on the wagon's seat, while wishing she'd chosen a less judgmental tale.

As the day had progressed, she'd droned on with

her book, not knowing how to manage a real topic of conversation. Her mind in the past week had been too divided, too busy—too worried. Now she had three nights with Beckman ahead of her, three days with him as well, and she wasn't ready.

Judging from his increasingly silent mood, maybe he wasn't either.

The inn was lovely, and Sara was made keenly aware Beckman—the male half of "Squire and Mrs. Sylvanus"—knew exactly how to manage himself there. He greeted the innkeeper with the perfect blend of cordiality and condescension to guarantee attentive service, and the suite of rooms they were shown to was comfortable, spotless, and possessed of an enormous bed. Tea and scones with jam and butter appeared within minutes of their baggage being brought up.

Sara glanced around the room, noting a fresh bouquet of roses on the sideboard and lace curtains on each window. "This is every bit as nice as Three Springs itself."

"I would tolerate no lesser accommodation for you." Beck eyed her across the little sitting room, and Sara understood clearly: The Subject Had Changed. "There's something I've been wanting to do, Sarabande Adagio. Will you allow me some privileges while we're away from Three Springs?"

Her expression must have given her thoughts away, for Beck smiled.

"Not that," he said. "Well, yes, *that*, soon and in all its glorious permutations, but we'll settle in here first, bathe, have our meal, and enjoy some anticipation, if that's acceptable to you."

He was sophisticated enough to enjoy anticipation, while Sara experienced worry.

"That's acceptable." She swallowed, because five syllables had left her mouth dry. Beck sidled over to her, his walk predatory and just plain... erotic.

"Let me be your lady's maid, Sarabande." He leaned in and ran his nose along her jaw. "I want to take your hair down, and I don't mean simply take the pins out to free your braid. I want to see it completely unbound, your hair in all its glory. The frustration of never having seen you thus, the anticipation of seeing you thus, has kept me up nights."

The husky, intimate note in his voice made her insides flutter, but she didn't move, didn't glide over to their luggage, find her hairbrush, and set it into his waiting hand.

She'd never glided in her life.

"Beckman, I don't know..." Beck's fingers brushed along her nape.

"You don't have to know." He pressed a kiss to the top of her spine. "You just have to trust that I'll know, and when the time comes, you'll know too. Let me." He got down to business, relieving her hair of pins with deft dispatch. He piled his finds neatly on the vanity then guided Sara by the shoulders to sit on the stool facing the folding mirror. He fished in her traveling bag, while Sara watched in silent alarm as he produced the hairbrush.

"I've ordered you a bath," Beck said, his hands on her shoulders drawing her back against his thighs. "And I've a few things to see to while you soak, but the tub will be put in the bedroom, and if you shut the door, dinner can be set up out here. Will that suit?"

"Of course." Good heavens, what did people talk about in situations like this?

"I want to make this weekend special, Sara." Beck got her braid free, and it uncoiled down Sara's back until he caught it in his hands and untied the ribbon at the end. "I realized as we approached the town that where you see the beauty of the place, I see only the many, many times I left my homeland from these shores, or came back to it, exhausted in body and spirit, wondering what the point was of the excursion."

He paused as he unbraided three thick skeins of hair. "Sometimes, I wondered what the point of my entire excursion on earth was. Portsmouth was so pretty, so bright and busy, while I——"

He gathered her hair up in his hands. In the mirror, Sara watched as he buried his nose in bright, coppery tresses.

"While you?" She wanted to hear the rest of his recitation, wanted it badly enough to lose sight of her worry.

"My brother had found me in an opium den, doing my utmost to shuffle off this mortal coil. For much of the journey home, the drugs were leaving my system. At the time, I thought it fitting I should endure such an ordeal while at sea."

This was important, also sad. "There is opium in Portsmouth, Beckman. There's opium in any town with an apothecary, and many people believe a small amount has no untoward consequences."

He dropped her hair, and in the mirror seemed to stand very tall behind her. "There was sunshine in Portsmouth, blinding sunshine, the gulls wheeling overhead, the hum and bustle of commerce on the dock. There was something of the essential goodness of an English town. I think sometimes I was saved by a delayed case of homesickness."

"Saved?" She raised the question, because her heart would have said a part of Beckman, as competent, hale, and confident as he was, was still at sea.

Beck's mouth tipped up in a wry smile. "Your hair should be a wonder of the modern world." He resumed running his hands through the unbound mass of it. "It's every bit as soft and silky as I imagined, and how other women must envy you its beauty."

"It's just hair." Nowhere near as important as the words Beckman had given her regarding his past. She wanted to pry, to ask questions, to rant at him that doubting the gift of life was beneath him and a sin and something he must never do again.

Except she had entertained the same doubts herself.

"I used to brush out my little sisters' hair," Beck said, smoothing the brush through her locks. "Ethan was their favorite, since he was the oldest, but then he left, and Nick went a little crazy, so I became the consolation big brother. You can't tease a sister as hard when you've braided her hair."

"You probably can't taunt a brother as hard when he's braided your hair, either."

"Verily." Beck put the brush aside a few moments later and stroked his fingers through her hair. "I was brilliant and just didn't know it. I spiked my sisters' guns with a hairbrush."

"Is Nick still a little crazy?"

His hands paused in her hair then resumed their slow caresses.

"Yes. I think maybe he is, but there's hope, since he and Ethan are at least talking, and maybe when he sees Ethan survived his banishment, Nick can get on about his life."

"Banishment?"

"Banishment." Beck's touch became more businesslike as he divided her hair into three thick sections. "My papa found it a useful tool with his sons, and I've been regularly banished myself—until Nick fetched me back from Paris."

"Beckman?"

"Love?"

"Why did Nicholas fetch you back from Paris?"

"Ah." He began to braid her hair. "I asked him once, because I wondered the same thing. Going to France was very risky, and the earl has two other legitimate sons, so I was clearly expendable. Nick simply did not agree with Papa's assessment that I'd sort myself out in time. George had just left the schoolroom, and Dolph was still with his tutors. Nick was unwilling to carp at them to see to the succession. Hence, I needed to be retrieved."

"Your brother fetched you home so you could remarry?" Sara could not keep her distaste for his brother's motives from her voice. "Why couldn't your idiot brother do his duty by the title? He's the heir."

"Since I went up to school, Nick has been hinting and warning and outright lecturing me he will not be having children. It's most of the reason why I married. The spare's purpose in life is to provide that service if the heir can't. I gave it my best try, or so I tell him and Papa, and I failed. That's where I leave the discussion, and now Nicholas is marrying, apparently, but the lectures haven't stopped."

"I would like to meet this somewhat crazy brother of yours," Sara said. "I would tell him what I think of his selfishness."

"Nick isn't selfish, but his situation makes him seem so sometimes." Beck sounded as if he were trying to convince himself of this. "When you finish your bath, don't dress. We'll serve ourselves, if that's all right with you."

"Of course." Sara rose, relieved and a little surprised when Beck took her in his arms and just held her.

"My thanks."

"For?" She wanted to glance up, assess his mood, but his chin was resting on her temple, contentment in his sigh.

"Letting me take down your hair, coming here with me, letting me hold you."

Letting him?

"It might come as a surprise to you, Beckman Sylvanus Haddonfield, but you are a comely man, full of charm and clean about your person. Spending time with you like this is no hardship. No hardship at all." Though it was a challenge. Moment by moment, whether he was sharing his past, taking down her hair, or merely holding her, it was a challenge.

"You're so fierce." Beck's smile curved against her brow. "But your bath will be here soon, and I'd best be about my errands." He patted her backside, a curiously endearing gesture, and stepped back. As he took his leave, a troop of maids and footmen brought in Sara's bath and washing water, leaving her to soak in peace and to wonder what errands the Haddonfield spare was about.

Eleven

By the time Beckman had returned to their rooms, the tub was gone, a tea cart laden with dinner had been set up near the window, and Sara was beginning to fret a little at his absence.

"Miss me?" He set down some packages and crossed directly to wrap his arms around her. "Your fragrances are enough to drive me to distraction, Sarabande."

"You've bathed as well." Sara got a nice whiff of bergamot, citrus, and Beck. She buried her nose against his sternum and wondered when his embrace had come to feel like home and a private adventure rolled into one.

She tilted back to peer up at him. "Just how tall are you?"

"A bit shy of six and a half feet." Beck peered right back at her. "I'm not the runt in my family—that honor belongs to George, who's all of three or four inches shorter. Nick is taller."

"God in heaven. The poor man, no wonder he's somewhat crazy."

"Why do you say that?" Beck slipped his arms from

her and moved to shrug out of his jacket. Sara's hands went to his shoulders, helping him out of his coat then turning him to unknot his cravat.

"A man that size will have little privacy," Sara said. "He's always visible, and people likely see only his size, like people see only my red hair. You are tall enough to know what that feels like, to be seen only as an oversized physical specimen. Even North is regarded by most as more brute than gentleman, at least until they hear him speak."

Beck lifted his chin, suggesting to Sara that other women had assisted him out of his clothes. His cuff links came next, and then his waistcoat.

"Tell me, love," Beck said as she started on the buttons of his shirt. "Are we to allow me any clothing during our meal?"

Sara dropped her hands and stepped back. "I beg your pardon. I wasn't… Oh, dear…"

"Dear heart," Beck said, pulling her into his embrace, "you may undress me any time. My dressing gown hangs on the back of the bedroom door, and then I'll be at least as unclothed as you."

She nodded, face flaming, and Beck sat to tug off his boots.

"Were you your husband's valet?" Beck asked as Sara brought him his blue velvet dressing gown.

"I was not." She took a surreptitious sniff of his fragrance from his dressing gown. "I liked sleeping in your dressing gown. It's very warm and soft." She sniffed again, crushing it to her nose. "And it bears your fragrance."

Beck grinned, rose, and tugged his shirt off over his

head. "Naughty, but flattering. And here I resent your dressing gown no end and can think of nothing other than getting you out of it." His breeches, stockings, and smalls were gone, just like that, leaving him naked in the middle of the sitting room.

"Beckman…" Sara turned her face away, another blush gracing her cheeks. "You are shameless." Also beautiful and desirable.

"So you be shameless too." Beck padded to her side and took his dressing gown from her hands. "Enjoy a little peek, Sara. Get some ideas for how you want to spend the rest of the evening, hmm?" He shook out his dressing gown and shrugged into it, while Sara did, indeed, risk a glance at him before he belted it at his waist.

Dinner was simple but satisfying. They talked as they ate, about the book Sara had read, about their shopping itinerary for the next day, about the city of Portsmouth, which Beck seemed to know thoroughly. They also talked of sights on the Continent they'd both seen, finding on at least two occasions they'd stayed in the same inns, though not at the same time.

"Why didn't you use London as your port of call?" Sara asked. "Portsmouth had to be a little remote, given your family lives in Kent."

"When one wants anonymity about one's comings and goings, London is not one's first choice. Then too, I got in the habit of putting in at the smaller ports."

He crossed his knife and fork on the edge of his plate. "Shall we take in a little evening air?" He rose, not waiting for her answer but holding her chair for her and wrapping her hand in his. "It's dark enough we'll have privacy on the balcony."

He was right on two counts. While they had talked and eaten and talked some more, night had fallen. Then too, their inn was on the edge of town and their room at the back. From their balcony, they could see the moon rising over the fields and pastures used by the inn's dozens of coaching horses.

"Pretty night." Beck settled his arms around Sara, holding her back to his chest. "And lucky me, I'm in the company of a pretty lady." His lips grazed the side of Sara's neck, and just like that, the pleasant meal with the congenial gentleman was over.

"Beckman, we need to talk." She pulled away from his embrace, relieved he let her go without resistance.

"I'm listening." He came to her side, where she stood against the railing, facing out toward the moonlit countryside. He didn't try to touch her, but Sara was abundantly aware of him nonetheless.

"You asked earlier did I valet my husband," Sara began. "And you let it drop when I answered in the negative."

"I am bent on seduction, Sara." Beck's voice held a hint of humor. "What was I doing, bringing up the man you chose for your mate, and your intimate ease with the business of helping him undress? Not well done of me, but I was curious."

"I never…" Sara glanced at him in the moonlight and saw his expression was cool, for all the humor in his tone. "That's what we need to talk about. You need to understand the way I was married."

"Unhappily," Beck said. "I wish for you it could have been different, just as I'm sure you wish the same for me." He didn't want to belabor the subject, which sparked Sara's curiosity regarding Beck's brief and ill-fated marriage.

Sara crossed her arms over her chest and prepared to be more honest than she had thus far. "My marriage was not unhappy, Beckman, it was miserable, filled with bewilderment at first, and loathing, and then— thank God—a towering indifference to anything save the ways and degrees in which Reynard's decisions impacted my survival, Polly's, and Allie's. He was my intimate enemy, by most lights."

"You did not want to be performing on stage," Beck concluded, and in the assurance of his tone, Sara understood that he was not merely being sympathetic. Beckman had been forced to perform somehow, perhaps solving the family problems, perhaps in his marriage.

Was he still being forced?

"I did not want to be performing on his terms, certainly," Sara agreed. "And then Allie showed up, and it became perform or starve. I did not want to learn what desperate measures starvation might inspire in my husband."

Beck tucked her braid over her shoulder. "That sounds ominous."

Sara merely nodded, because the private performances were her most personal shame. Those and the things Polly had suffered because her sister could not protect her.

"I don't like to think of it, though you need to know I do not come to this situation of ours with a great deal of experience."

"Not with a great deal of good experience," Beck

said. "It can be my privilege to address that lack, if you'll allow it."

"I'm going to allow it." The words were true, but they sounded far more confident than Sara felt. Far more calculating. "You have to understand, Beck, it's... I'm selfish about this attraction between us. I'm indulging a curiosity, nothing more."

He gazed out over the cool, silvery landscape. "You're taking your pleasure from me, striking a blow at the weasel you were forced to support with your music. I understand."

"You don't." Sara shook her head, amused at his words, sad though they were. Reynard's teeth *had* been a trifle prominent. "But you aren't wrong, either. You are a confection, Beckman. The male version of a woman's dreams. Handsome, charming, kind, generous... It would be better for me did you scratch more in public, swear, have a fondness for cock fights, or put your muddy boots up on my tables."

He turned so his backside rested against the balcony railing. "My sisters would skin me where I stood if I behaved like that. You deserve a man who is well-mannered, clean, and considerate, Sara. Every woman does."

"You aren't simply well mannered, clean, and considerate. I think I've made my point as well as I'm able, particularly with you standing there in the moonlight in just your dressing gown."

"Having trouble with rational discourse, are you?" Beck slipped an arm around her waist. "That's a start."

"Naughty man." Sara rested her head on his arm. "We are agreed, then, our expectations of each other are low and transitory?"

"Are you trying to wave me on my way before I've even shown you pleasure, Sara?"

"In a sense, yes." Sara thought of the letter she'd received a week ago, the letter she was going to have to deal with. "Your stay at Three Springs is temporary, and I might have reason to find a different post at any time. You've pointed out that Allie is isolated, and her art would prosper were we a little nearer civilization. This is a… frolic, Beckman. A frolic in which you've already pleasured me witless."

He shifted, putting himself between Sara and the balcony railing. "Love, I haven't begun to pleasure you witless."

He eased his arms around her waist, the character of his touch becoming seductive. He didn't merely hug her; he let her feel the slow glide of his hand on the thin material of her dressing gown, starting at her midriff and working his way around her ribs, down to her waist, over her hips, then around to rest on the upper swell of her derriere. "Let yourself come closer." Beck tugged on her. "Much closer."

She gave him her weight, her trust, and a bit of her heart, keeping her cheek against his chest. She could hear his heart beating a slow, reassuring tattoo and feel the tempo of her own heartbeat rising. One of Beck's hands slid up her spine and rested on her nape, where his thumb made slow, languorous circles.

"You don't have to be certain, you know." His voice was suited to darkness, low, sensuous, and soothing. "If you're uncomfortable, Sara, you tell me to stop, and I'll damned well sleep in the stables."

"I won't tell you to stop," Sara assured him, though

it was almost as if he were daring her to reject him, so insistent was he on reminding her of this. She offered him assurances in false coin, though, because in the past week, between fits of worry over Tremaine's missive, Sara had tried to puzzle out her reasons for consorting with Beckman Haddonfield. The best she could do, as she'd told him, was that she was using him in some manner to recover from her marriage. Reynard had left her dreams in tatters, her body exhausted, and her spirit hurting.

She would treat herself to the attentions Beckman offered, learn something of dalliance, and see what it was like to be held in affection by a man she respected—nothing less, and nothing more.

When his fingers stilled on her nape, she put aside her musings, waiting for his next word, his next breath, his next anything.

"A lady can change her mind, Sara," Beck whispered, cruising his lips over her closed eyes. "At any time, she can change her mind."

Provided she *had* a mind left to change. Beck's hands framed her face, his thumbs feathering over her cheeks and jaw. The care in his touch, the unhurried, savoring quality of his explorations turned Sara's knees unreliable and her spine into a lyrical, lilting melody. When Beck settled his lips over hers, she had a sense of sinking, of going under and drowning in pleasurable sensations.

He commanded all of her attention by virtue of showering all of his on her. He was touching her, breathing her, tasting her, wrapping his body around hers in such a way Sara felt him surrounding her every sense—sight, scent, hearing, taste, touch. She became filled with Beckman Haddonfield.

How long they stood there kissing, Sara could not have said. Long enough to leave her clinging to him, desperately needing more and clueless how to find it.

Beck broke the kiss and tucked her under his arm. "I've been waiting lifetimes for this, Sarabande Adagio, and for what follows now, we need and deserve a bed."

❦

Beck had not exaggerated. For him, his extravagant statement was simple truth. Sara wasn't his usual fare—a discreet widow or a titled lady out for an evening's romp. She wasn't one of Nick's hopefuls; she wasn't anything Beck had allowed himself before.

She was decent. Good. She was choosing him for herself, and he wanted to be worthy of the honor.

He also—God help him—hoped she was choosing *him*, Beck Haddonfield, not simply a randy and convenient male whose discretion could be trusted in the morning, but a person. This was greedy and foolish of him—he invariably stumbled when dealing in sentiment—but he was honest with himself out of habit, and it wasn't such a sorry thing to want.

To be a person to one's lover.

And for that reason, he'd changed his mind when he'd gone out on his errands. He'd retrieved Sara's packages and bathed, as intended, but he had not stopped by the common room and procured for himself enough brandy to ensure the evening would start with a pleasurable glow.

He'd taken his courage in one hand, his self-discipline in the other, and for the second time in his life, he'd resisted the temptation to get drunk his first night in Portsmouth. The decision was paying off, in the acuity of his senses, in the clarity of his will and the sure knowledge he would recall every sigh and caress Sara graced him with the whole night through.

He searched her face in the moonlight, seeing desire, but also uncertainty in her eyes. If he'd made that stop in the taproom, would he have missed the uncertainty?

"I want to see you. All of you, Sara."

She nodded but made no move to take off her dressing gown. Ah, well, he'd ever been one to enjoy unwrapping pretty gifts.

Slowly, his fingers went to the sash belting her dressing gown. He tugged it free then pushed the robe off her shoulders and tossed it onto the foot of the bed. Her nightgown was old, plain, and, in keeping with the warmer weather, came only to her knees. He knelt before her and slid off her slippers, one at a time. Rather than rise immediately, he nudged the hem of her nightgown up and ran his cheek over the smooth skin above her knee.

Heaven help him, even her knees smelled good— tasted good.

Sara's fingers tugged at his hair. "That tickles."

"What about this one?" Beck nuzzled the other knee. "Is it ticklish too?"

"Yes." He suspected she was trying not to giggle.

He wanted to hear her giggle. Wanted her giggling, laughing, crying, and yelling in his bed. He wanted her free there to be herself in every respect.

"Are you ticklish here?" he asked, rising and running the edge of his thumb along her ribs.

She flinched away. "Are you?"

"It will be your privilege to find out. Perhaps you'd like to start by removing my dressing gown?"

The humor left Sara's expression, replaced by wary curiosity.

"You've seen me before, Sara. All of me, and not just across the barnyard."

"We're not in the barnyard." Sara glanced at the bed fleetingly, as if it might burst into flames—which possibility Beck dearly treasured. She took a breath then reached out her hand and tugged the belt of his dressing gown free. It fell open, but she didn't immediately take it from him.

She studied the bed this time as if it were a map, not a common piece of furniture. "We're going to do this, aren't we?"

"If you allow it." Beck's tone was level, as if he waited on her to choose between different flavors of ice. "As you allow it."

Because God knew, left to his own devices, he'd toss her back across the bed, fall on her, and commence rutting. He was grateful again he'd not had that brandy, though Sara might have benefited from a tot.

Slowly, so slowly he wanted to scream, Sara's hand flattened against the bare skin of his midriff then eased around to his back. Her fingertips left a trail of heat, and when she stepped closer, her scent came with her.

"You'll have to tell me what to do." Sara rested against him, only her nightgown between them now.

"You have only one responsibility." Beck settled his hands on either side of her neck. "*Enjoy yourself.* You wanted to use me. I want to be used. Tonight, you say what you want, Sara, and you get it."

She slipped the blue velvet from his shoulders, tossed it across the foot of the bed, then took a step back.

Beck unwrapped his gift, peeling the flimsy old nightgown off of her as if it were the finest silk, lifting it from her as if to reveal the most gorgeous courtesan, not a tired, no longer young housekeeper with a daughter nearing adolescence.

"Glorious." Beck smiled at her, a glad, spontaneous smile shamelessly laden with lustful appreciation. She was not a girl; she was a woman in her prime, lovely, abundantly curved, and willing. "But your hair is up, Sarabande, and I promised myself tonight it would come down. Sit you in the middle of the bed and indulge me."

He patted the bed rather than toss her onto it—this time—and went into the other room. When he came back, Sara sat in the middle of the mattress with the covers drawn up under her arms.

"That won't do. Out into the lists with you, Sarabande. I've brought my weapon." He brandished her hairbrush.

"Is there a reason why you can't unbraid my hair while we're in our dressing gowns?"

"Yes." Beck's great weight dipped the mattress as he bounced into position directly behind her.

"And the reason would be?"

"You'll see," he murmured, reaching for her braid. Except Sara wouldn't see his reason, she'd feel it, as would he. Arousal was already pooling in his blood, so Beck silently admonished himself to slow down.

"Where did you get off to," Sara asked, "before dinner, while I bathed?"

"I took care of my own ablutions," Beck answered, relieved Sara was up to conversation. "And retrieved a few things I'd sent for. God above, I adore your hair, Sarabande." He was unraveling her loosely plaited braid.

"It feels good," Sara admitted on a sigh. "When you brush it like that. I've not felt my hair down on my naked back in ages, though."

"Like it?" Beck picked up the mass of her hair and swung it lightly across her back. He played for a few minutes, bunching the abundance of her hair in his hands, burying his face in it, and draping it over her back and shoulders then letting it brush over his groin.

"I'm engaging in perversions back here," Beck said. "Do you know how arousing your hair is when I brush it across my cock?"

"No." She took in an unsteady breath, while Beck caressed himself again with her hair.

"It burns, Sara." His voice had lost some of its teasing quality. "Brands me. Makes me want to brand you. Over and over again."

He gathered her hair and swept it over her right shoulder, then shifted, kneeling up and bending over her. He intended that she feel his erection along her spine. He did not intend the wave of possessiveness that swept him when he embraced her like this.

"You are in this state as a function of brushing my *hair*?" She sounded curious rather than intimidated—curious and maybe a little pleased with herself. "Beckman?"

"Hmm?" He'd curled down over her so his lips were near her ear.

"Are you done with my hair?"

"Not nearly."

"Are you done brushing my hair for now?"

This question took some time to absorb.

"Yes." Abruptly he dropped his arms and sat back on his heels.

"Might we get under the covers?"

"God, yes."

Beckman shifted again, and Sara scrambled around to climb under the covers with him. Her unbound hair took some managing, but the sensation of it sweeping along his shoulder and belly nigh unmanned him.

"Now what, Beckman?" Sara aligned herself to his side, her hair cascading over his chest and stomach.

Beck angled up off his back, gathered her against him, and rolled them. "Now, we make love."

He didn't give her a chance to reply but lowered his head to seal his mouth over hers. Polite teasing slipped from his grasp. He was kissing to arouse, and so—thank a merciful heaven—was she.

"Don't hold back," Sara whispered against Beck's neck. "Tonight I don't want you to be careful or restrained or gentlemanly. I want more, Beckman."

"You'll have it," he assured her as she closed her teeth over a pinch of his shoulder.

He insinuated a hand between their bodies, only to have Sara seize it with her own. "Yes." She clamped his fingers over her breast. "That. Please."

When he gently squeezed then closed his fingers more definitely around her nipple, she pushed herself up against his cock. "Beckman…"

He kept up his attentions to her breast, until Sara was undulating rhythmically against him, flaying his self-control before he'd even gotten down to business. He'd wanted to go slowly, to savor and cherish and honor her with his caresses and his self-restraint. He'd planned to pleasure her, to pleasure them both, but gently, because she was without recent experience, and this was their first complete encounter.

His plans went up in bright, reddish-orange flames.

"Come here." Beck shifted to his side, leaving Sara on her back. He could kiss the hell out of her this way and use his hands to better advantage. She took to the shift in positions like a duck to water, hooking a leg over his hips and rolling toward him.

"Better," Beck growled as he filled his hand with the curve of her derriere and brought her closer.

"Beck, I want…" Sara's fingers closed around his shaft, and Beck felt a moment's panic.

"You can have that," he assured her, gently untangling her fingers, "but later, love. Just a little later."

When she would have protested, Beck spiked her guns by brushing the backs of his fingers over the curls at the apex of her sex.

"Beckman?" Her undulating ceased, surprise in her voice.

"I want this to last," he tried to explain, exploring gently. "If you have your way with me precipitously, I won't do you justice."

Sara blinked, looking momentarily puzzled as he shifted his grip on her so his fingers could dip lower.

"You're ready for me." He didn't keep the smugness from his tone as he swiped a pair of fingers in a long, slow caress up her damp sex. Sara's body shuddered, and he repeated the caress, studying her as he did.

"You like that. What about this?" He dabbled at the opening to her body, gently, but not too gently for a woman becoming aroused.

"Do that again," she said, closing her eyes. Beck obliged by easing a single finger shallowly inside her.

"Better?"

"Not better enough." She arched her hips against him as he continued the same fleeting and shallow penetrations. When he limited himself to those teasing caresses, she pushed against him as if asking him to speed up, or for the love of God, to *enter her*.

Cautiously, Beck brushed his thumb over a spot higher up.

"Push harder," she muttered, grasping his hand and anchoring it against her. "Right there, Beckman, *ah, God, yes, right there.*"

"And there we go," Beck whispered, pleased and relieved, because God help him, Sara was so bloody snug, he hadn't been sure quite how to go on.

"Don't you stop," Sara hissed through her teeth. "Please, Beck, you can't…"

"I won't." He leaned over, kept up his stroking, and took her nipple in his mouth. He pleasured himself more than her, suckling greedily and drawing firmly in a rhythm that counterpointed the movements of his hand.

"Beckman…" Her fingers clamped around his wrist, her back arched, and her hips thrust up hard against his hand. His control nearly slipped when Sara began to make low, soft noises of pleasure and need and greater pleasure still.

"Everlasting, merciful…" Sara rolled to lay panting on her back, turning only her head to gaze at him. "God above, Beckman Haddonfield. You should be banned by royal decree." She rolled back into him, tucking herself against his chest, and hiding her face against his body.

Despite the arousal roaring through his body, Beck was pleased. Pleased for her, pleased for himself. Embracing her, he was reassured he had the patience to see this through, and the determination. He gathered her against him and swept her hair over her shoulder.

"You're all right?"

"Buzzing," Sara replied. "Once more, in very short order, buzzing. You?"

"I will be," Beck answered. God willing, he would be *soon*. "But I'm concerned."

"Hnn." Sara's tongue found his nipple, and by the lazy way she stroked him, Beck knew he'd chosen his moment well. Sara would not know a concern now if it kissed her on the lips.

"It's not a serious concern," Beck went on, "but I'd like your agreement to humor me, Sara."

Sara sighed contentedly. "Right now, you can have anything you please of me, Beckman. I am powerless to refuse you."

Beck smiled, his imagination taking off with that

offer. "I want you, Sara, more than I can recall wanting anybody or anything, but there's only one way I will have you."

She raised her face up to peer at him, the gravity in his voice perhaps penetrating her haze of well-being.

"What are you about, Beckman?" She reached up and brushed his hair back from his forehead. "And you needn't be diplomatic. Have I disappointed you?"

"Does this feel like disappointment?" He wrapped her fingers around his shaft.

Sara smiled wickedly. "No. That feels like the sweet shop is still open for business."

"Not to you." Beck answered as sternly as he could, but he had to close his eyes as Sara's fingers stroked lightly over the head of his cock. He caught her hand with his, stilling it, but not making her turn loose of him.

"What do you mean, Beck?" The beginning of hurt laced her tone, and Beck was relieved to know he had her attention.

"You have to promise me, Sara, you'll let me have the reins for the next little while." He kissed her cheek to soften his words and to take in a gratifying whiff of her fragrance.

"Didn't I just give you my reins? And the whip and spurs, along with a few lumps of sugar?"

"You did." Beck smiled despite himself. "But I want to be inside you, Sara. Want it so badly my eyes are crossing, and if you get to showing your enthusiasm, I could hurt you."

"That is nonsense," Sara began. "You are being overly…" But he held her gaze and slowly stroked her hand over the entire hard, thick length of him.

"I'll sleep in the stables," he threatened. "I'll sleep in the Solent rather than hurt you, Sara. You can't undermine my control on this, not this time."

She frowned, maybe sensing there was a compliment, a reason to be pleased in his words, and then he saw her put it together: she could drive him beyond reason were she too enthusiastic. Her, Sara Hunt, retiring, rusticating, widowed housekeeper.

"I will abide by your direction," she said gently. "No matter what, Beck. You can trust me on this, for this once at least."

He kissed her to hide his relief. In bed at least, he'd never disappointed a woman. And he really would sleep in the stables before he'd start now. Carefully, he shifted over her and settled between her legs.

Sara's hands came to rest low on his back. "What do you want me to do?"

"You can kiss and pet and carry on all you want above the waist." Beck nuzzled her throat. "Below the waist, you don't move unless I tell you to. Not a wiggle or a tease, Sara."

"Below the waist, I am your statue. I will come to life only at your command."

For several minutes, he tried to content himself with easy kisses.

"I like kissing you." Sara brushed his hair back and levered up to capture his mouth again. "Like it a lot."

As did he, but Beck's concentration was fixed on the territory Sara had given into his exclusive control. As she settled into the kissing and let her hands roam over his back, Beck gradually eased himself more snugly against her sex. The urge to thrust—to push into her and keep pushing—was nearly overwhelming, but he contented himself with nudging, then nudging again.

"This is harder than I thought it would be, this holding still," Sara said against his neck. He angled up on his arms to regard her.

"Is it too difficult?" *Let alone hard.*

"No." Sara smiled slightly. "But what is the problem? I want you inside me, Beckman."

"This is the problem." He did flex his hips then, and by rights—she'd had a child, for pity's sake—he should have begun to slip into the sweet, wet heat of her.

Sara cocked her head on the pillow. "It doesn't hurt. Do that again."

He did, watching her face closely, waiting for the telltale wince.

"Again."

He gained a bit of entry but saw her expression change fleetingly. "I'm hurting you."

"No. It's just different, that's all. Again."

He complied, hamstrung between increasing arousal and the certain conviction—as closely as her body wrapped him—he had to be hurting her. She wasn't hurting him, though; God above, just the bloody opposite.

"Don't stop, Beck," Sara said, but he could hear the caution in her tone as the head of his cock was now lodged blissfully inside her.

He tried to think.

"Close yourself around me," he suggested, settling down on his forearms.

Sara hugged him to her more tightly.

"Inside, too, Sara. Here." He gave her a minute thrust to demonstrate.

"Close myself?"

"Grip my cock with your sex. Like you don't want me to pull out." She comprehended that, and Beck felt the snugness of her contract around him. Had he been a Papist, he would have started saying the rosary on behalf of his disintegrating wits.

"Do that again, slowly, as if you could pull me into you, then let me go."

She did it, and he experimentally eased forward as she relaxed.

"That works," she reported, starting up again.

It *worked* too bloody well. It worked to arouse him to the point where his entire being was an exercise in self-discipline. By the smallest increments imaginable, Sara's body eased around him and admitted him to her intimate depths.

"Are you in pain?" Sara's hands were anchored on his buttocks, her face tucked against his chest.

"Bliss," he managed. But as soon as he let go, the bliss would implode into ecstasy. He couldn't do that until he was sure he wouldn't hurt her. "Can you move just a little on me now?"

"Like this?" She rolled her hips conservatively.

"Just like that," Beck rasped. "Until you're comfortable."

Or until he died, because all this holding back would surely kill him.

"I'm comfortable." She set up a tidy little rocking. "I just…"

"What, love?" Beck dropped his forehead to hers. "Tell me. Please."

"I want more." Sara let go with a luxurious undulation and sighed against his neck.

Sainthood loomed within Beck's grasp, but he declined for the greater pleasure of making love to the woman in his bed.

"I think we've earned a little more," he said. "But you hold still now. I don't want to take any chances."

Immediately, she quieted and waited for him. When he flexed on a long, slow thrust, she moaned softly and melted around him. "Better," she pronounced.

Thank you, God.

Beck found a rhythm, keeping his movements slow and languid but not letting himself open his eyes, not when the sound of Sara's sighs alone was driving him beyond reason.

"I want to move, Beck." Sara took his earlobe in her mouth and gently nipped him. "Just a little." He nodded. His jaw was clenched too tightly for speech.

Sara didn't warn him, though, that she was going to wrap her legs around him, lock her ankles at the small of his back, and use her considerable leg strength to anchor him to her. She added "just a little" movement to that shift in position, and Beck was lost.

His thrusting picked up depth and speed, and his arms locked behind Sara's head.

"Don't let me hurt…" He felt Sara's fingers lace with his own, grounding him.

"Love me, Beckman." She turned her head to kiss the heel of his hand. "Let go. It will be all right."

She clasped him with the interior muscles he'd shown her earlier, and Beckman was undone, dissolved in pleasure and passion when he felt Sara's body coming apart with him.

His restraint abandoned him as Sara's body communicated its delight, gripping and pulling at him, proving to him graphically that his satisfaction was her own.

When he could not have sustained any greater experience of fulfillment, Beck hung over Sara on his forearms, stroking her hair as he pulled the breath back into his body by force of will.

God help him…

"Did I hurt…?"

Sara's fingers brushed over his mouth then trailed around the back of his head to urge him down against her shoulder. While he waited, panting, for his wits to reassemble, she shifted her hips slowly, maybe treating herself to a little more pleasure, and surely answering Beck's question the most convincing way possible.

"That's all right then," Beck said, realizing it might be a little afterthought of an orgasm making her quiver around him like that, not just erotic sensitivity. "You're all right."

She kissed his throat and cuddled into him.

He lifted up a little—the woman needed to breathe—but Sara's fingers tightened in his hair, and so he lingered. He kissed her eyes and her cheek and her mouth, suckled her earlobe, and nuzzled her eyebrows. He closed his eyes and listened to her breathing, then buried his face in the fragrant cloud of her hair.

He could stay there, in that bed, feasting his senses on her forever. His cock was softening, but still Sara's body held him gently, and he knew the temptation to start up again, to ease from the bliss of fulfillment to the bliss of anticipation, again and again.

She would not thank him, though. Not tomorrow, maybe not even the day after.

"I'll be right back," Beck said, kissing her mouth one last time. Carefully, he uncoupled from her body then crossed the room to retrieve the wash water. He tended to himself, his cock still sensitive, then wrung out the cloth and sat on the bed at Sara's hip.

"Covers back."

Sara complied, barely, so Beck had to reach beneath the covers to hold the cool cloth gently against her sex. "Now, I wish we had a chandelier hanging over the bed."

"You want to peek?"

"I want to memorize the glory of you," Beck said. "And I want to make sure you're not... sore."

"Stop worrying." Sara's smile in the moonlight was radiant. "I am not sore, and I will not be sore, and so far, I like this dallying business rather a lot."

"Well, that's a relief." Beck turned the cloth over, giving her the cooler side. "I did not want to spend our remaining nights here playing cards."

Or drinking. The thought slipped past his postcoital glow, puzzling him, for all it was the truth.

"You're frowning. We can play cards if you insist."

"It isn't that." Beck returned the cloth to the basin and climbed in beside her. "Budge up."

"As we're truly good friends now, I suppose?"

He arranged her straddling him, and bless the woman, she snuggled right down against his body.

"We're friends, at least," Beck said, wrapping his

arms around her. He wasn't a man who begrudged his partners affection, but neither in the usual course was he exactly interested in lingering in a woman's bed. Still, he didn't question the pleasure he took in Sara's willingness to fall asleep in his arms. Didn't deny he enjoyed stroking that glorious hair down her back long after dreams had claimed her.

He did, however, wonder why he felt as if, for the first time in his life, he'd unwrapped a lovely package, chosen and decorated just for him, and had been utterly delighted with his present.

Incongruous as it was, he felt as if he'd made love to an innocent—not that he had any experience to go by there—to a woman who'd waited just for him, and saved all her passion and regard just for him.

Which, considering Sara was a mother well past the first blush of youth, made no sense at all.

Twelve

THE WEEKEND FLEW BY, WITH SATURDAY SPENT IN AN exhausting marathon of shopping and Sunday spent largely recovering. Sara saw firsthand that Beck excelled at anything associated with commercial endeavor. Whatever they purchased, he had it sent to the inn and packed on their wagon so there would be no delay Monday morning loading and rearranging the wagon's contents.

The way he spent money was to Sara nigh virtuosic. He didn't waste it, though, he spent it, invested it. He bought the better quality product, assuring her more durable goods were the better bargain, even if they cost a little more.

She agreed and raised her sights accordingly.

For North, Beck dropped off measurements taken from the man's boots at a little hole-in-the-corner establishment on a side street.

He purchased bolts of cloth for dresses, drapes, and everything in between, then moved on to sheets, towels, table linens, and other household goods. Sara noticed many of the merchants knew him, though a few made mention of not having seen him in some time.

"You are good company." He passed her a tot of cognac at the end of their busy day and joined her with his own on the balcony. "It's rare I can go shopping with a female and not end up wanting to run howling to the nearest taproom."

"It's rare I can go shopping with a man and not want to shoo him howling to the nearest taproom. With you, though, it isn't shopping so much as provisioning, and in the quantities you were buying today, you had the attention of the merchants."

"True, and with a pretty lady on my arm helping me make my choices."

A pretty lady the clerks kept referring to as his wife. He'd let them—and so had Sara.

They sipped their drinks in silence, standing side by side on the moonlit balcony.

"When, exactly, do your menses next befall you?"

A day ago, Sara might have taken exception to such a question, but now, it struck her as a simple measure of their intimacy.

She thought a moment, then named a date. "Why?"

"We're taking precautions to minimize the risk of conception." Beck set his drink down without finishing it. "Timing is important."

She trusted him to understand the details of that timing at least as well as she did. He was canny that way, and had she not known differently, she would have thought him married for far longer than the few months he alluded to.

"Will you tell me of your marriage, Beck?"

"What do you want to know?" His voice was even, but in his posture, Sara detected the slightest bracing.

"Who was she? How did she die, and do you still miss her?" *Did you love her to distraction, and is she the reason you look so sad sometimes?*

He was silent for a moment, as if arranging answers from least to most painful. "Her name was Devona Brockwood, and her grandfather was the Marquess of Whitfield, her papa in line for the title. When her papa died, she fell under the guardianship of her uncle, and he had several daughters close to Devona's age. It was decided she would be married off posthaste, because she'd already had a Season."

"Posthaste?" Sara didn't like the sound of that.

"I was considered an adequate match. Her stock had fallen with her father's death—her father had not seen to her settlements prior to his demise—and my sense was she was grateful for my attentions. Had her father lived, I've no doubt a duke's son or the son of a marquess, at least, would have been required."

And Sara had to ask. "Was she pretty?"

"Very."

Damn him for his honesty, though she thanked him for it too. "But?"

Beck's smile was sad. "But I was not yet one and twenty. All I knew was that by the rules of any society, once I married her, I could swive her regularly, sport about Town with her on my arm, and be the envy of my friends from university. She was eager enough for the match, and I was anxious to provide my father and brother an heir. We married on less than three months' acquaintance."

"Many marriages start out with less," Sara said gently, because Beck's disgust was evident in his voice.

"They do, but her death was a blessing in a way—to her, if no one else. She loved another, and there was no means by which we could have been happy."

Ah, God. The oldest recipe for misery on the planet, and the one seeing the greatest circulation. "And you did not know this when you married her?"

"Of course not. I knew I was to become an instant adult, by virtue of having captured my bride. I'd come into an inheritance at twenty, finished university, and was hell-bent on proving to my father I was more worthy of his respect than Nicholas. A bride with a baby in her arms was to be my capstone achievement—provided, of course, the baby was a boy."

"You were young."

"I was an arrogant idiot," Beck countered, "which is precisely why I never discuss my marriage, much less think of it if I can help it."

Even though, years later, it still fueled his flight into the opium dens of Paris?

"I'm sorry your marriage wasn't happy." Sara curled her arm through his and rested her cheek against his bicep. "We're so easily hurt when we're young. We dress and talk and carry on like adults, but inside, we're not very adult at all."

Beck settled his arm across her shoulders. "And yet by the time you were twenty, you had a small child, had toured much of Europe, and were the support of your family."

"I was impersonating an adult. There was no one

else on hand for the role. Take me to bed, Beckman. We're both weary, and this talk is not cheering."

She hurt for him but knew not how to say so without offending his male pride. Or perhaps she wanted the confidences to cease flowing between them, lest she impart a few more of her own.

❧

Devona had been so pretty, like a perfect caricature of English beauty. Blond, willowy, soft-spoken, and gracious. She'd been every young gentleman's dream of the ideal wife. But never, in several months of marriage, had she said those words, "Take me to bed, Beckman."

Such a realization might have engendered rage in years past, or guilt—barges and buckets of guilt—or resentment. Tonight, Beck felt only gratitude for Sara's company, and sadness for a young couple whose union had been doomed by immaturity.

Beck undressed his lover with simple courtesy, and after he'd brushed out Sara's hair, he rebraided it, but only after he'd indulged his pleasure in its unbound state. When they shed their nightclothes and climbed onto the bed, Sara tucked herself against Beck's larger frame and hiked a leg across his thighs.

"Did you enjoy today?" she asked, flipping her braid over her shoulder. She settled against him as his arms went around her, then found a comfy spot for her head against his shoulder.

She fits me, Beck thought, resting his cheek against her hair. She not only fit him, she was easily affectionate with him, at least behind closed doors. Maybe this was a maternal quality, this simple affection, or maybe it was a Sara quality. In either case, it was one of the things he enjoyed about her most, the way she gave and accepted affection.

"I enjoyed being with you today," Beck said. "But no, haring all over town, haggling, it reminded me too much of my past, and that in truth, Three Springs should not be my concern."

"But your father is your concern, and this is how you can feel close to him as he slips away."

"Plain speaking, but accurate. Nita writes that he sleeps a great deal."

"So he's not in pain." She shifted up on the pillows and tugged on Beck's broad shoulders. "Cuddle up, Haddonfield, as we're great friends and all."

A little tentatively, he did as she bid, resting his cheek on the slope of her breast. She linked her arms around him and hugged him to her.

"Tell me about your papa," she said, threading her fingers through the hair at his nape.

Slowly at first, Beck did. He started out with expected propaganda, reporting all of the earl's most impressive accomplishments, the bills he'd seen enacted in Parliament, the sound advice he'd given the king or the regent. From there, Beck drifted closer to more personal recollections, until, an hour later, he was wondering aloud why his father had waited until death was knocking at his door to hold Nick accountable for securing the succession and marrying.

"You will sort this out with your brothers." Sara kissed him again. "You like them too much not to, and they like you as well."

"And you know this how?" Even her breasts bore her luscious fragrance.

"You said when Nick retrieved you from Paris he saved your life, Beckman. He will be the head of the family, and he will need your support. You're the one who has actually seen the family holdings overseas. You're the one who has met this factor and that competitor. You're the one with the better sense of your younger sisters and the men who could make them suitable mates. While Nick has been off tending to whatever, and Ethan has been banished, you've been minding the family concerns."

She turned facts on their heads, sounding very brisk and practical while she did. "That's one way to look at it."

"Ask Nick sometime how he looks at it," Sara said. "For now, I need to move you. My arm has gone to sleep."

"My apologies."

Sara pushed at his shoulder. "Roll over. I'm going to rub your back."

"You are?" It occurred to Beck she might be sore, so he acquiesced. He could ask her, of course, but his mood was a little off for lovemaking, and the shops would be closed tomorrow. They'd have all day to indulge his selfish impulses—and hers.

"Go to sleep, Beckman." Sara's hand began to knead his shoulder. "It will all be here in the morning, as will I."

Usually, the idea that his troubles would greet him upon rising was not cheering. The way Sara said it put things in a different light.

⁂

Beck woke up the next morning spooned around Sara, a pleasurable novelty made all the sweeter by the breeze coming through the balcony doors. His erection was seated along her sex, and before she was fully awake, Sara was subtly moving against him.

Trusting she would tell him if he was asking too much, Beck shifted minutely behind her, wrapped an arm around her waist, and began to ease his way inside.

"Good morning," Sara murmured, bringing his hand up to settle over her breast.

"Good morning," Beck politely rejoined, pushing more firmly into her body. "It's a lovely day."

"Beautiful," Sara agreed sleepily. She contracted her sex around him and sighed—contentedly, he thought—as he gained a deeper penetration.

"Is this…?" Beck paused while he focused on easing his cock that much deeper into her heat.

"Beautiful," Sara assured him, closing her fingers over his on her breast. "Just… lovely."

He hadn't made love to her before in daylight. He wanted to, of course. He wanted to make love to her so he could see the sunlight on her face and not just on the erotic curve of her spine. He wanted to put her on her knees and fill her so deeply she groaned with the pleasure of it. Wanted her atop him, her hair drifting over them both, and he wanted her…

He slipped his hand out from under hers and closed her fingers around her nipple, then let his palm glide down over her belly, to her sex. His fingers found the seat of her pleasure, and in slow, glancing caresses, he began to drive her toward completion.

Beckman almost regretted it when he felt Sara surrender to her orgasm, so greatly had he been enjoying the lovemaking. He let himself join her, though his own orgasm became more intense for the control he tried to maintain over his body.

"You all right?" He stroked a hand down her spine when he could speak again, knowing she was unused to this much sexual activity, regardless of how he tried to contain himself.

"Blissful," Sara said, sounding well pleasured and smug. "How do married people behave in company, Beck, when there's all this between them in private?"

It struck him as an odd question. Sara had been married far longer than he had. Odd—but flattering.

"They start off with a honeymoon," he said, "and have a little privacy in which to gain their balance. But I believe a certain kind of misbehavior is the signal attraction of the married state for most people. Stay put and let me tend you."

Lest he ravish her the livelong day.

"I want to devour you," he said as he tidied her up. "Visually at least, if not otherwise."

"You need your breakfast," Sara informed him. And yet she parted her legs farther and didn't push his hand away. "Why shouldn't you look?" she asked, watching his face. "I like to look at you. Love to, in fact."

His gaze shifted to assess the truth of her statement, only to find the demented woman was smiling radiantly.

"I love the look of you when you're dressed for town," she said while his gaze traveled from that smile back to the damp, pink glory of her sex. "You're handsome when you're all country-gentleman-about-his-business. I love the look of you at breakfast, teasing Allie, ready to storm off on your list of tasks. I love the affection and exasperation I see in your eyes when you argue with North, or harry him off to the hot springs for his medicinal dip…" She might have gone on with her list of "I loves," except Beck closed her knees and wrapped his arms around her legs.

"You are going to need a medicinal dip," he declared, thinking he himself could do with a cold swim. God in heaven… The sight of her… so fearless and… generous. "I'm going to order you a bath, see about our breakfast, then scare us up a conveyance suitable for a drive along the water. Will that suit?"

"It will suit wonderfully."

He rose from the bed and caught her—true to her words—admiring the view shamelessly. When they'd finished breakfast and Beck was leaving her to her bath, he paused at the door.

"Sarabande Adagio?"

"Beckman Sylvanus?"

He wanted to give her something, something in return for holding him in the darkness and all of those "I loves" in the light.

Something she would not reject as beyond the bounds of a frolic. "I'm already regretting we must leave this place tomorrow, and when the summons comes from Belle Maison, I will regret that too, and not just for my father's sake." And then he slipped out the door, giving her privacy and taking some for himself as well.

༄

The day was idyllic and sleepy, like a Sunday in late spring should be, but warm enough to make the shore breeze comfortable. Beck hired a horse and buggy to take Sara up on the headlands for a picnic, finding a depression surrounded by stubby trees near a hilltop to spread a blanket. The view from the nearby cliff top was at once private and spectacular, with the sun bouncing off a sea of white caps and the town spread out below them.

Sara brought her book, and Beck read to her, her head on his stomach as he lay back on the blanket. He hadn't packed wine for some reason, but felt as lazy and relaxed as if they were on their second bottle. He set the book aside, thinking perhaps he'd read his audience to sleep, and let his hand stroke over Sara's hair. Her eyes drifted open, and she turned so her cheek was on his stomach.

Her hand came up to shape him through his breeches, and Beck had to close his eyes. A gentleman wouldn't ask anything of her today—hell, a gentleman would not have swived her silly before she even broke her fast. A gentleman...

She was undoing his falls, and he didn't protest, but he did have his limits.

"You need to recover," he managed. "I mean it, Sara."

She paused, frowning, then extricated him from his clothing, which was a delicate challenge when he was more than half aroused.

"You need something else entirely," she said. She got her mouth on him, but to Beck's relief, she desisted abruptly. He watched with silent curiosity as she took his hand and wrapped it around his shaft, then shifted around so she was lying on her back at right angles to his chest.

Slowly, slowly, she eased her skirt up over her bent knees, and God in heaven, the woman wasn't wearing drawers. She let her knees fall open, and let go a sigh.

"You wanted to look this morning," she said. "There's no reason why you shouldn't, Beckman. No reason you shouldn't touch."

She tossed all modesty aside and began opening the buttons down the front of her bodice, while Beck watched, speechless and increasingly aroused, as she pushed her clothing aside until she was lying in a pagan tangle of flesh and fabric, exposed to the sun and his hungry eyes.

He did not resist what she offered, but feasted on the sight of her. He looked, he touched, he tasted. He put his hands on every inch of her, took down her hair and draped it over every inch of him. He brought himself to orgasm more than once just looking at her, brushing his fingers over her sex, her breasts, her derriere, her mouth. She refused him nothing, obliged his every request, seeming to understand that in this situation, trust and arousal were bound together for him.

"You're going to burn," Beck cautioned when he lay naked, spent for the third time, his hand caressing the firm curve of Sara's bare buttocks.

Sara smiled over at him and wiggled under his hand. "Not in the biblical sense."

"I'm not usually so…"

"Lusty?" Sara's smile broadened. "Amorous? Passionate?"

"Horny." Beck's smile was embarrassed. "Selfish, hedonistic."

"For God's sake, Beck." Sara's smile faded. "It's a beautiful spring day, you're a healthy young man, and a little friskiness doesn't make you your half-crazy brother."

His eyebrows shot up as he considered the possibilities she was raising. Had he checked his lustier impulses to avoid sharing Nick's tendencies?

"You're not like him," Sara said, seeming to read his mind. "He discards women as easily as old boots, to hear you tell it. He goes for the jades and widows, almost as if he doesn't deserve a good woman's affections. You know better."

Put like that, Beck... *pitied* his older brother, a novel and not entirely unwelcome perspective. It was easier than judging Nick, and felt closer to the truth. His hand closed on the firm curve of Sara's derriere, and she undulated again like a cat seeking attention.

"I have discovered"—she closed her eyes—"I like it when you pinch me."

"Here?" He pinched her, not hard.

"Yes." Sara arched. "There. And my... breasts and other parts."

Those parts. While he'd pleasured himself several times with her assistance in this protracted bout of friskiness, she'd yet to demand anything of him. And how odd was it that a woman married for eight or nine years wouldn't know her own pleasures?

Beck smoothed his hand over her again. "Your husband was a selfish cretin, Sara. You deserved better."

"I won't argue that." She rolled over, which left

his hand resting right over her pubic curls, and Beck lectured himself not to start in with her. So far, he'd petted, caressed, looked, and looked some more; he'd kissed, tasted, and teased, but he hadn't done anything that might irritate her tender parts.

Hadn't needed to, not for his own pleasure anyway. It was a revelation, at least to a man who'd taken lovers on four continents.

"I haven't played like this before," he said, wondering when the brakes had been disconnected from his mouth.

"I haven't either," Sara said, fondling his flaccid cock. "It gives me ideas about those hot springs, Beckman. I hope you are prepared to be a sparkling-clean fellow in the near future."

He hooked his arm around her neck and pulled her to him, in charity with Creation at her words. A feeling expanded out from his chest, of beatitude and humor and overwhelming affection for the woman half-naked on the blanket with him. It crested, and subsided before his fool mouth opened and embarrassed him trying to express it, but it didn't fade entirely.

Not when they dressed each other, teasing and laughing; not when they drove back down to town, sitting too closely on the buggy's seat. Not when they made slow, quiet love that evening; not when they fell asleep tangled in each other's arms that night.

Only when Sara laughingly declined his proposal of marriage over breakfast did Beckman's newfound joy in life abruptly diminish.

Thirteen

"It came on Friday," Polly said, handing the little letter over to Sara in the stable yard. Beckman was in the barn, dealing with the inventory and the horses, while Sara dealt with an ache inside that had no cure.

"I wanted to read it, to hide it, and to burn it," Polly said, keeping her voice down.

Sara glanced at the address, knowing it was from Tremaine even before she opened it. "Thank you." She put it in her skirt pocket then drew it out again when she saw Polly regarding her with steady compassion.

"You had a lovely weekend, didn't you, Sara?"

Sara considered the manor house as she and Polly approached it, as well as the outbuildings, gardens, and every other feature of Three Springs that appeared exactly as she'd left it just days ago. "The weather was gorgeous, Beckman is a consummate quartermaster, and Portsmouth shows to good advantage when one has rusticated as long as we have. What about you?"

She put the question as casually as she could, but there was a difference about Polly, a peacefulness that hadn't been there a few days before.

"We managed," Polly said. "Allie is going like a house afire on her new painting."

"What did she choose for her subject?" Sara's gaze drifted upward, to where the third-floor windows gleamed silver in the last of the evening light.

"Soldier. North professed to be hurt, that she'd consider his horse a more worthy subject than he. She's probably already dreaming of the next study. She'll be relieved to know you're home."

"Let her sleep, but, Polly?"

Sara met her sister's gaze, on solid ground now that the first few difficult questions had been answered—or dodged. "My thanks, my very sincere thanks for looking after Allie and Three Springs. I hadn't realized how much I needed to get away."

Polly turned toward the eastern horizon, to where two stars were visible against the darkening sky. "Did it go well? With you and Beckman? I can have North thrash him, you know, if he... misbehaved."

"Or didn't misbehave? He was everything I could have hoped for, Polly. A completely, thoroughly enjoyable companion." At least until breakfast that morning, when he'd completely, thoroughly bewildered her with his proposal.

"For somebody who spent the weekend with a thoroughly enjoyable companion, you look tired and sad, Sara. Let's get Tremaine's letter over with, and then I'll tuck you in with a posset."

Sara had wanted to forget this letter, too, but Polly was right: ignoring the threat Tremaine posed was not prudent. She followed Polly into the kitchen and glanced around.

"Where's North?"

"Soaking," Polly said, putting on the kettle. "It helps his back, and he promised Beck he would."

Sara tore open the letter, scanned it, and handed it to Polly.

Polly frowned. "It's pretty much the same. Greetings, he's been remiss, would we consider a visit, how fares Allie... I don't detect a threat in this, Sara."

"He has those portraits, Polly." Sara sat at the table, feeling as if her little weekend in Portsmouth happened to someone else a century ago. Somebody whom God liked and spared a little joy every once in a while—a lot of joy, in fact, and a generous portion of pleasure, too.

"He's had years to use those portraits," Polly replied. "He doesn't mention them, and he may not understand what he has in them. Drink your tea, and where's Beckman?"

"I expect he's anywhere I'm not." Sara did not want tea. She did not want to dissemble before her sister, either. "I think I hurt his feelings, Polly. I know I did, in fact."

Polly was silent for a moment, stirring a fat helping of sugar into her own cup of tea.

"I used to be a nice person." Polly sat, pushed Sara's teacup closer, and covered Sara's hand with her own. "Now I'm old and mean, and so I say: Better his feelings hurt than yours, Sara."

"You're still a nice sister." Sara smiled wanly and sipped her tea.

༄

"The prodigal returns." North's voice came not from the pool itself but from the shadows to Beck's left, where the boulders were gathered along the water's edge. "All that wagon travel put you in need of a soak?"

"Greetings, North." Beck sat and tugged at his boots. "And yes, I am in need of a soak."

"Maybe you didn't get much rest this weekend," North mused, "what with all that procurement to tend to?"

Beck threw his boot in the general direction of North's voice.

"Cranky," North observed, "but you've good aim. I take it Mrs. Hunt did not haul your ashes, Haddonfield, which must have come as a blow to your considerable charm."

Beck fired the second boot at a higher velocity then nigh strangled himself getting his neckcloth undone. "She hauled everything I own or ever coveted, right out to the dung heap."

"She's *trifling* with an upright young sprout like you?" North put a world of dismay into his voice, and Beck was glad no lethal weapons were at hand.

"Stubble it, North." Beck heard something rip as he yanked his shirt over his head. "I bloody proposed to the woman, and she bloody laughed and told me I mustn't tease about such things on an empty stomach."

Even North was temporarily silenced by that admission.

"You proposed?" Then, "You proposed *marriage*? The 'do you, Beckman, take this woman…' sort of marriage? To Sara?"

"That general idea." Beck stood naked, fists clenched at his side, wanting to break something—or someone. North would have served nicely, except his back was already fragile. Then too, Beck, as usual, had no one else to talk to.

"Fast work, if you ask me." North ambled out of the shadows, in a state of complete undress. "Maybe a little too fast. Shall we?"

"Why weren't you already soaking?" Beck asked as he waded in. The heat felt good, but it made him realize how tense he was, how primed for violence.

"I come here to think." North carefully negotiated the bank, and Beck could see well enough to realize the man was still moving gingerly. Very gingerly.

"You idiot," Beck chided, "what did you do while I was gone? Patch up the west boundary wall by yourself?"

"You'll see I did not when you ride out tomorrow and make sure the entire estate is exactly as you left it on Friday." North eased one large foot into the water. "Now about this premature proposal you bungled so egregiously. I take it your manly charms were in adequate evidence to impress the lady?"

Beck had to smile at North in an avuncular role, or perhaps at the fool who'd heed North's advice. "You are going to diagnose my love life?"

"Somebody had better. Sara is a sensible lady, and sensible women don't turn down proposals from toothsome lordly pups like yourself."

"What are you?" Beck found the underwater ledge and lowered himself to it. "Five years my senior? Three?"

"I am millennia your senior in experience, as is evident by my ability to perceive you rushed your fences."

"I married a woman I knew far less well than I do Sara." Which did not refute North's point.

"And how did that turn out?" North asked, finding a seat several feet away, where the water would not be as hot.

"Disastrously, for her, anyway." And for him. In some ways, it turned out worse for him.

"Maybe Sara doesn't think she merits a man of your station. I, for one, am hesitant to ask any woman to shackle herself to me, and you must allow I am not the worst creature to crawl across Creation."

"Not quite. Our womenfolk like you, so you must have some endearing qualities. In deference to your sensitive nature, I will refrain from enumerating same, but minding your sore back is not one of them."

"A sore back will heal. A botched proposal will lie there, dying by inches, unless you revive it."

"Or put it out of its misery. I cannot fathom why she turned me down, North. I am a toothsome lordly pup, for all she knows, and the next thing to an earl's heir."

North shifted to sink lower in the water. "You want to see a woman fidget, you ask her a question beginning with 'Why did you…?' Shuts her up faster than a loud fart in the churchyard."

He fell silent, while Beck began to *think* rather than simply rant.

"I'm wealthy," he said. "Not just comfortable, North. I've filthy, leaking pots of it, more than I could spend on three wives."

"And the great good taste to keep this vulgar state of affairs to yourself." North grunted as he shifted under the water.

"I'm not ugly."

North sighed, as if finding a more comfortable position—or tolerating another man's brokenhearted maundering. "I will allow you your petty conceits regarding your appearance, which is passable."

"I have all my teeth."

No comment.

"She says I'm kind, and I get on with Allie."

"Allie is a tolerant little soul. Witness: she likes me."

"Adores you and your horse, at least one of whom is passably good-looking."

"A female of discernment."

Beck swirled his hand through the steam rising from the pool. "I wonder if it's not so much that Sara won't marry me, and more that something impedes her from choosing freely."

North was silent for a few heartbeats. "Haddonfield, you have your moments of inspiration, few though they are in number. Did you bring your nancy soap?"

"My future is imperiled here, and you want to scrub up?"

"I fail to see how your love life, as you call some pretensions toward romping, will benefit by my eschewing a good wash. I can be both sympathetic and clean. How much do you know about Sara's first marriage?"

"I know Reynard was a cad who exploited her shamelessly," Beck said slowly. "He was selfish in all the ways that matter—every one of them—and she hasn't said it, but she was relieved when he died." For which, Beck of all people did not blame her.

North shrugged in the water, causing concentric ripples to fan away from him. "Maybe she's just reluctant to remarry. Were you going to get that soap?"

Beck rose in a shower of steaming water. "You don't have to dissemble with me, your enfeebled lordship. I watched you try to navigate that bank."

"I don't want to go sailing onto my arse when I'm naked as the day I was born, and have only you to lend assistance."

"Idiot." Beck slogged to the bank, retrieved the soap, and lobbed it across the water at North. "Your back is killing you, and you are afraid if you fall, you won't get up."

There was silence from the water, perhaps because North was as appalled as Beckman himself at this bald pronouncement.

"Not killing me, precisely." North put the soap to use on one muscular arm. "But muttering threats to that effect. I might have overdone it a bit riding into town on Saturday."

"On horseback," Beck pressed, rejoining him in the water, "or did you for once show a little common sense and take the wagon?"

Another silence.

"If it wouldn't threaten you with permanent lameness, I'd thrash the daylights out of you, North. What can you be thinking?"

"Well… as to that." North swished around in the water to rinse. "I wasn't really thinking."

"Oh?"

"No, I was not. Soap?"

Beck swiped it out of his hand and began scrubbing vigorously. "Did something rob you of your feeble wits?"

"Someone." North's teeth gleamed as he smiled wistfully in the dark.

"Hauled your ashes, did she?" Beck paused to smile back at him, relieved at least somebody had enjoyed their weekend—more like two somebodies.

"Not quite." North's smile faded. "But she appended a little lecture to our dealings, you see, and I was disconcerted to be told I needn't be proposing, for she'd turn me down flat were I to wax inconveniently chivalrous. I'm well suited to a little rustic diversion, but not the kind of man who need offer marriage. I believe this rejection was offered in an attempt to encourage my dishonorable attentions on future occasions."

He shut Beck up for about five long seconds, because a speech of that length from North required pondering.

"Sorry, North." Beck pitched the soap onto the bank. "You didn't even get to propose before she was handing you your boots."

"Rather puts your situation in perspective."

"Women." It was said in unison, part prayer, part curse, and all bewilderment.

❧

"I think North's back is finally improving," Sara said as she helped Polly with the last of the tidying up after supper.

"It should have taken days, not weeks." Polly blew a strand of hair out of her eyes. "He is the most stubborn man I've ever met, and if it were getting cooler, not warmer, I doubt his back would be healing at even this rate. Shall we have a cup of tea?"

"We shall not. I'm going to tuck Allie in, and then get the laundry handed around."

"Wasn't Allie supposed to do that?"

"She did the chickens for me instead. I don't think she's cut out to be a housekeeper. She will always choose the outdoor task over the indoor task."

"You're outside plenty." Polly rinsed out a washcloth, and started going over the counters one last time while Sara did the same with the table.

"I am, but if I were keeping house in a less rural setting, say in Bath or York, I'd be a creature of the house, and the maids and footmen would be the ones beating the rugs and so on."

"And are you thinking Bath or York might bear consideration?"

She was. With a third polite, ominous letter from Tremaine, Sara was indeed thinking of housekeeping elsewhere. Sara glanced at Polly over her shoulder and saw her sister expected an answer.

"When did you get so perceptive, little Polonaise?"

"When I turned sixteen. I do not want to leave here, Sara. The place is just coming to life, and Allie is comfortable here."

"She doesn't know any better." Sara finished the table and draped her rag over the back of a chair. "Would you be as attached to Three Springs if North weren't here?"

"Would you be as anxious to leave if Beckman weren't here?"

"Ouch."

"Yes." Polly wrung out her rag within an inch of its wet little life. "Ouch."

"I don't think North will stay much longer, Polly." Sara kept her tone gentle, though she hurt for her sister.

"I'm counting on him leaving." Polly crossed her arms and leaned back against the counter. "Not really counting on it, but assuming it will come to pass. I just hope…"

"There was your first mistake." Sara surveyed the kitchen tiredly. "No hoping, Polly, you're less likely to be disappointed that way."

"What a cheerful lady you've become. Since your little visit to Portsmouth, you've been distracted, Sara."

"Since getting Tremaine's first letter."

Polly studied the pots that hung from the rafters like so many weapons in an armory. "So answer the man. Don't give him an excuse to come calling and start charming Allie away from all good sense."

"God in heaven." Sara's expression blanked with dismay. "You don't think he'd follow in Reynard's footsteps?"

"If he follows in any of Reynard's footsteps," Polly rejoined darkly, "I'll cook him a meal he won't live to digest."

Polly took herself off to bed on that note, leaving Sara to deliver the various piles of clean laundry around the house. But Sara considered the prospect of trundling up and down several sets of steps, several times, and possibly running into Beckman—polite, friendly Beckman, whose eyes in the days since they'd been to Portsmouth always held a hint of a question—and decided Allie could handle that chore in the morning.

Allie could not, however, write a reply letter to Tremaine St. Michael.

Directing her steps to the library, Sara tried to draft the letter in her mind. She got out pen, paper, sand,

and ink, and stared at the blank page, then managed, "Dear Tremaine."

Dear Tremaine? *Dear?*

"I thought you'd be in bed by now." Beckman stood at the door, looking tired, damp from his nightly soak, and wary.

Sara gave him a tentative smile. "Trying to see to some correspondence. Do you need the desk?"

"Just some ink." Beck sidled into the room and propped a hip on the desk, surveying her. "So how fare you, Sara Hunt?"

The question was there in his eyes, and a hint of concern too. Sara stared at the inkwell rather than look on either. "I'm tired. You?"

"Tired as well. May I ask you a question?"

She braced herself for some scathing inquiry, though his manner was not belligerent. "Of course."

"It's been nearly two weeks since we returned from Portsmouth." He picked up the inkwell, a once-elegant little silver bottle dented with age and use. "Was that single weekend to be the extent of your frolic with me, Sara?"

Sara felt the civility of that question, the dispassion of it, start minute fractures in the region of her heart. "I told you we weren't to attach significance to our dealings, Beckman. You knew that."

He set the inkwell down just out of her reach on the desk. "Sara, I've missed you."

The fractures cracked so abruptly Sara was surprised her pain wasn't audible. "You see me at every meal. I see you."

"You look through me at every meal," Beck said.

"If you are not interested in continuing our liaison, then you have only to tell me. I will leave you in peace, if that's what you want."

"What I want…" What she wanted was impossible, particularly with Tremaine's threat hanging ever closer. She rose, that being necessary if she was to leave the room—and the man sharing it with her.

"What do you want?" Beck prompted, closing the distance between them. "Tell me what you want, Sara, and I'll do what I can to see you have it. I'll leave if you like, though I'd as soon not abandon Three Springs yet."

"I don't want you to leave." She was positive—*certain*—of that much, but only that much.

"Let me hold you." Beck didn't wait for her permission but took the last step between them and enfolded her in his arms. He urged her against his body, and Sara slipped her arms around him.

God in heaven, *she had missed him*. More than she knew, more than was rational.

"Better," Beck murmured, his hands moving over her back. "Talk to me, Sara. Put your arms around me and talk to me."

Her tired brain started making a list: His bergamot scent, his heat, his strength, and the way he pitched his voice. His blue, blue eyes, the way firelight caught red highlights in his golden hair.

"I've missed you too."

"What else? You missed me, but you've not wanted to let me know it, Sara. What else is going on in that busy mind of yours?"

She shook her head and held him more tightly.

"I have a few things for you." Beck slid his fingers around her wrist. "Things I meant to give you in Portsmouth, but the moment never presented itself. Nothing of great value, but they aren't items I can use or give to another."

She wavered, and he waited. He didn't tug on her wrist, wheedle, or start in kissing, any one of which would have given her something to brace her resistance against. Instead, he held her with silent patience.

Sara's objections—she had them, surely she did—tossed down their weapons and limped off the field of common sense.

He held her hand as they passed through the house.

"This place is positively sparkling," he said, "and the gardens and lawns have come along as well."

This was the cunning flattery of a man who knew that a woman kept house so that others might enjoy the results.

She returned fire as best she could. "To say nothing of the acreage. You and North have been working miracles, but I never noticed North's tendency to be contrary before you arrived. He delights in it."

"He's not used to taking orders or having anybody to discuss his ideas with. We're reaching accommodations, but it's an education for us both."

Sara glanced around his sitting room and moved to light some more candles. "Because you are used to being listened to?"

"Leave them." Beck took the taper from her hand. "And yes, Sara Hunt, I am used to being listened to, at least when I'm on the earldom's business. But you are my business now, and the silence between us is not comfortable. Come."

Beck led her by the wrist into his bedroom, then rummaged in his wardrobe to retrieve some packages. He put them on the bed, sat on the mattress himself and patted the place beside him.

Such an innocent gesture, his big hand patting the quilt.

When Sara sat, Beck passed her a paper-wrapped parcel. "These, I made myself. My brother calls them house Hessians, and they're based on his design, with some improvements. Three weeks ago, the mornings were chilly, and... well. Open them, see what you think."

"I've never seen the like..." She withdrew a cross between a boot and a slipper, fleecy on the inside, suede on the outside, with a sturdy sole. "These are lovely and practical, and I wish I'd had them last winter."

"They do keep the feet warm, and though they get worn, they'll last. This one next." Beck passed her another parcel.

A set of new brushes and combs, followed by a green velvet dressing gown and a flannel nightgown that would wrap her from nose to toes. The last package, though, contained a summer nightgown of soft, soft cotton. Flowers were embroidered along the neck and bodice in an intricate, colorful pattern of gold, green, and red that repeated around the hem.

"This is too fine, Beckman." Sara traced the exquisite needlework with a single fingertip. "You cannot give me something so costly."

So intimate.

"I can't exactly wear it myself, and you need new ones, Sara. You need a new wardrobe, in fact, and should let me take the lot of you up to Town to see to it once the hay comes off."

"Hush." Sara leaned into him, gathering the nightgown to her nose and bringing his bergamot scent with it. When a man spoke for a woman's wardrobe, that woman had better be his wife if she wanted to preserve her reputation—or her sanity.

And Sara would not be Beckman's wife. She'd made a joke of his proposal, and he'd let her. Bless him and confound him for letting that sorry moment remain unremarked.

"Thank you, Beckman."

"You like them?"

She nodded, her nose buried in the nightgown. His arms came around her, and she snuggled into him.

"I almost bought you a violin," he admitted. "I can leave mine here instead, and you'll play it when you have some privacy, if you've a mind to."

"I won't play it." Sara sat up, feeling a queer hitch in her chest. She *should not* play Beckman's violin. "But it's a generous thought."

"I'd like to hear you play." Beck smoothed her hair back. "Let's put those brushes to some use, shall we?"

He never issued her orders—he never had to. Sara set the nightgown aside. "I should tell you no."

"You'd be telling yourself no. Will you put the nightgown on for me?" Beck's lips descended to the side of her neck, a brush of tenderness, heat, and bergamot. Sara cast around for the reasons why she should deny him—deny them both—and came up empty-handed.

When she said nothing, Beck turned her by the shoulders. She felt his hands moving on the back of her dress, slowly exposing her skin, her laces, and her shift to him.

"Let me." He knelt before her and drew off her half boots, then untied her garters and rolled down her stockings. Sara's hands of their own accord winnowed through his hair then slipped over his jaw before he sat back.

He had shaved recently—for her?

Her mind started adding to that earlier list: the feel of his hair in her fingers, the rhythm of his breathing as he grew aroused, the skim of his hands anywhere on her person.

"Now up." Beck drew her to her feet, slid her dress up, her shift and stays off, and just like that, Sara was naked before him in the candlelight. His gaze traveled over her slowly, his expression starkly reverent. He dropped the pretty nightgown over her head and stepped back.

When Sara met his gaze, he spun one finger in a slow twirl, and Sara obediently turned in a circle. The nightgown made her feel feminine and graceful, billowing softly with her movement then settling against her skin. When she met Beck's gaze again, his hands were on his falls, one eyebrow arched in question.

The kind thing to do, the decent, appropriate, honorable thing to do, would be to kiss his cheek, thank him sincerely, and get the devil back to the safety of her bed.

The lonely, cold, empty safety of her bed.

Fourteen

"MY TURN, SIR." SARA SAW APPROVAL, ANTICIPATION, and all manner of lusty things in Beck's eyes. Her fingers shook slightly as she slid his sleeve buttons from his cuffs, and shook even more as she undid his falls. When she knelt to take off his slipper boots, his hand glanced over her hair, and she had to concentrate, focus her mind, and think to draw her next breath.

She rose and leaned in, pressing her forehead to Beck's sternum. "I shouldn't let myself do this."

"You shouldn't deny yourself this," he countered, stroking his hand down her braid. "Not tonight. With me, not ever."

Ever with Beckman could end any day, given how his father was failing. On the strength of that thought, Sara started on his shirt buttons. When she'd worked her way up from the bottom button, she parted the linen and pushed it to the side so she could lay her cheek over his heart. His hands settled on her shoulders, kneading gently, and she felt the tension of the day ebbing.

Beck kissed her cheek. "Enough thinking. I believe you were in the process of undressing me."

She pressed a kiss to his bare chest and slipped the shirt off, then ran a fingertip down his sternum. "In just the few weeks you've been here, you've put on muscle, and you were in fine condition when you arrived."

Beck drew in a breath at her touch. "As long as you like what you see, I won't complain about resembling a stevedore."

Sara wanted to linger, to inspect and tease and play at sophisticated games having to do with pleasure and anticipation.

More than any of that, though, she wanted to kiss him. She stepped in close, wrapped a hand around the back of his neck, and stretched up on her toes to touch her lips to his. His arms closed around her in earnest, and he sealed his mouth to hers with a growl.

"Breeches," Sara whispered against his neck a moment later. "Have to get you out of them."

He took her hands and set them on his waist, but didn't stop the progress of his lips over her eyes, cheeks, chin, and brow. Rather than look down, Sara found his waistband and pushed his clothes off him. He stepped back only long enough to free himself from them altogether then swooped in to resume kissing her.

"Bed," Sara reminded him.

Beck scooped her up, tossed her onto the bed, then climbed in behind her. "God above, how I've missed you."

Sara did not want to talk with him, or rather, she wanted to talk too badly, to lay her burdens across his muscular shoulders. Beckman would accept those burdens—he was a man in the habit of accepting burdens—but he'd want answers first.

Sara lay back and lifted her knees, feet spread on the bed.

"Don't make me wait, Beckman."

§

A man who'd traveled to many a foreign port developed both an ability to observe his environs and an instinct for when something, some small detail was out of place. Beck had learned to listen to that instinct.

A nervous horse could signal that ambush lay around the bend of a sleepy provincial road. A serving girl a little too friendly might be a hint that the fancy English gentleman's wine had been drugged.

Sara's responses, hesitant, then eager, and now nearly desperate, were setting off an indistinct alarm in Beck's mind. She hadn't explained two weeks of apparent indifference, hadn't apologized for it, hadn't assured him there would be no more of the same. She hadn't made any reference whatsoever to his failed proposal either—though he knew damn well she hadn't taken it as a jest.

Those silences on her part should matter, though Beck's body wanted them to matter *later*. Sara brushed her fingers up his erection, sending a cannonade of pleasure over the deck of Beck's thinking brain. She took him in her hand, then, a broadside to his reason, and tried to tug him closer to her body.

He resisted. "Tell me you missed me."

"I've missed you, Beckman Sylvanus Haddonfield," Sara whispered near his ear. "I missed the feel of you."

She tugged on him again. "In my hands, in my body. I missed the scent of you, the taste of you. I missed the feel of your hands on me, missed the sound of your voice in the dark."

He needed desperately to ask her why, if she'd missed him, she'd held herself at such a distance and not even considered his proposal.

He needed *more* desperately to join with her again. She undulated against him, a bodily plea for consummation that echoed his own dearest desire. Her hands ran over his back, hips, and buttocks while her teeth scraped up his neck.

"Please." Sara arched up and hugged him to her.

"Easy," Beck cautioned. "No rush."

"Want you."

Love now, talk later. "I'm right here, love." He gave her the first increment of penetration, then stilled and waited for her body to accommodate him. When her breathing slowed and he felt her sigh softly against his neck, he let himself glide another half inch deeper into the glory of her heat.

"You." Sara kissed the side of his neck, and her body relaxed further, her trust in him manifest in her willingness to give him unilateral control of this most precious intimacy. He gave a slow hitch of his hips and gained another half inch, then another.

He advanced and waited, advanced and waited, his arousal a steady burning in his whole body. Even so, he could spend an eternity just joining his body to Sara's and know no frustration; it felt that right to be making love with her.

When he was hilted inside her, he went completely

still and gathered her against him. To have this closeness with Sara was sweet, dear, and more overwhelmingly precious than anything Beck could recall. He tried to find a name for what he felt, for the sense of being in the one place, with the one person, he was supposed to be.

Homecoming.

The term settled in his mind, and he began to move in her. Slow, steady thrusts that had Sara groaning softly beneath him and undulating in counterpoint to him. He plied her with monumental patience and self-restraint, bringing her to orgasm easily then letting her recover while he barely moved. When she'd found her balance, he eased her up again, then let her recover once more.

"I'm being greedy." Sara brushed his hair back from his forehead and stretched beneath him. "We both need our rest."

Beck nuzzled her shoulder. "Are you *complaining*? Are you suggesting I've kept you awake, Sara Hunt?" Though he had, and she needed her rest.

"I've kept you awake, but I feel boneless now, Beck. Light and warm and…"

"And…?"

"Happy," Sara conceded. "It makes no sense, but I feel happy."

He kissed her cheek and wondered why happiness in the arms of a lover should make no sense. "I will endeavor to make you happier still."

The tenor of his lovemaking shifted, became more… serious.

"Beck…" In her breathless whisper, Beck felt Sara's

body gathering for yet another bout of pleasuring. "I'm content, beyond content. More would be too much… Beckman?"

"Hush." He levered up on his arms and gazed down, frankly staring at the place where their bodies joined. "I say when it's too much, Sara. Trust me."

He picked up the tempo by increments, watching her face in the glow of the candles, then watching the thick, glistening length of his cock sinking into her heat.

"Beck…" She arched up and wrapped her arms around his neck. He capitulated this time, folding down over her, thrusting into her with banked force.

"Too much…"

Never too much, not with her. Beck drove himself into her, even when her body seized around him, even when she dug her nails into his back and moaned against his shoulder. Her contractions became deeper and stronger; then she fisted around him in one interminable spasm that sent him over the edge.

Beck felt his orgasm start in that drawing-up sensation at the base of his spine; then pleasure swamped him, running right up his center and off into the infinite reaches of his body. He heard someone groan—him?—and bucked and throbbed as his seed left him, heard another groan as he tried to draw in air to sustain him while the pleasure built and built.

It didn't end, it just… diffused, becoming more and more softly focused until every particle of him was light and warm and… happy.

God, yes, he was happy.

"Don't move." Sara patted his buttocks, and that

made him happy too, a little stroking caress Beck felt all over.

"Can't move," he murmured against her shoulder. "Not yet."

"Good."

The infernal woman found other ways to touch him. Ran her tongue along his neck, drew her toe up his calf, and nuzzled his ear, but they were little touches, the gestures a woman thoroughly wrung out by passion could offer.

"I'm crushing you."

"I love the weight of you. It's comforting, when my body feels so overcome it might float away."

He didn't believe that, not when there was fifteen stone of him comforting her like so much filleted mackerel. Sending up a sincere prayer for strength first, Beck levered up on his forearms. "You all right?"

Sara brushed his hair back. "You ask me that when you've pleasured me witless. I am fine. Witless, but fine."

"Good." He kissed her nose and carefully extricated himself from her body. "I'm fine too. Don't move."

"As if I could." Sara lay on her back, knees bent, gaze on him as he crossed to the hearth.

He scrubbed himself off briskly, taking in the sight of her sprawled without a lick of modesty—or worry—then did a much more careful job with her.

Sara watched him as he hung the cloth over the edge of the basin. "Next time, I will tend to this washing-up business."

So there was to be a next time?

Beck blew out all but one candle and crawled over the mattress to cover her again with his body. "Next time, I will pleasure you so witless you won't be able to speak, much less move when we're through."

He braced over her, tucking her face against his collarbone and laying his cheek on her crown. "You're truly fine? I become enthusiastic at times."

"You become..." Sara kissed his throat. "Breathtaking, spectacular, unbelievable. You truly ought to be the subject of a royal proclamation."

He rolled them so Sara was atop him.

"Maybe I won't pleasure you out of your speech." Beck buried his fingers in a fistful of her hair. "You spout such flatteries, and a man needs to hear them sometimes. Particularly when the woman in his arms is so very breathtaking herself when she's about her pleasuring."

And when she's not.

"Ah, Beck..." Sara tucked herself against his chest. "You are the sweetest man, the most dear, and the most dangerous."

Sweet and dear were flattering. When he'd unplaited her braid and indulged himself with a long session of stroking her hair, Beck fell asleep wondering if being dangerous in Sara's mind was really a good thing.

He came awake slowly, convinced Heifer had found his way to the bed and was flicking his tail over Beck's cheek. When his eyes opened, though, the single guttering candle revealed North's saturnine features as he used a lock of Sara's hair to brush against Beck's nose.

North looked diabolically dark and unhappy—darker and unhappier than usual. He gestured silently with his thumb toward the sitting room, waiting until

Beck nodded before he turned to go. Beck shrugged into his dressing gown and mentally catalogued the list of emergencies that could merit this unprecedented intrusion—Allie falling ill, Ulysses coming down with colic, Polly going missing?—then paused by the bed and tucked the covers up over Sara's shoulders.

Beck closed the door between the bedroom and the sitting room, ready to offer North a whispered tongue-lashing, but the expression on North's face stopped him.

"Allie? Polly?"

"No, lad." North's eyes, usually so guarded and mocking, held regret. "Your dear papa has gone to his reward, and I fear it is my sad duty to be the first to address you as Reston."

"Papa?"

"I am so sorry, Beckman."

"It isn't… unexpected." But Beck's lungs were fighting to draw breath, and his hands had a sudden sensation of emptiness. His guts felt empty; his life felt empty.

"The rider from Linden is in the kitchen," North went on, gaze on a carrying candle flickering on the low table. "He said your brother Ethan and your sister Nita were with the earl, but the old fellow just slipped away quietly in his sleep. The funeral will be on Friday."

"I want…"

"Anything you need," North replied. "Name it."

He wanted his papa. Wanted another acerbic lecture assuring him his father loved him, forgave him his many shortcomings, would be there to forgive him again when he stumbled, because Beck always, eventually, stumbled. And the earl always found some way for him to redeem himself, to allow them both the fiction that someday, the stumbling would be over.

"Beck." North laid a hand on Beck's arm, and it was enough—one simple gesture of caring from a man who lived a study of indifference was enough—to make the earl's death more real.

Beck shook his head at nothing in particular, but when he felt North draw him closer, he leaned on his friend.

"I'm having Soldier and Ulysses saddled," North said. "You can be at Linden before dawn, and the baron's stables will provide remounts. You can make that funeral if you leave now and the clouds don't obscure the moon."

Beck pulled away, though he wanted to cling, curse, or possibly put out North's lights. "Gabriel, I don't want to go."

North nodded, a world of sympathy in his expression. "You don't want to, but you need to. I'll pack your clothes. Polly is putting you together some food. You might want to say something to Sara."

Beck glanced at his bedroom door. What would he say?

"Let's get you dressed," North suggested. North did most of the dressing, while Beck stood there, silent and passive. "You know the roads between here and Kent?"

"I do."

"You going to wake Sara up?" North tied a simple knot in Beck's neckcloth. "I can wake her, if you'd rather."

"Let her sleep."

"At least leave the woman a note, Beckman." North passed him his riding boots. "She's in your bed, for pity's sake, and you won't be here in the morning with any explanations."

North wasn't judging Sara's location, but by his tone he was mightily definite on the obligation Beck had to leave a note. Beck *wouldn't* be here in the morning. In all likelihood, he would never be here again.

"A note, then." Beck pulled on his boots, wishing for all he was worth he could stay in that bed beside Sara until morning, wishing she could make this journey with him. What an odd reaction to a very expected death.

He wanted—he needed—to at least see her before he left his rooms, because for all he knew—and quite possibly for all Sara cared—he wouldn't be coming back.

"I'll be down directly." Beck stood and glanced around his room, as if he'd find answers by inventorying his surroundings.

"Get your shaving gear," North said. "I'll fetch clean clothes for you from the laundry." Beck nodded his acquiescence then didn't want North to go—to leave him alone.

"My thanks, Gabriel."

"Beck?"

"Hmm?" Beck left off eyeing the door to the bedroom again, torn between wanting to wake Sara up and the greater kindness of letting her sleep.

"The rider in the kitchen," North said. "He'll call you my lord, and Lord Reston, and he'll be wearing a black armband." He didn't have to add, because Beck understood clearly, those small ritual courtesies were going to hurt like hell.

"I know that." Beck let out a breath. "And so it begins."

"You'll manage, because you have to, and because your papa expected you would—also because you've no bloody choice." The last was offered with a hint of the typical North dissatisfaction with life, but it gave Beck a ghost of a reason to smile.

North left him alone, without further reassurances, but the warning had been needed and kind. Beck *was* the Bellefonte heir now, complete with courtesy title, and Nicholas, God help him, was the earl.

Beck stayed in his sitting room for maybe five minutes, trying to gather his wits, then gave up. There was no way to go from making love to Sara, sleeping with his arms wrapped around her, to dealing with the earl's... passing.

His *death*.

"Papa is dead." Beck said the words experimentally. "Papa is at peace."

That was true too, he realized, gathering up his shaving kit. "Papa is at peace, and he's gone. And I never said I was sorry for all the times I let him down."

He grimaced, because these soliloquies were not fortifying him in the least. He gave one last look at his bedroom door, squared his shoulders, and left the privacy of his chambers. He stopped in the library, thinking to pen Sara a note, but when his candlelight fell over the surface of the desk, he saw somebody had set out the writing paraphernalia already.

Sara, he recalled, when he'd come down here looking for a pot of ink.

"Dear Tremaine?"

Who in the bloody hell was Tremaine, and what did he mean to Sara?

Voices drifted up from the kitchen, Polly and North speaking in the quiet tones of people who didn't want to wake the rest of the household. Beck wanted to crumple up the paper but left it, thinking he'd pass a message to Sara through Polly rather than alert anyone to what he'd seen. Still feeling a sense of unreality, he directed his steps to the kitchen where the buttery, domestic scent of breakfast cooking hit his nose.

"My lord." The rider, looking haggard and wind-blown, stood.

"Jamie." Beck recognized the old groom he'd worked with for two years at the Linden stables in Sussex. When the grizzled former jockey would have bowed, Beck pushed at his shoulder and wrapped him in a hug. "You're too old to hare across the shires like this."

Jamie smiled up at him. "Not too old to bring you the good news as well as the bad, Becky, me lad."

Becky, me lad. The grief and shock eased minutely. "What good news could there possibly be?" Beck eyed the black armband on Jamie's jacket.

Jamie grinned from ear to ear. "Your wee brother has hisself a countess, Beck. Married a few days past and got word of the deed to your papa before the old earl cocked up his toes."

Beck rubbed his jaw in wonder. "Nick is married?"

"At your granddame's town house. Wee Nick wanted it done proper, so the lady's father couldn't cry foul."

"This is... good news. Interesting good news."

"They'll be expecting you at Linden by first light," Jamie went on, "and they'll have remounts waiting for you. The baroness said you're to break your fast with her, regardless of the hour, and I'd not vex the lady by ignoring her, were I you."

"Wouldn't dream of it." Beck's mind struggled to keep up with the conversation, even as Polly set a stack of griddle cakes with butter and honey before him.

"Eat," she said. "You don't want to, but you need to."

Her unwitting quote of North had Beck smiling distractedly, and he did as she ordered, not because he wanted to or needed to, but because refusing her efforts would hurt her feelings.

North came in from the laundry, a tightly wrapped bundle in his hands. "Your clothes. Polly, be a love and pack the man a couple of flasks, brandy in one, sweetened tea in the other. He'll need some comestibles he can eat in the saddle too."

Polly moved off without a word, but Beck had to wonder what she was thinking.

Did she know who Tremaine was? Was he Polly's dear Tremaine too? A cousin? An uncle? If the ladies had a relative who could offer them aid—and the relative had declined to do so—Beck was going to...

He wasn't going to do anything except... except finish his meal and go to his father's funeral.

North came in from the back hallway just as Beck was taking his empty plate to the sink.

"Horses are ready," North said, "and you're as ready as you'll ever be."

"Amen to that." Beck's eyes went to the stairway, and as if he'd conjured her, Sara appeared, her slipper boots first, followed by the green hem of the velvet dressing gown Beck had given her earlier in the evening.

"Beckman?" Sara's expression was sleepy and curious, and her hair—her glorious, unbelievably lovely hair—spilled down her back in cascades of fiery beauty.

"I'm off to Belle Maison," Beck said, holding out a hand to her. Unmindful of Polly and North disappearing to the back porch, he wrapped his arms around her.

"Your father?"

"Gone." Beck closed his eyes and thanked God for this chance to hold her before he left. She didn't say anything but held him to her, her arms around him, her face pressed to his collarbone. The great hard knot of loss in his throat eased another fraction. "I wish…" He stopped and swallowed, then soldiered on. "I wish you could come with me."

Sara leaned back to brush his hair with her fingers. "I wish I could spare you this, go in your place and spare you the loss of your father. And I will remind you to not take chances as you travel, Beckman. One funeral at a time is more than enough."

"Yes, ma'am." He kissed her cheek, touched by her warning and fortified as well. "Do something for me?"

She nodded, holding his gaze when he would have given anything to hear the words "Must you go?" from her even once.

"Sleep in my bed tonight?"

Another nod, accompanied by a blush. He was

relieved he didn't need to explain or bargain or suffer her refusal.

"I'll be off, then."

Before he could turn to go, Sara caught his arm and looped it over her shoulders. "I'll walk you to your horse."

"Horses. I'll lead one, ride the other, and make better time. Linden will provide fresh horses, and I should make the funeral at Belle Maison by Friday."

"Your half-crazy brother might be completely crazy by then."

"To say nothing of my sisters." And Ethan—God above, at least Ethan had been with the earl at his death. That had to count for something.

Beck grabbed his coat, and they reached the back porch. Seeing North patting Soldier over at the mounting block did something to Beck's insides. The hastily consumed meal threatened to rebel, but just when the question became pressing, Sara slipped her hand into Beck's.

She squeezed his fingers. "I'll keep you in my thoughts and prayers."

"And you will be in mine," Beck replied, relieved to have some sentiment from her suggesting… what?

That they meant something to each other. Something that would transcend distance and parting. Because this was parting. He'd never represented that it could be anything else, except when he had offered her the entire rest of his life and all his worldly goods.

"Safe journey." Sara hugged him again, kissed his cheek, and settled back, wrapping her dressing gown around her.

"Godspeed," North echoed, stepping back to let him climb aboard Ulysses. "If you lose the moonlight, don't be stupid. Put up until dawn, which will be along soon enough."

"Yes, Gabriel." Beck swung up onto his horse and accepted Soldier's reins from North. He saluted with his crop, blew Sara a kiss, and trotted off into the night.

North watched as Polly sent a pitying look at her sister then turned to get back to the house where she'd, no doubt, be making use of her handkerchief where North had no opportunity to comfort her.

When Sara started to cry, North wrapped his arms around her, tucked his worn handkerchief into her hand, and fashioned a lengthy list of curses that included full moons, elderly earls, stubborn lordlings, and even more stubborn housekeepers.

✦

"His penmanship is exemplary, and he says the funeral was lovely." North frowned at Beck's note. "How can a funeral be lovely, of all the perishing nonsense? His brother's wife is lovely, his sisters are lovely. Lovely, lovely, lovely. Here." He thrust the note at Polly, who passed it to Sara. "I have work to do, and you lovely ladies can decipher this. If I'm not back by midday you may assume the piskies have stolen lovely me for their own."

"Mind you don't miss the meal," Polly called as he stalked from the kitchen to the back hallway. She sipped her tea—Sara had flavored this batch with bergamot—while Sara read the note. Gabriel needed to be alone—never had God fashioned a man more suited to being alone—and Sara needed company.

Sara scanned the note and sat back. "It's as North indicates. Pleasantries and platitudes, but at least Beckman writes those."

"To North, he can't really write much else. It hasn't been a week, Sara. He may write more when the edge of his grief has dulled."

"I know." She managed to put a world of loss into two words, though Polly heard the hope Sara would never admit, too. "I wrote to Tremaine."

About time. "Good."

"You don't know what I wrote."

"You're overset," Polly said gently. "The man you care for has gone to bury his father, likely never to return, and you're worried for him. You're also worried for us, and Beckman isn't here for you to confide in."

"I wouldn't do that, Polly." Sara picked up her teacup, holding it under her nose as if she were sniffing the rising steam. "If Beckman knew what lay in our past, he'd have no choice but to take himself off to his titled life and put as much distance between us as he could. His father dying when he did was a mercy."

"He was the spare in truth a week ago," Polly said. "The heir has finally married, and so Beck's only presumptive now. I truly don't believe it matters to him, in any case, or he would have married by now."

"He did." Sara's misery was audible. "And she died, and I'm sure he loved her."

This was news, and likely some of the explanation for how distracted and distant Sara had been since coming back from Portsmouth. "She didn't die recently."

Sara shook her head. "Years ago, and he hasn't remarried or settled down. I believe he's still attached to her memory."

"He's talked about his dead wife with *you*?" Polly's protective instincts were stirring, though this was exactly the kind of confidence she might have treasured from Gabriel North.

"I asked. He answered only the questions I put to him, but in what he didn't say, I can tell he has feelings for her still."

Polly topped up Sara's tea when what she wanted was to rail against the lunacy of the male gender generally. "So he has feelings for her, but she's gone, and it's you who can't wait to dive into your green dressing gown each night, and who has started wearing your new bootish things all over the house. It's you who looks down the drive a hundred times a day, and you who has slept in his bed since the night he left."

"I want the scent of him—I want even just the scent of him."

They were probably the most honest and private words Sara had said to Polly in years. Polly wished she didn't understand them so easily.

"Sara, he could well come back." Polly did not believe these words, but a loyal sister had an obligation to be kind as well as honest.

That Sara didn't bother arguing caused more alarm than relief. "Tremaine wants to come for a visit, and I did not wave him off, not exactly."

"*You didn't?*" Polly rose, stalked across the kitchen, whirled, and stalked back. "Don't you think such a drastic measure called for a little consultation first,

Sarabande?" For Tremaine to visit when Beckman—
Lord Reston—was not on the premises made no sense
if Sara feared Tremaine's intentions, and yet Beck
wasn't offering to return.

Sara rose as well. "He will not visit. You wanted
me to write to him, to assure him all was well, but
he won't believe those assurances unless he hears
something approaching a welcome. All is well, Polly,
we're managing now, and Three Springs looks better
than it has in decades. I reminded him that a housekeeper hasn't the authority to invite guests, which is
the simple truth. He won't come, but if he did, now
would be the time for him to see we're not in need of
his avuncular resources."

Polly stopped short and narrowed her eyes on her
sister. "You're bluffing, then." There was some sense
in Sara's position—they'd bluffed their way through
many a daunting circumstance—also some risk. "Did
you explain this to Beckman?"

"Explain what to Beckman?" North's rasping baritone cut through the tension in the kitchen.

"There's a remote possibility we'll have company,"
Polly said, giving Sara time to form her answer.
"Family might drop by, briefly, one hopes."

"Family?" North's green eyes narrowed. "I've
known you ladies for going on three years, and
now family pops out of the woodwork? I'm just the
steward, so the goings-on here in the house could
not possibly affect me, you understand, yet I admit to
curiosity. Who is this family?"

Just the steward. Polly wanted to have at him with a
rolling pin.

Sara answered with enviable composure. "His name is Tremaine St. Michael, and he's my late husband's half brother. He has been writing lately to inquire as to Allie's well-being, and in his latest letter has suggested he'd like to visit. I said we appreciated his concern but intimated that a visit wouldn't be appropriate, given our positions here."

"You hope he won't visit," North countered abruptly. He regarded Sara, then Polly, then Sara again, his frown deepening. "Mind you warn the child. I was thinking to take her into the village with me this afternoon, if you ladies don't object?"

"Of course not," Sara replied, but she'd glanced at Polly first, and Polly had no doubt that North, being North, had seen that too.

∽

"I cannot fathom why the earl didn't fire that lot of vultures." Ethan handed Beck a drink, which Beck sipped, sighed over, and set down.

"That is fine libation, Mr. Grey." Though a cup of Polly's stout black tea would have been finer.

Ethan shrugged. "One grows used to what comforts money can command. Did any of the terms of the will surprise you?"

"Your presence surprised me." Beck bent forward to tug off his boots. He was staying with Ethan at his London town house, the invitation coming as another surprise in a week full of them. At Nick's request, both Ethan and Beck had stayed in Town for the reading of the late earl's will.

"I've had some chance to get to know our new sister-in-law." Ethan's big feet appeared beside Beck's on the low table—this was the private lair of a man in charge of a bachelor household, after all. "I think Wee Nick has met his match, and I'm not inclined to wander too far afield until he acknowledges this."

The new Countess of Bellefonte, Leah, was pretty, kind, smitten with Nick, and very much up to the new earl's weight in mischief and marital machinations. That alone would have recommended her, but she'd also taken charge of the logistics of the earl's funeral, so the Haddonfield family could more effectively manage its grief.

Beck leaned his head back against soft leather and listened to the fire crackling in the hearth. What was Sara doing on this cool and cozy evening? Had Allie taken the slop bucket to Hildegard?

"Nick still carps at me to see to the succession."

Ethan eyed him dispassionately. "You're a reasonably appealing fellow. A wife solves a few problems."

"And creates others," Beck shot back. "Or are you prepared to march back up to the altar yourself, Ethan?"

"As you no doubt know," Ethan replied evenly, "when a man is lonely for certain pleasures, he need not assuage them with a wife."

"That isn't lonely, that's merely randy, and you well know the difference." Beck knew the difference too, much better than he had even weeks ago.

"I know the difference, but in my marriage, I was far lonelier than I've ever been in the unwedded state."

Beck peered at his brandy. "I have to say I came to the same conclusion, though I was married just a few months."

"And I, a few years, but they were long, long years. What happened to your wife?"

This was a question a brother shouldn't have to ask, not because it was impertinent to inquire, but because a brother—any brother—ought to know these things.

"She was carrying another man's child when we wed," Beck said, closing his eyes. "And I did not learn of this until we'd endured our honeymoon and I'd gone up to Town in deference to my new wife's wishes. She was not... *easy* in my presence. I wasn't gone three weeks before Nick told me he'd dropped in on my household, looking for me, and she was entertaining a gentleman in a compromising manner. He didn't get a look at the man's face, for which we can all be grateful."

Though it had fallen to Beck to notify the poor bastard of Devona's passing—at his wife's dying request.

Ethan crossed his feet at the ankle, a man apparently comfortable with secrets Beck hadn't intended to share with anybody. "And being Nick, he went after the man with guns blazing?"

"Being Nick, he blistered my wife's ears for all to hear. Until then, she'd thought I was the Berserker of the Bedroom's younger brother and at no risk for siring the next earl. Nick set her straight, and things went to hell from there."

"I'm sorry."

It was the same damned platitude Beck had heard over and over again, but when he glanced at Ethan—a brother and a fellow widower—there was a world of understanding in his blue eyes.

"She didn't kill herself outright." Beck stared hard at his drink. "She took steps to make sure she lost the child, but she also lost her life as a consequence. I have not acquainted Nicholas with the specific consequences of his actions, and he has atoned for them in any case."

And there was peace of a sort in that realization. For years, Beck had assuaged his own guilt by blaming Nick for interfering, blaming Nick for presuming and assuming and generally being Nick.

Bold Nick, stubborn Nick… *protective* Nick. Nick who now had his own problems and had only been trying to help.

"Atoned by retrieving you from one of your less successful journeys." Ethan cursed softly in the direction of stubborn idiot younger brothers generally, rose, and refreshed his drink. He cocked an eyebrow at Beck, who shook his head. He'd barely touched his brandy, despite being in the midst of a discussion that might make a man very thirsty indeed.

Ethan dropped down right beside Beck on the sofa. "Did you love her?"

For reasons having to do with red-haired housekeepers and difficult partings, this question had been on Beck's mind for much of the last week. His first inclination was to offer Ethan a shrug, a platitude, and the sort of smile that would allow the question to remain essentially unanswered. Ancient secrets were one thing; recent revelations were quite another.

"I was young. All young men are romantics in some corner of their souls. I loved her the way an ignorant young man loves a foolish young woman, but in hindsight, I can see it was more that I fancied the notion she would make me an adult and capable of giving Bellefonte his heir. I did not love her—I did not *know* her—but I loved the idea of her."

Ethan nudged Beck with his shoulder. "I've never considered there are actual advantages to being the bastard. This business of the succession weighs heavily between you and Nick. Too heavily."

"I told him to swive his countess." Beck raised his glass to take another sip of his drink, then changed his mind and set it aside. "He looked so haunted, Ethan, I about wanted to cry."

"He and Leah will sort it out," Ethan murmured, but Beck knew damned well that was a hope on Ethan's part, not a prediction. It was Beck's hope, too. "What will you do about your Sara?"

"She is not my Sara." Maybe she was Tremaine's Sara? "I will find some project or other that requires travel on the Continent, or perhaps head north before cooler weather arrives. Scotland is beautiful in high summer."

Scotland, for all its beauty, was also as good a place as any to be miserable, there being a liberal sprinkling of whiskey distilleries amid the glens and valleys.

"Will you be here in the morning?"

Would he? Beck did not want to return to Belle Maison, where a bevy of sisters was trying to deal with their father's passing. He did not want to visit one of Nick's smaller properties, there to idle about with memories and regrets. He did not want to impose further on Ethan's hospitality now that the will had been read.

And he was bloody damned if he wanted to freeze his parts off come grouse season, tramping about on some arctic Scottish moor.

"I will not. I haven't paid my respects to Lady Warne, and she should have a full accounting of the state of Three Springs."

"You are being stubborn, Beckman." Ethan tossed back his drink and went to an escritoire over by the windows. "Nita sent some correspondence for you out from Belle Maison. My baby brother has apparently become a man of parts."

Beck did not want to deal with his factors, did not want to fashion a reply to the stewards and agents who handled his various commercial endeavors. He wanted to get blind, roaring drunk, though he knew that to be his personal version of the road to hell.

Ethan passed him a packet of letters. "You're welcome to stay here, you know, or you could bide a while at Tydings."

This was another load of peach trees, another attempt to close a distance that had formed without either Ethan or Beckman willing it. To give himself time to come up with a response—Beck did not want to bide at Tydings, an extraneous uncle to two little boys he'd never met—he sorted through his correspondence, coming to an abrupt halt at the third epistle in the stack.

A note from North.

The hope that shot through Beck was pathetic.

"You've had some news?" Ethan asked as he resumed his place beside Beck.

"Probably a note of condolence." Beck eyed his drink but didn't pick it up. He slit the seal rather than wait until he was alone in his guest room. A slashing backhand scrawl took up exactly two lines.

*Reston, get your lordly little arse back here.
Trouble's afoot.*

> *North*
> *PS: Sincere condolences on
> your loss.*

Seven words: Get your lordly little arse back
here. They rocketed into Beck's awareness from two
directions. First, worry suffused him, pushing past the
grief and restlessness. If *North* said trouble was afoot,
if *North* asked for reinforcements, then Sara might be
in danger.

"You looked pleased," Ethan observed. "Fierce,
but pleased."

"I am." The second tangent of Beck's reaction to
the note was more than relief, it was soul-deep satisfaction at the realization that Three Springs was where
he wanted to go. The place wasn't nearly restored
to its former glory, and North's summons—it was
nothing less—suggested Beck still had a contribution
to make there. "I'll be heading south again."

"I see." Ethan studied the decanter. "As it happens,
I have business south of Town myself. I'll ride out
with you in the morning, and we can call on our
new sister-in-law together. You are leaving in the
morning, aren't you?"

"At the very first light."

Fifteen

"THEY'RE ALL DEAD." NORTH REGARDED THE SCATTERING of feathers and chicken parts at his feet. Old Angus scowled alongside of him and bent to wrap a length of twine around the culprit's neck.

"I've seen this one in town," Angus said. "He begs at every door, poor blighter. Somebody set him in the henhouse, knowing he'd be so hungry he'd get them all."

The dog's hide was filthy and matted, crisscrossed with scars and sporting clumps of burrs. The damned beast was as stupid as he was huge, sitting docilely at Angus's feet, as if he'd no clue what had befallen his dear, late friends, the chickens.

"You want I should shoot him, Mr. North?"

The dog seemed to like that suggestion, lapping eagerly at the back of North's hand and giving a pathetic little woof of enthusiasm.

"Miss Polly will want him dead. She serves up a chicken regularly," North fumed. The dog cocked his head, regarding North curiously.

"Have the boys toss him in the warm end of the

pond," North said. "Scrub the daylights out of him, and brush out those burrs. If we feed him some regular meals, he might turn out to be a decent watch dog."

"Save us digging a sizable hole if he can manage that," Angus said. "I'll see to the chickens."

"And I'll fetch us more in town this afternoon, but the first time he digs into the coop, he gets taken into the woods, Angus."

The dog woofed again and capered around happily, nearly tugging Angus over in the process.

North aimed his scowl at the chicken coop, which showed no sign of forcible entry, no sign the dog had dug under the fencing, no sign of a loose board or post. Angus had the right of it: somebody had kindly unlatched the door to the coop and set the starving dog among the chickens. And the beast had been in the pen for some time. The water in the chickens' bowl was gone, most of the eggs in the nests had been broken, and the dog had been resting contentedly among his trophies when North came upon him.

Sleeping off a chicken drunk, North thought with a reluctant smile.

His smile faded as he reflected that Beckman Haddonfield had better get himself back to Three Springs, lest the ladies be left defenseless when North departed.

❧

The old earl had been wise to send Beck on far-flung errands, because travel gave a man time to think as nothing else could.

After spending long, hard hours in the saddle—the

Downs were becoming very familiar to him—Beckman concluded he was not simply returning to Three Springs to finish an errand for Lady Warne.

He also was not resuming the simple dalliance he'd enjoyed with Sara previously. He wanted more, and she likely did not. This put him again in the position of the odd man out, the extra brother, the intemperate son who had to be kept busy elsewhere, the little boy listening at keyholes, hoping for notice from those he loved.

Beck considered his options and decided those secondary, shabby, minor roles were no longer good enough. He'd offer Sara marriage—again, but without leaving her the option of turning it into a joke—and she would have two choices. She could be his bride, the mother of his children, and most important woman in his future, or she could become a bitter-sweet memory, one of the happier parts of his past.

He was virtually certain she'd turn him down again, but he deserved more than the occasional furtive coupling, and—quite relevantly—so did she.

The question was, could he convince her of that?

"Haddonfield." Gabriel North approached from the barn, his expression more forbidding than usual. "Glad you're back."

There was an entire lecture in North's green eyes, but likely because Allie had pelted straight for Beck's arms and was at that moment barnacled to his back, North mustered his version of discretion. "Polly will want to feed you. I'll take your horse."

But Beck didn't let him off so easily.

"I'm glad to be back."

This provoked North to a twitch of the lips. "Allie, introduce Mr. Haddonfield to your latest portrait subject. Those of delicate sensibilities shouldn't come upon such a beast all unawares."

Beck lingered with Allie, admiring the enormous brindle-coated canine named Boo-boo, then admiring the filly, who had indeed grown even in Beck's short absence. He admired the new chickens as well, and paid his respects to Hildegard.

"Aren't you hungry?" Allie asked, swinging his hand. "We haven't had a single batch of muffins since you left."

Suggestion hung heavily in the air. The sun was dipping closer to the horizon, and there was nothing in the house to dread. A man was entitled to get his bearings though—before facing the woman who held his heart in her hands.

"I could use some sustenance," Beck allowed. Allie dropped his hand and headed for the back of the house at a dead run, the dog woofing and bounding along beside her.

"So you came back." Polly's greeting was not what Beck expected. She eyed him up and down, the dispassion in her gaze a trifle unnerving. "I expect you're hungry, so you'd best wash your hands."

She disappeared into the pantry with a swish of her skirts. North came in from the hallway, smelling slightly of horse.

"She's gotten more fierce," Beck said. "One can hardly conceive of it."

"She and Sara are feuding over some family issue." North went to the sink and washed his hands. "And Allie's birthday approaches, so the household is in a state of high anticipation. Allie has, after all, acquired a puppy, so what other wishes might come true on her birthday?"

And *where* was Allie's mother, so that Beck might endure her less-than-enthusiastic greeting as well?

Polly emerged from the pantry, bearing a plate stacked with sandwiches. She set it down on the counter then untied her apron. "I'm off to help Allie sketch Boo-boo. Wash up when you're done, because it's Maudie's half day."

North watched her depart with the sort of wistfulness that the dog—another simple beast—reserved for its supper.

"And just how did Allie acquire her adoring friend?" Beck asked, taking the sandwiches to the table.

North followed, and judging from the way the man took his seat, his back was at least no worse than when Beck had left for Belle Maison.

"I found him in the chicken coop, nigh insensate from his excesses." North picked up a sandwich and regarded it for a philosophical moment. "That beast is a force of nature akin to a Channel storm in the form of a dog. He ate all the chickens."

Beck paused midreach for his own sandwich. "He ate *all* the chickens? And you didn't put a bullet in his canine excuse for a brain?"

"Considered it." North chewed thoughtfully. "A dog on the property is not a bad idea."

"A chicken-eating dog?"

"Any dog will eat chickens if he's starving and enclosed with a sufficient quantity of them." North offered no further explanation but shot Beck a questioning glance.

"We're alone," Beck said, and wasn't that just a fine state of affairs when a man traveled two days over hill and dale in the broiling sun on the strength of seven words that had yet to be explained? "Your note—a monument to literary subtlety, by the way—mentioned trouble."

North, being North, had to finish chewing then take his bloody damned time selecting the exact perfect next sandwich.

Beck waited. Even knowing he had yet to face Sara, something in his gut was glad to be… home. To be *here,* rather, where his lordly arse might be of some use to people he cared about.

"My note got you back here," North observed. "The dog wasn't the first incident. Someone put him in the chicken coop, knowing he was so underfed he'd wreak havoc. Before that, the smokehouse went up in flames, which might have spread, except Angus and Jeff had just drained the cistern to scrub it out, and the entire back side of the barnyard was sopping wet as a result. You know about the harrow that mysteriously loosened its own bolts, and we found a length of tin relieved of its nails on the barn roof."

The sandwich was good. A tangy portion of cheddar with mustard and a sweet, smoky slab of ham between two slices of fresh, yeasty buttered bread. Beck set it aside unfinished. "Is there more?"

"Unfortunately, yes. We're working on repairing

the roof of the springhouse, among others, and had replaced the supports, as the damp got to them, which isn't unusual in a springhouse. Somebody sawed through the new lumber, such that when Cane climbed up yesterday to start tacking down the shingles, he damned near came a cropper."

"And a heavier person would have," Beck said. "Say, you or I?"

"Precisely." And Beck knew what he was thinking. A fall from the roof for a man with a bad back could be tragic, not merely inconvenient.

"Motive?" Beck asked, frowning in thought.

"Damned if I know." North started on his third sandwich. "It can't be ignored that this difficulty started when you arrived to put the place to rights, Haddonfield. I've been here for almost three years, the Hunts for longer, and they can't recall any of this nonsense happening, much less a plague of it all at once. We get on well enough with the neighbors, and the ladies are well regarded in the parish."

"After does not mean because of."

North nodded at Beck's aphorism and kept chewing.

"I understand we're haying tomorrow, North?"

"The fields east of the ponds," North clarified. "We've spent most of your absence cutting and raking, and now it's time to put up what's on the ground and cut down what hasn't been scythed yet. The weather can't hold fair much longer, and it's actually a decent crop."

"We're due for some good luck," Beck said. "And since there are more fields to scythe and rake, I'd say some help from Sutcliffe would be timely on several counts. We should bring over Mrs. Grantham too. She's a favorite with Polly and Sara. But tell me, North, before we're interrupted, what you make of these happenings."

Having demolished three sandwiches, North rose and stretched. "I've poked around but can come to no conclusions. Whoever did this is sneaky as hell, but like you, I'm stumped regarding a motive." North crossed his arms and studied the ceiling beams where Polly's pots gleamed in precise order of size. "Your family is managing?"

Now, Beck gathered, when they had no audience, North would bring up the late earl's passing.

"We are," Beck said, rising. "His lordship's death wasn't unexpected, but neither was it… entirely anticipated."

"And how is the new earl?" North asked as they crossed the backyard to the barn.

"He's an idiot." Beck said, though—curiously—not without affection. He felt a stab of affection for this barn too, where he'd kissed Sara Hunt's tears and held her as a man holds a woman he desires. That thought damned near had him returning to the house and bellowing his arrival to the lady herself.

But, no. He would not assume she'd be glad to see him.

"My brother has decided his marriage must be in name only, though I doubt he'll succeed at this scheme. His countess will sort him out in short order."

"Leave it to a female," North said, scratching the filly's silky neck gently. "Our females are feuding."

Our females. "You mentioned this. Any idea over what?"

"You should winkle it out of Sara." North's mouth flattened into a saturnine grimness. "I gather it has to do with her late husband's brother, but that's not the whole of it. Sara is considering taking another post."

"North…" Beck pushed away from the stall door. "Can we walk a bit?"

North looked uneasy at this request, no doubt because he knew Beck was done with privacy and discretion. It was time for some answers, before North's reticence got somebody hurt.

The barn door opened, letting in a shaft of late-afternoon sunshine.

"Beckman?"

Sara stood there in a simple sky-blue dress, her hair catching every ray of sun, her smile tentative but genuine. Peeking from beneath her dusty hem were the toes of the boots Beck had made for her.

"Mrs. Hunt." Beck offered her a bow, knowing that despite all good intentions to the contrary, interrogating North would have to wait for another day.

❧

Sara fell into bed exhausted and relieved. Beck had been friendly over dinner, clearly glad to see her—who wouldn't be glad to put a parent's funeral behind him?—and willing to take his cue from her.

Though she'd had no cue to give him. She'd missed him to the marrow of her bones while he'd been gone, and yet now that he was here, he became so much blond, handsome temptation.

She was tempted, of course, to steal into his bed, and that temptation was hard to resist. She was more tempted, though, to tell him Tremaine St. Michael was asking to come skulking around, threatening to unmask secrets the Hunt womenfolk had long ago agreed never to divulge.

And yet, Sara was not about to become further entangled with a good man, and Beck was a good man, without revealing her past—all of her past—thus costing her Beck's regard.

Her mind whirled with the burden of her tangled loyalties and longings, but weariness dragged her under in short order.

The next thing she knew, she was being lifted from her bed.

"Who...?" Her mind tried to grasp what her senses already knew: the clean scent of bergamot, the feel of a big, muscular body, the care in the way she was touched, all told her who it was cradling her against his chest.

"Hush." One word in a rumbled whisper, then the fleeting sensation of lips pressed to her forehead. She subsided as Beckman padded with her from her apartment, then out into the kitchen and on to the front stairs. Sara soon found herself deposited on Beck's bed, her nightgown summarily drawn up over her head.

Beck tossed off his dressing gown. "Now you may berate me, just as soon as you welcome me home in truth." He crouched naked over her and commenced kissing her before Sara could formulate a response.

Ah, God... Missing him was too tame an expression for the need clawing at her. They needed to talk, they needed to gain perspective on their situation, to reach an understanding as to its temporary and inconsequential—

His tongue teased at her lips, delicately, gently, and Sara couldn't hold her miserable, prudent, painful thoughts in her head. She kissed him back, letting every scintilla of her passion for him show in her response.

"Better," Beck growled, smiling against her lips. He abandoned the pretense of gentility and ravished her mouth, then shifted to his side and set his hand to plundering across her breasts and torso even as he continued to kiss, nuzzle, and bite.

"Beckman…" Sara tugged at his hair and got no response, so she tugged harder, until he did pause, frowning at her in the moonlight.

"You're fertile now," he said. "I know. But I've missed you." He regarded her more closely. "I wasn't going to do this, you know. I was going to let you decide whether to come to me, but I fear your stubbornness is the equal of my own. I haven't seen you, haven't kissed you, haven't held you for almost two weeks."

He'd kept track of her cycle, better track than Sara had herself. "I've missed you too," Sara said, leaning up to kiss his cheek. "How was the funeral?"

"Must we?" He rolled to his back but brought her with him by virtue of the arm he'd slipped around her shoulders.

Yes, they must. They must *also* talk, for his sake at least. "That bad?"

"No, not really that bad. In some ways it was good, because we were all nine of us, even Ethan, together. Nick has married a very sweet woman who will, I think, end up being his salvation."

"You're happy for your half-crazy brother?"

"Cautiously." Beck trailed his fingers over Sara's

face, making her recall that she'd missed the exact feel of a callused hand on her cheek and jaw. "He's damned stubborn, but there's been much ground recovered between him and Ethan, and between me and Ethan, for that matter."

"You sympathize with your brothers," Sara said. "They've both been prodigal in some way, and so have you."

"Touché." He traced her lips with a single finger. "May I please swive you silly now?"

Please, God, yes. "You may not." Sara rustled around under the covers to straddle him and cuddle down onto his chest. "Nor will I ravish you just yet."

"My disappointment defies description," Beck murmured, stroking a hand over her back. "No one else has asked about the funeral, though North inquired generally after my family."

"North has been preoccupied of late."

"How much of his past do you know, Sara?"

The question was reluctant, an intrusion of practical concerns and a possible test of Sara's loyalty.

"He carries an impressive title," Sara said, "but has for some reason stepped away from it. I don't know why, but I trust him, Beck. He was the first man about whom I could say that in many years. Polly and Allie trust him too."

"As do I, though I have to wonder if he's cut off from all family."

As Beckman had often been? "Such a fate strikes me as unbearably bleak."

"Bleak." Beck angled his chin, so she could get his earlobe in her mouth. "So he stays busy and tries not to think about family. When did you acquire this little trick?"

She was alternately biting and suckling on his earlobe, inflicting on him attentions he'd inflicted on her.

"I've been storing up things I'd like to try with you if you came back." Sara eased off and curled up on him.

"If I came back?" Beck's frown was audible.

"I don't have plans for you beyond this night, Beckman."

A long silence ensued, during which Sara tried to make herself leave his bed. She'd notified two hiring agencies of her availability for a post in the West Riding. Not even Tremaine would think to look for her there.

"What are your plans for me, then, for this night?" Beck leaned up and kissed her temple, as if he'd kiss her thoughts.

"To have my wicked way with you, except, given I might conceive, I'm not quite sure how to go about it."

"I have a few suggestions," Beck murmured, his hand moving around to the front of her and finding her naked breast. Within minutes, Sara was gliding her wet sex over the hard, hot length of him, while Beck plied her breasts with mouth and hands.

"This is…" She was panting, aroused, frustrated, and determined all at once.

"Hmmm?" He took a nipple in his mouth, as if he could play with her for hours.

"Beck…" She slid a hand behind his head. "I want… I want you inside me."

"No, you don't." Beck shifted his hips against the

mattress when she would have tried to slip herself over him. "You want to come, and you're having to do more of the work yourself this way. Allow me to remedy the situation." He pulled her down to kiss him, kept one hand on her breast, and slipped the other between their bodies.

"Yes…" Sara felt his thumb on the seat of her pleasure and slowed the undulation of her hips to find a rhythm with him. In moments, she was rocketing up, climbing toward satisfaction.

"You too," she whispered, teasing her fingers over his nipple, feeling him arch into her hand. She cast off first, hanging over him, keening as she moved on his cock and his fingers, her hair falling forward as passion washed through her. When she lay spent and panting on his chest, he gathered her hair and brushed it to one side.

"Again," he whispered, "but easy." He moved slightly under her, and Sara knew she should be doing something—kissing him, petting him, synchronizing her hips to his—but she was too undone. His hands shifted to her hips, and his grasp there provided her the encouragement she needed to join the languorous slide and pull he'd set up.

"No more than that," he said. "Let me do the work."

She sighed, content to feel him moving easily against her sensitized sex. Without her making any effort, she felt arousal gathering again, fueling her to more enthusiastic movement.

"No." Beck slowed his tempo more. "You let me."

She relaxed, and like a long, slow wave coming to shore, he built their arousal until it broke over them, gently and at length, bringing a deep sense of pleasure, satisfaction, and joining, though he hadn't even been inside her.

A sense of coming home, Sara reflected when he'd tidied her up—the prodigal returning.

"Go to sleep," Beck rumbled, his voice resonating against the ear Sara had pressed to his chest. "I'll get you back to your own bed before the household wakes up."

Sara forced her eyes open despite the appeal of that offer. "Beckman, there are things we must discuss."

He spent a moment considering then reached around to tuck the covers over her bare back. "This is probably the only place we have privacy, and you have my undivided attention."

"They're difficult things."

"So let's tackle them now, when we have some time and we're in charity with each other. I am in charity with you, in case you couldn't tell." He hitched his arms more snugly around her, and the sense of being treasured and protected almost cost Sara her resolve.

But he was right; his bed was the best place they had for this discussion.

"I am ready to end this aspect of our dealings, Beckman." A beat of silence followed, then Sara felt his fingers circling gently on her nape. "Beckman, say something."

"Do you have my successor picked out?" Beck asked, his tone almost amused. "Somebody less inclined to interrupt your sleep, perhaps?"

"There is no successor. It's just… I have a daughter,

and cavorting with you sets a bad example for Allie. I
simply haven't had the discipline to resist."

"I pride myself on my irresistibility." Beck drew
the covers over her again. "But you aren't making
sense, love. I intend to be underfoot here for the rest
of the growing season at least, and having enjoyed my
attentions, I doubt your self-discipline will keep you
out of this bed—and don't think I'll make it easy for
you. And, Sara? I'm going to propose again, too, so
man your defenses as best you can. Or woman them."

"Don't tease me," Sara wailed quietly. "I'm serious,
Beck. You have to leave me alone."

"Reasoning with you hasn't gotten me very far, and
you are a very reasonable, rational, self-disciplined sort
of lady. I'm not teasing you, Sara. Who is Tremaine?"

Sixteen

AT FIRST BECK THOUGHT SARA WAS STIFFENING WITH indignation, but then he realized she'd started to cry, softly, miserably, making him regret the shot he'd taken in the dark. But having gotten a response from her, he decided to press his advantage, though North had already told him Tremaine was Sara's deceased husband's brother.

"You must be very upset, Sara"—he stepped around the word *frightened*—"to be casting me aside like this. Talk to me, and I'll listen. I promise."

He kissed her crown and prayed she'd believe him.

"Tremaine is Allie's uncle," Sara said, levering up to reach for a handkerchief on the night table. Beck forcibly restrained the urge to take the ripe fruit of her breast into his mouth, because they were—God help them—*talking*.

"Has he threatened you in some way?" Beck didn't see any point in subtle questioning, and given the recent events at Three Springs, he was quickly coming to conclusions of his own.

"He has not." Sara sat back on his lap, and Beck

obligingly raised his knees to support her. "Or not overtly. He's written to inquire regarding Allie's well-being, and Polly's and mine, and suggested he'd like to take a more active role in Allie's upbringing."

"I'd do the same should Nick's countess be widowed, but Allie's been without her father for several years now. What has Tremaine been up to?"

"He says only that he's been putting the family finances in order." Sara tossed the handkerchief back to the night table and leaned back against his knees, closing her eyes. "In truth, I think he's been looking for us, and it took him this long to find us."

"Tell me about Tremaine St. Michael, love." Beck smoothed her hair from around her shoulders, leaving her breasts exposed to his gaze. That she didn't notice was a measure of significant upset.

"I wish I could." Sara rolled off him and tucked herself along his side. "I've met him only three or four times, when we came across him on the Continent. He's like Reynard, and not like Reynard."

Beck angled an arm under her neck and drew her closer. "Explain."

"Reynard was wily, conniving, and determined," Sara said, "but he also had a pragmatic streak. If the prize became too costly, he'd shrug, mutter a curse or a joke, then find some other scheme to focus on. Tremaine is wily too, but he's... quiet. No Gallic bursts of temper, no little slips or asides to give away his game. He's cold, Beck. Not just reserved, but cold."

"And why would such a man take an interest in a niece?"

"Because she's a prodigy. She paints as well as

Polly ever did at her age and even better. She paints too well."

"He'd exploit that?"

"Reynard would have. He exploited me, and he exploited Polly."

"So here I am," Beck said, "trying to get under your skirts while this Tremaine may be trying to take your daughter away?"

"I'm not wearing skirts." Sara had smiled against his shoulder, thank God. "But yes, should Tremaine decide to impose on us here, I cannot present a picture of maternal devotion while I'm stealing into your bed."

"And he's on hand, this Tremaine, to keep track of who's sleeping where?" Beck brought her hand to his mouth and kissed the back of it, then her palm, then her wrist.

"He could show up at any point," Sara said, her cheek heating where it touched Beck's arm. "I told him we are doing quite well here at Three Springs. I did not tell him I'm looking for a post in the north."

The hell she was. "Why not invite him here?"

Beside him, Sara went still. "I very nearly have, and now I think he'd like nothing better. He'll charm Allie and tantalize her—she still recalls our trip to London when she was little more than an infant. Tremaine could take her back there, promise her lessons and ponies…"

Beck shifted to cover her. "Hush. Tremaine has no legal claim on the child, and you are a good mother. A wonderful mother, and Allie will not choose him over you."

She clung, and she didn't argue. Beck took both as progress. "Sara?" Beck's nose was against her temple.

"Beckman?"

"I'd rather he be right here under our noses, where we can keep an eye on him and know what he's about."

He'd used the word *we*, used it as carelessly as another man might have referred to his favorite horse as a he, not an it—then he waited to see if she'd object.

"I honestly don't know what to do," Sara said. "If he can be convinced Allie is thriving here, and a lawsuit for guardianship of her would be unavailing, then he might take himself off and at least wait until Allie is an adult to attempt his schemes with her. Polly says female artists are becoming less and less accepted, at least as professionals."

Beck silently cursed the departed Reynard, because even from the grave, the man's perfidy was ruining Sara's happiness. "Sara, you have to have considered that Tremaine could snatch her from under our noses and pack her off to the Continent, claiming she's his child or that he has guardianship of her. Court orders can be forged. Would he do such a thing?"

Sara was quiet for a moment, likely adding new fears to her already long list. "I don't know him well enough. I was always too busy getting ready for the next performance or wondering what Reynard was about to fret much over Tremaine when he made his rare appearances. Polly thinks I'm overreacting, but she has her reasons for wanting to minimize the cause for alarm."

And then it became time to ask a difficult, if obvious, question.

"Do you suspect Tremaine of instigating all the trouble we've had here lately?"

She did not hesitate, and that in itself was daunting. "It would serve his interests to unnerve us. It would put us in a frame of mind to believe his promises of providing for Allie, keep us off balance and uncertain."

This was hardly a ringing endorsement of dear Uncle Tremaine. Beck considered what was at risk and considered how frightened Sara was.

Also, how far away the West Riding lay during its interminable winters.

"You could marry me, Sara." He brushed her hair back as he spoke. "I'm a match for any damned half-French, agitating, wastrel uncle. Allie and I get on well."

"Damn you." Sara's voice was soft, pained, and barely audible because she'd buried her nose in the crook of his neck. "The heir to an earldom does not marry a housekeeper, Beckman."

"I'm only an heir in a technical sense. Nicholas will be anticipating a blessed event in no time, mark my words. Besides, this is England, and I can marry whomever the hell I please, assuming she's willing."

And not too stubborn for her own bloody good.

"Marriage to protect Allie is a noble offer, but we've both been badly burned by holy matrimony, Beckman. Allie will be grown and likely married herself in a few years, and then where will we be?"

"Married." Beck dipped his head and kissed her. "Hopefully in a bed very like this one, attired as we are now and not wasting time chatting the night away when we could be making our own family."

She kissed him back, likely to shut him up.

"You'll at least consider it," Beck pressed when he eased back from the kiss. "Promise me, Sarabande."

"Considering guarantees you nothing."

This was not true. The knowledge that Sara would consider his marriage proposal, even if only to protect her daughter, guaranteed Beck an endless supply of sleepless nights and difficult days.

He turned his head so his cheek rested on hers. "Considering gets me your honest attempt at thinking things over, and I'm after your promise, not your answer."

"Then, yes." Sara wiggled so she fit more closely under him. "I will consider your offer as a means of keeping Allie safe from her uncle's machinations, I promise.

"Good enough," Beck said, shifting them so he was spooned around her. "Go to sleep, love. We'll sit down with the entire household in the morning, and things will look brighter."

"Now you worry about rest." Sara fitted her bottom to his groin as he wrapped his arm around her waist. "You weren't so worried about sleep before, Mr. Haddonfield."

"We needed the other too." Beck kissed her ear. "And I can guarantee you we're going to need it again before morning."

⤜⤏

"Is there anything more conducive to producing bodily misery than a solid bloody week of haying?" Beck stretched out his weary body in the lovely heat of the springs, the hotter end of the pool suiting him wonderfully.

"War, perhaps," North suggested from his spot on the submerged ledge. "Childbirth, one supposes."

"A hangover I had the first night I landed in Baltimore." Though Paris made Baltimore look like a romp. "Did we bring soap?"

"You brought it," North said, but he sloshed his way to the bank and fished it out of their pile of towels and clothes, then tossed it to Beck. "And you've grease on your back from trying to prop up the wagon when the axle broke, Hercules Haddonfield."

"It didn't break," Beck said, scrubbing off with the soap. "Or did you see something I missed?"

"I was too busy watching all the help from Sutcliffe flirt with our cook," North intoned darkly. "You are correct, though, the axle was cut most of the way through, which is a considerable sawing job."

Beck made thorough use of the soap and lobbed it at North, who caught it one-handed.

"Have you considered sending to your brother the earl for assistance with things here?"

"I have not. Nick is newly arrived to a state of holy matrimony and not coping well with the shock." He dunked to rinse off rather than admit he'd almost sent word to both Nick and Ethan.

"He's your family, Beckman," North said as Beck's head broke the water. "I don't know how much longer I can stay, and it isn't as if you haven't investigated all of Creation in the interests of the family businesses."

North's tone was ominously reasonable.

"Little business projects aren't quite in the same

league with apprehending criminals," Beck said, though a trip to Budapest or Virginia or the Levant or Stockholm did qualify as more than a little business trip.

North made quick use of the soap then began sloshing toward the bank. "If I stay in here much longer, I'm going to look older than old Mrs. Hibbert at The Dead Boar."

"An improvement Miss Polly would surely regard with favor," Beck quipped, but he too was soon drying off with a bath sheet. He'd just gotten his breeches buttoned and pulled on his boots when a piercing scream rent the evening air.

"What in God's name?" Beck saw confusion and concentration on North's face.

"That's Allie," Beck said. The screaming went on, unceasingly, as Beck took off at a dead run toward the manor. He could hear North pounding behind him, but having the advantage of size, he outpaced him by several lengths by the time they'd reached the barn.

Allie stood along the back wall, where Boo-boo's dog pen had been constructed. The dog sat at her side, looking puzzled, his pink tongue lolling from his mouth. Polly was calmly trying to talk Allie into shutting up, while Sara wielded a long hay fork in the general vicinity of a black snake coiled between the child and the adults.

Beck crossed to the child, picked her up, eased back around the snake, then thrust the child into North's arms. She quieted immediately, her screams mutating into sobs while she clung to North's neck like a burr.

"North," Beck said over Allie's sobbing. "Hand the child to her mother, and let the ladies go outside, if you please."

North complied, crooning to the child and patting her back as he handed her off. Sara whisked Allie from the barn, Polly and the dog at their heels.

"Big bugger," North said when they had some quiet. "Never did fancy snakes."

"It's a black rat snake." Beck eyed the creature, which was writhing slowly in the dirt. "They get even bigger than this, at least in Virginia."

"What's an American snake doing here, for pity's sake? My ears will never recover."

"It's scaring the wits out of a little girl," Beck said grimly. He grabbed the snake behind its head and lifted the thing carefully. "And probably looking for mice and rats to fill its five-foot-long belly. Come along, you," Beck addressed the snake. "You've apologies to make."

"Coming out." Beck raised his voice to warn the ladies. "And bringing our new pet with me."

Allie's face was still buried against her mother's neck, so she was unlikely to immediately understand Beck had brought the snake out of the barn.

"Beckman," Sara spoke very sharply, "can't you take it away?"

"I will, but I thought Allie might want to see him when he's not so upset."

"The snake?" Allie ceased crying long enough to peer at Beck. "Eeeeuuuw."

"He's actually quite a fine specimen," Beck said, not going any closer. "Though I'm sure in India I saw snakes much longer and bigger around than this little fellow. He's far from home though, and not likely to survive the winter."

Allie regarded the snake with a blend of revulsion and curiosity. "Where is he from?"

"Virginia, the eastern United States. Sailors sometimes bring them on board ship. They're keen to eat up all the mice and rats, and unlike cats, they don't leave scent everywhere they go. This kind is usually shy, but they can bite. Would you like to pet him?"

"No." Allie stretched out a single finger toward the snake as she spoke. "Is he slimy?"

"Touch him and find out. He's without any family, if he had ears they'd be broken from your alarum, and he's far from familiar surroundings. I'd say he's due a little kindness."

And damned if Beck didn't feel a pang of pity for the rubbishing snake.

"I'd say he's due to be put on a ship back to Virginia," North muttered, but he must have understood what Beck was about and dutifully stroked his hand over the snake's black scales. "Shall we name him?"

"He's smooth," Allie said, quickly withdrawing her finger then passing it over the snake again. "Mama?"

Sara met Beck's gaze, a world of conflicted maternal feelings in her eyes, but she petted the snake as North had. "He is smooth, and he catches the light on his scales."

That bestirred the artist in Allie, and she eyed the snake more critically.

"What shall we do with him?" Beck asked. "I can send him back to his Maker, Allie, or I can find somebody in the village going to Portsmouth and put him on an outbound ship."

North sent him a look that clearly indicated the sharp end of a shovel would be a much simpler solution, but Beck waited for Allie to make up her mind.

"Send him home," Allie decided. "If he has family, they'll miss him."

"Oh, for the love…" North put his fists on his hips and glowered at the snake. "I suppose he'll need a little snake palace to bide in until his royal barge departs, and a name." He took the snake from Beck like so much dirty washing. "As the name Boo-boo is taken, and Screech lacks a certain dignity, his name will be Milton, and I will find him a suitably impressive dwelling and take him into the village tomorrow, there to begin his homeward odyssey, about which he will no doubt write at great length, setting a trend among all the fashionable, well-traveled black rat snakes."

He stomped off, lecturing the snake about getting ideas above his lowly station, while Beck silently applauded a very convincing reestablishment of the status quo.

"Quite an adventure for you." Beck held out a hand to Allie. "I suppose you want a snake now for your birthday instead of a pony?"

"A pony?" Allie's eyes grew round, and she began to chatter volubly, completely missing the wink Beck shot Sara and Polly.

The topic of Allie's birthday figured prominently at the dinner table, with various outlandish suggestions being made regarding her gifts and appropriate activities for the occasion. North joined the group midway through the meal, having constructed a wood and wire cage for Milton.

"He's taking a nap after his ordeal," North reported.

"He's been rendered temporarily deaf by a certain young lady's stunning propensity to summon help, as have I. Ah, I see you left me a dollop of potatoes and three entire green beans. I'm touched."

Polly rose, smiling. "There's more."

North reached over and slid the butter away from Beck's plate toward his own. By tacit agreement, the adults were not going to discuss the broken axle or the snake at the table, not while Allie remained among them. But when she'd disappeared to take Hildy her scraps, Beck glanced around the kitchen.

"When Allie has found her bed, I'd like the rest of us to convene in my sitting room."

Sara nodded, resignation and worry reflected in her gaze.

"Sara and I will be doing the dishes tonight, Polly," Beck said. "You've cooked for a legion all week and can use the time to get off your feet."

"Excellent suggestion," North said. "Though perhaps you'd take a turn with me in the garden rather than get off your feet?"

A glance passed between them, one Beck didn't try to parse, though North was a fool to walk away from a woman who looked at him that way.

When Beck was left alone in the kitchen with Sara, he did, indeed, set to clearing the table and washing the dishes.

"You sit too," Beck said, stacking plates at the table. "I'll tend to this, and you enjoy a second cup. I wanted to talk with you first, though, before we open discussion with the others."

Sara rose and slipped her arms around his middle.

"I've never been so grateful to see another person in my life as I was when you came skidding into that barn, Beckman. That idiot snake kept slipping and slithering off the hay fork and glaring at me and waving his tongue about…"

"You would have gotten him," Beck assured her, setting down his load of dishes to return her embrace. "He was as upset as you were, though."

"Polly wanted to get an ax."

"A shovel would have given her longer reach, but all's well, even for the snake."

"You handled it beautifully." Sara held him a moment longer. "Thank you."

"My pleasure, but, Sara? The broken axle on the wagon today? It wasn't an accident, and I suspect this snake was purposely put where Allie and Boo-boo like to play."

"I haven't asked Allie for the details. I gather the beast was somewhere in the vicinity of the doghouse."

"It could be coincidence. The snake might have come in on a wagonload of goods shipped into Portsmouth, but I don't think we can take that chance."

"What are you saying?"

"If the snake was put here deliberately, then we've escalated from malicious mischief toward replaceable property, to a threat of real harm to Allie or you ladies. Even nonvenomous snakes have a nasty bite, Sara. They're carnivores, and the wound can easily get infected."

Sara dropped her arms from Beck's waist and stepped back. "Somebody wants Allie *dead*?"

"Or doesn't care if harm befalls her, which suggests to me we're not dealing with a greedy uncle."

"How do you figure that?" Sara moved off to pour herself a cup of tea, her movements mechanical, her eyes unfocused.

"Why would Tremaine stir up so much trouble to get his hands on a talented artist then put the artist herself in harm's way?"

"I don't know."

She sounded so forlorn, so uncertain. Beck silently cursed whoever had let the snake into the barn. The scare to Allie was likely to be quickly forgotten, not so the scare to her mother.

"I think we need to have a serious talk with one Tremaine St. Michael, Sara. Sooner rather than later."

"You want us to confront him?"

"I do, but here, where we've got some support and we can keep a close eye not just on Tremaine but on Allie as well."

"You're determined to invite him here?" Sara worried a thumbnail between her front teeth. "Is that necessary?"

"I think it is. I wanted to discuss it with you first."

"I could take Allie away somewhere."

He understood the impulse to flee but understood as well that it seldom resulted in a real solution—and wasn't that an insight to be pondered some other fine, long day? "And if he was able to find you here, using your maiden name, what will you do when he finds you there too?"

She glowered at her teacup. "I'll go to America with the damned snake. It's my job to keep Allie safe, and I'll go to the ends of the earth to do that."

She wasn't arguing, which Beck took as an

indication that she was closer to emotional collapse than even she knew, so he took her teacup from her and wrapped her in another hug. "The ends of the earth are not as worthy of inspection as one might think. It's time to stop dancing around silences and innuendos, Sara. We'll get St. Michael here, on our turf, and determine his motives. My brother is an earl, my step-grandmother a marchioness, and my pockets are full to bursting. I'm connected to more damned titles than you can count, and I will bend all of my resources to see that Allie stays safe with you."

"It's so complicated," Sara whispered against his neck. "Why does it have to be so complicated?"

"It isn't complicated. Either St. Michael ceases his nonsense, or I'll see him behind bars or in the ground."

Sara cuddled closer, which might have been a sign of progress except for the realization that if Allie were once again safe, then Beck's greatest leverage for gaining Sara's hand in marriage would be gone.

Seventeen

THE HAYING WAS SUCCESSFULLY COMPLETED, THE barns and sheds and even the house sported repaired or replaced roofs, the walls and fences were again sturdy and straight, and the crops matured in the fields. Summer eased past the solstice and into July, hitting the lull between haying and harvest when life should have been sweet.

At Three Springs, since the evening Beck had explained his intent to invite Tremaine St. Michael for a visit, every adult on the property had lived with an underlying sense of tension. The lack of further destructive mischief only made the anxiety greater.

There was good news, at least for Beck, in that Nicholas had reconciled with his new countess.

"You are still determined to leave?" Beck asked as he and North rode in from the eastern barley fields.

North patted Soldier's dusty neck. "I am. I thought you'd have matters wrapped up by now, and St. Michael has apparently gone to ground."

"He's on his way here."

"He's on his way…" North's scowl was thunderous.

"This man puts a little girl in harm's way, he's on his way here, and you didn't think to mention this to me? The women will draw and quarter you, and I'll sharpen their knives."

"I got his letter in the village today. Seems he's been walking the Lake District or some such, and he's happy to grace us with his presence as of the first of next week. You are duly warned, so what will you do about it?"

"Fret prodigiously."

"Just so, and I appreciate the warning. But you'll still go."

"Soon," North said, his eyes straying to the back of the manor house. "When you've routed the enemy, I'll move along, so you'd best be looking for a new steward."

"You were going to stay through harvest," Beck reminded him as they turned their horses into the stable yard.

"I was going to try, but it isn't working out that way."

Beck regarded him as closely as one could regard North, given his ability to mask his feelings.

"Is Polly angry with you?"

North swung off Soldier. "She is not, or not as angry as she should be. She's… brokenhearted, and that I cannot abide. The sooner I'm gone, the sooner she'll realize I was a complete waste of her sentiments."

"Gabriel…" How did Beck, of all people, tell another man that leaving didn't solve anything?

"There is no good outcome for us, Beckman," North said as he ran up his stirrups. "The most honorable thing I can do is take myself off and let her get on with her life."

"You aren't even giving the woman a chance, North. At least tell her the truth of your situation—whatever that might be—before you go, so she has a reason for your departure other than her own failings."

"God." Clearly, this possibility had not occurred to North. He rested his arm over Soldier's muscular neck and bowed his head as if exhausted. "She'll blame herself, won't she?"

"The good ones do. The worthy ones." Just as Beck had blamed himself for his young wife's decisions.

The realization went through him like a dose of strong medicine. He felt the relief of it, the absolution of it settle into his soul while North stood braced against his horse.

"I sometimes wish I'd gotten on that ship with the damned snake."

"But you would have left my flank exposed," Beck said. "So blame your situation on me, but please consider the terms of your parting. What affects Polly affects Sara and Allie, and me as well."

"You should have been a vicar." North loosened Soldier's girth. "Inducing guilt is one of their most highly cultivated skills."

"You should have been a marquess," Beck said, letting instinct have free rein.

North shook his head as he took Ulysses's reins from Beck. "If I'd been a marquess, I would never have met Polly Hunt, never have built my first snake palace, never have soaked away my aches and worries with you and your nancy damned soap. Being a steward has had rewards being the marquess would never have. I've brought in crops I saw planted and tended, cared personally for beasts and buildings, and developed an appreciation for the people closest to the land. It hasn't been all bad, Beck. In fact, in some ways, I've been happier here at Three Springs than I ever would have been as Hesketh."

Hesketh. Hesketh was indeed a venerable, much-respected marquessate. "And you'll miss it," Beck warned. "Worse than you miss Hesketh's holdings."

"That I will." North's eyes strayed to the house again before he led the horses into the barn. In that single glance, Beck had seen a peacefulness in North's eyes, an acceptance that boded ill for the man's future. North was going to leave, and there would be no talking him out of it.

Beck's situation with Sara wasn't leaving him peaceful in the least. When he kidnapped her to his bed, she was a sweet and passionate lover. She never sought him out at night on her own, though, and in her embrace, Beck felt an increasing desperation. He reminded her of his proposal regularly, and she renewed her promise to consider his offer if ever she believed Allie in danger.

But that was before Beck had an acceptance of his invitation from Tremaine St. Michael. He broached the topic as lunch was finishing up, when he had Sara and Polly to himself in the kitchen.

"Ladies, we're to have a guest."

Sara looked up sharply from where she was sorting the silver back into a drawer. "Your brother?"

"Tremaine St. Michael has accepted our invitation to visit, and he'll be here on the first of the week." He was looking right at Sara, so he saw her stiffen and close her eyes. Polly set down the plate she'd been scraping into the scrap bucket and muttered an "excuse me" before leaving the kitchen at a fast clip.

"Let her go," Beck said softly. "She'll find North, and I've already warned him."

"I was hoping..." Sara bit her lip and took up the plate-scraping Polly had abandoned.

"You were hoping St. Michael had fallen from the face of the earth," Beck finished for her. "Apparently, so was Polly."

"Polly is in a difficult position," Sara said, keeping her gaze on her task.

"Because North is leaving?"

Sara straightened and moved on to the next plate. "That, but also because Tremaine is coming. Polly cares about... all of us."

"And we care about her, but what aren't you telling me, Sara?" Because as sure as Gabriel North was a man with problems, Sara was still keeping secrets.

She finished with that plate and reached for the next, then stopped and turned her back to him. His arms were around her before she got her apron untied.

"Talk to me, Sara." He drew her against him. "For the love of God, no more silences. Please talk to me."

❦

Sara felt Beckman behind her, solid, strong, and secure. Were the issue anything less than Allie's safety, and were it anybody else demanding Sara's confidences, she would have gone right on scraping Hildy's supper into a bucket.

"Please talk to me."

Sara nodded. He gave her a moment, probably knowing she needed to gather her courage, her wits, her breath.

"There are paintings," she said, glad he couldn't see her face. "Tremaine has them. Reynard gave them to him for safekeeping when he fell ill, or Tremaine stole them, I know not which."

"What sort of paintings?" Beck said, misgiving in his tone beneath the calm.

"Nudes. Of me."

Nothing about his embrace shifted. Not one thing. "Nudes are acceptable artistic subjects."

"Nudes of some statue might be. Nudes of mythical gods and goddesses are allowable. Nudes of one's neighbor aren't. Nudes of one's housekeeper aren't. With those paintings in his possession, Tremaine can ask pretty much anything of me, Beckman, and I'll comply."

"Polly feels responsible?"

"She was young and angry and didn't see the harm. The poses are such that my face isn't quite visible in any of them." Nor was it quite obscured.

"How many?"

He had to know one painting was enough to destroy a woman's life.

"Three." Sara turned in his arms and laid her cheek against his chest. "They're good, almost charming."

"Is this why Polly stopped painting for others?"

"Part of it. Most of it."

Beck pressed a kiss to her temple. "So we'll buy the damned paintings."

"Why should he sell them to you?" Sara asked

miserably. "He can have the cow, so to speak, by holding on to those three pictures."

Beck was quiet for a minute, his hands stroking idly over Sara's back. "How does he have title to them?"

She went still when he posed the question—a simple question. Or was it? "What do you mean?"

"Provenance is the first thing any reputable collector will want to prove." Beck took half a step back and led Sara over to the table.

"The dishes…"

Beck was out the back door in three strides, bellowing for Maudie, who came from the carriage house at a trot.

Beck pointed toward the kitchen. "The dishes, my girl. And mind you don't be getting the lads in trouble." She bobbed a blushing curtsey and scurried to her task.

When Sara had been escorted to Beck's sitting room, the door firmly closed behind them, she had the sense the real inquisition was about to begin.

Beck settled beside her on the sofa. "Let us discuss provenance. The painter owns the painting unless paid a commission. In this case, I doubt Reynard commissioned the works."

And why, in years and years of being mentally dogged and harassed by those infernal paintings, hadn't Sara once considered this?

"He did not, though he could argue he was owed the paintings for putting a roof over our heads, that sort of thing."

"He didn't put a roof over anybody's head," Beck shot back. "You did."

"But what belongs to me belonged to him, as my husband, so he was owed, not me."

"In the absence of a contract of some sort, that's at least debatable. Polly is family, but if Reynard sold her paintings in addition to your performances, then she earned her keep."

"He did, or he sold most of them."

"We have a situation where you and Polly are both bringing in income, but you think Reynard somehow had title to the paintings Polly created? What sort of man would rely on that reasoning to keep paintings from the women who should have them? And what sort of uncle would use those paintings to control women he ought to have been assisting for the past several years?"

"Reynard's brother," Sara said shortly. "Possibly—I don't know, Beck, but it's my rosy fundament that will hang in some drawing room if Tremaine decides to be difficult."

"Is this what has been bothering you?" He phrased the question delicately, though Sara suspected he was asking if this was why she hadn't accepted his proposal. Proposals, plural.

"It bothers me, yes." Haunted her, more like. Sara forced herself to ease her grip on Beck's hand. "It bothers me terribly."

"Did you pose for these paintings?"

"Of course not, though I could see why you'd ask. Polly was on hand, backstage, before I'd perform sometimes. She and Allie both saw me in all manner of dishabille, and at the coaching inns, quarters were often cramped and privacy limited. No one thought anything of it."

"But your trust was somehow betrayed. Do you think Reynard put her up to it?"

"I don't know. It isn't something we talk about." One of many things they didn't talk about, at least until recently.

"I am beginning to think nobody talks about anything on this property," Beck muttered. "Will Polly confide in North?"

"I don't know that either. Somebody should explain this to him. He's family."

"If she doesn't, I will."

"What about the others?"

"They don't need to know. How much does Allie comprehend of these difficulties?"

"Not much." Sara chewed a thumbnail. "I hope."

"Somebody is going to have to explain to her that discussing her art with Uncle Tremaine is not well advised. Her little studio is going to have to be dismantled for the nonce."

Well, of course, though Sara had been too upset to see even this far ahead. "We can do that. How long do you think he'll stay?"

"It's England in the summertime. Who knows? I can summon reinforcements if we need them. Lady Warne might enjoy taking a hand in things."

Sara stopped mistreating her thumbnail as one more confidence went flying past her common sense. "I'm scared, Beckman." She pitched against him. "I'm scared for me, Allie, and Polly, and even a little bit for you."

His arms came around her; his scent tickled her nose. "Don't be scared for me, Sara. Get those paints

put away and stored somewhere St. Michael won't
find them."

Sara let Beck go find North. As relieved as she was to
have this secret aired, she'd also noted that now—when
the respectable suit of an earl's son might have faced
Tremaine down—Beck hadn't renewed his proposal.

Which was of no moment, really. She still could
not have accepted him.

❧

"Did Polly tell you about the paintings?"

North glanced up from where he was cleaning
his bridle in the saddle room, but his expression was
harder than usual to read.

"She did."

"I can offer to buy them." Beck lowered himself
to sit beside North on the plank bench. "Our
womenfolk will do anything to keep those paintings
from becoming public, though, and establishing that
Tremaine *doesn't* have title to them will make them
public indeed."

Which, of course, he hadn't pointed out to Sara.

"Polly says Sara's face isn't clear in any of them."
North eyed his reins, which looked perfectly clean to
Beck. "Sara's hair will give her away to anybody who
knows the artist."

"Polly's upset?"

"Oh, one might say that." North went silent for a
moment. "I've never seen her cry before."

"Christ." Beck leaned back against the wall. "I will
be more relieved when this is over than I was to get
home from Virginia."

"Too many snakes?"

"Slavery, in all its brutal splendor, with no softening fiction I was among Bedouins or South Seas' cannibals. My father's chums from school, no less, slaveholding and quoting Scripture to support it at table."

"Polly and Sara felt like slaves. They don't want Allie to suffer that fate."

"I won't allow it," Beck retorted. "You won't allow it."

"Allow?" North blew out a breath and settled back beside Beck. "Just who are we, Beckman, that we're allowing and not allowing matters in the lives of the Hunt womenfolk?"

"Damned if I know."

❧

"I shouldn't be here." Sara stared up at the ceiling of Beck's bedroom, having held her fire until his door was safely closed behind them.

"Nonsense." Beck shucked his dressing gown and climbed in beside her. She wasn't volunteering to take off her nightgown, so he pulled her to his side clothed as she was. "You asked me to leave you in your own bed only when Tremaine is underfoot. I will miss you badly in this bed starting tomorrow night, so I'm gathering rosebuds while I may. Or Sarabuds." He kissed her nose, hoping to lighten the mood.

"I'm bleeding."

He absorbed that, though it wasn't the first time the topic had been mentioned between them.

"Cramps?"

"A little," she said and turned away from him onto

her side. He spooned himself around her, settling his hand over her womb.

"Sorry, love. I wish I could hurt for you. You're worried about Tremaine?"

"Of course." She sighed and rolled over to her other side, tucking her face against his chest. "I hate the waiting, and I'll hate having him about, and I'll hate not being able to spend my nights with you."

"One is encouraged to hear that last," Beck said, drawing her braid over her shoulder. "You leave a man to wonder, Sara Hunt."

"Don't wonder. Be assured, Beck, when Tremaine shows up, our dalliance is over."

Beck gathered her closer, getting a whiff of flowers and worry for his trouble. "I want to marry you."

"It doesn't help, you know?" Sara's index finger began to draw patterns on Beck's bare chest. "You need to stop proposing to me and consider when you'll move on about your life."

"I'm about my life now," Beck rejoined. "This very minute I'm about my life, Sara."

"This very minute you are depriving yourself of sleep so I might scold you yet again for being unrealistic."

"For caring about you?" Beck shifted, covering her with the warmth of his naked body though she lay on her side. "For loving you?"

Silence, and then tears. Quiet tears eased from her on long, careful breaths, while Beck held her and wondered why on earth a woman would cry to know she was loved. They fell into exhausted slumber without finding an answer.

❧

Tremaine St. Michael had been at Three Springs for two days, and Beck was increasingly perplexed by him. He was a man of odd contrasts, physically, socially, intellectually.

He'd bowed very correctly over Sara's and Polly's hands, but swept Allie up in a tight, protracted hug. He was reserved with Beck and North, but possessed of a quick, dry wit as well. Physically, he was built like a dragoon—tall and well muscled—but he moved with peculiar quiet. His features were at odds as well, with eyes and hair of such a soft, lustrous dark brown as to appear black, but high cheekbones, a Viking nose, and a jawbone that looked descended from Vandal antecedents. His voice was a unique blend of growling Scots burr and graceful French elision.

Nothing about the man added up, though Ethan's letters claimed Tremaine St. Michael knew the Midlands wool trade inside and out, and was profiting accordingly. Toward the ladies, Tremaine was unfailingly polite, but to Beck's practiced eye, Sara and Polly were both avoiding the man.

Which left him often in Beck's company, or Beck's and North's.

"That end is too hot," Beck said, pointing off to the water on his left. "Here, however, it's just right. Bring the soap, will you, North?"

"Soap I can carry," North said. "You can haul your own damned spirits." He fired a pocket flask at Beck and finished undressing.

"There's a ledge here." Beck sank into the water. "It's just made for man's weary fundament. I don't know if the Romans put it here, or Mother Nature, but to me, it's the best feature on the property."

Tremaine took a seat beside his host. "So far, I have to agree with you."

He sank down on a long sigh and leaned his head back against the stones.

"You could fetch a pretty penny for the property based on the springs alone," Tremaine said when North had taken a place several feet away on Beck's other side.

"Drink?" Beck uncapped the flask and passed it to his guest.

"Mighty fine," Tremaine declared, his burr showing more clearly. "So, now that we're great friends, Haddonfield, drinking by moonlight and larking about like pagans in your grandmother's springs, tell me why my brother's widow won't give me the time of day."

"Plain speaking," North growled. "Have to give him points for that."

"Drink." Beck passed North the flask. "And hold your tongue, old man."

North obliged and passed the flask back.

"It's complicated," Beck said carefully. "I think it has to do with items that came into your possession after Reynard's death."

"Items?" Tremaine took a swig from the proffered flask. "That doesn't narrow it down. Reynard sent me scads of things over the years, particularly after he married. His fortunes improved, I gather, and he had nowhere else to hoard his treasures."

"You still have these things he collected?" Beck asked. "Because by law, unless he willed them to you or conveyed them overtly, I believe they belong to his wife and daughter now."

"One comprehends this." Tremaine had to be reminded to pass the flask along by Beck taking it from his hand. "I have a load of plunder for Sara and Allie to go through and sort, at least. There are paintings, too, which I gather might be Polly's work or purchased for her. I'm surprised she isn't still painting—she's very good. Reynard considered her every bit as great a find as Sara."

"How did Sara feel about being found?" Beck asked. He sent the flask on to North without partaking.

"Gentlemen…" Tremaine's voice took on a hint of steel. "We can agree my brother was a rotten excuse for a man. He lived off his womenfolk, exploited them shamelessly, and refused to let them rejoin their parents when his scheme became obvious to his young wife. I offered to see the ladies back to England at one point, but Sara refused to go."

"She refused?" That made no sense, like everything else associated with Tremaine and his infernal brother. Beck passed the flask back to his guest, though trying to inebriate St. Michael into confidences was likely a lost cause.

"For two reasons." Tremaine took a goodly pull before elaborating. "First, I gather Reynard had written to the senior Hunts, lamenting Sara's difficult temperament, her lack of gratitude for his hard work on behalf of her art, her lack of dedication to her God-given gifts, and so forth. When Sara wrote to them asking if she could come home with her daughter and sister, her parents replied with a scathing lecture about a wife's vows and familial sacrifice. I gather the damage has become permanent."

"She's written to her parents recently," Beck said, though her epistle barely qualified as a note.

"She has," Tremaine replied. "I paid my respects to them on my way down here, but neither Sara nor Polly has asked after them."

"Did they ask after her?"

"I have a letter from them." Tremaine closed his eyes and sank lower in the water. "I'm not to pass it to Sara unless she inquires."

"So prompt her to ask," Beck growled, getting up from his seat and leaving North and Tremaine to share the remainder of the brandy. Beck retrieved the soap and started scrubbing himself briskly.

"You think I should?" Tremaine sounded genuinely perplexed. "I was hoping the ladies would accept my aid rather than go running home to Mama and Papa."

"Why?" Beck submerged and came up. "Three females are a substantial expense."

"Because to me," Tremaine said levelly, "they are due the support. It is not an expense. It is a privilege, and thanks to a lot of bleating, stinking sheep, I can easily spare the coin. You have family coming out your ears, Haddonfield, both brothers and sisters, an old granny of some sort. My family in France is gone—mostly murdered in the fruitless march toward a republic—and what few second cousins I have in Scotland regard me as a bloody Sassenach." He dropped into a soft burr. "These women, Allie in particular, are all the family who will claim me."

North swirled the water and shot Beck a thoughtful

look. Beck dunked again, then passed him the soap and traded places with him on the bench.

"You are an orphaned *comte*?" Beck asked.

"I don't use the title."

"You need to talk to Sara," Beck said. "You mentioned two reasons she wouldn't accompany you to England. What was the second?"

"The child." Tremaine tossed the empty flask onto the bank. "By the law of any civilized land, a man's legitimate progeny are his to control, period. Sara would not risk antagonizing Reynard lest he separate her from her child. And he would have, much as it shames me to say it."

"Happy for him, the man is dead," Beck said, "else I should have to see to his demise myself."

"For observing the law?" Tremaine caught the soap when North pitched it.

"For exploiting a seventeen-year-old girl who'd just lost her brother," Beck began. "For parading her all around Europe like some musical whore, for using Polly and her art just as badly, for being an obscene perversion of what a husband should be, for coming between parents and their only surviving offspring—need I go on?"

Tremaine submerged and stayed under long enough for North to murmur, "I won't let you drown him, Beck. He's no more Reynard than you or I are."

Excellent—if irksome—point.

"I can't argue with you, Haddonfield," Tremaine said when he'd whipped his hair out of his eyes and tossed the soap onto the bank. "I want to. I want to protest you're being too harsh, my brother meant well, his wife was an ungrateful no-talent schemer, but I can't. Reynard was raised under difficult circumstances, and he did not rise to the challenges in his life. For all that, Sara still probably blames herself for what befell her and her sister and rues the day she ever sent for Reynard."

A beat of silence, and then Beck asked, "She *sent* for him?"

"She hasn't told you this? Reynard used to gloat to me in his letters about it." Tremaine disappeared under the water again, coming up closer to the hot end of the pool. "Sara had heard of Reynard. He'd some success managing a pair of brothers who played violin and viola, and she expected he could do the same for her and her brother. No doubt, she thought he'd find them some engagements around London, start them off on the private parties, that sort of thing. A young lady performing in a concert hall might not be the done thing, but a brother and sister making music in private homes before Polite Society is another matter."

"A reasonable expectation from her viewpoint," Beck said.

"True." Tremaine climbed back up on the ledge. "But Reynard saw much greater potential for income by taking one violinist—a young, lovely female with dramatic red hair—and marching her all over the Continent, where women can and do perform professionally. If he'd taken Sara and Gavin, they would have supported each other against him and been much more difficult and expensive to handle. So he chose Sara and took the brother aside, explaining the boy owed it to his sister to step out of Sara's path. He similarly closeted himself with Sara and said she needed to free her brother from worrying about her, focusing on duet literature, and so forth. Reynard promised her Gavin would be a better musician on his own two feet rather than pandering to his sister's lesser talent."

"Perishing, sodding, bloody, contemptible hell." Beck shot off the ledge and slogged to the bank. "How can you recount this perfidy so calmly?"

"The picture emerged slowly." Tremaine followed Beck and North out of the pool and accepted the bath sheet North tossed him. "I did not see much of my brother, but we'd cross paths occasionally on the Continent. He wrote often though, dropping a hint here, a detail there. He did regret Gavin's death, though, of that I'm sure."

"I thought it was an accident." Beck stopped drying himself, unease wrapping around the anger in his gut. "Sara told me Gavin's death was an accident."

"She no doubt wants you to believe that." Tremaine pulled his shirt over his head and stepped into his breeches. "Gavin was supposedly cleaning his gun the day after Sara accepted Reynard's proposal, and the thing went off. The boy left a note encouraging his sister to take her chance for happiness with Reynard, and asking his parents to forgive him."

Beck strode off and stood a few paces away, rage and sorrow ricocheting in his mind while curses in five languages clamored for an airing. North handed Tremaine his boots, gathered up the soap and the empty flask, then caught Tremaine's eye and jerked his chin toward the manor house.

They left Beck alone and half-naked in the dark, the silence of the night screaming around him.

Eighteen

"He has a letter from your parents."

Sara knew that voice and that scent, but did not know Beckman would accost her while she lay in her own bed. She opened her eyes when Beck climbed into that bed, spooned himself around her, and gathered her close.

"Get out of this bed."

"Polly's off somewhere," Beck said, smoothing her braid over her shoulder. "Allie's fast asleep. I checked."

"You…" Sara tried to roll over to glare at him, but he held her gently in place.

"I expect your sister is trysting with North at the springs. I hope she is. We should try it sometime."

"You should get out of this bed," Sara insisted. "Allie has the occasional nightmare, and when she does she comes looking for me."

"She'll find you, but one wonders where this argument was all the nights you spent in my bed, Mrs. Hunt. Aren't you interested in your parents' letter?"

"No." Sara flopped the covers for emphasis.

"Mendacity in domestics is a terrible problem." The dratted man kissed her ear.

"Beckman…" The mere sound of his voice, the slightest hint of his scent, and some of the tension Sara had carried since Tremaine's arrival left her body. "I'm not interested in another sermon from my father."

"Your husband is dead. What can your father sermonize about?"

That stumped her, which was a relief, because their increasingly frequent nocturnal arguments bit at her composure far more than she'd ever allow Beck to see. He seized the advantage of her silence.

"We had an interesting chat at the springs, your brother-in-law and I." Beck's hand kneaded at the base of Sara's spine, where her menses left her feeling achy. "He freely admits to having a store of items sent by Reynard for safekeeping, and admits those items are yours, Allie's, and Polly's."

When Beck touched her like that, it was hard to form words, much less think.

"It costs him nothing to admit such. Next he'll be insisting we accompany him back to Oxford to look over this treasure trove, and then we'll be virtual prisoners."

"He asked me if he could buy you Three Springs," Beck went on, his hands working *magic*.

"Asking and producing the deed are two different things."

"Sara, the man has no other family."

Sara rolled over then, mostly to reclaim her powers of speech and thought. "Beckman, you acquit him of all the trouble we've had here and find him worthy of trust and confidences and God knows what else, all because you've splashed around in the springs together? Forgive me if I'm slower to trust. His brother was similarly charming and kind and interested only in my welfare, until he'd sprung his trap, leaving my life in ruins, my brother dead, and my parents believing every lie Reynard spun, while my sister…"

"Sara?" Polly stood at Sara's door.

"God save me," Sara muttered.

"My apologies," Polly said. "Allie's not in her bed."

"She's not?" Sara sat up in an instant, scooting to the side of the bed. "Could she be at the privy?"

"Not likely," Polly said. "She's been warned not to leave the house at night."

"Dear God…" Sara was almost off the bed before Beck stopped her with fingers wrapped around her wrist.

"Wait." He reached for his dressing gown with the other hand. "Think first, Sara. We'll find her. Where's North, Polly?"

"He thought he saw a light in the barn and was going to investigate, but Allie wouldn't take a lantern out there without permission, not with all that hay to catch on a single spark."

Beck kept his grip on Sara's arm when she would have bolted for the door in her nightgown. He handed her the green dressing gown and then her slipper boots. "Your sister will need a shawl, Polly, and a lantern. I doubt she'll let me leave this house without her."

Sara nodded affirmation of that notion, and Polly disappeared.

"I'm going to see if Tremaine is in his bed," Beck said, standing to yank on his breeches. "You will not panic, Sara, do you hear me? Allie was in her bed not fifteen minutes ago, and she can't have gone far by moonlight."

Unless, of course, she was bundled onto Tremaine's horse and heading for the first ship out of Portsmouth. Sara kept that thought to herself as Beck escorted her to the kitchen and saw her into Polly's keeping, while he went to see if Tremaine—alone in all of Creation—was yet abed.

"St. Michael is not in his bed," Beck said, anxiety in his eyes, "so you ladies take the lantern, and I'll find North. You will remain on the back porch, though, until you see my signal. If you fear I've come to harm, you lock yourself in the carriage house with Angus and send Jeff for help on foot."

He turned to go, but Sara stopped him with a hand on his arm. All the years she'd been married, all the years she'd been a mother, she'd felt a lack. Men had desired her; men had paid money to hear her perform. They'd offered her pretty compliments, some of them even sincere.

But no man had put himself at risk of harm for her or for her daughter. For Beckman to walk into certain danger for her or for Allie was an awful blessing, much harder to accept than Sara would have guessed.

"Be careful, Beckman. Please, for the love of God, be careful."

He kissed her soundly on the mouth and slipped out into the darkness.

❧

Beck's slipper boots made a noiseless approach easy in the thick summer grass, but as he neared the barn, he heard voices murmuring. First, Allie's light tones drifted through the darkness, relaxed and curious, though her words were indistinct. Then came the peculiar rumble of Tremaine's bass burr. Their conversation was clearly amiable, and Beck was calculating how best to get closer, when North stepped from the shadows, a finger to his lips. He gestured toward the barn, and Beck nodded.

By slow increments, they stole nearer, until they were in the dense shadows of the first empty stall, close enough to hear every word.

"Do you know what my papa looked like?"

"A lot like you," Tremaine said. "His hair was not as reddish, but more brown, and his eyes were not as… they weren't as pretty. But in here"—he paused—"there it is. I brought this in case you might want it."

"That's my papa?" Allie's voice was wondering. "He looked just like that, too."

"I think your aunt might have painted it. It's good enough to be her work."

"Aunt is very talented with portraiture," Allie allowed absently. "He looks happy."

"He generally was. He tried to paint too, you know, when he was young."

"I didn't know." Allie's tone was arrested. "Why did he stop?"

"Hard to say. The times were very difficult in France—they still are—and lessons and materials were not easy to come by. Then too, he was never satisfied and felt anybody else's work was better than his."

"It's hard," Allie said, "to be the student and feel like you always botch it up. Aunt says I have to be patient, and I'm getting better, but I'm not supposed to talk about my painting with you."

"Whyever not?"

North would have risen then, but Beck stopped him with a shake of his head. Instead, he indicated they should shift a few feet closer, so the child and her uncle were in view.

"Because you might try to make me paint for money," Allie said, "the way my papa made money from Aunt's work and Mama's music. It wasn't well done of him."

"They've told you about that, have they?"

"No." Allie's voice shifted as she rummaged in the trunk. "I sleep in a little alcove, and they often think I'm asleep when they're up late, talking. When I ask, they always say nice things about my papa, but they won't look at me when they do. At night, when it's dark, they half-say things to each other about him, and he wasn't very nice sometimes."

"He wasn't. Nobody's nice all the time, though, Allemande. I tell myself he was doing the best he could."

Allie fell silent, and Tremaine, hunkered before the trunk with her, was apparently going to leave her to her thoughts.

"What else do you have in this trunk, Uncle?"

"A few things I thought your mama or your aunt might want," Tremaine said. "There are three little paintings your papa sent me right before he died, some perfume he bought in Venice, an inkwell with a bear on it—I think he bought that with you in mind—a little decorated teapot. Sundries, I suppose, but these things caught my eye when I was packing."

"They're for us?" Allie's voice was muffled as she went diving again for treasure.

"I believe they are yours. Yours, your mama's, and your aunt's, but certainly not mine."

"Don't suppose you use lady's perfume," Allie muttered. "My goodness, I remember these…"

"Allie…" Tremaine's tone held amusement. "I meant to bring this trunk out sometime when your mother could supervise dispersal of the contents, but the moment never presented itself. Why don't we get you back to bed, and we'll make a project of it in the morning?"

"Yes, Uncle, but you should know I get up quite early." The lid of the trunk came down, and Tremaine hefted Allie to his hip.

"If you get your sheets dirty because you tromped around the yard tonight, you'll get us both in trouble."

"Tremaine." Beck stepped into the light, having surprised Allie at least.

"Mr. Haddonfield." Allie grinned from her perch on Tremaine's hip. "Hullo."

Beck smiled at her. "Hullo, princess. My lecture about not leaving the house alone after dark must have slipped your memory."

"But I'm not alone." Allie hugged her uncle, who was looking chagrined and protective of his niece.

"No harm done," Tremaine said. "I'll just take Allie back to her apartment and make apologies all around."

"And explanations," Beck suggested, reaching for Allie and transferring her to his own hip.

"Beckman?" Sara's voice sounded from the barn door. "Is everything all right?"

"So much for my lectures about staying on the porch. In here, Sara, and you needn't worry. Allie is merely having a midnight chat with her uncle."

"Hullo, Mama." Allie's grin dimmed. "Hullo, Aunt. Is Mr. North coming too?"

"I'm here." North emerged from the shadows. "Though I believe I'll be seeking my bed."

"Not so fast."

Five adults and one child turned to survey the figures coming down the ladder from the hayloft. The going was difficult, because each man was clambering down while trying to keep a double-barreled pistol trained on the assemblage.

"Tobias?" Polly spoke for the group, her voice laden with incredulity. "Timothy?"

"Hold yer tongue, Miss High and Mighty," Tobias spat. "We'll just be taking the girl here. Set her down, mate, and back away from her."

"Not on your miserable, craven, cowardly lives." Beck turned so Allie was shielded by the sheer bulk of his body. "Murder me before these women and this child if you like, but I'm twice your size, and I take a lot of killing."

"As do I," North echoed, smiling evilly.

"And then there's the girl's uncle," Tremaine chimed in, "who has years of neglecting her circumstances to atone for."

"There's three of 'em," Timothy noted, apparently for the first time.

"We got four shots atween us, Tim," Tobias said. "They'll not do a thing."

From the corner of Beck's eye, he saw Boo-boo regarding the scene with sleepy puzzlement.

"A stray dog could kidnap the child more effectively than you two," Beck scoffed, catching North's eye. North nodded ever so slightly and shifted his position.

"Where are you going?" Tobias waved his pistol between North and Beck.

"I've seen enough of this farce," North began in his most scathing tones. "You two are the most imbecilic, ridiculous…"

"Boo-boo!" Beck literally threw Allie into North's arms. "Treat! Boo-boo, treat!"

The dog started baying and jumping around, Tremaine grabbed the women and hustled them from the barn on North's heels, and Beck put himself between the twins and those they had held at gunpoint.

"Make the dog shut up, Toby!" Tim fired his gun at Boo-boo, who thought the noise was great fun indeed, barking louder than ever, until Tim discharged his second bullet in desperation, then pitched the gun at the dog.

Beck wrenched Tobias's gun from his hand and cocked the hammer.

"Both of you hold still." Hearing Beck's voice, Boo-boo fell silent as well, tilting his head as if to ask why the game had been suspended.

"The dog is still hungry enough to snack on whatever's to hand." Beck picked up Tim's spent weapon without taking his eyes off the twins. "As much as I'd like to let him have at you, for your own safety, get in the empty stall."

Tim eyed the dog. "Do as he says, Tobe. That beast didn't like us none when we brung him here."

"Hush, you!" Tobias hissed. "We never seen that damned dog. Never."

"You were seen with the dog in the village," Beck improvised. "Your boots, doubtless, will match the prints found near our burned smokehouse. You will not be able to account for yourselves on the days when trouble befell us here, and I'm sure, if I ask around on the docks in Portsmouth long enough, I'll find somebody who sold you a black rat snake, traded you for it, or lost it to you in a card game."

"Tobe…" Tim was already in the stall. "He knows about that snake. I told you the snake was a bad…"

"Shut up!"

"In the stall, Tobias," Beck said. "Now. My finger itches worse with each moment I consider the harm you did a helpless old woman's property, much less the scare you put into the ladies who never did you any wrong."

Tobias was inspired, perhaps by the absolutely genuine menace in Beck's voice, to join his brother in the stall. "You never paid us our wages," Tobias sneered. "Your hands ain't clean."

"Your wages were left at the posting inn," Beck said, closing both the top and bottom halves of the stall door and bolting them. "If you owed a prior balance there, you might have taken it up with the innkeeper. What, no witty riposte, gentlemen? You disappoint me, as does my own unwillingness to murder you outright. Be warned, I will shoot you should you give me the slightest provocation. The very slightest."

He left them with that to think about, detailed Jeff and Angus to watch the prisoners, and headed for the house. On the back porch he paused, gazing up at the starry night and wishing he could take more than a few minutes before joining the others inside.

Because with this problem solved, he had no excuse for tarrying here at Three Springs. Tremaine was no threat, no matter what Sara thought, and Tobias and Timothy were at least on their way to the Antipodes.

And Sara had a letter from her parents, likely inviting her to raise Allie at home in St. Albans.

The sense of turning his sights on home, and being both relieved and disappointed to do so, was familiar to Beck. Before it swamped him, he forced himself to open the back door. Sara alone waited for him at the kitchen table, a tea tray sitting before her.

"Where is everybody?"

"North said something about needing decent attire when he calls on the magistrate in the middle of the night. Tremaine offered to accompany him," Sara replied. "Polly took Allie to wash her feet off, and then they were headed for bed as well."

"And you?"

Sara shuddered minutely. "I want to know what you've done with those two, and I want to know what Allie was doing out in the barn with Tremaine. She was told…"

"And you were told," Beck interrupted gently and poured a cup of tea. He added cream and sugar, stirred, then wrapped both of Sara's hands around the cup. "Drink."

While she complied, he fixed his own cup.

"Tobias and Timothy are locked in a stall under guard, and no, it's not one they could climb out of, assuming they're bright enough to look up while considering escape. Jeff and Angus have a loaded pistol between them to encourage cooperation in the prisoners."

Sara's shoulders slumped. "Thank God."

"You were worried for them?"

"For you." She glared at her teacup. "I was worried for you. You argued with them and wouldn't let go of Allie, and then we were running, and I heard a gun go off... North said to stay at the house, then told us you'd confined those two at gunpoint, and if he hadn't..."

"And I said to stay on the porch," Beck reminded her. "But your worry flatters me. As for what Allie and Tremaine were doing in the barn, Sara, you'd best ask them. He showed her some mementos gathered by her father, though, and she was all set to ask him more questions about Reynard."

Sara nodded, wrapping her arms around her middle. "Of course, his trump card, the deceased papa, to whom he was never close, but Allie wouldn't know that."

"He answered honestly," Beck said, and it occurred to him to wonder why Sara wasn't with her daughter when the child's welfare had been so overtly threatened. No doubt she wanted to give Polly time with the child, because... because...

The answer landed in his head like exploding ordinance.

"What would you have me say, Beckman?" Sara rose. "I will never trust the man. While I know that isn't fair—it isn't even rational, God knows—I can't change it, either."

"Will you ever trust me?"

Her answer was a long, pained silence.

"I see." Beck got to his feet, feeling decades older than when he'd stolen into Sara's bed. "Very well, then. But, Sara?"

She raised miserable eyes to him.

"Two things. The paintings, the ones you're so afraid of? Tremaine has them right out in the barn. He told Allie he'd brought them with some other valuables, because he thought you might like them."

She blinked—nothing more, and Beck wondered if she even comprehended his words. "What else?"

"If you want to join me in my bed tonight," Beck said quietly, "you are very welcome there, as always, but I'm done carrying you half-asleep where you can damned well get yourself wide awake."

He leaned down and brushed his lips over hers, gently, lingeringly.

If his intent had been to take the sting out of his words, he failed miserably. Sara's tears started before the sound of Beck's retreating footfalls had faded.

Nineteen

IN THE FIRST PAINTING, A NAKED WOMAN STRADDLED a low-backed dressing stool. She sat in a shaft of sunlight, bowed over to brush her hair, her back to the viewer. The hair itself was glorious, fiery red, molten white, burnished gold, and everything in between. It hung in a cascade to below her hips, catching every sunbeam in its highlights. By contrast, the rest of the scene was in deep shadow, giving the painting an ethereal, dreamy quality.

In the second image, the woman stood in the same brilliantly lit full-length window, her back again to the viewer. She had on a filmy peignoir, and the sunlight pierced it easily, so she might as well have been nude, so clearly were her curves and hollows delineated. Her violin was tucked under her chin, her body curved up as the other hand held the bow poised over the strings. The stillness conveyed in her body, juxtaposed with the sense of the bow about to strike music out of silence, made one want to not only savor the beauty of the painting, but to *listen* to it as well.

"This one has always been my favorite," Polly said

as she joined North where he stood before the third painting in the ladies' parlor.

"It's lovely," North agreed, slipping an arm around Polly's waist. They'd had a week since Tobias and Timothy were bound over for the assizes, a week to say good-bye.

Polly cocked her head. "I've always thought the cat is particularly good."

North considered the image of the same woman, curled on her side amid a pile of pillows and blankets. Her face was obscured by the arm she'd flung over her head, but a cat lay nestled in a tidy counter-circle in the curve of her unclothed body. The marmalade cat was arguably the same color as the woman's hair, but the artist had given the cat's coat a subtle, muted glow, while the lady's hair streamed over her body with brilliant glory. Even so, while the cat was clearly contented, the woman was just as clearly exhausted, and again, the contrast made a good painting fascinating.

"Have you seen the one of you and Soldier?" Polly went on, her head resting on North's shoulder.

"I have." North turned his face to inhale the scent of her. "I wanted to see these before I left, though. They are brilliant, but you will please not tell Sara I peeked."

Polly shifted closer. "I'm leaving as well."

"Where are you off to?"

"Tremaine has asked me to inventory the things he has from Reynard, and I'm going," Polly said. "I might see our parents while I'm gone, and I might decide to find another post as cook."

"You've had a falling out with Sara?"

Polly smiled slightly. "She asked me to go, probably hoping I wouldn't be as upset when you left. She's considering her options as well, but she doesn't know I'm thinking of not coming back."

"Polly..." North did not at all like the idea of the three Hunt ladies splitting up. But Polly put her fingers over his lips before he spoke.

"I have been happy here, Gabriel, but sometimes not so happy too."

"Thus sayeth we all."

"I will think of you," Polly said, turning to slip her arms around his waist. "I'll dream of you."

"You will forget me," North admonished. "The sooner the better. If what Tremaine says is true, you'll soon have some money from selling Reynard's plunder, and you can reestablish relations with your parents. And you're lovely, Polonaise. You can have any man you please."

"Hush."

"I want you to be happy." North kissed her forehead—only her forehead. "I need you to be happy."

Polly shook her head and stepped back. "You need me to let you go."

"I do." He surveyed her features warily. "You'll manage?"

"Of course." Though her smile was a painful, forced thing. "I'll not see you to your horse, though. You have other good-byes to say."

And in the few beats of silence that followed, North wanted to say he'd write, to give her his direction, to tell her something of his plans, but he couldn't. For all he knew, he was riding to his death, and he would not involve her, nor would he be so unkind as to give her hope.

"God be with you." He half turned, as if to go, hesitated, then turned back, gathered her into his arms, and settled his mouth over hers. He didn't plunder, but neither did he content himself with a mere gesture. With his kiss, he let her know he'd dream of her, worry for her, pray for her, and miss her every day and night he had left on earth.

Then he stepped back, gave her a grave bow, and left.

✺

"So when are you leaving?" Allie's tone was casual, but in her watchful expression, Beck saw the question was not.

"What makes you think I'm leaving?" Beck asked. They were lounging on the fence outside Hildegard's wallow, watching her nurse her twelve new piglets.

"Mr. North left, Uncle Tremaine left, Aunt is leaving."

"I have family elsewhere, Allie. Soon they'll have use for me some place besides Three Springs."

"We have use for you here," Allie shot back. "All of us. We have use for Mr. North too, but his younger brother is in trouble."

"He told you that?"

"He's my friend," Allie said, her gaze on the piglets. "He told me the truth."

"Truth is sometimes uncomfortable," Beck said carefully, but he'd surreptitiously studied the paintings in the days since North's departure, and studied the three Hunt ladies with particular care. There were some truths that needed to be aired, regardless of how uncomfortable they might seem.

Allie peered at him. "More like the truth is always uncomfortable, at least at first."

"I'll miss you when I leave. That's a truth."

"I'll miss you too. And it will not be comfortable."

She fell silent, regarding the pig where she lay, piglets rooting at her greedily.

"Mama cries," Allie said, her voice soft. "At night she thinks I'm asleep, and Aunt is asleep, but Mama cries. I've asked her what's wrong, but she just smiles. I don't know what to do."

Beck felt the misery that had taken up residence in his gut spike, hot and painful, up toward his throat. He hadn't resorted to the bottle yet, but the temptation loomed with enormous appeal as he considered the uncertainty on Allie's face.

He slipped a hand to her shoulder. "Sometimes people just need to cry, Allemande."

"She used to cry," Allie said. "Before we got our house in Italy, she cried a lot. But she didn't cry when Papa died. I did, though."

"I cried when my papa died, princess. My brother did too, and he's bigger than I am. We all cried."

"Does it still hurt?" Allie asked, regarding him gravely.

"It does, though I don't think of only the hurt when I think of him. I think of his laugh, and his silly jokes, and the way he'd stay up with a colicky horse, even though he was the earl. I think about the good things, not just the parts that hurt." To his surprise, his words were the truth. Two months after his father's death, it wasn't hurting as much to think the earl had gone to his reward.

"I wanted my papa to be proud of me," Allie said. "I painted as best as I could, and Papa liked what I did, but Mama yelled at him when she saw what I'd done."

"Cried over that too, did she?"

"No." Allie shuddered against Beck's side. "And it was worse when she didn't cry. Aunt helped me, though, and I think that made Mama mad too."

"Seems the two are connected sometimes, loving someone and being frustrated with them."

"Hildegard doesn't look frustrated. She looks tired."

"But at peace." To the extent the mother of twelve could ever be at peace. "You're very close to your aunt, aren't you?" Beck offered the question, knowing he shouldn't be tempting the child to reveal confidences.

"I love Aunt Polly, and she loves me and Mama. I'm glad I have family, but sometimes…" She scuffed her half boot on the bottom fence board. "I wish you and Mr. North and Uncle didn't have to leave."

Beck had nothing to say to that. He wished he didn't have to leave too.

❧

"You will be back," Sara assured her sister as they stood outside The Dead Boar waiting for the post coach. "Go paw around Reynard's treasures, sell whatever you think needs selling, then come back to us."

"Sara…" Polly eyed her sister and saw a woman holding on by a thread. "I may not come back. We've discussed this."

Sara's smile was resolute and not at all convincing. "You might walk away from me, Polonaise. In fact, you should have walked away from me long ago, but you won't leave Allie."

"It hasn't worked, Sara." Polly held her sister's gaze. "Being here with you and Allie, I put my life aside, thinking this *was* my life. Being with Gabriel, or rather, not being with him, makes me realize I'm just existing here. I haven't really painted in years, haven't flirted, haven't slept past dawn because God knows, somebody has to get the bread in the ovens, will she, nil she. I haven't heard a foreign language, unless you count the Yorkshiremen who came through last summer. I'm dying by inches here, no matter how much I love you and Allie."

"You're tired," Sara said. "We're all tired, and you need and deserve a break. Go to Oxfordshire and exorcise Gabriel's ghost."

"Will you manage?" The question North had asked Polly herself wasn't nearly adequate to cover all it needed to.

"Manage the house, of course. Lolly and her mother will keep the kitchen functional, and once Beckman goes, there really won't be much housework. It will be back to weekly dusting, weekly laundry, weekly marketing."

"About Beckman." Polly glanced around and saw they would not be overheard. "You are making a mistake with him, Sara. Just as I made a mistake thinking I could be happy cooking at Three Springs for the rest of my life."

Around them, passengers secured their luggage at the back of the coach, then climbed inside.

"I'm older than you," Sara temporized, "and I had my chance to wallow in my art, Polly. Beckman is an earl's son, and my past leaves me ill-suited to be anything more than a diversion for such as he."

"You are being ridiculous. You think you're doing this for Allie, or for me, but, Sara, I *promise* you, she and I would both rather you gave Beckman the truth and trusted to the consequences. He'll not disappoint you."

"Maybe he wouldn't, but then what, Polly? He should be on about his life if anyone should, but instead of walking away puzzled, he'll feel honor bound not to walk away, and that's worse."

Polly resisted the urge to shake a woman who didn't know when to think of herself. Above them, one of the porters cursed roundly as a bag came tumbling down, nearly striking a half-grown boy.

"For the love of God, Sara. You think you know, you think you can predict another's heart, you think you've made the best choice, but it's all so much arrogance and cowardice driving you. Talk to the man, I beg you. If not for my sake or yours, do it for Allie's. She's in danger of shifting all the affection she had for North onto Beckman, and he's ready to bolt as North has."

"Allie's affection lies with you, Polly."

Polly held up one gloved hand. "Don't play that card, Sara. We agreed not to trade in that coin, and we've done well by each other so far. I love you, I want you to be happy, and I am begging you to talk to Beckman. Please."

The head porter called "five minutes" as the fresh team was backed into the traces. Beck came striding out of the inn, Allie's hand in his as she trotted to keep up with his longer paces.

"We bought you lots and lots of goodies, Aunt!"

Beck bent down and hefted Allie onto his hip to close the distance more quickly, the sack of food from the inn's kitchen in his other hand.

"Your trunk is loaded?" Beck set Allie down when they reached the coach.

Polly nodded at the luggage rack on the boot. "Up there. Hug me, Allemande, and promise to be good. I will want to hear about your paintings."

"Good-bye, Aunt." Allie hugged her fiercely around the waist. "You'll write and tell me of all the things Papa collected?"

"I promise, Allie. Sara." She hugged her sister but said nothing more.

"And you, Beckman." Polly turned to him. "Walk me to the leaders." She gestured to the powerful pair in the front harness. Beck obligingly held out an arm and led Polly away. In the noise and bustle of the inn yard, the short distance was enough to make their words private.

Polly glanced back at Sara and Allie. "I can't ask you to look after them, but I can ask you to be patient. There are things Sara needs to…"

Beck stilled her with a single finger to her lips. "I know, or I know much of it, and if Sara won't confide in me, I can't make her."

"You can encourage her," Polly said. "You can understand she's been alone with her burdens so long she doesn't know how to put them down. I was little more than a child, Reynard worse than a child, and then Allie came along…"

Polly let the words trail off, lest she say too much.

From the look on Beckman's face, perhaps she'd said too much already.

∽

Beck had a retort ready for Polly's little homily. He was mentally building his defenses day by day against the moment he'd leave Three Springs, but Polly's words hit him low in the gut. He knew what it was to keep making foolish decisions out of sheer emotional exhaustion, bad habit, and lack of obvious alternatives. That kind of inertia and despair had damned near killed him.

"I can't make her trust me, Polly. I've tried what I know to do, and she remains steadfastly opposed to confiding in me."

"Try confiding in her yourself." Polly leaned up and kissed Beck's cheek. He hugged her to him briefly before he handed her up into the window seat he'd reserved for her.

"Safe journey, Polonaise." Beck's height put him more than level with the window. "And, Polly? I got a brief note from North in the morning post, and he's reached his destination safely, though he didn't elaborate. If I hear further, I'll let you know."

Polly's face broke into a surprised smile as the coachy cracked his whip and the horses clattered off at a bone-shaking trot.

Allie slipped her hand into Beck's. "You made Aunt smile. What did you say?"

"I wished her safe journey and told her if I heard more from North, I'd let her know."

"Will you let me know?"

"He'd want me to."

"I really miss him."

"I know, princess. I miss him too."

❧

Late August would have been the last precious weeks of the summer lull, because the fruit and grain weren't ready to be harvested yet, except Beck's red winter wheat had to be planted before harvest. He was glad for the backbreaking work of plowing, glad to fall into bed exhausted every evening after his soak or swim, glad for a way to numb himself that did not involve liquor or worse.

He was not glad to toss much of each night away, despite his burning fatigue. He willed Sara to come to him, and more than once, sat up, grabbed for his dressing gown, and started down the dark corridor toward her room, only to stop himself.

He'd done nothing to deserve her mistrust and much to earn her trust. Polly's last words rang in his memory though, urging him to confide in Sara. As he tried to rehearse what that might sound like, he gained an appreciation for the magnitude of the task he was requiring of Sara. He was still wrestling with himself mightily when the weather turned autumnally cool, then rainy, then downright chilly.

"Fall grass will come in good for this rain," Angus observed.

"And the wheat will get a nice start," Beck agreed as they stood in the barn, listening to the rain drumming on the roof.

"And then we'll bring in the corn and be glad for

winter. Those boys of Lolly's must have grown four inches each this summer."

"Polly's cooking and lots of fresh air."

And it could have gone on like that for hours, meaningless small talk, cleaning the harnesses *again*, inspecting the irrigation ditches *again*. Watching the rain, Beck admitted to himself he was dawdling around the barn, looking for another excuse to avoid the house. But soon the crops would be in, then the fruit harvested, and who knew if there would be any more rainy afternoons like this one?

"Keep an eye on the infants." Beck shrugged into an oilskin. "Allie cheats terribly, and the boys are only so gallant."

"Will do," Angus said with a wink. "And we won't come for supper until the bell rings."

Beck sloshed across the stable yard, into the back gardens, wondering what, exactly, he hoped to accomplish. Since her sister's departure, Sara had become increasingly reserved. Allie wasn't painting, and there had been no further word from North.

"I could do with a nice hot cup of tea," Beck said when he found Sara in the kitchen. "And I don't suppose there are any more muffins?"

"In the bread box," Sara answered, her glance sliding away from him. "Butter's in the pantry."

"Join me?" Beck disappeared into the pantry, then brought himself, butter dish in hand, to stand beside her. "You've lost weight," he said, frowning down at her nape. "I can see it here." He touched the top of her spine. "All the more reason you should have a muffin with me, Sarabande."

"One muffin won't hurt." She arranged the tea tray and set the butter and basket of muffins on the table.

"In my sitting room." Beck picked up the tray and was on his way up the stairs before Sara could protest. "I've laid a fire, and it's a chilly day," he said over his shoulder.

He built up the wood fire in his sitting room while Sara poured, then settled himself beside her on the sofa. She didn't exactly move away, but neither did she relax against him.

"What did Polly have to say?" Beck asked when Sara passed him his teacup.

"She's safely arrived," Sara said, gaze on her drink. "She says there is a considerable cache of items, some of it rubbish, but most of it quite valuable. Reynard was collecting from places subsequently devastated by the Corsican's passing or occupation."

"Any violins?"

"She hasn't said."

"I'm leaving mine here." Beck set his tea aside and reached for a knife and a muffin. "In case you get the urge."

"Thank you."

"That's all?" He buttered both halves of the muffin and passed her one. "Just thank you, no protestations you'll never play again? That your art is lost to you? No ordering me to keep the damned thing where it won't tempt you?"

"It's a nice instrument." Sara took a cautious nibble. "I heard you playing it last week, and you're good. You should keep it, but I can't make you do anything."

Beck wanted to smash his teacup against the far

wall, because he couldn't make *her* do anything either—not one damned thing.

Confide in her.

"I'm not as competent as you were," Beck said. "I heard you play on two occasions, you know. I went the second time because I could not believe the evidence of my ears the first time."

"You heard me?" Sara's cup and saucer hit the table with a clatter.

"I was frequently on the Continent when you toured, Sara." Beck risked a glance at her and found her face pale, her eyes full of dread. "Why wouldn't I have treated myself to your performances?"

"They were ridiculous," Sara said, her voice glacial. "Perversions of what music should be."

"Any woman who can play the *Kreutzer Sonata* from memory is not ridiculous, though I agree, your costumes were not worthy of your talent. The private performance was particularly troubling in that regard."

Sara's chin dipped, as if she'd suffered a sudden pang in her vitals. "You attended a private performance?"

"When a woman's playing is touted as able to restore a man's lost virility, an ignorant young man isn't likely to turn down his invitation. I assume they were Reynard's idea?"

"He was always after me to take a lover," Sara said miserably. "A wealthy, besotted lover who would shower me with trinkets and baubles. Better yet, he wanted me to have many lovers, who would compete with one another for my favors."

Many lovers, as if the risk of disease, pregnancy, or

mistreatment was of no moment. Beck set the knife he'd been holding on the table.

"Not enough for him to prostitute your art, but he must pimp your body as well. Thank heavens the man is dead, and thank heavens you withstood his selfish plans for you. Would you like another muffin?"

"Another muffin?" Sara's tone was incredulous. "You bring up some of my worst memories and offer me a muffin?"

"You won't accept anything else from me, Sarabande," Beck said softly. "Would you like to know some of my worst memories? Probably not, but I will share them with you in any case, because I have lost my well-honed ability to thrive on silence."

"Well-honed?" Sara's tone was more bewildered than indignant, so Beck marched on, his anger for her warring with his frustration with her.

Beck poured himself more tea and gestured with the pot. "When I was a mere boy, I learned why my father was banishing Ethan, and got a stout boxing of my ears when I tried to tell him he was wrong. Not long after that, I learned my youngest sister was a by-blow, then learned the earl's solicitors were blackmailing him over it. It seems my lot in life has been to collect secrets, Sara, and I find it a distasteful pastime."

"My private performances weren't a secret from you," Sara said. "They just never came up."

"This is true." Beck stirred cream and sugar into his tea and sipped in an effort to calm himself. He was letting his emotions tear at his composure, and anger wasn't what he wanted to convey to Sara. "I could not care less about those private performances, Sara, though I'm sorry you were subjected to them."

She nodded, clearly not willing to argue with him in his present mood.

"For the love of God, Sara, when I say I do not care, I mean I do not hold it against you that you earned coin for playing half-naked before leering idiots. You should have been paid handsomely, at the least." Beck set his teacup down very carefully, and went on in precise, dispassionate tones.

"When I first beheld you here, I had a sense of what the French call déjà vu, of having seen you before, and I had. I'd seen the Gypsy Princess perform, though it would have been almost six years ago, on my way back from Budapest by way of Vienna. My companion for that stretch of the journey insisted we take in your performance, and I, ever willing to dawdle on my homeward journeys, assented. The house was packed, all levels of society turning out to hear you."

He stopped, pulling himself back from the memory. "Cost of admission to the private performances was exorbitant, obscene—much like your costumes."

Sara wasn't blushing. She looked like she wanted to clap her hands over her ears and flee the room.

"Sara, you were magnificent, your talent obvious even to my relatively undiscerning ears. Your hair had been arranged artfully, and had just as artfully come undone as you plied your instrument with wild, passionate, exotic melodies. Then, just when the entire room was roaring and clapping and pouring out its demand for more, you brought us to hushed stillness merely by holding your bow poised above the strings."

He risked touching her, a brush of his fingers over the knuckles of her clenched hands. "The heartbreak that poured from your violin thereafter tore at me, made me nearly weep for my distant home and feel again every regret I'd ever known. I've since realized that for a man to overcome his regrets, he must first acknowledge them. Your performance was the first step on my journey home, Sarabande Adagio. I've yet to take my last."

She gave him no reaction, but rather, sat staring at her hands like a monument to silence. Beck withdrew his hand.

"I care very much that you were alone, Sara, without the support of friends or family when you needed them. I care that you were exhausted and exploited and made to cast your pearls before swine. I care that you had responsibility for your sister thrust on you when you were least equipped to deal with it." His voice dropped, becoming bleak. "I care that you bear the sorrow of all of this, the pain and anguish of it, and you won't let me even hold you as you do."

Beside him, Sara made a sound, a low, grieving sound, from deep inside, a sound Beck recognized. When she might have pitched to her feet and bolted for the door, Beck manacled her wrist and drew her back down beside him, looping an arm across her shoulders and drawing her close to his side.

Confide in her, Polly had said. Confide in her, put into her keeping all the silences and secrets and private burdens of one man's lifetime. Beck kissed Sara's temple for courage—or possibly in parting—and kept speaking.

"I was married, you'll recall." Beckman spoke quietly, as if his previous volley of verbal arrows hadn't been launched directly at Sara's heart. "But you do not know my wife was in love with another, a relation of some sort. She married me because her family would not approve the match with her beloved, and she'd already conceived his child. She was desperate but thought I'd tolerate a cuckoo in the nest, if it ever came to light."

He fell silent, his lips skimming along Sara's temple.

"She told me as she lay dying she thought she could bed me and pass the child off as mine, but when it came time for the actual intimacies, she couldn't stop crying, and I... couldn't. I just couldn't. Nick happened upon her a few weeks later with her lover, having no idea my marriage was unconsummated, and confronted my wife with her responsibility toward the Bellefonte succession. In all her worry and upset, it hadn't occurred to her that burden might fall to us, and her bastard might inherit the earldom. She tried to rid herself of the child, but ended up ridding herself and the child of life."

"I'm sorry." Sara voice was small, brittle with pain, but she would not leave him in the midst of this recitation—she could not.

"I was sorry too," Beck said on a sigh. "I was sorry enough before the marriage, always trying to outdo my brothers, all unbeknownst to anybody save myself and possibly my father. After the marriage, I was even sorrier. I went from frequent heavy drinking to incessant inebriation. I bet on anything, gambled my personal fortune away and back each month, swived any willing female... I was a disgrace."

"You're not a disgrace now."

"But I have a disgraceful past, Sara," Beck reminded her gently. "Aren't you going to hold it against me, judge me for it, cast me away for sins I've committed? It gets worse, you know. My father was at his wits' end and devised one journey after another for me after Devona died. I became the Haddonfield remittance man, sent far from home and hearth lest my excesses be too great an embarrassment to my family. There was always a token task to see to, always a veneer of purpose to my travels, but I was mostly sent forth because decent families do not leave inconvenient children on hillsides anymore. Not in this civilized land of ours."

And yet, Sara had the sense Beckman was on a hillside, a high, lonely hillside with sheer drops only a few feet away.

"But you learned so much," Sara protested. "You couldn't have been drunk the whole time."

"I wasn't. I always set sail with good intentions and usually gave a decent accounting of myself, until I was homeward bound. Then I'd fall apart, thinking of the churchyard where Devona was buried, thinking of the child she lost, thinking of how disappointed my father must have been in me."

Another silence, this one more thoughtful.

"I was simply too weak to deal with my disappointment in myself," Beck said. "And in my family. They owed me, you see, owed it to me to ensure I was happy at all times. Life owed me happy endings, and I owed nobody anything. One can see my expectations were bound for readjustment."

How she hated the dry irony in his voice. "What happened?"

"I tried to kill myself." Beck drew his hand down her arm and back up again, in a slow caress that made her shiver. "First with whiskey, then absinthe, then opium, then any and all of the above. Nick fetched me home as I was about to succeed at my goal, and left me at Clover Down to recover, then marched me down to Sussex to work in the stables of an old-fashioned estate fallen on hard times, much like this one."

Sara felt a shudder pass through her; he likely felt it too. "You could have hung yourself from the nearest barn rafter."

"Might have, but I'd been given responsibility for the livestock. All I had to do was get up each morning and look after the beasts, and it… soothed me. They did not know of my past, did not care. All they cared about was whether their oats appeared on schedule, and that much I could manage. I could manage to be civil to the other stable boys. I could look after a scrappy little runt pig until it no longer needed to be fed from a bottle. The pigs have ever been charitable toward prodigal sons."

"You grew up."

"Perhaps, or I realized I could serve some purpose if I'd sober up enough to be of use. Then too, I found in Sussex, working each day on a specific patch of land, using my own wit and will to make the place healthier was much better for me than sailing off to foreign ports to carouse with strangers. I had never been successful running from my regrets, but I found some measure of peace in rising from the same bed, day after day."

"You needed something to care about."

"Apparently so." Beck nuzzled her temple. "And someone to care about, someone to love."

She went still beside him and remained silent. In that silence, she felt her heart sinking like a stone bound for the bottom of the sea. If she had viewed a continued liaison with Beckman as difficult before, it had become impossible with his raw truths and unvarnished trust.

"I do love you, you know," Beck went on as the ache in Sara's chest threatened to choke her. "And I think you must love me a little, too, Sara, or you would not have given me your virginity."

Another instant of silence as the import of his words cascaded through Sara bodily.

"God help me." She scooted forward and again would have left the room, but Beck put his hand on her nape, not gripping, just a warm, careful weight.

"I beg you, Sara." He took a breath, his lovely, precise voice dragging like a rasp over Sara's soul. "I *beg* you, do not lie to me now. Do not lie to yourself."

The fire hissed and crackled on the hearth, the rain pelted the windowpanes, and the wind soughed around the corner of the house. In the warmth and solitude of the cozy sitting room, Beckman fell silent, and Sara...

Gave up.

Gave up pretending it didn't hurt so badly to be without him, didn't devastate her to consider his leaving, didn't leave her howling in endless inner darkness to sleep one floor and a load of regrets away from him each night.

She loved him. He'd carried her secrets for her,

waited for her, and now, in the face of his relentless pursuit, she just… gave up. Gave up her loneliness, her fears, her insecurities, and her bondage to a past that had come to cost too much. She curled back against him, along his side but facing away, because she could not bear for him to look upon her eyes. She felt Beck shift to curl himself around her on the sofa, the warmth of him providing a comfort beyond words.

"A man can't tell if a woman is chaste. I've been promised a man can't know for sure," she said, barely above a whisper.

"I couldn't tell with my body," Beck said, "though I suspected, but with some other sense, I knew. You were like a gift, just for me, not like a woman who'd had a child with a man she loathed."

"Reynard assured me our affection for one another would grow after we wed, though when he whisked me off to the Continent, it soon became apparent his affection was for the coin I could bring him. Being married to him gave me a veneer of respectability, but I think he sensed that if he forced me, I would take Polly and go, regardless of the folly involved." She hoped she would have, and hoped equally some vestige of honor had informed her late husband's unwillingness to assert his intimate marital rights. "So you knew about Allie all along?"

"I still don't know about Allie," Beck countered, wrapping an arm around Sara's waist. "I only suspect and worry and wish I could help."

"Reynard got to Polly." Sara heaved a sigh the dimensions of the universe. "His strategy was to divide us, divide our loyalties, so Polly would fall in with his schemes and set herself against me. She was so young, Beckman. A child, and it never occurred to me Reynard would seduce a fifteen-year-old under his protection."

"He cannot be dead enough to suit me."

How she loved Beckman Haddonfield. "Once Polly conceived, Reynard was of course off on his other liaisons," Sara said. "He nearly destroyed her, nearly destroyed us both. She tried to talk herself into hating me, but when his perfidy became undeniable, she hated the child and herself and me—and him."

"For the last, we can be thankful."

"If that kept her alive, then yes, we can be thankful even for a hatred like that." Sara found herself lifted bodily and settled on Beck's lap. "She nursed her baby but couldn't really open her heart to Allie, not as a new mother."

"Hence the subterfuge was made easier," Beck said. "The child was yours and legitimate, but alas, as a legitimate child, also under Reynard's authority. He went along with the scheme to put you, Polly, and Allie more firmly under his control, and probably saw the advantages to him from the start."

"Of course," Sara said, burying her face against Beck's shoulder. "I think so far as he was capable, he loved Allie, but then when we visited England, she began to draw, and her talent was obvious."

"That must have hurt you, to see such tangible evidence of her relationship to Polly."

"No." Sara shifted slightly. "The art is what drew them back together. Polly matured a great deal and loves Allie every bit as much as I do. But as my child, Allie would be legitimate, as you say. As Polly's, she'd be a scandalous indiscretion and reflect poorly on Polly and me both. I'm not sorry we did what we did—even Allie seems to understand the why of it—I am sorry Reynard exploited the situation for his own advantage."

"It can't have been easy." Beck's lips found Sara's crown. "Raising another woman's child while she looks on."

"It wasn't, particularly when that woman is your younger sister and blames you for the child's existence, when she's not blaming herself, then berating herself for feeling any resentment, and on and on. It was during one of our periodic feuds that Reynard suggested to Polly the various nude studies of me."

"They are breathtaking."

He *would* focus on that, and he wasn't wrong. "What a tangled web."

"We'll untangle it."

He might have been referring to enlarging Hildegard's wallow, for the simple conviction in his tone.

"We?" Sara tried to wiggle off his lap and was gently restrained. "Beckman, I have lied to you, about myself, my daughter, my sister, my past, my marriage. You have no responsibility to me or mine. None at all."

"You are entitled to your privacy, Sara, but I'm going to ask you a question, and would have truth from you or nothing at all."

"Don't do this." Sara tried to leave him again but was again gently dissuaded. "Beckman, you aren't thinking clearly. You aren't considering your situation."

Beck looked straight at her, and God help him, his every emotion was in his beautiful blue eyes. "Sarabande Adagio Hunt... I love you. I love you, and I want to marry you if you'll have me. Do you love me?"

She reared back, surprised.

"I can live with not marrying you," Beck went on. "I can ask you to marry me twice a day for the next fifty years, or fifty times a day for two hundred years. The only real question is do you love me? Because if you love me, there is no way on God's green and beautiful earth that I will walk away from you. There is no foreign land I will visit, no vice I will descend into, no family project I will turn my hand to. You are my home, and I was put on this earth to love you." He slipped his arms from around her, leaving Sara at sea and desperate to find the shore.

"Do you love me, Sarabande Adagio? Can you love me? A drunk, a fool, a man who drove one woman to take her life and that of her unborn child, a man who nearly killed himself rather than admit his family loves him and he them? Can you, do you, love that man? For he certainly loves you."

She shook her head slowly from side to side, her face turned from him. In the patient silence, a tear fell from her jaw onto the back of her hand.

"I love your courage," Beck said softly, lifting her hand to kiss the spot where the tear glistened in the firelight. "I love your determination, your fire, and your tremendous heart. I love your passion and the way you protect your own. I love your unbending integrity and your tender feelings, your—"

Sara pitched into him, wrenching sobs breaking from her. He encircled her in his arms while she cried for the exhausted, bewildered, mean, angry years of her marriage. She cried for herself and Allie and Polly. She cried for her brother and her

parents and for the girl she'd been and never would
be again.

And then she cried in relief, because she could, because
Beckman Haddonfield must truly love her to hold her
this way, to bear her secrets and Allie's and Polly's. To
trust her and wait for her and trust her yet more. When
she had cried herself out, she rested in his arms, absorbing
the warmth and strength of him for long minutes.

Beck's chin came to rest on her crown. "Shall I take
that for a yes?"

"You may." Sara unwadded the handkerchief she
didn't recall Beck passing to her. "But I want to say it."

"I want to hear it. As often as you like, for the rest
of my life."

"I love you, Beckman Sylvanus Haddonfield," Sara
said, her voice hitching in the aftermath of her tears.
"I love you, Beck."

"Practice as often as you please. I love you, and I
will love hearing you say it."

"I love you." Sara rose and extended a hand. "I
love you. I will always love you. It's a rainy afternoon,
we have hours of privacy, and I love you."

In the years to come, they often stole away for
hours of privacy on rainy afternoons. Sometimes Sara
would play her violin for Beck, and sometimes they'd
pass hours in loving each other without words.

Other times, they'd talk, and Sara would drowse on
Beck's chest, enthralled with the music of his voice and
the melodies of his hands on her naked body. Whether
they loved silently or with noisy, unbridled passion,
secrets never again had the power to separate them or
to dim the love they shared for the rest of their lives.

Author's Note

A significant question for me as this story wandered into my imagination was whether there are child prodigies among the painters. Mozart is the quintessential musical wundkerkind, but I hadn't come across his like elsewhere in the arts. I asked the art historians in my family (we have two) if they knew of such, and the example that came immediately to mind was Pablo Picasso. A little nosing around also brought to light the example of Sir Thomas Lawrence, who was contributing to his family's upkeep significantly with his sketching by the time he was ten years old. Sir Thomas went on to lead the Royal Academy, and his portraits continue to delight us to this day.

A yet more interesting case was that of Angelica Kauffmann, a Swiss-Austrian lady who became one of two female founding members of the Royal Academy. By the time she was thirteen, Angelica was painting portraits professionally, and she went on to trade portraits with Sir Joshua Reynolds. Alas for the ladies, when the two female founding members of the Academy died, it took more than a century for that august body to again admit a female artist as a Royal Academician.

Acknowledgments

I love this story, love a tale of people wandering far from home for all the wrong reasons, people who then (eventually) find the courage to come back to the love they need and deserve. Credit goes to my editor, Deb Werksman, for choosing Beckman and Sara's tale over some less unconventional offerings, and for making time in the middle of a tempest to give the story a thorough buffing.

As always, Skye, Cat, Susie, and Danielle are manning various oars to row the manuscript along, and I cannot thank them often enough.

I'd also like to thank my parents, who early and often in my childhood loaded as many as five children into a station wagon and drove us coast to coast of a summer holiday. We learn things when we leave home, and we learn things when we come home, too.

About the Author

New York Times and *USA Today* bestselling author Grace Burrowes hit the bestseller lists with both her debut, *The Heir*, and her second book in The Duke's Obsession trilogy, *The Soldier*. Both books received extensive praise and starred reviews from *Publishers Weekly* and *Booklist*. *The Heir* was also named a *Publishers Weekly* Best Book of The Year, and *The Soldier* was named a *Publishers Weekly* Best Spring Romance. Her first story in the Windham sisters series—*Lady Sophie's Christmas Wish*—received the *RT* Reviewer's Choice award for historical romance, and was nominated for a RITA in the Regency category. She is hard at work on more stories for the Windham sisters, and the Lonely Lords, and has started a trilogy of Scottish Victorian romances, the first of which, *The Bridegroom Wore Plaid,* was named a *Publishers Weekly* Best Book for 2012.

Grace lives in rural Maryland and is a practicing attorney. She loves to hear from her readers and can be reached through her website at graceburrowes.com.